WINTERHAWK

Death in Arcaria

SL Gervais

For more books in the series check out my website at SLGERVAIS.com

CHAPTER 1

Dren was shaken from her encounter outside the tavern. The stranger's words ran through her mind: They are killing those with magic. If the prophecy points to you, you must get out of the city.
A paper lantern crunched under her foot as she crossed over the street. She glanced up at the faded remnants of bunting still attached to buildings, just out of reaching distance, where they would remain until the next strong gale obliterated them completely.

She paused for a moment as her mind took in the space where a bakery had once stood. It had boasted the tastiest honeycake in the city. Now it was nothing more than a heap of wooden beams lying at jaunty angles underneath collapsed masonry.

From the sanctuary of the keep, she hadn't realised the extent of the landslips and tremors or the havoc they could wreak in a densely packed merchant district. She tried to avoid picturing those families waking up in the morning only to find everything that they had ever worked for had been destroyed overnight. It wasn't her problem though.

She was glad that she hadn't put down roots in this

cursed place. It made it easier to move on without being burdened by memories. Her mind crept back to unpleasant thoughts: how Artra wanted nothing to do with her and Toran's betrayal. Her mood darkened. She had to keep moving. There was nothing left for her in this town.

The city was bustling with people eager to buy and sell and she knew a tailor near to the port who wouldn't ask too many questions about the provenance of her tunic. Trade continued whether buildings were falling down or not. Turning a corner, she spotted the rail of shabby clothing that would provide the disguise she needed. Pushing past piles of fabric and second hand clothes, she worked her way through to the back-shop.

'Haven't I paid you people enough?' came the irritated grumble from the workshop. 'What do you want with me this time? You know I pay my taxes.' The speaker lowered his voice. 'And most of the time I pay almost all of them. Even the ones I don't think I should have to pay.'

'Marcos, it's just me, Dren.' She pulled the soldier's tunic over her head and thrusted it towards the sallow skinned man. 'I'm looking to trade this in.'

'Back to your old ways, eh Dren?' he said, his moustache twitching upwards with a slight smile. 'Didn't think you would last the course.'

'Say, how did you know where I've been?'

'People talk. Your snowball fight is legendary among the merchants. Never had any time for Lord Hathron meself. Always thought he was a cut above as if he forgot that he came from the same streets as the rest of us.'

Dren's ear was drawn to the sound of a spinning wheel in a side room. Marcos' three sons were busy at work patching and mending second hand garments for sale. They had learned to thread a needle before they were old enough to walk, a fact Marcos didn't tire of telling to whoever cared to listen. He waved a hand towards his sons.

'Can't get those useless lumps to leave home. Their mother still spoils them. What wife could ever hope to be good enough?' The boys looked up from their fabrics and smiled at the man whose only concern in life was their happiness. Then they resumed their work without missing a stitch.

'So what's been happening while I've been away?' Dren handed over her cloak and tunic for inspection.

'To be honest, I've been struggling to keep the rain off our heads. There's only so much coin to go round. People are too busy fixing up their crumbling houses to bother about whether their clothes fit. Anyway,' he said, feeling the quality of the tunic and weighing up his profit, 'I'd be running a risk taking this off your hands. I mean, if I were to get caught...'

Dren was no fool when it came to Marco's tactics. 'I'm sure the profit margin will more than make up for the risk.'

They settled on a price that tended strongly to favour the tailor but Dren was in no position to haggle. She needed rid of the identifiable garment before it attracted too much unwanted attention. There was no telling who would be out looking for her, especially if there happened to be a reward for her capture.

Marcos scooped out a handful of coins from a creased

leather wallet and handed the small bundle to Dren. The coins could last a month if she was careful. He invited her to pick a set of clothes from the rails outside. Dren selected a bright green tunic from the rail, then picked up a blue coloured hood and a vivid red cloak. She inspected the garments closely. Once she saw Marcos had lost interest in her, she replaced the items with drab coloured ones, which she quickly put on before leaving the stall. She didn't know who she could trust here and, as much as she enjoyed Marcos' company, she would rather the man was unable to provide a full description should any soldiers come asking for her.

CHAPTER 2

Seema the monk awoke to the chorus of birdsong outside her small window. It was still dark but her day had now begun. She creaked over onto her knees. Sitting up with her legs stretched out in front of her, she leant forward to touch her toes, folding her body in half until her head rested on her knees. She felt the satisfying crack as the pose released the tension in her vertebrae.

Once she finished stretching, she moved on to her personal prayers. Although short in duration, her simple ritual was as full of heart and meaning as an hour of weeping and extravagant praying from anyone else. She felt her Creator smile upon her at the conclusion of her devotion, the same ritual she had carried out every morning since she had taken up her calling to become a monk, many moons ago.

Seema couldn't say how long she had been a monk. She no longer concerned herself with earthly chronometry, but rather thought of things in terms of the spiritual realm. For the followers of an eternal god, time was an elastic concept which meant that meals were either served stone cold or incinerated.

Luckily someone had the foresight to install a gong in the monastery for coordinating worship. Upon hearing this signal, Seema stood up and placed her simple brown robe around her shoulders, tying it closed at the front with a woven cord, its intertwining strands reminding her to pursue a course of harmonious unity.

She rolled up her sleeping mat then dipped her fingers into the water bowl. She washed the sleep out of her eyes and dried her face with a rough cloth before exiting her cell to join the steady stream of monks heading for the prayer hall.

Striding through the airy marbled corridors, Seema didn't stop to notice the stained glass overhead or the paintings of birds, plants and animals that adorned the walls. She was fully focused on getting to the hall in one piece. It wasn't easy being the tallest person in a monastery designed for the petite and nimble. Her fellow monks glided effortlessly through the marble hallways as if skating on a sheet of ice, while Seema tried her best not to slip on the polished tiles. Some mornings were more successful than others.

As a child, Seema would never have been called graceful. Being taller than her peers and clumsy with it, she was always the one who would get the blame when the butter dish turned up broken. She was the one who would get picked last for games since she could never catch the ball without it slipping through her fingers like water.

It wasn't that Seema went out of her way to be different. It just seemed to come naturally to her. When she first heard the Creator calling her to become a monk, she had thought that this meant she would finally be among people just like herself. It came as more than a mild disappointment to discover that, even among those on the very fringes of society, she was still something of an outcast. But Seema told herself that the Creator didn't make mistakes and had made her that size for a reason.

Seema shuffled into a space beside her elder. Petra smiled at Seema with that beatific smile. She was the closest thing Seema had to a friend. Not that anyone here was deliberately unkind. All the monks had a remarkable capacity for tolerance and love but it was only with Petra that she felt she could show her fears. And of course she knew the Creator was also well aware of her defects, having created them. She quickly cast the hint of unspoken bitterness from her mind.

Her belly rumbled in anticipation of breakfast. Seema immediately made the sign of the blubberfish and tried to immerse herself fully in the morning devotions, ignoring the sideways looks and whispers of the other monks.

The pitch of the chanting rose and Seema joined in. The union of one hundred voices giving thanks to the Creator rose up and filled the mosaic cupola overhead.

A bead of sweat trickled down her back. The heat from so many bodies made the atmosphere sticky. Seema scratched her fingernails through the rough material at an itch underneath her robe. She closed her eyes and tried to focus on the music but the unscratchable itch was still there.

She glanced over to check whether Petra was looking at her. When she saw that she wasn't, Seema gave another scratch through the fabric to try to get some relief.

The itching grew hotter and hotter until it became

like a burning. Throughout the prayer, she tried to control her will, and master her urge to claw at herself like an animal. Overwhelmed by the physical discomfort of the itch, she came out of her meditative state. She looked around the hall to see whether others were feeling it too but the chanting monks were a picture of calm serenity. She tried every meditation technique to clear her mind, but it was no use. She simply had to scratch. And she didn't care who was watching.

As she ran her nails up and down the fabric, an image came unexpectedly into her mind. It was a shoe. Not an everyday sandal but a good, sturdy, walking shoe.

It was then that she recognised the itch. It had been over a decade since she had experienced it but it was the same feeling.

When she was about ten years old, Seema had pulled her six year old sister out of the icy River Upp, freezing herself half to death in the process. It was this small but heroic deed that caused the Creator to start talking to her.

That call had started off as an itch, a physical sensation that no amount of scratching could relieve. In the end, she tried speaking to the Creator and, when she did, much to her surprise, the Creator answered her back. The voice told her to pack a few possessions, say farewell to her family and join the monastery.

Other monks had been surprised at the Creator's choice. But, Petra assured her, the Creator didn't need a thousand lukewarm voices in the choir. She called people who could do a job and do it well and that included Seema. The good and the exemplary were chosen to be the Creator's representatives on earth, leaving the rest of the population largely untroubled by religion.

But today of all days she had to ignore the itch for this was a high holy day for the order of monks. The Order's sacred task was to guard a scroll known as The Winterhawk Prophecy. Today the scroll would be unfurled for its annual reading, to prove that no harm had come to it.

A gong signalled it was time for silence. A hush fell over the hall as the high priest in long robes the colour of a fire-moon approached the platform. Two novices carried the carved wooden scroll box with trembling fingers.

"Bring out the key," the priest commanded.

Two monks in white ceremonial robes bordered with gold stitching brought out a wrought iron key on a chain. They bowed under the weight of it and a third monk assisted turning it in the lock.

As the scroll was brought to the dais, the high priest cleared her throat.

'Brothers and sisters, as you know, our order was started with the sole task of looking after the prophecy until the day that it is fulfilled. I know this is a job that each and every one of you takes incredibly seriously."

Seema tried to concentrate on the priest's words but the scratching had done nothing to relieve the itch. In fact, it seemed to be moving around like an ant evading her fingernails.

The priest continued. 'Here are the words spoken by the prophet on the day the sun turned black:

'This is my warning and my promise to you. The Creator looks around and groans at the state of her world. Under human's care, even the animals are once again at war with one another and the earth is not at peace with itself.'

No one would notice if she scratched her back, would they? Just one tiny little scratch.

'The day will soon come when humanity is on the brink of war, the very earth will shake and groan and open up to swallow the arrogant and humble alike.

'Even the birds of the air and the trees in the forest will take sides.'

The itch travelled into a hard to reach place in the middle of Seema's shoulder blades. She bit down on her top lip. She had to ignore it. Today of all days was not the day to stand out.

'But, out of this chaos, salvation will come as an outsider. It will not be like you, neither will it be born among you. It will not be accepted by you but despite this, it is the one whom the Creator has chosen to redeem humanity.'

Her spine tingled as the itch spread round her face. Her cheeks reddened as Seema clasped her hands firmly behind her back. *It is a mere sensation. Nothing is real. Feeling is all in my mind.*

'Even though you shall mark, reject, and betray it, it holds your fate in its hands.'

The itch made its way into Seema's nose. She took a couple of breaths, sniffing deeply to shift it. The itch responded by tickling her nostrils. It was almost unbearable. *I will not sneeze,* she willed herself. *I will not destroy the sanctity of morning prayers.*

'It shall peacefully destroy your divisions and your festering rivalries without shedding blood by its own hand. Thus shall you recognise it when the time comes.'

'Amen,' said the monks in peaceful unison.

'A-a-a-a-a-achoo!!!'

CHAPTER 3

Dren headed back towards the harbour, all dressed up in her newly-acquired clothes but without the faintest idea what she was going to do next. Although she couldn't explain what was driving her, something was calling her to leave. It was no more than a whisper blowing in her ear but its message was clear. Like the sound of a far-off drum beat carried towards her by the prevailing winds, it was urging her to leave.

You must get out of the city.

Maybe what she really heard was the call of the sea. She had heard sailors talk about this before. The sea would lure them in and, before they knew it, they were many miles away from shore with only thin planks between them and a watery grave. Logic told her it was best to ignore sounds in her head that she didn't understand.

All about her, the harbour was bustling with life. After the Blubberfish celebrations, the fisherfolk reverted to their summer way of life. Most would fish near the shore, laying crates to trap crabs and lobsters in safer waters for a few months before once again yielding to the call of the deep and venturing out to deeper seas.

Today they were taking advantage of the dry weather to mend their nets and clean their boats at the quayside amidst the sound of the seabirds and the waves breaking against the harbour walls.

The pungent smell of seaweed was ever present and Dren sniffed deeply, the salty air bringing back memories of summers long ago. She walked the length of the quay, past the whistling, catching fragments of stories and the jubulant cheer of those blubber fisherfolk who were still in celebratory mood. Although they were rivals at sea when it came to landing the biggest catch, here on land they were simply old friends catching up with one another after months spent apart.

The happy mood was contagious. Dren almost got caught up in the holiday atmosphere which rippled through the air. It was only when she saw the winterhawk flag flown from the tall masts indicating the ships' allegiance to the City of Drabsea, that she felt guilty about having cast off her identity for a purse-full of coins and a set of second-hand rags.

She had chosen a loose-fitting woollen tunic and a washed out pair of grey trousers which she wore over her hose for extra warmth. A faded cloak, tied off with a rope belt completed the look. Her hair was still short from the last cut at the keep and she knew that she would still be easily mistaken for a boy.

The feeling of guilt didn't last long. At the smell of fresh seafood being roasted by the harbour wall, she gave her inside pocket a pat and followed her nose. The soup from the tavern had barely warmed her insides. She could afford to spend a coin on some freshly landed fish. As she approached the fire, one of the sailors indicated a space on the ground and invited her to sit with them.

'Welcome soldier,' said a sailor whose face was creased with wrinkles. He raised his mug of ale at Dren's arrival. Seeing Dren's puzzled face, he explained, 'It's your boots that gave you away. Military issue. Plus your hands betray the fact you've had an easy life. Take a seat boy.'

Despite being mis-gendered, Dren couldn't argue with the sailor's observation. Compared with most trades, a soldier had regular meals and less heavy lifting. Of course, the downside was the possibility of an early grave. However, she didn't think a sailor who spent the worst months of winter at the mercy of an unpredictable sea would welcome such observations from a deserting soldier who had only ever experienced peaceful times.

She took a seat on the ground beside a small fire in the hope of sharing some of their catch. She would play along with their assumptions. Now was not the time to correct the pronouns.

'You can call me Cap'n. And this here is my crew,' he said pointing towards an assortment of drunken figures all seated next to a large barrel of beer.

The Captain took a mean-looking knife from his belt. 'You'll be looking for food then?' He leaned over the fire and sliced a piece of pinkish meat from what looked like a giant tentacle. The captain offered this to Dren along with a bowl filled with more recognisable shellfish.

Despite her hunger, she wasn't convinced by the tentacled flesh but didn't want to offend her hosts. Tentatively, she took a bite of the meat. It didn't taste too terrible. She swallowed it then took another bite.

'That's good fish. Tell me, what do you call it?' she asked as she chewed.

The older man hesitated and looked around as if waiting for someone else to volunteer the information. The others held their breath.

'We call it sea monster.'

Dren stopped chewing and looked at the man.

'Sea monster?'

'Aye, like a giant snake but with tentacles.'

Dren immediately spat the half-chewed meat back into her bowl as a few of the sailors shuffled awkwardly on their bums.

'At least we now know it's not poisonous,' said a young-looking man with blackened teeth.

The captain shot him a venomous look.

'Well, not immediately poisonous, anyway,' he added, taking a swig of his drink. The sailor didn't look to be much older than Dren.

Dren's face turned green. The old captain tried to reassure her. 'Look, we were about to try some of it ourselves but it would have been rude to have taken the choice cuts and leave you with the scraps. You are the paying customer, after all.'

Something about the mention of monsters piqued Dren's curiosity and, depositing the rest of the meat back into the bowl, she asked the captain to tell her more about the monster.

Placing his hands into his pockets, the captain got himself into a comfortable position and started to speak in a deep and resonant voice.

'The blubberfish were moving fast in the water and we had been following them for a number of weeks, waiting for them to settle in a grazing spot. Strange thing was, they wouldn't settle anywhere, just kept on swimming, as if something was disturbing them. We would cast our nets and, time after time, they would come up empty. Then we tried the rod and again, nothing. It was as if all the fish had disappeared. Hunger was ever present in our thoughts.'

And then one day we saw it. Just a dark shadow. But that was enough. We knew we were being followed by a sea monster. That's what had been eating the herring and scaring away the blubberfish.

'So I gave my crew a choice. Either we kill the sea monster or it would kill us.' The captain paused for dramatic effect and raised his arms high.

Dren listened patiently, mesmerised by the storytelling even if she didn't quite believe what she was hearing.

'It was waiting for us to grow weak so it could eat us too. And so we cast our nets by the hull of the boat where we had seen the shadow hiding. But it just squeezed itself thin like a squid and slipped right through the holes.

'If we could not capture the beast with our nets, we would have to outsmart it. So I steered a course towards colder water. I guided us into the ice fields and there I put down anchor among some shallow reefs. And then we waited.

'For three long, cold nights we sat up with hunger in our bellies, afraid to sleep in case the monster lunged for us after dark. But the waiting finally paid off. One morning, by the early rays of sun I saw it. Frozen solid, it had floated to the surface.

'So there was no dramatic fight with the monster?

It just froze to death?' Dren couldn't keep the disappointment from her voice.

'Wait!' exclaimed the sea captain, afraid to lose his audience, 'I haven't finished yet.' He cleared his throat and continued. 'We pulled the monster aboard. It took all of the little strength we had left. The beast had the body of a snake and the tentacles of a giant squid. I got me knife and hacked off one of its massive limbs. As the sun came out, its green scales shimmered like emeralds in the light.

'But the rising temperatures melted the ice crystals that were keeping the beast in its deep sleep. The severed tentacle came to life, writhing and dancing around the deck, whipping anyone in its path. I had to tie it to the mast to stop it moving. But I should have realised then that the beast was not yet dead.

'When the creature had been out of the frozen water for a day, it regained its senses and the reanimated limb thrashed about on deck, nearly knocking over the mast as it threatened to capsize us. It must have realised I was in charge because it raised itself up to its full height then lowered its terrifying blood-red head to meet me with its forked tongue hissing fearsomely.

'Red?' Dren interrupted once more. 'Thought you said it was green.'

'Hush boy, this is my story and I'm not done telling it. It was red and green like rubies and emeralds and it was as tall as the mast and as broad as the ship. As it fixed its eyes upon me, I thought I had taken my last breath. At that moment, Klevor over there...' he pointed his beer mug towards a crewman, 'comes up behind it and knocked it clean overboard with an oar, leaving nothing behind but a piece of tentacle I had hacked off with my cutlass.'

'So, no one else has seen the sea monster?' asked Dren.

'Well, no,' admitted the captain. 'But that's why we brought back the meat as proof.'

Dren thought about whether any of this could be true. She hadn't known about the existence of the Wynyms before they had appeared in the woods never mind what monsters or giant squids might roam about the depths of the ocean. Yet how could she trust this drunken group of sailors when all she had was their word and a roasted piece of something that looked suspiciously like squid?

'And that be how we caught it,' he said, the captain's voice returning to its normal pitch. 'What's wrong, lad. Aren't you hungry?'

'To be honest, it's not to my taste.'

'Maybe it needs a bit more salt?' said the crew woman sitting beside the captain.

Dren gave a feeble smile. Despite her hunger, she had no plans to eat any more sea monster. She wrapped it up in a napkin and placed it in a pocket. She would dispose of it later, out of sight.

Then the voice in her mind started up again, nagging at her to go. A thought occurred to her. 'Say, would I be able to get passage on a boat.'

'Well that depends if you'd be any use,' the captain replied. 'Have you ever sailed before?

'No, I haven't,' Dren admitted. 'But I can swim,' she said brightly.

This brought on a round of laughter from the crew.

'If you need to swim, then the boat's already sank. I'm afraid we're full, I've got all the men and women

I need here. Plus we're not going anywhere for a few months yet. We've only just got back and there's the husbands and wives to see to. But why would a soldier like you be wanting passage on a boat?' The captain's eyes narrowed. 'You're not a wanted man, are you?'

Dren cursed herself for not having introduced herself with a cover story. 'If I were a wanted man, would I be sitting out here in the open talking with you all?'

'No, I suppose you wouldn't,' conceded the captain but still looked at Dren with suspicion, as if he might be missing out on a lucrative bounty.

'To be honest, I just want to travel and see the world.'

'Ah, I was young like you once.' The man relaxed. 'But there's nothing out this way except treacherous water and icebergs. You could always try going north, I suppose. But why you would go there unless you had to is a mystery to me. They 'aven't got no sea.'

'What do you mean, north? I thought it was just mountains up there. There's not a way over them, is there?' Dren felt a tingle of excitement at the conversation. She tried to keep calm despite the drumbeat in her head speeding up.

'Of course you can't go over the mountains.' He scowled at Dren's ignorance. 'You have to go through them. Don't they teach you soldiers nothing of our history? The mountains are riddled with tunnels. The Wynyms used to mine them for gold and gems. Horrible little people. Even underground was too good a place for them. Not that you see them so much no more.'

Dren couldn't help agreeing with the sea captain.

'When the gold ran out they boarded up the entrance tunnels. Greedy verminous beggars, is what they are.

Probably still hiding down there somewhere.'

Dren thanked the Captain for the food and decided to make herself scarce before anyone had the chance to question her story further. The crew turned their attention back to their drinking. No one else seemed to be in a hurry to try the sea monster, she noted.

She wrapped up the remainder of her uneaten dinner along with the stale rolls she had salvaged from the keep and placed the parcel inside the lining of her sea-blue cloak. Oddly enough, the garment seemed to have been altered by a previous wearer to include numerous concealed pockets. She couldn't fathom why anyone would need so many secret hiding places.

She bid farewell to the captain and his crew. Her mind was made up. She was going north.

CHAPTER 4

Seema felt every eye turn to judge her as the holy scroll was secured away for another year.

'I'm sorry Petra, it was an itch that got into my nose.'

Petra raised an eyebrow. 'Itch, you say. Hmm, I'll take that as my sign. Come child.'

Seema took Petra's outstreched hand. The old monk led her forward and the crowd of worshippers parted to let them through.

'Where are we going?' whispered Seema growing alarmed as she realised the elder was taking her up to the platform. 'I just need a tissue.' She gave her nose a scratch but the itch evaded her attempts at relief and moved back down towards her legs.

A murmur started up among the monks as Petra made her slow way up the carpeted steps towards the dais. She was now dragging a reluctant Seema by the hand. 'How's that nose of yours doing?'

'Much much better, thanks. Think it was just dust.'

'And the itch?' Petra stopped abruptly and Seema almost collided with her. Then Petra's smile lit up her face and she continued pulling Seema up towards the high priest who was waiting expectantly at the top.

The itch continued to travel downwards, picking up intensity as it went. Seema's cheeks were on fire with embarrassment but it was nothing to match the burning in her legs. By the time their climb ended at the top of the platform, she felt like ants were attacking both feet. Suddenly it didn't matter who was watching, she flung off her sandals, grabbed the sole of one foot and then scratched like a furious wildcat.

'My child, do you want to draw blood or do you want to satisfy the itch?' Petra took hold of both hands and a cooling sensation flooded Seema's body.

The high priest approached them. 'Petra, child of the Creator, you have the floor. What message do you bring?'

'Last night when I had said my nightly prayers and extinguished the evening candle, I was gripped by a sudden, unrelenting dream. I saw an iceberg. It was bobbing along with the flow, unaffected by the other icebergs around it, content just to drift.'

Seema didn't like standing on top of the platform. She was too far away from the other monks to read their faces, but she could read the thoughts as they floated around the room and they weren't kind.

Who does she think she is?

'Then a current gripped the iceberg and sent it hurtling towards the shore. It landed on the beach with a crash and great chunks of ice shattered onto the land. Then I saw a tiny flea crawling off the iceberg.'

'And what does this vision mean, sister,' asked the high priest.

Petra's black eyes twinkled. 'The thing about an iceberg is that what is visible on the surface is only a fraction of what is going on underneath the water. In the vision I heard Seema praying non-stop for an end to the world's ills. Then this morning when I saw her scratching and I remembered the flea, I realised the Creator had sent us a message. It is Seema's calling to go out of here on a mission.'

There were gasps around the hall. To be called was indeed a momentous occasion. For most of the monks it only happened once in their life. A warm round of applause started up.

Seema felt ill. Petra was overreacting to a simple allergy.

Then Petra placed a hand upon her shoulder. 'I think you should go,' she said quite simply.

And with that blessing, the monk knew that there was no denying it. On this most holy of days, she had indeed been called by the Creator for the second time in her life.

'Child, you must leave today but, before you go there is something I must give you. And, of course, we mustn't forget the most important ritual.'

'Whatever you need me to do, Petra, I am willing.'

She put her two hands on Seema's shoulders and gave them a squeeze. 'Breakfast!'

As Seema bit into her grain bread spread thick with beanbutter, she felt her heart overflowing with joy. She didn't know what the Creator had in store for her, but to be called to go on a journey was a great honour indeed.

She would have preferred to slip out quietly and unnoticed, avoiding any fuss but the others wouldn't hear of it. Especially, as they pointed out, her shoes were worn through to the sole, she hadn't possessed a cloak since she was a child and hadn't been outside the monastery since she had taken her vows. As a stream of well-wishers came to her table wanting to shake her hand. She stood up and wiped her buttery palms on her robes.

'Now remember this,' Agnes warned her as she handed her a fat clamshell purse with a golden clasp. 'You can't just take things without asking. You have to pay for them. Otherwise you'll get into trouble.' Seema didn't rise to the patronising tone. It wasn't as if she had been born inside. She did know how the world worked. At least she thought she did. The monks were meant to live simple lives devoid of earthly pleasures and possessions and yet this purse was stuffed full of gold coins. But now wasn't the time to question where it had come from.

'And remember that men outside are not as virtuous as the ones that live here. They want more than just prayer from your lips.'

Seema smiled at this. Although the monastery had managed to avoid public scandal, it was certainly not without want of trying from some of the younger monks, both male and female. Again Seema gave a bow of thanks for the words of wisdom she had received. Did they really think she was so naive?

'Sorry about these.' Emra handed her a hastily crafted pair of leather sandals. 'They don't make many that are-' she paused to avoid saying whatever had first come into her mind before continuing, 'in your size so I had to improvise. These should get you through the milder season at any rate.

Seema thanked the monks warmly as they wished her well and made the sign of the Creator over her head. Despite their kind gifts and warm wishes, she couldn't help sensing that they all thought she'd be back again before the sun set tomorrow. It saddened her that they underestimated her.

In spite of her awkward appearance, Seema was highly sensitive to the emotions of those around her. She could read in their faces things which others thought they had managed to conceal. But, more than that, she could also read their thoughts. It was a precious gift that very few monks had and, the ones who did were very careful not to let others know about it. It was a sure-fire way to ensure nobody ever got close. Most people didn't like the idea that the Creator could see inside your head. They preferred to keep their dark thoughts private. The idea that a friend could know something you hadn't even admitted to yourself was a worrying thought indeed.

What was supposed to be a gift from the Creator was, in practice, a curse. It hurt her to look at her fellow monks and know that not one of them thought her capable of surviving outside by herself. They were all afraid she would embarrass them. Yes, she might trip over her feet and spill her soup down her robes but she would show them she was worthy of the responsibility placed on her by the Creator.

After the crowd had left, Petra handed her a long object wrapped in cloth.

'What's this?' asked Seema.

'Just something I kept from my younger days in the hope that one day I would escape from this cursed place. Now you get to do that for me. It gladdens my heart.'

Seema took it and opened the wrapping. It was a cut length of willow to use as a walking pole. Intricate carvings were etched along its length.

Seema was thoroughly puzzled by Petra's revelation. Never before had her mentor uttered the slightest complaint about living here and hers was a mind she had no business prodding. It just wouldn't be right. Seema thanked Petra as she turned the smooth stick around in her hand. It was just the right height for her which was strange as Petra was bent over with age and couldn't have possibly used the staff herself. No explanation was offered and Seema knew better than to ask. Some things only made sense in time. She had faith in that.

She also had faith in herself. She bid farewell to her mentor and took her first step towards the city. She would make them proud. Especially her doubters.

And with that thought, the lace in her new sandals worked its way loose. With her next step, she stood on the end of the binding and lurched forward. The momentum sent her tumbling over an embankment. The rest of the monks were probably watching behind the monastery's large windows no-doubt trying to keep a solemn expression on their faces as they sniggered at her misfortune.

The embarrassment by itself was bad enough. But, what made it a hundred times worse, as she rolled faster and faster down the hill was the speeding cart hurtling round the corner.

CHAPTER 5

'What in the name of-? Are you badly hurt?' came a concerned voice from above. Seema counted the bones in her body to take her mind away from the ache in her head. She didn't seem to have any more or less than the last time she had counted so she smiled up at the voice and beamed. 'No, not badly hurt, thank you. Just a little dusty. Now, if you'd be so kind as to fetch my walking staff, I'll be on my way.'

As the man made sense of this heap of robes, he realised to his horror that he had just run over a monk. The thought quickly dawned on him: *They'll be wanting compensation. If I had only killed her outright no one would have been any the wiser. This could cost me half my house.*

Seema struggled to her feet as the man left his cart to search the bushes for her staff. She was perturbed by what she heard him think although she realised she might have misunderstood him, given the pain in her head. Why on earth would he wish to harm her? Couldn't he see it was just an accident, that she didn't mean to collide with his cart?

In her years of isolation, she had forgotten how strange the ways of the world were. Then the doubts started to creep in. Maybe she should have given this trip a bit more thought after all.

She dusted herself down as the mule hitched to the cart stamped impatiently. She raised her arm out to scratch its ears only to pause upon hearing the man shout.

'Wait! Don't touch her. She bites, that one does.'

She snatched her hand away from the reach of its teeth, lent along the animal's back and grabbed hold of its harness.

'Hey! What are you doing?' he shouted, gesturing for her to stop.

Seema merely smiled and slackened the buckle.

The donkey gave a snort as the pressure was released from its aching muscles. It breathed a deep sigh of relief and nosed her arm in thanks,

'Well now, I've seen it all. You religious folk must have an affinity with the animals. She's been foul tempered since we bought her. Responds to nothing but the whip.'

'Her harness was too tight,' said Seema in a soft voice. 'There's always a reason with animals. They're never born bad. You just need to take the time to listen to them and figure out what's wrong.' She stopped talking before she could be accused of lecturing him. She had been warned against doing such things in the wider world as it was often needed yet seldom appreciated.

'Listen to them? I suppose you're going to tell me the donkey spoke to you or some such thing?'

She fired him a look that stopped him in his tracks despite it being delivered with a smile.

'I think you'll find that animals don't speak, regardless of what fables your mother told you.' She didn't add that, despite their lack of speech, she could read the thoughts of animals easily enough. However, she had learned years ago that, especially in the spring, their minds were firmly fixed on one thing. And that was the one thing that made her blush.

She shook her head. 'I know how to treat an animal. We have a small farm in the monastery,' she said to stop the man's mind dwelling on the mystery of things. 'You should be able to place one hand between the collar and the skin otherwise it'll chafe. How would you like to walk about with your belt tied tightly around your neck?'

The man's face reddened as if he didn't know whether this was a threat or not.

'Now,' she added before the man had a chance to refuse, 'Are you going to give me a lift or what?'

Seema had already hoisted herself onto the back of the cart and was beaming expectantly. Reluctantly, the man climbed aboard and set them moving with a dunt to the donkey's ribs, although, in the presence of the animal-loving monk, it was more a gentle nudge than his usual kick.

The cart gradually built up speed. The merchant didn't strike up much of a conversation and Seema was happy to ride in silence. After being shut away from the world, there was just so much to take in and her eyes were hungrily feasting on the sights.

After a few miles, they approached the waterfront. 'I'm only going as far as the port,' the driver announced.

'Then that's where I'm going too,' said Seema, shielding her eyes with her hand as she scanned the horizon. The glow of the sun over the low bank of cloud illuminated the small fishing boats bobbing up and down on the water. It had been a long time since Seema had last seen the sea but it looked as vast and changeable as she had remembered.

'Where are you headed for?'

'I'm heading wherever the Creator wills me to go,' she said, turning to look at him with a faraway smile.

After another mile, he guided the cart to the edge of the road and announced that they had arrived.

Taking great care not to trip for a second time that day, Seema gathered up her cloak with one hand, picked up her staff with the other and successfully managed to dismount. She bid the man farewell with a sign of blessing and walked in the direction of the sea wall.

Seema surveyed the array of coloured boats moored in the sheltered harbour, masts stretching up towards the sky like a forest of leafless trees in winter. Deck hands were busy painting, hammering and fixing the fishing vessels ready for the following season. She walked past rows of clawfish crates stacked high on the pier, the fresh smell of warm seaweed bringing memories flooding back. But this was not a day for dealing with ghosts that had lain buried for so long. She turned away from the bustle of the sailors and made for the town.

CHAPTER 6

Several roads would take Dren north towards the Celestial City and into the mountains. The main highways tended to be used by merchants and were kept in a good state of repair. Regular patrols were carried out by the Kingdom Watch to deter robbers and thieves from helping themselves to the goods being transported. But Dren knew she had to avoid these at all costs, just in case her description had been circulated and anyone was out looking for her.

Another quieter route followed the banks of the River Upp but this flowed under the shadow of the keep. She wished to avoid rekindling troubling memories as well as avoiding running into Hathron. There would be no second stay of execution.

It would be safer to stick to the backstreets, at least until she had crossed over the boundary with Arcaria, a two day walk away. She could then follow the river to the Celestial City and, from that point onwards, she would be at the mercy of the gods.

But safer didn't mean safe. The city was full of hazards waiting to trap the unwitting and violent muggings were a daily occurrence. She raised her hood up over her head. She could probably pass as some kind of trader but she didn't want to give the impression that her purse was too full so she slowed her pace and hoped that her aging cloak might give the impression she was down on her luck.

She put her hand to her hip and felt something missing from her belt. She was very aware that she didn't possess a weapon. Like the sailors on the dockyards, most workers kept a small sword or knife hanging on display. However, it would be less usual to see a trader bearing arms. Their class tended to be more discreet. Concealed weapons were their preference.

As for actually carrying a weapon, Dren was now trained to kill and there was a risk that she might have to take someone's life. She didn't want to be forced to make that decision again. The image of the Wynym flashed into her mind. She steadied her breathing and cleared her head. The thought faded but, as usual, the feeling of disgust lingered in the back of her throat.

She passed a row of boarded up houses. She had only been away from the city for six months but a lot had changed in that time. People now hurried about from one place to the next as if tomorrow might never come. There was an air of fear in town. She could feel it as readily as she could smell the stench of the rubbish which crowded the back alleys. She might come to regret the decision not to take a weapon but, all things considered, travelling without one would be the safer option at present.

As she rounded a corner and continued towards the central market place, a hush descended. For a moment everything went strangely quiet. Dren couldn't quite put her finger on what had changed. And then the ground swallowed her whole.

******

Seema had no particular route in mind as she meandered through the city, taking in the sights she hadn't seen in a long time. She was happy just to be out walking in the fresh air. There was a distinctive style to the Drabsea architecture with row upon row of overcrowded houses. Some of the original buildings were several stories high and painted white to contrast with the deep blue of the sea. They gleamed as the sun reflected off the dazzling exteriors.

But, in contrast with how she remembered the town, other structures had appeared in between the tall buildings. Some of these were no more than makeshift shelters, hastily erected to fill the gaps where earth tremors had torn down whole buildings. The city groaned under the weight of the loss.

Seema began to feel overwhelmed by the sheer number of thoughts and feelings she could sense coming from the throng of people all around. She tuned them out as best she could. It was hard to describe the experience to those who didn't have the gift. It was like visiting a cheese market in the height of summer where it quickly became hard to tell one pungent blue cheese from another. And so it was with thoughts. In a crowd, one thought blended into another and another until it became like a soup.

Taking long, loping strides, she soon reached a space where the crowd thinned out. Despite her apprehension, she was experiencing true freedom. Here temptation was all around her whereas, in the monastery, there was no real alternative to always doing the right thing.

Seema didn't often find time to contemplate her place in the world. But now, as she surveyed the market stall with its boxes of fruits, rolls of cloth and every kind of hot meat smoking on a grill, she thought of all of the other occupations she could have found herself in. Her family were educated people. Her mother had been a teacher and her father did whatever job ensured the rent got paid on time.

But it was an unspoken rule that family was an unwanted distraction to contemplation and prayer and she had not seen them since the day she left. Monks were encouraged to cut all ties with the outside world. She hadn't questioned the tradition but she did wonder about her younger sister from time to time. Was she married? Was she happy? Seema had saved her life all those years ago when she had pulled her out of the sea.

And then a feeling intruded at the back of Seema's mind. It was a sensation of panic but it wasn't her own. Something was not right. She turned to find the direction where the feeling was strongest and tried to follow the trace of the emotion, even though she could not make any sense of it. The feelings intensified as she passed under an arch before it was extinguished like a candle blown out by the wind.

Only then did she realise what she had been sensing. An entire row of houses had been reduced to a dusty pile of rubble. Everywhere, people were running and screaming but worse than the blind panic was the unmoving limbs sticking out of the rubble. It was a terrible sight and what she had been hearing had been the panicked thoughts of those trapped within the buildings as well as those frantically trying to rescue survivors.

Seema took in all of this in a fraction of a second. Then she gathered up her cloak and ran as fast as her tightly laced sandals permitted towards half-collapsed houses. She grabbed hold of large rocks with both hands and passed them along the line of volunteers. Soon, a crying child emerged. He had been passed out of a hole made by his parents, howling and covered in brick dust but at least he was alive. The volunteers increased their efforts and the hole was widened. Eventually, his parents were pulled to safety, both bleeding from head wounds but mercifully alive. Seema made a sign of thanks to the Creator.

Then a warning shout rang out and Seema braced herself as the ground moved. A crack appeared between her feet and a gaping hole opened up like a wound along the street. She leapt to one side and it took all the balance she could muster not to fall into the rift. And then, as if standing on a wave of earth she was transported several metres along the ground before the tremor stopped and deposited her unceremoniously on the ground. The next thing she could see as she emerged from her daze was a dark hooded figure standing over her, holding out a friendly arm.

And, for the second time in her first day of freedom, she was helped to her feet by a stranger.

CHAPTER 7

Everything around Dren went dark and she felt the world give a shake. And then it stopped. She groped round about her and felt soft earth crumbling through her fingers. Above her head was something like dark clouds. For a worrying moment, she thought that the sky had fallen down on her head. She reached up to investigate, but rather than the soft clouds she had expected, her hand brush against rough cloth. She pulled at the material until she found an edge. She kept pulling and eventually found daylight.

Using her legs, she pushed herself upwards until her head and shoulders were above ground. She experienced the strangest sensation as if she was climbing out from her own grave. Luckily, the crevice was not very deep and she managed to heave herself out unassisted through clouds that turned out to be the awning from a shop which had fallen from overhead, trapping her in a sinkhole.

Dusting down her clothes, she ran her hands along her limbs, checking for bleeding. She was relieved to find nothing worse than a few bumps and scrapes. More alarming were the noises all around. Screaming filled the air accompanied by cries for help, indicating that others had not been so fortunate. She was lucky to have escaped with only bruises.

And then the earth moved again, catching her off balance and throwing her to the ground. She landed painfully on her face. Dazed, she lifted her head. A face stared back at her.

Dren jumped to her feet. An awkward silence fell and Dren realised she was staring at a woman. She stretched out her hand to the stranger. She took it and Dren helped her onto her feet. Dren felt very small as she raised her head to meet the woman's eyes. She towered a good arm's length above her.

'Are you okay?' Dren asked.

'I'm sorry, I'm just so clumsy on my feet,' said the woman sounding thoroughly annoyed at herself. Her voice was surprisingly soft.

Dren started to explain that it wasn't her fault but she didn't seem to be listening.

'We have to help those people.' The woman pointed at a spot in the ground where a house had stood just moments before. Now, all that remained was a pile of white stones and a stray dog sniffing the dust.

Dren looked at the rubble just to be sure but she couldn't see anybody. She turned back to the woman.

'Down there? But I can't hear anyone.' She gestured to where the crowds were running to pull people from collapsed buildings. 'Wouldn't we be better going over there, where the others are?' She looked back at the rubble. Surely no one could have survived underneath all that. 'If there's anyone down there, they're surely dead.'

She looked straight at Dren. 'You'll just have to trust

me then.' There was a note of authority in her voice that made Dren pay attention. 'There are people in there who are dying.' The woman grunted as she heaved herself out of the shallow hole. 'Others can help the rest but these people need us now.'

Dren's expression betrayed the fact that she wasn't at all convinced but she was in no position to argue. This was the tallest woman she had seen in her life and she spoke with a gentle but commanding voice. Even if Dren had been wearing her full battle armour, she would still have obeyed this woman. There was nothing for it but to follow her.

They spent an exhausting few minutes digging together, lifting rocks and shovelling dust and earth with their bare hands. Dren's hands sifted through chipped mugs and smashed bowls, which only hours before would have held breakfast. She picked out pieces of chairs and table legs. And then Dren touched something warm. It felt like a hand.

'I've found an arm!' she bellowed.

The woman moved in to have a closer look. 'I sincerely hope it's attached to someone. But you'll never find out if you stop now.'

Irritated by the woman's abruptness, Dren continued to dig, carefully trying to free whoever was buried here. Eventually, she unearthed the rest of the body. It was a man. He was covered in a fine grey dust from head to toe and he wasn't moving.

'I don't think there's anything else we can do for him now,' said Dren, trying to shield the woman from the sadness of the discovery.

But, before she could say any more, the woman reached forward and took the lifeless man into her arms. Cradling him like he was her own child, she shed a single tear which fell onto his face. Gradually, colour returned to the man's face. After a minute he began to take shallow breaths. Dren looked on in amazement. It was as if all he had needed was a good wash to remove the dust.

The man gave a cough, emptying his lungs of brick dust. He managed to sit up. A small boy whom Dren had passed on her way here appeared by their side.

'Papa!' he cried as the man blinked in the daylight. The survivor hugged his child and then turned to the two strangers who had just saved his life.

'What happened?' asked the man, trying to express both his gratitude and his sadness without there being enough words to say what he felt.

'I'm Dren and this is...'

'Seema.' The tall woman pointed her thumbs inwards. 'There was an earthquake and the ground moved causing the buildings to collapse. We heard you calling out and dug you out of the wreckage.'

Dren raised her eyebrows. The man had not been in a fit state to call out, but she didn't correct her.

'You should rest,' Seema continued, 'But first we need to move away from these other buildings. They might not be stable now the ground has shifted again.'

The man struggled to his feet with Dren and Seema helping to bear his weight. The young child followed clutching a doll as they walked a safe distance away.

'My house...' said the man in a desperate tone as he looked back at the ruins. The only part left was a solitary staircase, leading to nowhere.

'At least you have your life,' said Seema. 'And your son still has his father.'

'That is true.' The man held his head in his hands and started to weep. 'What was I thinking? I can't begin to thank you for saving me.' He coughed deeply from his lungs, bringing up black particles which he spat onto the ground. 'I can't repay you for what you have done but, when I have rebuilt our home, I would be honoured if you would come and visit me.'

Seema smiled. 'I shall, if the Creator wills it.'

Dren gave her a look, but the man seemed unfazed by her strange sayings. He nodded gratefully and walked off leading his son by the hand.

CHAPTER 8

When the man was out of earshot, Dren unclenched her fists. 'What does the Creator have to do with any of this?'

'Why, the Creator has everything to do with this. She who set the wheels in motion continues to grease them.' Seeing Dren's puzzled expression, she added, 'Do you think it was merely by chance that you met me today?'

'I would rather think that pure unlucky chance crushed the man under the walls of his own house. If I thought it was actually the will of some malevolent being then I might start to dislike the Creator.'

'You think the Creator wanted the man to suffer?' Seema sounded horrified.

'I just know I don't like the sound of your Creator much. If there was such a being then surely he would have stepped in and saved the man before his house fell and crushed him.'

'Firstly, the Creator's a she. What man do you know that has ever given birth?'

'Well no, but-'

'And the Creator isn't there to stop bad things happening otherwise how would we ever experience goodness? You can't have one without the other.'

Dren realised this was no ordinary stranger. She didn't feel like being preached at and tried to walk away but the woman followed her and continued her lecture.

'The events in this world are neither good nor bad. They just happen and whether they cause pain or bring happiness is purely arbitrary.'

'That sounds like a bit of a godless world to me.'

Seema ignored Dren's interruption and continued, 'We can either try to do good, like when we helped the man, or we can ignore his plight and go about our own business. Equally, we have the option to rob his house while he lies there dying. Life is all about the choices we make. And the Creator can help us make the right choices.'

'But what has the Creator got to do with what I did today? We only did what came naturally.' Dren rubbed her head.

'And is it every day that a monk appears out of nowhere and directs you to move rocks when you think it is futile?'

'I suppose not,' she conceded.

'I believe the Creator is calling us all to do great things. We can ignore that voice and let chance dictate the course of our lives, or we can ask for the Creator's help in all that we do and live the fullest life available to us.'

Dren supposed that what Seema said made some sense but it didn't explain everything. It would take more than clever words to convince her. She kicked a small pebble that was lying in her way.

Then she thought about how she brought the man back from death's door with her tears. She shook the image from her head. She was afraid that, if she asked, the monk might just have an answer that she wasn't prepared to hear.

At that moment, the skies darkened and heavy drops of rain poured down. Dren looked at Seema and they both ran for cover, eventually finding shelter under an archway. They hovered awkwardly, trapped together as they waited for the rain to stop. Not wanting to appear hostile, Dren changed the subject. 'So, what's with the robes?'

'These?' she looked down, a puzzled expression on her face. 'But we all wear these. We eliminate unnecessary choice so as to make better use of our minds.'

'We? You mean there's more of you?' The idea of a whole race of giant women dressed in robes who could bring people back to life with their tears both concerned and amused her.

'I'm sorry, I don't mean to laugh, I just... never mind.'

Seema's cheeks flushed red with embarrassment and Dren sensed she had overstepped the mark. 'Look, I'm sorry. I was rude. Are you hungry?'

She reached into her inner pocket and pulled out the parcel of food she had salvaged over the last few days.

'The bread is a little stale, but it's better than the stuff they're serving in the local taverns.'

'Thank you, that's very kind,' she said, taking a bread roll and breaking it in half. 'What's this purple meat?' she asked as she popped a piece into her mouth.

'That'll be the sea monster.'

'I see.' Seema stopped chewing.

'That's kind of what I thought,' said Dren. 'Although it's most likely just squid. The sailors were already quite drunk by the time I met them. I think they were just looking for an excuse to tell a good story.' She still didn't have the slightest desire to try any more, choosing a roll instead.

'Funny how sea monster does very little for your appetite,' said Dren.

'Yes, strange that.' They both let out a shared laugh.

Dren decided to donate the rest of the suspicious looking seafood to a cat which had been following her for a while, drawn by the smell of food. She placed the purple meat on the ground and watched the animal nibble a corner of a tentacle. No sooner had the cat tasted the meat than it gave a hiss, arched its back and ran off into a doorway, still snarling.

'I suppose that settles it then. No more sea monster for anyone,' and she kicked the tentacle into the gutter, glad that she hadn't eaten any more of the stuff.

'So what are you doing here?' Dren tried again to make polite conversation. 'Are you visiting someone?'

Seema gave a smile. 'I've left my home and I'm going on a journey.'

'Where are you going?'

'I haven't figured that bit out yet,' she said, gazing out into the distance.

'That sounds a bit like me. I'm trying to get as far away from here as possible.'

'Then maybe we were destined to meet,' she said, the laughter gone from her voice.

Dren thought back to their earlier conversation. 'So you think that that man's house was meant to collapse just so we could meet?'

She shook her head. After a moment of silence she spoke again. 'Perhaps the reason we both left our homes was so that child would still have a father tonight.'

After a short while, the rain let up and Dren decided she better start moving while it was still daylight.

'It's been nice meeting you. I wish you well with your journey,' she said not wanting to waste any more time.

As she was about to walk away, she noticed a shopkeeper approaching from a doorway nearby. When the man saw Seema, he made angry gestures and shouted at her to leave. Dren felt a pang of guilt when she heard the man demanding compensation for the murder of a prize rat-catcher. Seema exchanged a few words with the man and hurried to catch up with Dren.

'What was that about?' Dren asked.

'Oh, nothing important. Seems some folk are superstitious when it comes to monks. They don't like us hanging around in case we bring bad luck.'

'You're really a monk?' she said, glad to be able to change the topic before Seema figured out Dren's role in the cat's demise.

'Does that surprise you?'

Dren was relieved to discover there was a reason for her strange mannerisms. She had thought she was just odd. 'I was raised by monks when I was a baby, so I've been told. I was too young to have any memory of it. But tell me this, if you are meant to make people believe in the Creator, why do you live miles away out in a monastery where no one can see you?'

'Do you really need to see me to know that the Creator exists? Have you never had a little baby reach out its hand to grab your finger?'

'But that's...'

'Or smelled the wet grass just after a rainstorm,' she continued. 'Or had a stranger pay you a compliment that touched your heart?'

'I suppose,' she said reluctantly.

'Then you have experienced the mystery of creation.' She stopped and turned to face her. 'What more could I do to convince you than what is already visible?'

'So that's what god looks like? Babies and the rain?' She tried to look less sceptical than she felt.

'In a way, I suppose that they are. But what I meant was that these things are gifts of the Creator's abundance. By these signs we may know that we are cared for.'

This wasn't the kind of conversation Dren had been expecting. She would be polite for the short time they were going to be together.

Seema continued, 'I'm no different from you. I'm following the call in my heart and going where it sends me. Same as you.'

This was making Dren's head spin. Her life was nothing like the monks. 'But you wear robes and chant. I'm not anything like you.'

'These are merely outward symbols of what's on the inside. Think of the robes like a uniform. They symbolise that I have pledged my allegiance to the Creator. Same as a soldier's uniform represents his pledge to his ruler.'

Dren felt nervous at the mere mention of soldiers. Like the sailors down at the docks, could it be that the woman had also worked out what Dren was? Hopefully it was just a coincidence.

'So, what are you running away from?' asked Seema, changing topic.

'I'm not running away, I chose to leave.'

'Are those not the same thing?' she asked. And then

she squawked. 'My staff! I must have dropped it when I fell.'

Dren watched open-mouthed as she ran off in a panic towards the unstable ground. 'Wait!' she shouted after her. 'It's not safe.'

But the monk was already out of earshot. Still feeling a degree of responsibility, Dren rushed after her. When she finally caught up with her, she was peering down into a deep hole. Dren looked down and saw a wooden staff, broken in half. It was well out of even the monk's reach.

As much as Dren told herself that it wasn't her problem, she still didn't like to see her upset.

'It's okay, we can get another one,' she said.

But Seema shook her head. 'You don't understand. It was a gift. I only received it today and I've already lost it. I should have taken better care of it. I can't believe how stupid I am.' She sniffed and wiped her nose on the sleeve of her robe. 'If I can't be trusted with a simple stick, how can I be entrusted with anything bigger to look after?'

'You're not stupid at all,' Dren said, trying to console her. She started to put her arm round Seema's shoulders to comfort her then pulled it back as she realised she couldn't reach. 'Listen, I can make you a new one. The willow grows along the river by the woods. It should be easy enough to find a replacement.'

That's when she realised the consequences of trying to be nice. She had just invited her to travel with her for the next two days. And, when she saw the monk's face brighten, she didn't have the heart to change her offer.

'Come,' Dren said gently, leading her away from the edge. 'It's not safe here.'

Maybe it would be good to have some company, she thought. Even an unlucky monk with strange ideas was better than being alone. But, as she thought it, she realised the foolishness of it all. A giant monk as a travelling companion would attract a lot of unwanted attention. They would need to be extra careful to stick to the back roads.

Today was certainly not going to plan. Not that she had an actual plan but, if she had made one, it wouldn't have involved any of this.

They travelled briskly for the rest of the day. Seema clung to Dren's side, never questioning where they were going. Dren walked quickly hoping the monk would tire and leave her to carry on alone. Although Drabsea was a vast city, Dren was familiar with its streets and she knew how to navigate the shadier quarters with ease. Wearing her dark hood up over her head in case the rain came, she felt almost invisible. She could be anyone she wanted to be right now. She let her imagination run wild and pretended she was a spy with an important message to deliver to the king.

In this game, she would walk the streets, scanning for hazards, avoiding dangerous shadows where an assassin might lurk looking to wrestle the secret message from her before ending her life with the swift strike of a concealed blade. Then she remembered the note she had been meant to deliver for Toran. She hadn't even managed to do that right.

She sighed as she thought of Aimree. She really missed her and she had only been gone one night. She tried to avoid the thought that she might never see her again. And then she remembered that Toran liked her first and she really shouldn't be thinking about her like that.

The thought of Toran brought a scowl to her face. It wasn't like they were friends any longer. Toran's betrayal had released her from any obligation towards him.

The path grew dark and Dren realised the hour was getting late. They would need to find an inn for the night. Had she been alone, she would just have slept in a doorway again, but she couldn't expect a monk to sleep rough. She cursed herself again for having made such a rash offer. The monk was only going to slow her down and cost her money she didn't have.

As if she could hear her thoughts, Seema said, 'We should think about turning in for the night. But we'll need a cover story to avoid attracting unwanted attention. I get the feeling that your journey is more clandestine than mine.'

'You're not wrong there. But how do we avoid drawing attention to ourselves?'

'There is a way. But I don't think you're going to like it,' she said with a smile.

CHAPTER 9

Time and the whims of fashion had not been kind to the stables. What had once been an impressive building, frequented by well-to-do merchants and suppliers to the army, had become rundown and ramshackle. Rolled flakes of what little paint remained on its facade clung precariously to the woodwork. The owner had long since given up emptying the buckets under the leaks in the roof. It currently boasted a handful of underfed animals with the rest of the stalls abandoned to the weeds.

Horses had replaced donkeys as the transport of preference among the rich in town and the stable owner clearly couldn't afford to upgrade his stock in the current climate. His eyes lit up at the sight of potential customers.

Without being prompted, he led out the first animal for inspection. The donkey took one look at Seema, stamped its hind hoof on the ground and refused to move another step.

The merchant pulled on the rope, first with one hand and then two but it was clear to all the donkey was going nowhere. The man led it back to its pen, trying his best to smile while discretely cursing under his breath. He promised to return shortly with an even finer specimen.

'These rare breeds- so temperamental.' He shrugged apologetically.

He held the rope taught as he paraded a darker coloured donkey. This time the animal had a hood over its eyes. It gave the occasional kick but otherwise allowed itself to be led by the nose. Handing the rope to Dren, the merchant offered his hand to Seema and helped her up onto the animal's back.

'Let's see if he doesn't walk as sweetly as a lamb for madam,' he said through gritted teeth. This was meant more as a threat to the donkey than a promise to the customer.

As Seema mounted the donkey, sitting side-saddle over its back, the animal lurched dangerously over to one side.

The merchant tried to mask his worried expression with an awkward smile. 'If I may be so bold. This beast is possibly best ridden in the military style, forward-facing as if he were a thoroughbred horse.'

Seema looked uncomfortable as she grabbed its neck and swung her leg over the other side of the donkey. But with her weight now evenly spread, the donkey gave a relieved gasp as it finally managed to get some air into its lungs.

'Much better!' said the man smiling from ear to ear. He removed the hood and patted the animal's head, being sure to keep out of reach of the teeth. The donkey gave him a look of pure disgust then turned away to examine Dren with a suspicious eye.

'What's the donkey's name?' asked Dren, trying to act

the part of the groom.

'He's called Thunder,' said the trader.

'Is that because of his natural might and power?' asked Seema. At that moment the donkey's stomach let out an alarming rumble, followed by an explosion as his digestive cycle came to its natural conclusion in a steaming pile on the ground.

'Not exactly, Madam.'

Dren had to admit, her eyes had been opened as she watched Seema bartering. Her travelling companion was certainly able to hold her own when it came to driving a hard bargain. It was as if she knew the trader's next move in advance.

At times in the negotiations, Dren could have sworn that she was missing something, some obvious clue that revealed the trader's hand. Judging by his face, the donkey trader felt it too. He had no idea how this parochial monk managed to out-manoeuvre him at his own game. But Seema continued to smile serenely throughout and gave nothing away. When the sale was complete, Dren wasn't sure that the trader wasn't worse off than before the bartering had started.

The road through town was well maintained and relatively flat and they should by now be tucking into a hot dinner and downing a pint of something wet. However, by the time Dren had convinced their new purchase to walk in a straight line for at least some of the time, the last rays of daylight had almost faded completely from the sky. There was now no chance of making it to the inn in time for dinner. Resigning herself to going hungry, she coaxed the donkey along the stony road. She would never kick an animal, but she didn't think the donkey would extend the same courtesy to her and so she kept well out of reach of its legs. And for good measure, she also avoided its teeth.

'It shouldn't be long now, only another mile or so to the inn,' she said with a strained smile, forcing herself to remain cheerful despite the situation.

Seema looked almost ridiculous sitting atop the donkey. Dren was sure it couldn't have been a comfortable ride for her with only a padded sack for a saddle but, as it had all been her idea, she wasn't going to waste too much pity on her.

'Are you sure you don't want a shot?' asked Seema as she bounced precariously from side to side.

Dren would rather have walked barefoot through burning fire than try her luck on the donkey's back. Thunder gave her a defiant look as if daring her to even consider mounting him. 'It's probably better for me to walk in case anyone is watching us.'

Confident in their disguise, Dren took them along the main northern highway. She wasn't too keen on losing her peripheral vision but she made sure to walk with her hood up, just in case she was recognised by a passing soldier.

The inn came into view as they rounded a final corner. The building was a little crumbly around the edges with its paintwork now more grey than white. Yellow moss clung to every window frame and a dozen roof tiles were broken. But it looked perfectly adequate for their purpose. After all, she told herself, they only needed somewhere dry to lay their heads down for the night.

Dren held the donkey tightly by the rope and managed to get him to stand against the raised walkway at the front of the inn just long enough to allow Seema to dismount. She almost managed to do this without stumbling, but Thunder bucked at the last minute and the clatter of her boots as Seema bounced off the wooden deck would have been loud enough to wake anyone sleeping within.

The donkey gave a look as if to say he was only trying to help, which didn't fool either of his new owners. But they were both tired from travelling all day and neither had the energy to take issue with his lack of manners.

Seema approached the front door and knocked sharply. A shuffling of bolts and locks came from within. Then the aging landlady appeared. She looked them up and down before barking, 'There's no dinner. And the hot water's finished.'

That's fine,' said Seema with all the grace she could muster. 'I come to claim the right to rest,' she added.

The innkeeper hesitated. There was no denying the monk had every right to ask for shelter. However, this didn't extend to the scruffy youth she was travelling with and she told them as much. Had she seen them coming she would probably have closed the shutters and pretended to be asleep. Reluctantly, she beckoned Seema in. She took another look at Dren and pointed over to the stable then quickly closed the front door behind them in case Dren hadn't understood her meaning and tried to follow them in.

Dren groaned inwardly as she heard the bolt slide shut. She understood the woman's meaning all too well and turned in the direction of the stable. Given the run-down state of the inn, this didn't bode well for a good night's sleep.

CHAPTER 10

As Dren lay awake on the itchy hay bale, she knew she was in for a long night. The stable accommodation was more suited to those who slept standing up and weren't too bothered by the absence of hygiene. She wondered whether that would have been the time to admit that she was only disguised as a boy. But being herself wouldn't give them a cover story. How could they explain why a raggedy looking girl with a military hair cut was lodging with a monk? If anything, the truth would attract more attention than simply claiming Dren was a groom. She didn't want to lie to the monk, not even by omission. But they would shortly part ways so it wasn't as if Dren would have to keep who she was hidden for long.

The noises coming from the animals were relentless. Thunder seemed determined to win some kind of competition with the other three beasts who were stabled in the same barn. His braying ability was clearly something he was very proud of.

When he saw Dren looking towards him, he bared his teeth and pulled back his lips in what Dren could only imagine was the donkey version of a sneer. Maybe Dren was just being over sensitive, but it looked as though the donkey was mocking her.

The thought of Seema tucking herself into a freshly made bed made this even harder to swallow but she tried her best to be happy for her. Tossing and turning in an effort to get comfortable, she told herself she had slept in worse places. But it had been a long time since sleeping rough had been a normal part of her daily routine.

Something stabbed into her forearm. Thinking it was a sharp piece of straw, she tried to brush it away. That's when she realised something was biting at her skin. She slapped her arm and reduced whatever had been feeding on her to a crushed smear of blood and wings. She cursed the donkey under her breath. *Lice!* Of course it just had to have lice.

Finally, her eyes grew heavy, her surroundings blended into the void and she started to drift off to sleep. Just enough time had passed for her to fall into a comfortable slumber when she felt something warm against her arm. Confused, she blinked open a sleepy eye and looked up, only to see a donkey face looking straight at her. And then the smell hit. The unmistakable scent of urine assaulted her nostrils and Dren realised to her horror that she was lying prone in a pool of donkey pee.

Scrambling to her feet, Dren shook her fist at the donkey. Thunder was still mid-flow, creating a miniature river right beside Dren's straw bed. There was nothing for it but to curl up on the ground outside. If anyone wanted to steal the unattended donkey, they were welcome to him. She left the stables uttering a torrent of swear words. Both she and the donkey knew that Thunder had won that particular battle.

We'll see if you're still smiling tomorrow with half a ton of monk on your back, she thought as she rinsed out her sleeve in a trough before spreading out her cloak and lying down to snatch some sleep before morning.

The smell of fresh grass and damp earth disorientated Dren when she next awoke. Daylight flooded her eyes as she rolled over. Heavy footsteps approached. Blinking against the light, she was momentarily confused. Where was she and why was she lying on the ground? She felt a flutter of panic. A whiff of stale urine reminded her exactly what had happened. Where was the donkey?

'Did you sleep well?' asked Seema with a voice filled with far too much joyful enthusiasm for the time of day.

Dren was so stiff that she could only manage a slight nod of the head and even that hurt.

'I suppose it's authentic enough,' she continued. 'It does genuinely smell as though you've been around donkeys your whole life.'

A yawn prevented Dren explaining what her donkey had done. She was glad Seema hadn't felt the need to ask why she was sleeping on the ground outside rather than in the stables. She must have thought that Dren was playing the part well.

Seema, on the other hand, looked well rested after a night in a comfortable bed. No doubt she had already eaten. Jealousy welled up inside Dren. Weren't monks meant to sacrifice their own comfort for the sake of others? Why was she getting the raw end of the deal?

She hated to admit it but she was beginning to crave her morning bowl of chewsan. It wasn't exactly the taste that she missed, but she had come to appreciate its warmth and the way it filled her up. A hot bowl made with the newly ripened berries that she had picked fresh from the spice gardens would be just the thing right now.

'It's not the grandest of inns but I think even this one would draw the line at letting you near the dining room.'

Dren's eyes lit up as Seema placed a tray of breakfast down on the ground. Guilt crept over her for labelling the monk as selfish.

Her eyes grew wider still as she examined a couple of hard boiled eggs. The exotic looking patterns on the shell sparkled as they reflected the light. These were swiftly devoured followed by a thick slice of buttered bread washed down with a bowl of steaming cha. It was a welcome change from yesterday's meal of stale rolls.

Once she had finished eating, she thanked Seema and placed the used dishes back on the tray. In order to keep up appearances, it would be up to Dren to clear up. No one would expect to see the monk tidying up after her groom.

Carrying the dirty tray inside, she paused as her eyes adjusted to the dim light of the eating area. A group of merchants were seated at a large table and, if the muck on their boots was anything to go by, the rest of the visitors were farmers bringing their goods to market. No one even gave so much as a glance in her direction. The disguise was working.

After lingering for a moment just to be sure she wasn't being watched, she returned the tray to an empty table. None of the staff were paying her the slightest bit of notice either. When she was absolutely certain that nobody was looking, she helped herself to a piece of fruit that had rolled underneath a table before stepping back out into the sunlight.

It was time to play the part of the groom again. Entering the barn, she found Thunder feasting on some fresh hay. Dren deliberately kept out of kicking distance. When the donkey had eaten his fill, he gave a contented snort and stood upright, rubbing his nose against the wooden scratching post. Dren tiptoed quietly in from the side, trying to avoid spooking the wary animal and picked up Thunder's bridle which was hanging over the stall.

Hearing the crunching sound of footsteps in the crisp straw, the donkey looked over to see who was approaching and, recognising Dren, immediately lowered his nose back down to munch on the hay. Something told Dren that looping the bridle back over his muzzle was not going to be an easy task.

Unwilling to be upstaged by an animal she hadn't even wanted in the first place, Dren reached for her secret weapon.

Thunder raised one eye in Dren's direction, trying not to look too interested. His ears twitched at the sight of the ripe fruit Dren was holding in an outstretched hand. Finally his nose got the better of him. He gave a deep sniff towards the ripe piece of fruit, and made a quick movement forward, trying to snatch the prize. Dren immediately moved it just beyond the reach of the tethered donkey. Thunder snorted in frustration.

Slowly, Dren peeled the orange and made a very obvious show of putting half of the desirable fruit deep within her cloak. She offered the other half to Thunder who reluctantly allowed his soft neck to be patted. As Thunder meekly chewed on the segment he had earned,

Dren beamed at this small but significant victory. She placed the bridle over the donkey's head and led Thunder out of the stall by the reins.

The donkey offered no resistance as they walked together to the front door of the tavern to meet Seema who was ready and waiting. Without needing to use the steps, Seema swung her leg over Thunder's back. The donkey braced himself to bear her weight and the whole procedure was carried out with rather more grace than the previous night's dismount.

'If you like, we can take turns riding,' said Seema after they had travelled a safe distance away from the inn. 'You only need to travel as my groom when we are around other people.'

'To be honest, Thunder and I have only just negotiated a truce. It might be pushing my luck to try and ride him as well.'

'Speaking of donkeys, you smell like the rear end of one.' Seema blushed as she covered her mouth with her hand. 'I'm sorry, I didn't mean to be so...'

'Accurate,' Dren said, finishing her sentence. 'You're only speaking the truth. I'll walk downwind of you. Up till now I had been trying to avoid the river but we should be far enough away from the keep that I can risk having a wash.'

When they reached the edge of the city, the land opened up into an expanse of fields. These lesser travelled roads were not maintained to the same standard as the main highways and Dren felt sorry for Seema as the donkey bumped her over every rut in the road.

After a few miles, Seema suggested she might prefer to walk for a bit. Thunder gave an appreciative sigh as she dismounted. She grabbed a handful of long grass from the side of the road. He munched appreciatively and continued walking by Seema's side, looking warily out of the corner of his eye in case Dren planned on taking a shot.

They continued walking on foot until the sun sat high in the sky. 'Thunder's looking thirsty,' said Seema. The donkey's ears perked up at the mention of his name. 'Do you suppose there's a stream about here?' She wiped the sweat from her brow with a folded square of embroidered cloth. In spite of the short shower of heavy rain the previous day, the ground had already dried out leaving not so much as a muddy puddle.

'And I suppose I could do with a bath, before I start attracting flies,' said Dren.

As if on cue, the donkey gave a swat of its tail.

'Well that seems to have settled it,' said Seema with a smile. 'Let's find the river.'

CHAPTER 11

Dren didn't know this part of the countryside well. Although it still fell under the governance of the Drabsea administration, the villagers and farmers complained they received little from their rulers and yet paid the highest taxes. Their children had grown up to be naturally suspicious of strangers and Dren had never met a farmer who didn't take an instant dislike to her city manners and accent. There was no way they could turn up unannounced at a farm and ask for directions.

She looked into the distance and saw a field of grazing pasture. "If they keep animals in there, then they must have access to water. Let's see if we can't find a stream."

They reached the far corner of the field where a large trough was situated. There was no stream in sight.

Seema let out a thirsty sigh. "The water must be brought here by bucket. Never mind. At least Thunder can have a drink.' She led Thunder over to the trough.

The donkey peered at the muddy stone basin filled with brown water. He took one look at the swarm of dead flies floating in an oily sheen on the surface then curled his lip and wouldn't take so much as a sip. No amount of cajoling could convince Thunder to drink.

At that moment, a fly zipped past them. The donkey's ears twitched. The insect hovered for a brief instant above the basin then came to rest on the surface. This was the final mistake the fly would ever make.

The water stuck to the pads of its feet and, the more the insect wrestled with itself, the more its legs became hopelessly trapped in the residue floating on top. After a brief struggle, the fly grew motionless.

'Well, that's settled it then,' said Seema cautiously. 'If poor Thunder won't drink from it, we certainly won't be touching it.'

'But there must be a water source otherwise the farm wouldn't be here.' Dren tried to remain more optimistic than she felt. Her legs were tired and she was now very thirsty. She had carefully rationed the little water they carried but the supply was now exhausted.

'There's nothing for it but to keep walking until we find some.'

Changing course, she guided them in a north easterly direction. After what felt like much longer than it should have, she finally found what she had been searching for. The noise gave away the presence of running water, instantly lifting their flagging spirits.

Thunder didn't need to be told twice. At the sight of the clear stream, he pulled Dren over to the water's edge. Dren let go of the rope and both dropped to their knees and drank the clean water.

'Shall we stop here for lunch?' asked Seema.

'The area is too exposed,' said Dren, splashing cool water on her face. 'We should find a place with a little shelter just in case anyone happens to be looking for us.'

'Who would be looking for us?' ask Seema.

Dren said nothing. It was best if the monk didn't know she was assisting a felon.

When Thunder had drunk his fill, the three continued over the soft, pine covered path. Overhead, the birds sang brightly, undisturbed by the visitors below. It was peaceful and green, a different atmosphere from the shadowy Hinterwood.

As they walked, Dren looked about for any willow trees. But, to her disappointment, there were none to be seen. Seema's walking staff would just have to wait. But, truth be told, it was nice to have some company for a little while at least.

The river meandered until it almost bent back on itself, revealing a hidden clearing containing a small pool. This was fed by a pleasant waterfall, which was sheltered from prying eyes by established trees and thick foliage on either side.

'I think I'll take the opportunity to wash first,' Dren said as Seema knotted the donkey's rope around a tree next to some long grass. She waited for Seema to take the hint and leave her in peace but her head was in some faraway place and she merely smiled and nodded.

Dren gestured at her tunic but still there was no reaction from Seema. It wasn't until she removed her cloak and started to untuck her shirt that Seema realised with a start that Dren was looking for some privacy. Hastily, she announced that she would go deeper into the woods and pick some berries for lunch.

With Seema safely out of sight, Dren undressed, folding her clothes into a neat pile on the ground. They could also have done with a good wash but she didn't want to waste precious travelling time drying out clothes when she could be putting more distance between herself and the keep. She was still very much within hostile territory.

The running water was clear as glass and Dren was taken aback by the unkempt face peering back at her. As if to make sure it really was her own reflection, she put a hand up to remove a piece of straw from her hair and watched as the unfamiliar boy in the river did the same thing in reverse.

Dren was struck by how much she had changed from looking like a soldier in such a short space of time. The familiar doubts crept back in. Who was she kidding, pretending to be a soldier? She was a common street rat, nothing more. Although, if the architect was to be believed, she was also a warrior foretold by prophecy. The man was clearly under the spell of madness. She chuckled at the thought. And then there was that strange man who had grabbed her outside the pub. It was an odd encounter but he had obviously mistaken Dren for somebody else.

Dipping a bare toe into the pool, she shivered and instinctively rubbed her arms together to heat up. The temperature was still far from being pleasurable. She dipped both feet in the stream, feeling the smooth hard pebbles underfoot. She dropped to her knees and the water rose to her waist.

Soon though, the unpleasant sensation wore off and she ducked her head under, feeling the sharp rush of cold meeting her scalp. She waded over to the small waterfall and let the stream of water flow over her. Her skin felt clean for the first time in days as the force of the water removed the accumulated dirt and grime and donkey odour.

Combing her fingers through her hair, she realised it badly needed cut. Having become used to the neat military crop, she was dismayed to find how quickly her hair reverted to growing wild. Soon she would be unrecognisable. On second thought, maybe that wouldn't be a bad thing. Maybe she should let it grow out, buy a dress, chose a more feminine name and be done with Dren for good.

Scooping up a handful of small stones from the bedrock, she rubbed them over her body until she felt almost clean. Soap was a luxury she would have to do without for the time being. It was funny how only six months ago the thought wouldn't even have crossed her mind.

Further downstream, the river became reasonably deep and she swam a few strokes. Then she remembered Seema. She hoped she wouldn't come back too soon because she had no towel and would have to drip dry in the sun. Buoyed by the water, she floated over to the edge of the stream where she started to haul herself up the bank.

Her actions were interrupted by a twig snapping. Instinctively she crouched back down below the bank and ducked until the water covered her shoulders. Cover was limited here and the high bank meant she wouldn't see who was approaching until they were right on top of her.

The noise of the waterfall had masked the sound of the approaching intruder. She cursed her carelessness. What was she thinking leaving her clothes and donkey at the other side of the clearing?

She grabbed a couple of large rocks from the stream. If nothing else, she could use them to scare off an approaching animal.

A flock of dark-winged birds took flight above her head, startled by whoever or whatever was approaching. She questioned her decision not to bring a weapon as her mind raced ahead. What if it was more Wynyms, out for revenge? At least Seema's size would make them think twice before attacking. It would require half a dozen dwarfs to bring her down, with or without poisoned swords.

Her heart beat faster as the footsteps grew closer. Maybe it was only a hunter out snaring rabbits, or a poacher hoping to fish undisturbed.

The worst case would be if they tried to take the donkey. They would never be able to afford another one. Then again, Thunder would be more likely to bite them than to go off willingly. Unless, of course, they bribed him with treats.

As she pressed herself tightly against the bank, she glanced over at Thunder. Typically the stupid donkey didn't seem the least bit bothered. He was still happily munching away on the sweet moss and stubbornly oblivious to the approaching threat.

The footsteps stopped abruptly. A shadow appeared overhead, blocking out the sun and Dren could only make out a silhouette. She lifted the rock above her head and prepared to throw it at whatever was about to approach her.

'Dren!' exclaimed a female voice taking her by surprise.

To her utter horror, she realised that she recognised the voice. She lowered the rock quickly and held it in front of her to protect her modesty. She looked up and raised her other arm to block out the sun. It was Aimree!

How much had she seen?

'What in Kingdom's name are you doing down there?' she asked.

'Washing,' was the only thing Dren could think of to say.

'I'm so glad to see you. Everyone has been really worried about you since you took off so suddenly,' she said, her voice full of concern.

She thought this might be an appropriate moment to get dressed before they continued with the conversation. 'If you don't mind, Aimree, could you pass me a blanket? I'm starting to feel a little underdressed.'

Seema chose that particular moment to return, arms full of soft fruits. 'Dren,' she shouted, as if on cue. 'I'm back! Are you decent?

Aimree looked over to see where the voice was coming from. Then she froze, as if she had seen a ghost.

Seema took a single look at Aimree and dropped to the ground like a stone. She hit her head on the way down and knocked herself out cold, berries and gathered fruits spilling from her arms.

Thunder momentarily halted his chewing. He turned his attention back to Dren who shot him a look as if daring him to even consider grinning. Thunder merely snorted and returned to eating the grass.

Dren didn't mean to appear uncaring but she had her own priorities. Explanations could wait. Grabbing handfuls of river moss, she covered herself as best then, leapt out of the stream and dashed to retrieve her clothing.

Aimree could deal with the fainting monk.

CHAPTER 12

Eventually Seema came to, groaning as she rubbed her head. Her hand brushed rough cloth and she realised someone had wrapped a bandage tightly around her forehead. She must have passed out. Seema collected bumps and bruises the way other people collected flowers. She wouldn't worry about adding one more.

Looking up, she saw Aimree seated on the ground near to her, deep in conversation with Dren. Both looked to be about the same age. Had her little sister really grown so big in ten years? As she tried to sit up, Aimree rushed over to her side.

'Don't move. Just stay there and rest. Here, drink some of this.' She passed her a cup of hot sweet tea. Seema stared distractedly at the leaves floating on the surface. Aimree poured a second cup from a pot which was simmering over a small fire.

There was so much she wanted to say to her sister after a decade of lost time. Aimree was the reason Seema had been called to live as a monk in the first place. Pulling her six year old sibling to safety from the sea when she could barely swim herself was what earned her the affection of the Creator and her place within the monastery. But Seema detected a cold note of anger in her younger sister's face.

As she looked over at her younger sister, Seema saw something in the eyes looking back at her. She knew she shouldn't do it but she couldn't help herself. Ever so gently, Seema peeled back the layers of thoughts flitting across Aimree's consciousness and looked into her sister's mind. What she saw was like a slap in the face and the feeling almost sent her physically reeling.

Her sister's mind was full of bitterness, bordering on hatred. And it was all directed towards Seema.

How could her sister hate her? After all, she had saved her life. It was only then that Seema realised something for the first time. Never before had she asked herself what Aimree thought about it. Which was ironic, given her ability to tune into the thoughts of others. After all, Aimree had nearly lost her life and then lost a sister on the same day. Seema sighed, realising how unintentionally selfish she had been and thought of all of the birthdays and feast days they had missed sharing together.

But then she felt a pang of long-buried jealousy. Even as a child, it hadn't been difficult to see that Aimree had been her father's favourite with her graceful manners and dazzling smile. Aimree had inherited her father's charm while Seema had been burdened with his great height. She suspected he also had the gift of thought reading although they had never actually discussed it.

Truth be told, it was more of a burden. She desperately wished her gift had come with instructions. Seema had learned the hard way that, just because someone thinks they want something, it doesn't mean they actually do want it. Like the time when her mother desperately wished for a bit of peace and quiet around the house and Seema refused to speak for a week. Or when her father wished he had had another boy then yelled at her when she chopped off her long hair. There was a very fine line between a gift and a curse.

Her head was pounding as a result of more than just the impact with the ground. She tried to focus her attention back onto the Creator and restore her peace. She would address the issues with her sister later she thought as she drifted back to sleep.

******

Aimree had never gotten over the fact that the Creator had taken her sister from her. As a child, she had become angry and withdrawn. She grew up wrestling with these issues until they had settled just beneath the surface, allowing her to carry on as if everything was normal. Today however, her anger bubbled up from that deep place within and threatened to boil over.

'You know her then?' asked Dren as the monk let out another snore.

'Yes, she used to be my sister,' said Aimree with no attempt to disguise the bitterness from her voice.

'You never mentioned you had a sister. Wait, what do you mean, used to be?' Dren adjusted a blanket around her shoulders. Aimree, as usual, had come prepared for all eventualities.

'She was my sister before she ran off to join the monastery.' She stared at the fire, its flames burning with the rage she felt inside. 'I came home one day and they told me the Creator had taken my sister away. She didn't even say goodbye.'

'But Seema would only have been a child herself at the time!'

'Seema? Is that what she's calling herself these days? This is really too much.'

'Come on, give her a chance.'

Aimree's eyes narrowed. 'How did you end up hiding naked behind a donkey with her, anyway?'

'It's a long story and it's not how it looks.'

'Try me,' she said, looking her squarely in the eyes.

'Okay then. I bumped into her on the road north. Her walking staff had broken and she was pretty upset about it so I agreed to come with her until she found a replacement.' Dren fed a small twig into the fire. It glowed red and crackled. She tried to focus on the flames and not Aimree's rage.

'And the donkey?'

'I figured Hathron might send someone looking for me so we had to come up with a cover story. We bought Thunder and I've been travelling as her groom since then.'

'Well, you're right about one thing. They're certainly looking for you. We were all dragged out of our beds and questioned. The keep is in an uproar. I didn't tell them anything, though,' she quickly added. If she could convince herself that she had done nothing wrong, then maybe Dren wouldn't sense the deep, dark betrayal.

'What about Toran?' Dren drew closer towards the fire.

'I'm not so sure about him,' she replied, sowing the seeds of doubt. 'He's pretty angry about something. I wouldn't like to guess what he's capable of.' When Dren was finally captured by the authorities, she figured it would be better for him to suspect that Toran had a hand in it. After all, there was no point in him hating both of them.

She patted Thunder who was lying by her side. The donkey tried to sneak as close to the fire as possible.

'And what about you?' asked Dren. 'Did you decide to go for a walk in the hope that you'd stumble upon some men bathing, or was that not the plan?' Dren almost surprised herself that she hadn't come clean to Aimree about who she was. But Dren was enjoying the position that her acquired gender was giving her. It allowed her to speak her mind in a way that would be frowned upon if it came from a woman.

Now it was Aimree's turn to squirm. 'It certainly wasn't a sight I expected to see in the woods.' She paused and drew a deep breath. 'I suppose you could say I'm running away too. But I'd rather not talk about it.'

Dren knew better than to press her on the subject given her current mood. 'Where are you planning to go?' asked Dren, still with no idea of what had happened to Aimree to make her so certain she wanted to throw away everything. Soldiering was in her blood, and all she talked about was joining the Kingdom Watch.

'I did hear of somewhere once, in a story. But it's a long way away.' She picked up her pack and threw it over her shoulder.

'Far away, like the Celestial City?' Dren motioned for her to give him her bags.

'No, further away than that. The place I mean is over the other side of the mountains and then some distance away.'

Dren didn't like to point out that Aimree was doing the very thing she was so angry with her sister for doing. Must run in the family.

Out loud, she said, 'Well, I happen to be looking to go to the other side of the mountains too. We could go together if you like?' Dren took her bag and threw it over Thunder's back. If he wasn't going to be ridden, the donkey may as well be of some use. Even with Seema's impressive bargaining power, he had cost a small fortune.

'And what are you looking for over the other side of the mountains?' she asked.

'Somewhere I belong,' Dren said wistfully.

'Me too.'

There was enough daylight left to make it to the edge of Arcaria where they could find a place to spend the night but only if they hurried. There were risks for all of them should they be discovered. Aimree would be considered a deserter since she hadn't returned to the keep for a second night-curfew. And Seema was technically aiding and abetting, although she had no idea she was complicit in a crime. Hopefully there was an exemption for monks.

'Are you sure you want to come with us?' Dren asked while Aimree still had time to make it back to the keep if she found a main road and flagged down a cart. 'I don't want to pry into your business, but if you've not returned by tonight, they will treat you like a common criminal, same as me.'

'Thanks for your concern,' she said, 'but I'm no longer welcome in the keep and I will not live somewhere that doesn't want me.'

Her words struck a chord with Dren. Aimree was being treated exactly the way she had been. She was more than welcome to travel with them. 'In that case, we should set off soon and make some progress along the road before it gets dark. I better go get some clothes on,' she wrapped the blanket tightly around herself and stood up.

'I promise I won't look,' laughed Aimree.

Now it was Dren's turn to blush and not for the first time that day. Part of her wondered how Aimree had managed to take exactly the same route as she had, never mind how she had managed to make up the extra ground in such a short space of time. But she had no reason to question what was surely down to chance and coincidence. There would be plenty of time for explanations later on. Especially if they were going in the same direction. And she certainly hoped they were.

Walking over to where she had left her clothes, she noticed that her cloak had been moved. That's strange, she thought, surely the wind wasn't strong enough to blow it away.

Then she saw the burst seams right over the pocket where she had left the other half of the fruit. *Stupid animal! s*he cursed. Thunder must have chewed his way through the material and into the inside pocket while Dren was busy swimming. She felt foolish as she remembered the big show she had made out of teasing Thunder, showing him where she had put the rest of the fruit.

She looked over and saw the animal lying contentedly beside Aimree, curled up like a baby beside a warm hearth. She would make sure that was the last time she was outsmarted by something on four legs. *Your card is marked, donkey*, she thought. But she was also impressed that, much like herself, the animal would do whatever it took to survive.

CHAPTER 13

Dren felt better now that she was fully clothed. She combed her hair with her fingers, using the river water to smooth down her untameable fringe. She brushed the dust from her cloak and then walked over to the fire that Aimree had started. Aimree returned a short time later carrying a skinful of water she had collected.

'I thought I'd better make myself useful in case you had second thoughts about bringing me along,' she said with a grin.

'Well, we are an elite travelling unit, can't be carrying any dead wood,' Dren said managing to keep a straight face as she fed a couple of twigs onto the fire.

'That's a terrible joke,' Aimree said but laughed anyway.

Was this the right time to ask what had happened back at the keep? Dren was afraid to ask in case Aimree closed up on her again, or worse, decided not to join them.

But then Aimree leant in close and whispered. 'Can I ask you something?'

'Of course, you know you can ask me anything.' Her

heart skipped a beat and Dren uttered a silent prayer that Aimree couldn't hear how nervous she was.

'About what happened in the keep after you left. Did-'

Aimree stopped in mid flow as Seema's footsteps approached.

Dren cringed as Aimree deliberately turned her back on Seema. She hoped that Seema was still too groggy to notice her sister's hostile behaviour. But a small part of Dren was also angry with Seema for ruining the moment.

Seema looked at Aimree intently but said nothing.

'We better be getting on, then,' said Dren trying to defuse the tension. Having seen Dafine and Wudsam in action, she did not want to get caught in the middle of another set of bickering sisters. They struck camp and set off, all three walking on foot while Thunder carried the bags. They walked until the daylight had faded. When the trees blocked out what little light the moon provided, they agreed that they should make camp rather than risk becoming lost at night.

Dren picked a flat piece of ground just out of sight of anyone who might be following behind them on the trail. Two deserting soldiers couldn't afford to take any chances.

Silence surrounded them as they each built their own simple structures out of branches and ferns which they balanced against broad based trees. Aimree still refused to speak to Seema which made for extra work as there was no question of them sharing one shelter.

Seema untied their bags from Thunder's back and led him down to the stream where he drank greedily. Seema let him roll about in the water, where, free from his burden, he played contentedly before shaking himself dry, spraying beads of water around the campsite. Dren did his best to avoid the spray. There was something deeply unpleasant about the smell of damp donkey and she could have sworn the donkey was deliberately trying to soak her.

Seema led Thunder into a glade of tender young shoots and spent time talking to him and petting his soft muzzle as he munched away on the plants. Dren couldn't work out if Seema really liked the donkey or just wanted to avoid speaking to her sister. Either way, Dren was glad that, for now, the arguing had stopped.

Aimree had brought smoked slices of meat with her. It was a welcome sight. Now that her orange was gone, Dren's meagre supplies were finished. Being new to travelling, Seema hadn't thought to fill her pockets at the inn. Whether she was willing to lower herself to petty thievery in the future remained to be seen but sometimes hunger was the best teacher.

Aimree held out a smoked strip of meat to her sister when she returned from tending to the donkey. It was meant as a peace offering, but Seema shook her head.

'Thanks, but I don't eat meat on the odd days of the month- only what grows in the ground or comes from a tree.'

Aimree looked at Dren and rolled her eyes.

To make up for any offence she might have caused, Seema volunteered to take the first watch. Dren and Aimree retired to their respective shelters where they quickly fell asleep, their bodies and minds exhausted. Seema could just make out the stocky body of the donkey. She envied his carefree existence. Nothing troubled him except for the occasional biting fly. Her heart sank as she thought of her sister. She could sense that Aimree was deeply unhappy.

Time seemed to stand still as Seema waited for the minutes to pass. It left her with too much time to think. Although her natural instinct was to try to do something to help, she could only guess at what the root cause of the problem was.

Despite her ability to read the minds of others, she knew better than to go poking around in her sister's thoughts for the answers, as tempting as it was. In the past she had ruined any attempt her parents had made to surprise her on her birthday until eventually they had given up trying. As she got older, they wouldn't even bother wrapping her present.

The problem was she found it incredibly difficult to avoid interfering where she could see pain within a person. But she also knew it was best to keep a respectful distance, and hope that one day her sister would be able to talk over her problems when she was ready.

A small noise startled her and she almost screamed until the frog gave itself away with a loud croak. It launched itself into the river with a plop. What had she been thinking, volunteering to protect the group? She didn't know the first thing about keeping watch. But she was determined not to be a liability and wanted to prove her worth. She resolved to try extra hard to stay awake.

Seema cleared her mind and focused only on the present, feeling the cool sensation of the night breeze against her cheeks. The small dent she made in the earth underneath her proved that she mattered in the world. And for the first time in her life she became aware of the immensity of the universe.

She felt able to connect with the works of the Creator

in a way she had never done before. How can you appreciate what the Creator has done for you when you spend all day in a structure built entirely by human hands? She made a mental note to tell the monks about this when she got back home. And then she paused, wondering if she would ever see them again.

Once her eyes adjusted to the darkness and her ears tuned into the sounds of the night, it became easier to relax. She could differentiate the sounds of the insects from the other animals that called out to one another. The birds of the day had been replaced by the hooting of night owls. Occasionally she would hear the baying of something that probably had claws and teeth but sounded far enough away that it wasn't about to trouble their camp.

After a couple of hours she was on the verge of falling asleep. Her eyelids grew heavier and heavier until they flickered shut. Then *Bang!* A sound rang out that definitely wasn't animal in origin. She peered out into the darkness and then she saw it. It was the flicker of a lit torch and it illuminated a soldier. There was at least one but there could have been more.

Was this the right moment to wake the others? She wasn't sure. If it was a false alarm they wouldn't trust her again. As long as they all kept quiet, then maybe the soldiers would walk on by and not discover them. She held her breath and prayed that they wouldn't hear Thunder. The noise increased as the soldiers came closer to the makeshift camp. The light from the torch grew brighter but she couldn't move.

Just as she started to curse her decision not to wake the others, the flame went out. She held her breath. Then came the sound of cursing and fumbling. She froze.

Two voices came close and she strained to hear them. Then a torch flared into life and the soldiers moved away. Perhaps they had just been going to the river for a drink. Relief flooded over her.

It was time to wake Dren.

CHAPTER 14

After she had been asleep for what seemed like only a few minutes, there was a tap on her shoulder.

'Dren!' it was a woman's voice. The same voice called out her name again, this time with a note of urgency. 'You need to wake up!'

She sat up and rubbed the sleep from her eyes. A large figure loomed over her and for a moment she wondered where she was, then her panic subsided as she recognised Seema. Looking past her at the stars outside, she calculated she had been asleep for a few hours.

She turned back to Seema and noticed the fear in her eyes. 'What's the matter?'

'I thought I heard voices,' she said looking over her shoulder towards the tree-filled darkness.

Dren strained her ears to hear but the only sounds were the wind in the trees and the faint snores coming from the donkey.

'Maybe it was Thunder you heard?' she said, trying to reassure her.

'I wasn't aware donkeys talked in their sleep,' she

said, without a hint of amusement.

Dren had no desire to get out of her warm bed but, as it was her turn to take over the watch, she put on her torn cloak and willed herself to stay awake.

'Did anything else happen?' she asked.

'A group of soldiers passed by earlier but I figured it was just a routine patrol.'

'During the night? That's strange. I wonder why they would be out on patrol outside of the keep. What colours were they wearing?'

'It was hard to tell because of the darkness but I think they had trees on their tunics.'

That confirmed they had crossed the border. But, if Arcarian soldiers were out looking for Dren, then word had travelled fast. Unless it wasn't Dren they were searching for. She gave a glance towards Aimree's shelter.

In either case she would have to rethink their route for tomorrow. Just when she was about to probe further, Dren heard Seema's deep breathing. She was already out cold.

Dren tried to keep her mind from speculating on what would happen if she was captured. She wondered how the keep went about tracking down fugitives. Would they use the Kingdom Watch? Or maybe they would stick up posters like those nailed to the doors of shops advertising a reward for the capture of murderers and robbers. Her heart sank.

As the darkness closed in around her like a cloak, she found herself jumping at the slightest noise. Every time a leaf fell it commanded her entire attention. She was like a rock lion, ready on a hair trigger to pounce on its unsuspecting prey. Except the difference here was that the lion had the advantage of excellent night vision and, in this scenario, she was the prey.

It was hard to judge how long she had been awake for. Time seemed to drag and Dren shivered in the night's chill.

Eventually the stars indicated that there were only a couple of hours left until the sun would crest the horizon, bringing with it the dawn of a new day. This signalled the end of her watch so she got to her feet and walked over to Aimree's shelter. She looked so peaceful sleeping that she almost didn't want to wake her.

More than anything she wished that Aimree would make up with her sister. For one thing, it would make the journey go a lot quicker. Silence lengthened the days as well as the nights. Although she didn't understand what made such a popular recruit want to leave the keep, she was glad of her company.

Dren realised she was staring at Aimree. Reluctantly, she whispered her name and let her waken gently.

'It's time,' Dren said as Aimree sat up in the shelter and wrapped her cloak around her in preparation for starting her turn at the watch.

'Do you want me to sit up with you?' Dren asked despite her tiredness.

'Why? Do I look like I'm scared of the dark?'

Dren was taken aback by her tone. 'No, I didn't-'

'Sorry Dren, I shouldn't have snapped. It's just this business with my sister and all. I suppose it's weighing on my mind.'

Dren nodded then returned to her shelter. She wasn't used to Aimree being hostile towards her and she didn't like it. None of this boded well for a peaceful journey. Maybe she should travel alone after all.

She lay down, trying to get back to sleep. It was typical that her eyes had been heavy as lead throughout her turn at the watch but, the moment she tried to get back to sleep, she felt wide awake. The conversations with Aimree replayed over and over in her mind.

Just as she was finally drifting back to sleep, she was awoken by the sound of a donkey braying, which shattered the peace of the forest.

Thunder! What was the blasted donkey up to now? She jumped to her feet and grabbed her cloak. She was joined by Aimree. Together they ran through the woods into the spot where Seema had tied up the donkey. Thunder was there but he wasn't alone.

Dren dived for cover behind a tree, pulling Aimree with her. A group of soldiers dressed in the forest-green uniform surrounded the frightened donkey. One soldier had a hood over Thunder's head while a second grabbed onto the rope around his muzzle.

He kicked out but other soldiers holding sticks tapped him into line. Dren was pleased to see Thunder wasn't going to be taken without a struggle but he was outnumbered and eventually the soldiers managed to untie him and half drag him to his feet.

Dren and Aimree could only watch helplessly as their prize possession was led away deeper into the forest. Aimree made a move to follow them but Dren held her back and gestured for her to stay silent. There was no sense in giving away their presence when they were outnumbered.

Relief at not being discovered gave way to a sense of guilt. Dren ran to wake Seema to explain how they had lost their valuable asset but she shook her head.

'This is no time for explanations. We need to get out

of here.'

Without wasting a minute, they broke apart their shelters, taking care to disguise their footprints and erase any trace of having been there. It was only a matter of time before someone checked the surrounding area for the owner of the donkey.

'What do we do now?' asked Dren, more to herself than to anyone in particular.

'We have to get Thunder back, that's what,' said Seema. 'There's no telling what those soldiers will do with him.'

Aimree started to speak. Dren braced herself for the fight that would inevitably break out between the two. But, much to their surprise, Aimree simply said:

'I agree. Thunder needs us.'

Dren buried her own concern that this meant heading into an unknown city to rescue a donkey, when they themselves faced prison. Seema would also be in trouble if it was found that she had assisted them.

But when she looked up and saw the two expectant pairs of eyes staring back at her, her heart gave in.

'Fine, we'll go get the stupid donkey if he means that much to you. But we better hurry. They've already got a head start on us.'

CHAPTER 15

Thunder's frightened braying cut through the still night air like a knife. The trees on the outer fringes of Arcaria towered upwards, blocking out all hint of light in their race to be first to touch the sky. The branches knitted together overhead and it looked almost possible to walk from one tree to the next without ever setting foot on the ground.

Using the thick tree trunks as cover, Dren, Aimree and Seema followed as closely as they dared behind the soldiers. They were close enough to hear the odd swear word but too far away to be able to make out any of their conversation.

Being outnumbered two to one, they would have to bide their time. And if the soldiers took Thunder all the way into the keep's stables, then Dren didn't much fancy their chances of getting him back. Not that she would say this out loud. Seema and Aimree seemed particularly fond of Thunder. Dren reckoned that, if it was a choice between saving her or Thunder, then they would first go after the donkey and worry about Dren later.

Walking silently from one tree to the next, they

followed behind the patrol ignoring the aching leg muscles. The soldiers' presence kept any predators at bay meaning they covered a lot of ground over the next few hours. The soldiers were too busy trying to control the cantankerous animal to notice they were being followed.

Then, without giving any warning, the soldiers stopped dead. Dren paused with one foot hovering off the ground, afraid to put it down in case the rustle of leaves gave her away.

She held her breath and watched as the soldiers took off their expedition packs and threw them on the ground. As two of the larger soldiers tied Thunder's rope around a strong tree, the rest of the unit gathered up branches and started sweeping the ground.

'They must be making camp to get a few hours rest,' Dren whispered, trying not to give away their presence. 'They're beating away any snakes from the site. We need to get out of here before they come this way.'

'I don't see how we can,' said Aimree. 'We'll make too much noise if we try to run.'

'But not if we climb,' said Seema, pointing upwards.

Dren studied the large tree, its broad, low-hanging branches almost touching the ground. Scaling it shouldn't be too difficult for Aimree and herself who were no strangers to physical exercise but what about Seema with her long heavy robes? As the beating of the branches grew louder, Dren realised they had run out of options.

There was nothing else for it. She held out her clasped hands and made a foothold for Aimree who propelled herself upwards. She grabbed the branch overhead then swung her leg over, pulling herself up with ease. Dren then offered a hand out to Seema but she had already managed to hoist herself up into the tree.

Taking a running jump, Dren grabbed onto a low-hanging branch and hung on tight as she walked her feet up the rough bark of the trunk. Inch by inch she moved her hands higher until she reached a more substantial branch to climb up. Only when she had reached the denser foliage did she dare stop to catch her breath.

Directly below them, the soldiers were setting up camp. Dren watched them as they finished checking the area for danger, and moved on to constructing their shelters.

They weren't out of danger yet. If any one of the soldiers so much as glanced upwards, there was a high likelihood of being spotted. Dren pointed upwards to the top of the tree, indicating they should keep going. Aimree nodded and continued to scale the branches as if she were climbing a ladder until she reached a place high in the tree branches where the leaves would shield her from the archer's sight.

Watching from her vantage point near the top of the tree, Dren could barely make out the other two as they each found a place to perch among the thick branches. Dren tried her best to get comfy, wedging her back against the trunk and clamping her legs around the branch. Given how meticulous the soldiers had been scaring away the snakes from camp, she fully expected to be joined by a slithering reptile taking refuge up in the trees. She smiled despite herself.

Nothing about the tree made it suitable for sitting on. She empathised with the birds who built their nests up here. The ability to fly wasn't enough compensation for spending your life in a tree and eating worms.

Although she badly needed to close her eyes, she didn't dare relax in case she drifted off to sleep. The branch swayed in the wind. She winced at every creak and tried to stay as still as possible.

Then she made the mistake of looking down. Her head spun and she clung tighter. A fall from this height would most probably kill her, she thought somberly. Or, at the very least would leave her lying in an unconscious heap right in the middle of the soldiers' camp.

She looked down again and saw the soldiers dragging logs around the edge of their firepit. They made quick work of their task and, before long, had a good blaze going. The succulent smell of roasting venison was carried high up into the trees, stimulating the taste buds of those watching patiently from above.

'I'm hungry,' whispered Aimree from her branch somewhere above Dren's head.

Dren turned to where Aimree's voice was coming from. 'You've got all the food in your bag,' she said sitting up straight on her branch.

'I don't want to take more than my fair share.'

'You always did have the appetite of an entire platoon,' said Seema, joining in the conversation.

'What's that supposed to mean?' said Aimree sharply.

'Even as a six year old you would be the first to clear your plate and then try to sneak the bread off mine.'

Aimree didn't miss a beat. 'Maybe I was doing you a favour pinching your food. If you had cleared your plate every night, there's no telling what size you would have grown to. At least this way you can still fit through doors.'

'Maybe I should never have saved you from drowning,' she fired back in a manner very unbecoming of a monk.

'Shhh! Keep it down,' said Dren, unnerved by the ferocity of the sisters' bickering. 'You're making more noise than the soldiers.' Even though the soldiers' chatter would mask the odd noise, she didn't want to take any chances. 'Since we're going to be stuck up in this tree for a while, can't you at least try to get along?'

A temporary truce brought with it the silence Dren desperately needed.

Down below, the soldiers let their campfire burn low until one of the men stood up and relieved himself straight into the glowing embers. The fire hissed angrily, as if someone had stepped on a snake. Then it died, giving out one last breath of steam. Dren watched, slightly revolted and thought about a proverb she had once heard. She couldn't remember the exact words, but it went something along the lines that men should never be given the task of guarding the hearth. Not because women wouldn't pee on the flames when they thought no one was watching, but because it was physically impossible for them to do it without getting burnt. She sighed. Women were every bit as capable as men when it came to choosing to do wrong.

CHAPTER 16

Seema felt a wave of shame as she thought about the hurtful things she had said to her sister. They couldn't be taken back. Not now that the unspoken had been uttered.

A bolt of fear pierced her heart. What if the Creator had heard her words? Maybe She had read her heart weeks ago and knew that these words would be on Seema's lips. Maybe this was why She had sent her from the monastery, not on a journey but into banishment.

Panic rose in her chest and she held on tightly to the branch above, interlocking her fingers in case the nausea unbalanced her and sent her tumbling downwards. She closed her eyes, hoping the sensation would pass and, as she did so, realised that she hadn't performed any of her daily devotions since she had left the monastery. In a spirit of fear, she began to pray.

Oh Creator of the world, sustainer of the present and architect of the future, I cast off my own thoughts and come to you stripped bare. I wish only to serve you and you only. She began in her usual fashion, only, this time she wasn't quite able to say it and believe it to be true. She tried to centre herself and continued in prayer.

I thank you for sending me on this journey and giving us your tree to sustain us. I thank you for Dren, our guide, and for returning my sister to me.

She felt a sharp tap on her shoulder. Assuming it to be Aimree, she ignored the interruption and continued in prayer.

I ask for safety on the road ahead and that you may reveal your divine purpose to me so I may better serve your will.

She was assaulted by another prod, this one harder than before.

'Quit it, Aimree,' she whispered sharply, not wanting to lose the attention of the Creator.

Please give me patience with my sister. A series of painful jabs caused her to open her eyes and turn her head to reprimand her younger sister. Would that girl never learn to respect her elders? Seema looked over her shoulder and made out the outline of a cloaked figure sitting on a neighbouring branch.

'I said give it a rest!' she hissed.

The cloaked figure opened two large orange eyes and stared directly back at her.

******

Higher up in her tree top hiding place, Aimree sat in silence, desperately trying to keep still. The rough bark grated against her skin. After what she had seen she didn't trust the forest. There were too many unknowns, too many places for dark things to hide.

A lone wolf called out in the distance, its cry echoing out through the woods. At least wolves didn't climb trees, did they?

She surveyed the soldiers dozing by their fire,

unaware they were being watched. A chill ran down her back. What if she was also being watched? There was no telling what other nocturnal predators would also climb trees to hide at night. She remembered all of the stories of bears and grues and even ravenous bark scuttlers that she had been told as a child. Perhaps they were just tales designed to keep an inquisitive child from venturing anywhere near the forest but, right now, she believed every word.

The last time that she had explored the woods, she had been a soldier. But this time was different. She had left all of that protection behind her when she had decided to leave the keep. Now she was just like everybody else and that meant she was vulnerable. She told herself it was silly to be afraid of the woods. Better to be scared of things you could actually see as opposed to the fears created by an idle imagination. Even as she said this to herself, she shuddered at the thought of the tree snakes that inhabited these parts. It was rumoured they could swallow a person whole. Although a snake might have bitten off more than it could chew should it decide to eat her sister. She barely managed to stop herself from laughing out loud at the image that was forming in her mind.

The hooting of an owl brought her back to the present. The hurtful words she had exchanged with her sister had left her in a lonely place. She was back to being that scared child when half of her had been chopped off. The pain was every bit as raw as it had been the first time. But what stung now was knowing that this time she was partly to blame.

Aimree wrapped her cloak closely around her body. The argument had only warmed her head but her heart was chilled by their icy exchange. The problem was, there was too much pride inside her to even contemplate apologising for her unkind words. She hadn't asked for her sister to come back into her life.

And it wasn't just the argument. The more she thought about turning Dren in to the authorities, the more unsure she became. Could she have it on her conscience that she had killed a man and let Dren take the blame for it? Even though he thought he had killed the Wynym himself?

But she couldn't go back to the keep without bringing in Dren under arrest, Eigot had made that clear. The problem was that Dafine knew the truth and the truth had an inconvenient way of coming out. Could she live with the shame and the fear that one day Dafine might out her? She would just have to.

Down below, the captured donkey curled up in a ball to preserve its warmth. The sight of Thunder made her smile. She imagined his belly rising and falling as he slept, finally exhausted after hours of kicking and biting. Aimree hugged her knees to her chest.

Why couldn't Seema just have spoken to the soldiers and asked for Thunder to be returned to them? She was his rightful owner after all and she was sure the soldiers would be grateful to have the cantankerous beast taken off their hands. It was, surely, the most sensible option when all things were considered.

She thought again about the things her mother had warned her about, the hidden dangers in the woods. Then she thought about the dark secret she had hidden inside herself, the reason that she had run away from the life that had been mapped out for her. And she didn't know which to be more frightened of. A single tear ran down her cheek. She felt very small and surrounded by darkness. Then a single scream rang out from the treetops.

******

Dren patted her head. Was it rain or just a passing shower? At least the foliage above would shelter her from the worst of it. The night was growing colder and she once again cursed the donkey.

She weighed up their options. They needed Thunder back. Having come all this way they couldn't leave with nothing to show for their trouble. Plus, she didn't think she could cope for much longer with nothing but the two bickering sisters for company. At least she could talk to the donkey without fear of being ridiculed. Then again, Thunder did have a way of showing contempt with a flick of the ears. Still, it was better than being shouted at.

Her stomach was protesting the absence of a warm dinner. Although Aimree had brought a few rations with her, soon that meagre supply would be exhausted. If they stopped to hunt and took time to cook what they caught, they would be in danger of losing the trail of the soldiers or of being discovered. And, although the trees were covered in overhanging berries that were juicy and plump to the touch, she knew better than to eat one without being absolutely sure what it was first. She just hoped the others had as much sense. A deadly blackthorn could easily be mistaken for the sweet red berries which grew along the banks of the river.

They were at most a two day walk from the Arcarian Keep. Surely the soldiers would stop at an inn along the way and they could steal Thunder back. If there was one thing she knew about soldiers, it was that they wouldn't miss a chance for a warm bath and a good drink if the opportunity came their way.

She wiped another couple of drops of warm rain from her face. She hoped the soldiers wouldn't sleep for too long. It was hard to keep her eyes from closing and her head from bobbing. If they had been prepared for this, she would have brought a length of rope which they could have used to tie themselves to the tree. If Toran had been here, he would probably have gone on about his principle of maximum efficiency and attached them all to the trees using nothing but his boot laces. Dren felt a pang of emptiness which was quickly replaced by a bolt of anger. She didn't need Toran and she wasn't going to sit around wishing he was here. That particular chapter of her life was closed. In future she would just pack better, but that was a lesson for next time. And she sincerely hoped there wouldn't be a next time.

A piercing scream violently roused her from her thoughts. It sounded like Seema and something was very wrong.

CHAPTER 17

The creature in the cloak let out a high pitched squeak, its wide mouth revealed a jaw full of teeth designed for tearing. Once Seema started screaming, she couldn't stop. Finally, her legs told her to run and she scrambled to her feet. She groped around in the darkness for a higher branch to grab onto. Finding one, she pulled herself up. Her face brushed against something soft and furry. A pair of glowing eyes blinked open and another creature shrieked as razer-sharp claws tore at her hair. Seema clasped her hands round her head, trying to protect herself from whatever underworld creature was attacking her.

Leathery wings battered at her sides and frantically she prayed to the Creator for a safe delivery. If only she still had her walking staff, she could have tried to defend herself. How could she have been so careless? Her sister was right, they would have been better off without her. She was nothing more than a great big clumsy fool.

Then the creature was gone. She looked up in relief and, to her surprise, she saw Aimree battling with the winged beast. She wrestled it away from her face and threw it into the air. The creature swooped and rose before flying off to join hundreds of other furry creatures swarming high over their heads. The high pitched squeals of a feeding frenzy filled the air. 'Bats!' said Aimree, as she tried to catch her breath.

Concerned that Seema might be badly hurt, Dren clambered over leafy branches paying no heed to the drop below. She battled her way past flapping wings and reached Seema's branch where she wasted no time examining Seema's face as best she could in the dim light.

'You're badly scratched but the cuts don't seem to be bleeding.'

'We need to get out of this tree before they return,' said Aimree, testing the strength of the neighbouring branches. She pointed to the black circle of bodies in the sky. 'There are hundreds of them! We must have disturbed their roost.'

'What about the soldiers?' said Seema. 'They've surely heard the commotion by now. If we climb down now are we not just fleeing from one danger only to land in the midst of another?'

'Look, they're gathering rocks to throw at the bats,' said Aimree.

Although the bats were still screeching in a high pitched cacophony of sound, they couldn't rule out that the soldiers had also heard Seema's all too human screams.

'We need to keep going along the tree canopy,' said Dren, looking around for the safest way across to the next tree. 'Follow me!' Through the faint light of the moon, she picked out a route and started to crawl on her belly.

As Dren groped her way along the branches, hand over hand, her fingers stuck to a tarry substance on the bark.

'Bat poo! Of course! Why didn't we realise this before? We have to keep going until we find a tree without berries. They must be coming here to feed.'

She continued to make slow progress over precarious gaps. A large rock flew past Dren's shoulder, narrowly missing her. She froze, pressing her body flat against the branch. 'Have they seen us?' she whispered, sweat forming on her brow.

'Keep going!' shouted Aimree. 'We're under attack.'

Seema winced in pain as she followed Dren and Aimree from one branch to the next. How the other monks would laugh if they could see her now. Well, that wasn't strictly speaking true. They would more likely recoil in horror to find her climbing trees like a child and whisper disapproving things just out of her earshot. And in the past she would have agreed with them that this wasn't appropriate behaviour for a monk.

But it was funny how quickly your perspective shifted when you were actually hiding up the tree rather than sitting safely inside a monastery. Right now she figured she was the most qualified monk to assess what behaviour was appropriate.

Far down below, the soldiers were up and dressed. Seema caught a glimpse of Thunder being led away, oblivious to the drama unfolding above. She was too far away to read the soldiers' thoughts so she had no idea where they were taking him. Then the branch lurched violently and she clung on for dear life.

Don't look down, don't look down, she repeated to

herself as she followed Aimree. There was an obvious path across the branches, but her sister was so light. What would happen if the branch couldn't take her own weight? She tried not to think about it and continued to stare straight ahead as she inched her way through the treetops.

At this height, she could really feel how much the trees swayed in the wind. She knew they had to be flexible otherwise they would snap in a storm but right now that knowledge didn't help. Her fingers were sore from gripping branches. She had to pause again to gather her inner strength. When she looked up, Aimree was almost out of view in the darkness. She hurried to catch her which caused the branch to sway even more.

Damp patches of sweat formed under her arms. This was the last thing that she needed. It wasn't just the embarrassment of excessive perspiration, she knew well that animals could smell fear. She didn't need to be able to read their primitive minds to know that predators picked on the weakest in the pack.

She could still vividly picture the bat as it attacked her face. She could almost taste its rank odour. A life of prayer didn't adequately prepare the body or the mind for fighting off monsters. *They're living creatures, not monsters,* she corrected herself and tried to give thanks to the Creator for the bats but her heart wasn't really in it. The scratches on her face still stung, reminding her that nature and humans were still at war.

And then she slipped.

CHAPTER 18

Dren had never been particularly scared of heights. But this was the first time she had crawled along the thin end of a branch above a sheer drop, praying that it wouldn't snap as it swung wildly under her weight. Without daring to look down, she made a grab for an even thinner branch. It bowed dangerously but she swung and grabbed hold of the neighbouring tree.

Trying her best not to look at the forest floor or even to think about the fall that led straight to it, she grabbed the next bough and hauled her body safely across the gap and onto the next tree. She continued hand over hand amid the noise of the bats flapping over her head. Occasionally one would swoop down and she'd press her body into the tree branch until it passed.

Lines of sweat formed on the palms of her hands as she inched forwards. She hoped the other two would wait at a safe distance before following her across the forest canopy. There was no guarantee the branches could take their combined weight. In fact, she was almost certain they couldn't. There was a reason you didn't see fat squirrels.

Finally clear of the most immediate danger, she grabbed a thick branch and shuffled towards the centre of the tree, sucking in deep breaths of relief. She reached the solid midsection and stopped for a rest.

Aimree was managing without any hesitation. She admired the fearless way she pulled her strong body from one tree to the next. There was no doubt she was born to be a soldier. Dren couldn't fathom what had made her give up on her dream.

Seema, on the other hand, was definitely struggling. Her body shape indicated that she was much less used to physical activity. It didn't help that her heavy cloak kept catching on the smaller branches.

Aimree finally caught up with Dren and sat down beside her.

'I don't think we should go any further at height, it's too much for-'

Dren stopped mid-sentence. Seema was dangling precariously upside down from a branch, her fingers wrapped desperately around the thick limb. It was a long way down to the forest floor beneath her. If she fell now she would do more than break bones.

'We've got to go back for her!' shouted Aimree.

'No,' said Dren firmly, putting out her arm to stop her. 'If you try to walk along the branch, it'll bounce and she'll lose her grip. She has to do this herself.'

They didn't dare shout out in case they drew the soldiers' attention. All they could do was watch like helpless spectators as Seema wrestled with the branch, her sandals slipping as she tried to hook her heel over the bough.

'I can't take this anymore, I'm going to climb down and help her from the ground.' Reluctantly, Dren let go of Aimree. It was pointless to try and stop her once she had made her mind up. The branch Seema clung to looked thick enough to hold her weight but, the more she struggled, the more the branch seemed determined to throw her to the ground.

And then the worst happened. Dren could only look on in horror as Seema's fingers unclasped and she lost her grip. Dren just hoped that Aimree was looking the other way and wasn't about to witness the death of her sister.

Time stood still as the bundle of robes containing the monk fell towards the ground. Dren could neither cry out nor turn away. She could only stay numbly transfixed as Seema plummeted towards the earth like a seed pod in the season of birth.

In the distance, Dren thought she could hear a high pitched whistle. And then it faded while Seema continued to fall, caught up in her robes as she approached the earth.

An angry honking accompanied by the beating of large wings broke the silence. Dren watched wide eyed as two massive birds appeared from the woods and flew full at speed towards the falling monk. As they got closer, she could see that they were swans. One was the colour of pure snow while the other was its mirror image and as black as the night. Dren wasn't sure that she had ever seen a black swan before.

The birds folded back their wings and began to dive. Were they going to attack Seema? She had heard that a swan could break a person's arm with its powerful wings. How unlucky could one monk be?

But, instead of swooping at her, they dived underneath her, spread their wings and caught her on their backs. Dren stared at them in disbelief. The swans glided down with Seema on their backs. They landed gracefully on the carpet of pines. The force of this was enough to throw Seema off and she rolled along the ground, still tangled up in her robes.

It may have been an undignified landing but she appeared to be unharmed. Dren rubbed her eyes. Then, as if it was the most ordinary thing in the world, the swans pecked at some grass before stretching out their wings and flying off without so much as a backwards glance.

Dren slid down the tree and ran over and joined Aimree who was busy re-adjusting her sister's robes and brushing mud and leaves from her hair. Seema sat where she had landed, her head bowed, as if in prayer. Combined with the torn clothing and grazed face, she had the appearance of a wild thing. If they did happen to cross paths with the soldiers, it would be the soldiers who turned on their heels and ran off in terror.

'Seema?' Dren said in amazement, 'The swans! What happened?'

But it was like Seema couldn't hear her. She got to her feet and started to walk as if being pulled forward by some unseen hand. Dren and Aimree followed behind her with no idea where she was going. There was something about the deliberateness of her actions that made them follow without asking questions.

'What do you make of the swans?' asked Aimree. 'I've never seen a black swan before.'

'I'm not sure. Those swans had deep blue eyes. Swans don't have blue eyes, at least, I've never seen one like that before.'

Dren turned to Seema for her opinion but she didn't

seem to be listening to their conversation. She had that faraway look in her eyes again.

Eventually Seema came to a halt and pointed to a small path.

'There!' she said triumphantly.

'What is it?' asked Dren, thinking that she must be receiving messages from a higher power. She didn't understand how her faith worked but she truly believed she had just witnessed a miracle.

Seema gave a long deep sniff. 'Sausages!' she declared with a grin.

CHAPTER 19

The smell was coming from a charming wooden cottage. A grassy path wound its way up to the front door. On one side, was a rockery brimming with heathers of all colours. A pond teemed with fish as long as Dren's arm and a dozen hungry orange mouths flapped open, hoping for the arrival of food.

A thin wisp of smoke rose from the chimney and Dren could indeed detect the unmistakable smell of sausages cooking. She felt foolish for thinking it was a rush of divine inspiration which had led Seema here. Of course monks got hungry too.

Despite her other-worldly manner, Seema was becoming more and more human as Dren learned to see through the trappings of religion. Except of course, the small matter of being rescued by the swans. But maybe there was a perfectly rational explanation for that.

They needed to be on their guard here. Dren had no idea how they would be viewed by the Arcarians. There was always the danger that any one of the wood dwellers would turn them over to the authorities, simply for being foreigners. Dren stepped forward to knock on the front door. But just as she raised her hand, the door swung inwards and an old man with tufts of white hair and a neat beard appeared at the threshold.

'Oh, it appears I have visitors,' he said in a friendly voice although he didn't sound entirely surprised to see them. 'Do come in!'

Despite the house seeming incredibly small from the outside, it was deceptively spacious and all four fitted in quite comfortably although Seema did have to duck to fit through the front door. The man gestured towards four chairs set around a table made from a slice of a large oak tree. Fresh bread and butter had been laid out and all four places were set with plates. This struck Dren as odd. Had the man been expecting company in such a remote part of the forest?

'Please, help yourself to something to eat. From the state of your clothing, I presume you must have been on the road for a while.' He played with a cord around his neck.

'Thank you, but if you're expecting guests, we don't want to put you out,' said Dren without confirming the man's statement. She didn't want to give away too much information about who they were or where they had come from. And, as hungry as she was, she figured it was polite to decline.

However, Seema virtually elbowed her out of the way to grab a slice of bread. Without any hesitation, she grabbed a knife and shovelled on a thick layer of butter. Aimree, who was already devouring her slice, looked up at Dren's words.

'Yes, we don't want to put you out,' she mumbled, her mouth full of crumbs.

The man brought over a plate of sausages and placed them in the centre of the table.

'As luck would have it, these are hot and ready for eating.'

Seema reached over to take one with her fork.

Aimree shot her sister a look. 'I thought you weren't eating meat,' she said sharply.

'I never refuse hospitality,' Seema explained. 'It would be pure rudeness to impose my values on this stranger's kindness,' and with that she took a bite.

Aimree looked at her in disbelief but said nothing, more interested in eating than arguing with her sister.

Dren dropped the attempt at manners and speared a sausage with her knife. She blew on it to cool it slightly and then bit into it. It was the best sausage she had ever tasted. She wasn't going to stop and think about the wisdom of eating food offered by a complete stranger until she had filled her belly.

'Wild boar,' said the man, by way of explanation, 'Flavoured with herbs from the garden.'

The mention of a herb garden made Dren think about Dingwall. Come to think of it, there was a striking resemblance between this stranger and the architect from the Drabsea Keep. It was probably just that they shared the same rugged complexion that comes with working outside. Dingwall had never mentioned having any relatives in Arcaria. Although, if truth be told, he hadn't mentioned very much about himself or where he had come from.

Swallowing a second sausage, Dren thought she better introduce herself. However, she wasn't sure exactly what to tell the man. She didn't want to lie and give a false name. On the other hand, she didn't want to give away the fact that Seema was a monk harbouring two deserting soldiers. It probably wouldn't make a very good first impression.

As if he knew what Dren was thinking, the stranger saved her the effort. 'In case you're wondering, they call me Thurso. And you are very welcome in my house. In fact, I was wondering when you were going to turn up.' He walked over to the window and rummaged around in an old wooden box.

Before any of them could ask him what he meant, he pulled an object from the box. Seema's eyes widened in amazement. 'My walking stick,' she said as he handed it to her. She turned the smooth wood over in her hands. 'How did it made its way here? Wasn't it damaged? 'Thank you! But how did you...'

'I'm sorry, I should have introduced myself properly. I am the Woodwarder.' Seeing their blank looks, Thurso continued. 'I look after this entrance to the Hinterwood and I am the keeper of all things made of wood. The staff made its way into my possession. I fixed it up and I figured its owner would be along to collect it as soon as they realised it was lost. It looks like a valuable possession.'

Seema seemed to accept this explanation. Dren was less convinced by the man's vague words. But since he had made them a very fine lunch and didn't ask too many awkward questions about who they were, Dren figured she could tolerate a little strangeness.

Aimree wasn't as easily satisfied, however. 'You mean to say that you expected us to arrive at your door the very second the sausages had finished cooking?' she said, her eyes narrowing with suspicion.

'My dear, if I had wanted to poison you, I wouldn't have wasted my good sausages, if that's what you're worried about.'

Aimree looked embarrassed as if Thurso had known exactly what she was thinking.

'I think you'll find that the timing was your gain and my loss,' he added with a gentle smile.

'Yes, sorry about that,' said Seema. 'It was my nose that led us here.'

'Well, however you ended up at my door, be assured you may stay as long as you need. Weary travellers should take rest where they find it.'

'That's very kind of you, sir, but we're already behind on our trip,' said Dren.

'Well if your journey involves passing through Arcaria then I may be able to advise you on the best routes.'

'That would be a great help,' said Dren. 'The walking staff was not the only thing we lost and we think it might be going towards the city.'

'Thunder!' cried Seema without thinking as she remembered that he was still with the soldiers.

'But it's not even due to rain yet!' said Thurso.

'No, Thunder is...' She stopped herself before she said too much. Dren was already shaking her head at her. 'Never mind.' She cast her eyes down to her plate.

'Why don't we take a walk?' Thurso said to Dren as he rinsed an empty frying pan in a small sink by the window. 'I find it aids the body with digestion and the mind with thinking.'

Dren nodded in agreement and rose from the table, leaving Aimree checking over the bat scratches on Seema's face. At least they were back on speaking terms. There was nothing quite like a fight with a bat, a near death experience and a pair of mysterious swans to bring families closer.

CHAPTER 20

Thurso pulled on a coat then opened the back door. Again he tugged at the cord he wore round his neck. Dren caught a glimpse of a wooden whistle attached to the cord and she thought back to the swans. She wondered how she could bring this up in conversation without sounding irrational. Then her host pulled the high collar up around his neck and the whistle disappeared from view. The moment for asking questions had gone.

As she followed Thurso out of the house, the scent of jasmine filled her nose. The rear of the cottage was covered in climbing plants, mostly red veined forest ivy with its blossoming trumpets but Dren thought she spotted a blood-rose growing in one of the borders. It had been Dingwall's favourite flower and had to be specially imported from the Celestial City.

'That's a royal flower,' Dren exclaimed, unable to hide the note of surprise from her voice. She hadn't seen it growing naturally anywhere in the woods and she wondered where it had come from.

'Oh, that? Just a perk of the job,' he said without answering the question. Thurso was a wealth of knowledge about the Hinterwood. He explained that Arcaria was the first city to be built in the Kingdom.

'When the first people arrived here by sea, they found they preferred the shelter of the trees to the starkness of the oceans. The forest was cleared to the north and south to create the Celestial City and the city of Drabsea. But those who loved the trees the most put down their roots in Arcaria and didn't leave. Today, those who dwell in this region fiercely protect the forest and consider its wood to be more precious than gold.'

'Have you always lived here?' asked Dren.

'My ancestors have guarded the entrance to the Hinterwood for generations. I am aware of all comings and goings.'

As much as Thurso's easy-going manner made him appear trustworthy, Dren wasn't prepared to let her guard down completely. She changed the topic to make use of the man's knowledge of the area. 'Something's been stolen from us by a group of soldiers and we are trying to get it back.'

Thurso's expression grew serious. 'That is a serious charge,' he said, reaching up and examining a dwarf apple hanging from an ornamental fruit tree. 'A soldier convicted of stealing can be sentenced to death. Do you have proof of ownership of the...' he waited for Dren to fill in the blank.

'Donkey,' said Dren, not bothering to keep up the pretence any longer. If she wanted the man's help, it was better to be honest with him. 'We were camping in the woods and woke up to find a group of soldiers had taken him. We've been following their trail ever since but we lost them overnight. We just want him back so we can get on our way.'

'In that case, it might be tricky. Prince Erat is offering a reward for any strays found wandering in the woods. It seems that some new animal species have been discovered and the prince is very interested in examining them. The soldiers will be on route to the keep to trade him in.

'There have been a number of odd animals sighted recently. Equally, a number of wild animals have been abandoning the woods and running into town as if they're being hunted by something. The threat of rabid animals frightens people, so Prince Erat is very keen to have the animals rounded up for everyone's safety. I imagine your donkey will be headed straight for a cage. When they figure out he's just a regular ol' donkey they'll either sell him to a tannery or he'll end up in someone's stew.'

Dren's face fell.

'But I'm sure you'll figure out a way to get him back,' Thurso added.

Thurso continued along the path, whistling as he examined the flowers for dead-heads and kicked stray leaves from the path. This brought back memories of working in the spice gardens with Dingwall. The resemblance was uncanny. Dren had to ask, 'Say, do you know a man named Dingwall? It's just that you seem so alike.'

The man smiled. 'I do indeed.' At that moment a songbird fluttered down and landed on the man's shoulder. Thurso rummaged in a pocket and passed the bird a pink and blue pitted seed. The bird stretched out its wings as if bowing and flew off clutching the prize in its beak.

'I suppose you could call us cousins. We're distantly

related,' he said without offering any more detail.

They came to the end of the path. He pointed to a gap in the trees. 'See the flag pole in the distance?'

Dren nodded.

'Follow it and you will be walking straight towards the keep. However, you will also be walking straight into view of anyone who may be keeping an eye on me.'

Seeing Dren's worried look he added, 'Don't worry, they can't see you quite yet. I've made sure it's not that easy to spy on me. There are some things here that I would rather the authorities didn't know the precise details of, if you catch my meaning.'

Dren didn't want to know what illegal things the Woodwarder got up to all the way out here in the forest. She had enough troubles of her own without becoming embroiled in somebody else's criminality.

'Anyway, if you stick to the wooded edges of the path you should be able to make it to the market place without drawing too much attention to yourself. From there the keep is easy to find. Just remember to stay under the cover of the trees when you leave here.'

'Thank you for your help,' said Dren.

'Well, any friend of Dingwall is a friend of mine. But I have one last thing to give you. Come, let's go back inside.

In contrast to the bright sunshine outside, the interior of the wooden cottage was dark and it took Dren's eyes a few moments to re-adjust. Aimree and Seema were still sitting next to one another. Dren was relieved that she could now leave them alone without them coming to blows. They looked up together as Dren crossed the cottage floor towards them.

'We left you some bread.'

There was one dry heel left on the chopping board. Between them, they had finished an entire stick of butter.

Thurso wandered over to the carved box that had contained Seema's staff. 'Should be just about your size,' he said as he opened the lid and took out an item wrapped in cloth. 'At any rate, you'll grow into it.' He handed the large bundle to Dren who took it carefully in both hands.

Dren pulled back the cloth and saw that she was holding a magnificent bow, carved from a single piece of dark wood. She turned the bow in her hands and, before she had even touched the string, felt a vibration flow between the wooden bow and up her arms. She looked around to see if the others had noticed what had happened but Aimree and Seema were still sitting at the wooden table, oblivious to what Dren was experiencing.

As she drew the string back, a feeling of warmth poured up her arm. This bow just felt right. In the distance, she heard the unfamiliar cries of warriors and the whizz of arrows flying overhead. And, just as suddenly as the sensation had come over her, it was gone. She wondered how the others still hadn't noticed anything.

'This looks expensive. I can't afford to pay you for it,' she said still gripping it tightly. Then a thought occurred to her. Maybe she did have something she could give after all. She reached into her pocket and pulled out the triangular glass vial that Dingwall had given her before she had left.

'Does this mean anything to you?' Dren asked holding it out for Thurso to look at.

The man took it from Dren and his expression grew

serious. 'I would put that back on now, if I were you.'

'I'm not that fond of jewellery, to be honest.'

Thurso turned serious. 'If my cousin had anything to do with it, you most definitely need to be wearing it.'

'Your cousin? You mean Dingwall?'

'Second cousin once removed if we're being exact. That amulet will keep you out of bother. But only if you wear it round your neck. Otherwise you're broadcasting your whereabouts to anyone who's sensitive to such things.'

'What things?'

'Things we aren't meant to speak about.' He lowered his voice. 'Magic. Stops it leaking out of you. At any rate, that's the theory.' He took it from Dren and placed it around her neck then tucked it out of sight. 'Unless you've been trained, which I assume you haven't, this little vial captures any stray magic that decides to wander away from your body.' His broad smile returned. 'As for the bow, it's a gift. I don't expect any payment. Just don't go shooting anybody.'

Dren stared at him. Thurso looked her right in the eyes. 'I'm surprised that stone wasn't more your element. Still, who am I to judge? You are what you are. But I must warn you, beware the power of the weapon. It can have a strange effect on people who are unfamiliar with its ways. Remember at all times that you and you alone are responsible for your actions.'

Nothing more was said, but a flash of something unspoken passed between them. And then the spell was broken and the world resumed as before.

Dren remembered her manners. 'Thank you kindly for this magnificent gift.'

Thurso gave a slight nod. 'Sadly, its previous owner

suffered an untimely ending. No point in it languishing in a box when it could be of some use. It should fit underneath your cloak easily enough. I take it from the way you hold it that you're familiar with how it works.'

Dren nodded. 'But there are no arrows.'

The Woodwarder sighed. 'Do I have to hold your hand for you too?' He shook his head in mock despair. 'There's a fletcher in the city. Mention my name and he'll charge you double.'

Dren started to speak, but Thurso continued. 'Don't mention my name and he'll assume you're a common poacher or, worse, an assassin and sell your name to the authorities. It's your choice.' He looked over at Seema. 'And I'm no expert but, if I were you, I'd get those scratches looked at.

'Oh, these are nothing, I've had worse,' she said. But one dark look from Thurso and she added, 'Of course, you're right. I will find a healer in the city.'

Thurso beamed. 'I have very much enjoyed your visit. If you have a chance on your way back, do pop in to see me.'

'Oh we don't plan on coming back,' said Dren. 'We're only going one way.

Thurso looked at Dren and his smile never faltered. 'Yes, I'm sure you know best. Good luck finding your donkey.'

CHAPTER 21

'What do you mean I'm to be a kitchen aide?' Meela shrieked at her father. She threw the weighty sack of grain towards him.

The impact nearly knocked him off his feet. Meela's father stooped to pick up Meela's sack, then he started the long climb up the narrow stone staircase, which led to the merchant's storehouse. He did not want to be having this discussion right now.

'Just calm down now and listen to me,' Sefra said to his small but very vocal daughter who followed at his back.

'How can I calm down when you've just informed me I'll be peeling potatoes for the rest of my life?'

'But sweetness, you know I only want what's best for you. You are my only daughter.'

'If you loved me then you wouldn't send me to work in that dungeon. I hate you,' said Meela emphatically, placing her hands on her hips.

'Don't exaggerate,' he said, turning to face his daughter. 'It's a royal household, not a prison and, if you work hard and get noticed for the right reasons, you might be able to work your way up the ladder.'

'Am I not working hard right now, hauling sacks until my arms are sore and my back is almost breaking? Where has that gotten me?' Meela folded her arms. 'And the keep does have a dungeon. I've heard that Prince Erat beats servants who make mistakes and chains them up in it.'

'But that's nonsense.' He had always said she was as strong as a mountain goat and as wilful as three chained together. Meela's father began to worry that the solution for his business problem hadn't been pitched in the best way to his stubborn daughter. 'Someone's been telling you stories,' he continued. 'Anyway, you know I would have kept you working with me if I could afford it, but I've got your three brothers to think about and I wouldn't be able to feed us all if you stayed.'

Sefra was descended from a long line of traders who had survived in spite of difficult times. And times had never been harder than the present. The earth tremors damaged stock and orders often went unfulfilled. Overheads were up and profits down. What had once been a wealthy family business was now struggling to maintain a foothold within Arcaria. But, like the water rats that scuttled about in the depths of the grain cellar, he was shrewd. He would fight with whisker and claw to keep his head afloat when all of the other rats were drowning.

But Meela was no fool either. She knew he was only looking out for himself. He wanted her to persuade the head cook to buy from him rather than from the competition. He had hinted that, if she did well then he would buy her back. And he didn't stop telling her that, with her disability, a suitable marriage was never going to be a realistic prospect.

Meela had not grown up with her eyes shut. She always knew that her bad leg meant he would pick her brothers over her when it came down to it. Even without the leg, her father still had a dim view of girls' ability even if she was the hardest working member of the family. At that moment, the grain sack slipped from her father's hands as he tried to open the door with one arm. Meela caught it, saving it from tumbling and splitting its contents over the stairs.

'That's my girl, always said you were the most capable one in the family.'

Meela heard the empty flattery in his words and paused. Looking Sefra straight in the eye she said: 'Ok, father, you're right. I no longer work for you.'

Her father started to smile. His smile quickly faded, however, as Meela about-turned and launched the heavy grain sack down to the bottom of the stairs, where it burst on impact, scattering the valuable commodity over the stone floor below.

'That makes us even!' Sefra shouted out at her, enraged by the waste of the goods. 'At least you're not mine to worry about any more.'

*****

As they walked along the edge of the forest path, keeping to the shadows, Seema grew irritated. Here among the trees, her height was a disadvantage. She had to be on the lookout to avoid the low hanging branches. As if that wasn't bad enough, the incisions left by the bats had started to burn like nothing she had ever experienced before. When ignoring the pain didn't work, she moved on to rubbing at the cuts, but that technique didn't prove to be any more effective.

Although Seema had never experienced a hive of pack ants running up and down her face with their needle-like legs piercing her skin, she thought that it would be a relief to experience the age-old practice favoured by those who tortured the prophets, rather than the insidious pain she was feeling in her face right now. Finally, she had resorted to simply clawing at the scratches using her nails. It was worse than that cursed itch.

'Are we going to have to tie your hands together?' asked Aimree.

Dren looked over at them with a puzzled expression.

'To stop her scratching at her face,' Aimree explained.

'You know, I didn't even feel it until Thurso pointed it out.'

'Is it really as bad as it looks?' Dren was concerned by the inflamed welts which seemed to be getting bigger by the minute.

'It stings like a b-'

'Seema!' shouted Aimree, shaking her head in disgust. 'You're a monk, you can't say things like that.'

'I'm sorry but it's true. I'm in agony.' Seema was getting grumpy. 'If the worst that happens after being attacked by a bat bigger than my head is that I utter an occasional oath, then I think I'm doing pretty well.'

'Swearing just proves she is human after all,' said Dren, trying to take Seema's mind away from the pain. She also wanted to avoid the sisters getting into another full-blown argument. The Arcarian Keep was still a considerable distance away.

Luminescent toadstools crowded round the base of

the trees and a pervasive smell of damp filled the air. Dren didn't envy those who called this forest home. As they passed small cabins nestled between the trees, Dren knew they had to stay hidden as best they could from people much more used to the ways of the forest than they were. Hunters and log merchants posed little threat so long as they didn't venture too close. However, during the hot dry months of summer, the Kingdom Watch took up positions in tree houses to watch for forest fires. Although summer was still a month or so away, Dren didn't want to take any chances. It was safer to prepare for the worst and assume they could be observed at any moment. After what Thurso had said, she couldn't tell who else might be looking in her direction.

As they continued along the path, more signs of habitation appeared. Wooden cottages similar to the Woodwarder's were dotted about. Some of the larger houses had small rockeries, as if stone was a novelty in this part of the Kingdom.

It must be expensive to transport the stones all the way from the beaches of Drabsea or from the northern cliffs. That would mean a rockery was really just a show of wealth. She laughed at the idea of someone trying the same thing where she came from.

The forest floor undulated and Seema relied on her stick to stop her from tripping on more than one occasion. Dren squinted, trying to make out the detail. It was engraved with figures and animals. 'What's carved on your staff?' she asked.

Seema's eyes flicked downwards. 'This? It's part of the story of how we came to be. The rules forbid us from writing down the word of the Creator in books so people can't fight over the exact meaning. We get around this rule by carving the things we want to remember. It's become something of an art form,' she said, looking proudly at her staff.

'You mean, you're cheating the Creator?' Dren asked, innocently.

Seema looked aghast at what Dren was suggesting. But she had to concede the point. 'I suppose you're right, in a way. Even monks bend the rules when it suits.'

They walked side by side as Seema told Dren the stories behind some of the designs. As she talked, it dawned on Dren that Seema hadn't left them, despite having found her stick. She didn't know how she felt about that if she was honest. This was meant to be Dren's journey after all.

Most likely Seema would only travel with them a little further before returning to her monastery. She couldn't stay away for long, it would be like a fish going without water or a bird without air. And she did break up the awkwardness of being alone with Aimree. Dren still had to give a name to her feelings for Aimree. Dren couldn't work out if she meant any more to Aimree than just a friend. She certainly hoped so but there was no way of asking without setting herself up for a painful rejection and having a long hard conversation about who she really was.

'...and that's how the monastery was formed.'

'Right, yes.' Dren stuttered, aware that she had stopped paying attention. Hopefully a response wasn't required. To fill the silence, she tried to think of something to ask to keep the conversation going. She realised she did have a question that had been burning inside her for the last few months. In fact, ever since she had first heard about its existence.

'Can I ask you something?'

'Of course Dren, you know you can ask me anything. Especially if it takes my mind off the itching.' She clasped her hands tightly around her staff to avoid scratching.

'Well, I was just wondering. I read somewhere that the monks' duty is to look after the prophecy. Is that true?' She looked up at her. 'It's just, no one will talk to me about it.'

'You're right. That is our job. But the prophecy is nothing for you to worry about. It's only there to remind kings and queens of their obligations in the one language that they all understand.'

'What language is that?' she asked.

'Fear.'

CHAPTER 22

There was no question that the Wayfarers Tavern was a more elegant affair than the previous inn. Although, from Dren's perspective, anything would be an improvement from sleeping in a rat-infested stable.

As they walked towards the public entrance, Aimree took a look at Seema's face. The wound was glowing an alarming shade of red. 'Still itching?'

'Hurts like a...' Seema managed to stop herself just in time.

Aimree tutted as she turned Seema's face to the light. 'Hmm, there's signs of infection and some of the wounds are starting to weep. Probably best to keep your head covered, just in case they don't let us in,' she said, rummaging in her bag. 'I've got a piece of cloth in here. Wear it over your face and we'll just say you're our grandmother. Just hunch your shoulders and use the walking staff.'

Seema wrapped the cloth around her head. 'Eurgh, what's that smell?'

Aimree shrugged apologetically. 'Sorry, that's a cheese cloth. It was wrapped around my lunch when I left the keep.'

'And you gave me it for my face?' Seema snapped.

'It's not like we have much of a choice,' Aimree fired back. 'If they see the marks and think it's contagious, they won't let us in.' She closed up her bag.

'Okay sisters, I think you've made your point,' said Dren, once again playing peacemaker. She extended her arm. 'Would you care to take my hand, grandmother? Mind you don't trip on these steep stairs.'

'Thank you kindly, my child,' said Seema her voice rattling in her throat as she slid easily into character.

'Let me take your bag for you, grandma,' said Aimree, rushing to her side.

They shuffled up to the front door of the inn where they were met by the unusual sight of the innkeeper, standing watch over the entrance.

The man's pot belly was covered with a greasy apron. It may have been white at one point but it was now a sorry-looking shade of grey streaked with oily finger marks. Despite this, the thought of food made Dren hungry.

The man smiled as he held open the door for them but Seema hesitated. For an instant, Dren feared she was about to have a crisis of truthfulness. All she had to do was keep up an act. It wasn't exactly the same as lying to the man. But she needn't have worried. Seema, it turned out, was an expert actor.

'Standing guard?' said Seema, in a quivering voice. 'This must be a dangerous place. Come my little ones. We have not sunk so low yet that we need to stay in such a brothel.'

The man's smile wavered, the fear of losing three potential customers written on his face.

'No, ma'am, forgive the precautions but you are clearly not from around these parts. I don't mean to frighten you but-'

'Eh?' she squawked in an alarmingly loud voice, 'I can't hear you son, I'm a little deaf.'

He leaned in so she could hear and immediately recoiled from the smell of cheese. Trying to keep the revolt from his voice, he spoke a little louder. 'It's because of the creatures. They've been getting bolder and even venturing out from the woods.'

'Creatures?' said Seema softly looking up at the man in surprise, momentarily forgetting her charade. Luckily the innkeeper didn't seem to notice her slip-up. 'There's been an increase in wild animals coming into town. But they're strange, foreign beasts, not known about these parts. Luckily the prince has extra soldiers on patrol so your safety is guaranteed.'

'I'll be sleeping with a pointy stick under my pillow,' she added getting back into her character. 'Just to be on the safe side. Please have one brought up to my room immediately.'

'That's the strange thing,' said the innkeeper. 'It is said that some of them seem to be unharmed by the blade. Of course, I'm sure that's just talk. You know how soldiers are. Of course I'll find you a stick. I'll sharpen it myself.'

In keeping with appearances, they asked for two rooms, one for Aimree and her 'grandmother' and the other for Dren.

The innkeeper turned to Seema again. 'It's probably best that you keep watch over your granddaughter. There are soldiers dining at the bar tonight. They're not the best company for a young lady,' he said, oblivious to how patronising his words were. Aimree had to bite her tongue.

'Soldiers?' said Seema. 'That reminds me of a fellow I knew in my youth. He had the most charming smile and the largest-'

'Grandmother, that's quite enough,' said Aimree sharply, cutting her off mid flow. Aimree smiled apologetically and the innkeeper gave an understanding nod.

Once they were all safely inside and out of earshot, Aimree hissed, 'What on earth were you doing? Trying to get us kicked out?'

'I think you'll find, I was trying to get more information. I'll bet it's the same soldiers who took Thunder. What on earth did you think I was going to say? He had a large sword.'

'Sword my-'

'Goodnight,' said Dren. 'I'll be in my room if anyone needs me.' Never before had Dren enjoyed having a whole room to herself. She could overlook the fact that there was barely room for the single bed. Even if the view was limited by the mottled green darkness of an overhanging tree, at least she could choose when to draw the curtains.

'Lice-ridden no doubt.'

Dren could make out the muffled voices of Seema and Aimree who had finally made the long slow climb up the stairs to the adjacent room. She made a mental note not to discuss anything sensitive within such paper-thin walls.

The promise of a hot bath and cooked meal were both appealing prospects. However, they would have to wait. First she had to find the fletcher.

Knocking loudly on the neighbouring door, she explained cryptically that she was off to see to some business in town. Aimree was busy scrubbing the cheese cloth in a bucket of warm water which the innkeeper had brought all the way upstairs for them. Grandmother was going to be a demanding patron, it seemed.

On her way out the front door, Dren nodded to the innkeeper who had resumed his watch. Not that there would be much he could do when faced with immortal creatures except maybe to barricade the door and holler for reinforcements.

'We've got plenty to drink in here, young man,' the innkeeper called after her, unwilling to see a valuable customer leave to spend his change elsewhere. 'Nothing they have in the city that you can't find here. And if you can't find it here, you must be too drunk to see straight.'

'Business calls,' said Dren, patting the coins in her pocket.

'I see,' said the innkeeper with a knowing look. 'Mind there's an extra charge for late night visitors. That way, I don't have to tell your grandma what her golden boy gets up to after dark.'

Dren winced inwardly. That certainly hadn't been what she had meant to imply. She was quickly learning that they spoke a different language in Arcaria and she wasn't familiar with its nuances. She would need to be more careful with her words in future. Still, it provided a good cover story as to why she was slipping out and, apart from a nod and a wink on her return, it would avoid any awkward questions.

CHAPTER 23

The kitchens were situated in the damp underbelly of the Arcarian Keep barely separated from the River Upp by a crumbling stone wall. This closeness of the river resulted in a constant trickle of water dripping into the underground chambers.

Officially, this was a deliberate design, engineered to keep the kitchens moist to prevent the spread of fire. But Meela knew this was just an excuse for poor workmanship. The real reason was nothing more than short-sighted architecture designed by men who had never worked even half a day in a kitchen.

A permanent mist of spice enveloped the hottest part of the Arcarian Keep's kitchens. Not one bit of her aching body wanted to be here peeling potatoes. Meela's job was the lowliest in the kitchen, if not in the entire keep and nobody paid her the slightest bit of notice. But, despite fighting her father to the end, she had nothing but the bruises to show for her efforts. Sefra had already received payment in advance and he wasn't about to relinquish the gold that would keep his business afloat.

A dozen cooks, each with their own area of expertise

somehow managed to be heard over the incessant clattering of pan lids and the hissing of fat from dozens of roasting game birds. There was a pastry chef and a pudding chef, a dairy chef and a legume chef and chefs whose culinary creations were only fit for the eyes of royalty.

Meela's hands were numb from her basin of icy water and her ears rang with the sound of Jared's booming voice.

'Those were due up five minutes ago. If they take much longer, someone upstairs will likely starve to death.'

That's not so likely, thought Meela, *given the size of their bellies.*

'If that lamb waits about any longer, we'll be serving bleedin' mutton,' he shrieked at a poor kitchen hand who was struggling under the weight of the heavy cauldron.

The tall red hat worn by the head cook was visible from every corner of the kitchen. The hat was an unnecessary sign of rank as no one who entered the confines of the kitchens could fail to notice him bellowing out orders. If progress was too slow for his liking, a kitchen aide could expect a dig in the ribs with his rolling pin or, if he or she was unlucky, a clout on the head with a hot pan.

Jared carried a layer of grease about him, accumulated through working long hours with little time left over to sleep, let alone to wash. His hands were marked with the scars that came from years of wielding cleavers. As a general rule, Meela stayed out of his way wherever possible and refused to complain despite her frozen fingers nipping in the salty brine water of the potato barrel.

Suddenly, there was a rap at the service door. Usually it fell to the kitchen porter to attend to the numerous daily callers. Occasionally a beggar would appear looking for charity but most knew better than to try their luck at the keep. Those who didn't would be sent on their way with a kick to the rear. Other times, traders would bring up leftovers from the market, hoping to offload ripe produce before it spoiled.

'Well, why are you standing their gawping like a goat? That door won't be answering itself, will it?'

Meela looked about and realised the head chef was talking to her. She removed her hands from the icy water and dried them on the rag tucked into her waistband. Then she hurried over to the door.

'Mind and use the spy hatch, don't want the weather getting in.' This advice came from a nearby chef's aide who was icing flowers onto soft biscuits and knew better than to let herself get distracted with callers at the door.

Meela released the latch and the hatch folded downwards, allowing her a view of the impatient-looking pork merchant. He was still wearing his blood-spattered slaughtering apron. This made Meela feel a little queasy. Something wasn't quite right.

'For the love of goodness, open the door quickly, or would you have me freeze to the spot?' The man seemed strangely familiar and a warning was pulling at her mind.

'Ask him what his business is,' whispered the chef's aid who had appeared at her side, freely offering her experience. She was intrigued by the visitor now that he wasn't her responsibility.

'First, tell me what business you have here at the keep, sir,' Meela demanded firmly but politely.

'I've got a proposition for Cartha the porter, so fetch him for me. Quickly now!'

A flash of recognition crossed Meela's mind. She remembered the year when her father had ordered a fattened pig for her eldest brother's birthday. The merchant took them for ignorant country fools and tried to charge them double the price for the runt of the litter. When Sefra challenged him, he acted as if it was some conspiracy they had all hatched against him. Her father set the dogs on the fraudster and he was never heard from again.

Until now, thought Meela.

'Well, the porter's not here,' replied Meela, with an air of authority beyond her years. 'You could wait for him but he might be some time and the wolves are hungry this time of year. You'd best be careful what with the scent of the kill on your apron.'

The stunned merchant slowly regained his wits and turned to walk towards his empty wagon muttering, 'I'll just come back later.'

'Shall I pass on a message?' she shouted after him but received no answer. Meela noticed him stooping to pick up two empty baskets as he left. *Strange,* she thought, *doesn't look like he was here to sell anything after all.*

She latched shut the spy hatch and went back to her potatoes.

CHAPTER 24

The bell alerted all in the vicinity to Dren's arrival. A conversation fell silent as Dren entered the dark shop. A hooded woman left without saying a word. At least, Dren thought she was a woman but it was hard to make out much in the gloom. She suspected the lighting was deliberately set low.

Apart from the hooded figure who had hastily departed, there were no other customers. It was a workshop and not the kind of shop where people came to browse, that much was obvious.

A man she assumed to be the fletcher stood curled over a workbench at the rear of the shop. He was sharpening the point of an arrowhead with a whetstone. Bulges of muscles pressed tightly against the fabric of his cloth shirt. This would have made sense if he had been a blacksmith or a labourer, but his was a craft that required precision rather than brute strength. The size of the man was something of a puzzle.

To Dren's left were rows of sticks cut to various lengths, all with notches scored on one end to accommodate a bow string. The other end awaited the arrowhead.

The only other objects on display were contained within neat wicker baskets. Dren glanced in one and saw it contained feathers from various species of bird. She recognised the tail feathers of the spotted owl along with the camouflage plumage from at least three different types of hawk.

Sparks flew as the fletcher sanded the tip of the arrow in a slow, deliberate manner, not pausing in his work as he raised his eyes to look at the intruder. His musky odour filled the small space in the same way a wolf marked its territory with its scent.

'Can I help you?' the man's deliberate tones reached Dren's ears over the sound of grinding metal.

'I'm here to buy some arrows.'

After an uncomfortable pause, Dren brought her fist towards her mouth and coughed. As she did this she simultaneously lifted the cloak from her shoulder, casually revealing the bow.

'Are you out of your mind? There's no need to shout. Put that thing away before somebody sees it,' said the man. A hint of panic had crept into his voice. 'You know I should report you for even possessing that.'

Then he raised his voice to an audible level. 'Illegal hunting will not be endorsed or encouraged by this establishment. Creatures or no creatures.' He looked about him to check whether anyone else was listening in to their conversation.

Dren realised it was her turn to talk. 'That's a shame, because you come highly recommended.' She hoped a bit of flattery would go a long way. When this got no reaction she added: 'Thurso sent me.'

Upon hearing the name, the man's demeanour changed instantly. He stood up from his workbench.

'This way,' he said, in a hiss as he grabbed Dren's arm and manhandled her towards the rear of the shop. He drew a heavy curtain, hiding them from view.

He gave Dren a stern look, like a teacher reprimanding a pupil. 'Just what are you all about, flashing a concealed weapon? You'll have me lose my license. If anyone had seen it...' he tailed off. 'Anyway, down to business. What exactly are you looking for?'

'I want to buy some arrows,' Dren repeated, unsure of what the fletcher wanted her to say.

'Well I don't exactly sell fresh fish. Come now, I haven't got all day. What is your purpose?'

Dren's blank look caused the man to grunt in frustration. 'To wound, to maim or to kill? Ground runner or flying creature. Or...' he paused and the corners of his mouth turned upwards. 'Do you have a taste for the inedible flesh?'

Dren caught up with his meaning. 'No! Well, I don't know. Maybe?' Then she hurriedly added, 'But it's purely for self-defence.'

'Yes, yes of course' said the man who Dren still only knew as *the fletcher*. 'You'll take a dozen. They will be ready in a week. I don't keep that kind in the shop for obvious reasons. But be aware. They will have absolutely no effect on the creatures.'

Dren contained her urge to ask if they could be made any sooner. She didn't fancy hanging about town for a week for ammunition she wasn't sure she would need. But the man's tone didn't invite any more questions and the bow hung heavy on her shoulder. Feeling out of her depth, Dren hurried out of the shop, the tiny bell echoing her departure as the door closed behind her.

There was nothing for it but to return to the

Wayfarers. Although Dren was eager to see the city, she would be staying here all week which meant plenty of time to explore later. If the bow could get her in as much trouble as she suspected it could, then she wanted to return it to a safe hiding place as soon as possible.

Even though she was in a hurry, she avoided taking exactly the same route back to minimise the risk of being robbed. She had no desire for trouble to follow her back to the inn. The back road eventually led her round the back of the building. The inn was boarded up from behind, meaning all visitors had to report to the innkeeper. But, as Dren walked around to the front door, she noticed the burly man was absent. That could only mean one of two things. Either there had been trouble or it was dinner time.

Her nose started to twitch with the smell of cooking. She let herself in and raced up the stairs, still carrying the bow close to her skin. She intended to visit her own room first to hide the useless weapon under the bed but something made her turn at the top of the stairs and knock on the girls' door instead.

After a short delay, it was opened by Aimree. The sight of her puffy, red eyes took Dren aback. Had she been crying? The curtains were drawn and the room was dark.

'What's wrong?' she asked but Aimree raised a finger to her lips, bidding her to be quiet. Wordlessly, Dren was led into the room. She saw a motionless figure asleep in the bed.

Aimree's voice crackled. 'Just after you left her throat started to swell. When she couldn't get a deep breath I panicked. That's when I begged the innkeeper to summon a healer.' Her whispering voice trembled as she continued. 'According to the healer, the bat scratches are causing her to be very sick.'

'Can't they just clean out the dirt? What kind of healers do they have around here that are afraid to get a little blood on their hands?'

Aimree shook her head. 'It's not as simple as that. That kind of bat wounds is usually fatal. The toxins creep into the blood and slowly poison the heart. Seema just happens to have more blood in her body than most which is why she has lasted this long already.

'The healer gave her a strong draft to make her sleep which should buy her a little more time. But she needs a special herb to cure her of the sickness.'

'What herb is it?' Dren asked.

'It's called thale.'

Dren's hopes sank when she heard the name. It grew in the garden of the Drabsea keep but it wasn't easy to find in the wild.

'Well doesn't the healer have some thale?'

'That's the problem. It's a rare and expensive herb.' Aimree paced up and down the room, trying to look anywhere but at the lifeless figure of her sister. 'She doubts if we will find it anywhere in the city. If we could source some she would start brewing the antidote immediately but, without it, there is nothing she can do except try to make her comfortable.' She stopped walking and turned to face Dren. 'I need to prepare myself to face the truth. My sister's going to die.' The tears started flowing again.

Dren was taken aback. If they had still been in the keep, she had no doubt that Seema would have been cured by now. They had access to the best medicines and, even if she didn't agree with the physik's diagnosis of her own rash, she still had faith in his ability to heal the sick.

Not that she would say this to Aimree. She looked really upset and Dren didn't have the faintest idea of how to comfort her. A thousand thoughts ran through her mind but none of them seemed to be suitable. 'Aimree, listen to me. We're not going to give up on her. I'll find the herbs. How hard can it be?' A glimmer of hope lit up in Aimree's eyes. 'I just need to get into the keep somehow and get to the garden. They must have some there. How much time do we have?'

'A few days at most. After that she will just slip away.' More tears filled her eyes.

It seemed inappropriate to tell Aimree that she needed to get some dinner and work out a plan. Instead, she tried to sound in control of things. 'Leave it with me. I'll sort something out.'

'Thank you Dren. You truly are a hero. I mean that.'

Aimree looked so relieved that it made Dren cringe. What had she just promised to do? She walked out of the room and closed the door behind her feeling like a cross between a fraud and a fool. Would it not have been kinder to tell Aimree she didn't have the slightest clue how to break into a castle, steal some plants which may or may not grow there and make it out alive again? Then again, if she didn't, that would mean certain death for Seema. The least she could do was try.

CHAPTER 25

Dren walked down the stairs and straight to a seat in the last empty booth at the bar. It must have been payday as all around her were tables of men and women drinking to excess, empty pitchers piled high on ale-soaked tables. She couldn't afford to join in the merry-making but she would have one drink. The answer to her dilemma would most probably not be found in the bottom of the glass, but outside the inn lay hostile territory.

The weight of the bow pressed into her shoulder, a not-so-subtle reminder of its presence. She imagined holding it and drawing back the string. The string quivered as if lightening ran through it. Dren shook her head and brought herself out of her daydream. She cursed herself for forgetting to leave the useless weapon under her bed. But now that she was comfortably seated at a table with the prospect of food, she couldn't face the thought of an unnecessary journey back up the steep stairs. The bow would just have to stay where it was.

Lost in her thoughts, the words of the innkeeper startled her. 'Not so lucky today young man?' The innkeeper must have seen Dren's despondent look and assumed he had suffered a romantic disappointment back in town. 'Never mind, the night has only just begun.' He wiped the table with a damp rag. 'You'll be hungry, I suspect? Nothing like the thrill of the chase to work up an appetite.' And with that, he went off to fetch something that Dren could only hope would be edible.

He reappeared with a jug of ale, a generous slice of game pie and some more advice. 'You need to keep your strength up and get back out there. That's the wisdom that comes with age and many many knock backs.' The man gave another one of his winks as he placed the food and drink down in front of Dren before turning his attention back to the neighbouring tables.

A long table set along the back wall seemed to demand most of the innkeeper's time. A group of a dozen soldiers crowded around it. Most of them were older than Dren and all were extremely drunk. She watched with a pang of envy as they sang rowdy songs together. They wore no armour, only tunics in forest green indicating their allegiance to Arcaria. Despite this, their swords lay close to hand under the table. *That could have been me, enjoying a night with friends,* she thought. Instead, she had left that choice behind her and rolled the dice on a life of uncertainty.

Turning back to dinner, Dren once again wondered if she had done the right thing. Especially now that Seema's life was on the line. *If she had never met me, she wouldn't be in that state.* Picking up the meat-filled pie, Dren chewed listlessly as gravy oozed out and dripped onto the plate. All day long she had been looking forward to eating a hot meal but the weight of responsibility that had fallen afresh on her shoulders had taken away any hint of pleasure. Plus the soldiers were distracting her from thinking up a plan. They must have been drinking for hours as their language had grown ripe and their stories more and more outrageous.

She took a swig of her bitter ale. It was certainly stronger than the watered down version they were occasionally given at the keep. Dren finished the pie and the innkeeper refilled the tankard. She hadn't meant to drink any more only she couldn't leave until she had come up with a plan to help Seema. She stared at the bubbles rising in the drink, desperately hoping it would give her the inspiration and the courage she needed to be a hero. The problem was that, the more drinking she did, the more outlandish her ideas became. She even contemplated storming the castle, charging in atop Thunder, snatching up the plant and making it out again before the drunken soldiers could catch her. And then she remembered that Thunder was gone.

Excited shouts roused her from her negative thoughts, and she allowed herself to become distracted by the soldiers as they argued and boasted and drank. Dren noticed the battle scars and wind-burned faces of seasoned soldiers drinking to forget what they had seen sitting alongside the hot-headed youths who drank to forget they were still scared.

'And I ran it through with my sword but the beast never felt a thing. Kept charging straight at me. I had to dive out of the way. I've never seen teeth so big in my entire life,' said a thin man with a two day growth on his chin.

'I heard they managed to kill one of them last week.' The woman slurred her words as she downed her drink. Her knuckles were grazed. Presumably she was no stranger to a bar fight.

'Starved it to death,' said the soldier who was sitting at the corner of the table. The light was poor and Dren struggled to make out his features

'That's alright if you can catch one and persuade it to get into a cage in the first place,' said the thin man. 'Last one to try had his arm bit clean off, so they say.' This drew shouts of derision from the rest of the table.

The soldiers continued to banter back and forwards across the table. Then they moved on to another drinking game which involved emptying a whole glass while singing the Arcarian anthem. The game moved around the table, each soldier taking his or her turn. Finally came the turn of a mean looking soldier in the corner. When he leaned forward revealing his face in the light, Dren noticed his black eye. *Must have been fighting*, she thought.

Then realisation dawned and Dren felt a jolt of anger. The black eye wasn't from a punch. She saw the imprint of a circular rim. That was a hoof mark! This had to be one of the soldiers from the woods. She tried to master her anger before it got the better of her. Her training kicked in as she weighed up her options. For a start, she was outnumbered. And she couldn't risk causing any trouble while Seema was still at death's door. She had no choice but to bide her time and wait for the right moment.

It didn't take long before Dren's thirst for vengeance became overwhelming. Whether it was the pressure from the bow or the ale, she couldn't tell but she knew exactly what she was going to do. The offending soldier had drunk enough that he was bound to need to relieve himself at some point. That's when Dren would march up to him and demand he return Thunder. The donkey was her rightful property. Well, Seema had paid for him after all. The thought of her lying upstairs dying strengthened her resolve to right this injustice.

Caught up in the heat of her thoughts, Dren failed to realise that, sometimes, the rightful owner is just a name given to the stronger person. But, as the drink gave her false courage and the bow continued to weigh heavy on her shoulder, both exerted their own influence. Without Dren being entirely aware of why, she became increasingly convinced that this was the right course of action.

It wasn't long before Dren's plan was set in motion. 'I'm off to see a man about a mule. I'll be back in a minute,' said the soldier in the corner. When he stood up, Dren got a view of the hoof mark in all its glory.

This was her cue to rise from her table. She followed a discreet distance behind the soldier who walked out of the inn and headed towards the bushes. *The thief didn't even have the decency to go to the toileting hole around the back.*

Dren watched as the man unbuckled his belt. As soon as he had reached the point of no return, Dren crept closer to him, not entirely sure what her plan was but feeling her entire body burn with anger.

Dren hadn't anticipated that the seasoned soldier was used to operating whilst drunk. The man sensed someone behind him. The call of nature could wait. He turned quickly and pulled a small dagger out of his waistband. He held it in the casual manner of a trained killer.

Dren cursed herself for assuming an off-duty soldier would be completely unarmed. And then she felt the rage build inside her again and, grabbing the bow from under her cloak, brought it level with her eye and drew back the string as she raised the bow to point upwards at the man's head.

At exactly the same moment as the soldier, Dren realised that the bow was not loaded. In a way, she was relieved that she wasn't able to kill a man purely because she felt angry. But her relief was soon replaced by a dull pain which shook her temple as the soldier smashed his fist into Dren's skull. As Dren slumped to the ground, she tried to look at the positive side. If the soldier was still alive, he might still tell her where Thunder was. And then darkness washed over her and everything went black.

CHAPTER 26

A steady beat, like the sound of rain, filled the space in Dren's head which, until that point, had been empty of any sensation.

Drip drip drip.

She couldn't place the sound but it was persistent. Cold, hard earth pressed into her back and she realised she was lying on the ground.

She rubbed her hand along her body. Her clothing was damp to the touch. She opened her eyes and blinked but everything stayed dark. Was it night time? Why couldn't she see any stars? Trying to sit up, an explosion of pain struck her head. This must be one mother of a hangover. What had she been drinking? She would certainly avoid ordering it again. Then she remembered she had been hit.

She tried again to sit up, slower this time, but something was holding her back. Her limbs felt heavy and she couldn't move. Puzzled, she tried again. She felt tightness in her wrists and ankles. After a few moments of struggling, she realised she must be bound in some way. Had she fallen into the bushes? Then a voice came out of the darkness nearby.

'So, this was your plan was it? Nice work, Dren.' The familiar sarcastic tone at once frightened and reassured her.

'Aimree, is that you? What happened?'

'You mean you don't remember your drunken fight with the soldier? What in Kingdom's name were you thinking about taking that stupid bow with you?'

At the mention of the bow, Dren felt an emptiness across her shoulder where the bow had been. 'I know it sounds stupid but I couldn't think straight with that bow on my shoulder. I don't know why Thurso gave it to me. It was obviously meant for someone else. He virtually said as much when he gave it to me.' She knew it was gone yet still tried to feel about for it only to realise that her wrists were bound with rough rope. She stopped struggling as her movements made the rope bite into her skin. All around her was nothing but darkness. 'Where are we?'

'About twenty feet below ground.'

Dren was speechless.

'Haven't you worked it out yet? We're in prison!' Aimree's voice faltered and she sounded close to tears

'Huh? I don't understand. How did you end up here too?' now she was even more confused.

'I only came down to the bar to get some food for Seema. That's when I saw your new drinking buddies dragging your unconscious body across the floor. When they started to smash their glasses over your head, I tried to intervene and they decided I was aiding and abetting a criminal. The landlord turned a blind eye and I was bound, hand and foot, thrown roughly over someone's shoulder and carried up to the keep along with you. Although, I think I heard them dragging you along the ground.'

Dren felt her head. That would explain the strange bumps and cuts. She remembered she had threatened a soldier. And then she recalled the punch. After that, she couldn't remember anything more.

'I just hope the landlord doesn't kick out "grandma". She's too ill to be moved,' Aimree said, accusingly.

She wasn't blaming Dren for this, was she? Then again, maybe she was right. Why hadn't Dren tried harder to get Thunder back? The donkey had probably been tied up in the inn's stables the whole time the soldiers were drinking. Dren groaned at her own lack of thought.

There was a click, followed by a hatch opening. Dren's neck gave a painful crack as she turned towards the door. Faint green light illuminated the four walls of the bare earthen cell. The walls were woven out of thick tree roots. An anonymous hand casually tossed a couple of stale pieces of bread into the room. They were so hard they rolled along the ground before coming to rest just out of reach.

'Can I have some water please?' she shouted before the hand disappeared.

'This isn't an inn. Drink off the floor like everyone else.'

'But it's filthy!' she shouted back.

The voice just laughed and the hatch clicked shut, plunging the small cell into darkness once again.

'Please, my sister's sick, she needs help,' Aimree cried out as the footsteps disappeared. But her call went unanswered. 'I can't believe you let this happen,' she said to Dren. Her tone was full of bitterness.

She didn't need Aimree to remind her. If anything

happened to Seema, Dren knew she would carry the blame forever. Trying to lighten the mood she said, 'Hey, at least I got us into the keep.'

Aimree didn't respond and Dren decided it was best to leave her alone. She struggled against the tethers and at last managed to sit upright against the wall of the cell. Immediately, she regretted the decision as her shirt soaked up the dampness from the mossy tree roots that formed the walls of the prison. It was wet enough to chill her but there wasn't enough liquid to drink. All she could do was moisten her parched lips.

Just as she was beginning to wonder if Aimree would ever speak to her again, a high pitched noise sounded from nearby.

'Did you hear that?' Aimree said, sitting bolt upright.

Dren had thought she had heard squeaking earlier. But she thought better than to mention they might be sharing the space with rats. There was no sign of a mattress or blanket in the cell and they had no choice but to sit on the squalid ground like a couple of animals.

'Did you pick up the bread?' Aimree asked.

'No, I'm not hungry enough to eat off the floor yet.' Dren felt along the earthen floor for a drier space to sit. She reached as far behind her as she could but the whole floor was sodden.

'I didn't mean for you to eat it. I meant so it didn't attract vermin!'

'Aimree, if a rat wants to take a bite out of a piece of bread, I'd rather I wasn't holding the bread at the time.' She groped around in the darkness, stretching out her fingertips but she still couldn't reach the bread.

'Well you better sleep with one eye open in case the rat decides it wants a piece of you.'

'The hypothetical rat will be too full up on mouldy prison bread to bother eating me.'

'There's nothing hypothetical about the rat. You were lucky to sleep through it the last time but just wait until they start fighting. Then you'll know all about them.'

Aimree's last comment killed the attempt at conversation. Dren feared she would keep the argument going until they got out of here. That was if they managed to get out. There was nothing to do except wait for the hatch to open again. It was going to be a long night.

CHAPTER 27

Wiping her hands on the damp dish rag she had tucked into her apron, Meela bid good night to the kitchen staff. Her long day was over but it would only be a few hours until tomorrow's shift started. As one of the newer members of the household, it was her job to rise before the rest of the keep to boil up the porridge for the servants' breakfast. Stifling a yawn which told her she should go straight to bed, she exited the kitchen via the back stairs. There was something she had to do. Sleep would have to wait a little while longer.

A door led directly to the keep's gardens where a bright moon illuminated her path. The stillness up here was a gift after the noise and harsh shouting that dominated the kitchen but she wasn't up here simply to enjoy the peace. There was someone she had to visit.

The path came to an abrupt end at a recently erected fence which towered over her head. Spikes had been nailed into the top of the posts to keep out trespassers. Undeterred, Meela skirted around the edge of the barrier until she found the place she was looking for.

Looking around to make sure she wasn't being

watched, she removed a loose slat and slipped into the enclosure. The fence served both to keep those inside hidden from the casual prying eye as well as to ensure the security of its contents.

She squeezed her body through the tight space between the fence and the rear of one of the wooden pens. Again she checked that nobody was about before she walked around to the front. The sight of row upon row of cramped cages made her heart lurch the way it had the very first time she had accidently stumbled across them. These were nothing like the kennels situated beside the keep's stables. The well-fed hounds would bark at her approach, waving excited tails in expectation of a bone.

In contrast, these cages were cramped, squalid and the occupants mostly mute. She walked the length of the rows, taking in the pitiful sight, trying not to let her heart break. Soulful eyes stared as she passed by. Some looked up expectantly, hoping that this visit would bring food. Other animals cowered in dark corners, frightened and alone, having already given up all hope of being rescued. A few of the creatures gave a whimper as she passed but most knew better than to call out and risk a beating from the soldiers.

Meela was drawn to this terrible place, even though the sight of it had reduced her to tears the first time. She wasn't particularly prone to crying but this amount of suffering had affected her. She shared the pain of being held somewhere against your will, far from home.

She walked over to a cage which had been empty the night before. There wasn't even any fresh straw for the new arrival which looked like a cross between a bear and a horse. It was unable to use its awkward legs to lie down and so it stood, rocking backwards and forwards on legs too thin for its bulky body.

Each night she found herself drawn to visit the animals. Or creatures, as folk were calling them. Regardless of what people named them, she felt nothing but pity for the poor things. Some nights she was kept awake by their howling, as they called out in despair for help that would never come. Were they calling to their family, or crying out for their Creator? At any rate they were pleading for somebody to rescue them. It made her sad that she couldn't do anything.

But tonight they were strangely quiet as if they were too weak to care. Most looked as though they had simply given up fighting and chosen instead to lie down in a corner, hoping to die.

Eventually she found what she was looking for. It was nothing exotic or remotely dangerous, not like the rock lions or the wild Mamroose that shared adjoining cages. Instead, the recipient of Meela's visit was just a simple donkey who had no place in a zoo. When he had appeared here two nights ago he was wild and frightened. He had banged his head against the cage so hard that Meela was surprised he didn't knock himself out. But when he looked up and saw her, it had been love at first sight. He had instantly calmed as she spoke to him in a gentle whisper and made him a promise that, if she could, she would get him out.

'You don't belong in here,' she said out loud as she patted him on the nose and slipped a carrot through the bars. Technically it would be classed as stealing, but the kitchen wouldn't miss it. She must have peeled over a thousand already.

The donkey snuffed contentedly. Meela whispered

reassuring words to him as he crunched on his treat. Although he had a wild spark in his eyes, he had been well cared for. He clearly belonged to someone. She wondered how on earth he had ended up in here, alone and unwanted. Once she had proven to him that her hands and her pockets were indeed empty of food, Meela bid him farewell with a scratch behind his ears. She promised she would return again as soon as she could.

Next she turned her attention to the other cages. The animals were lying in their own filth. Why was nobody cleaning out the enclosures? There wasn't so much as a water bowl in sight. She sighed as she saw the condition of the long-tailed monkey's matted fur and the cramped cage opposite it was totally unsuitable for the armour-plated red back.

The thought that someone in power had decided that this was acceptable made her angry. What kind of leader was Prince Erat if he thought you could just lock up your problems in a cage and forget about them? You wouldn't treat a human this way. And then she thought of her father. Hadn't she warned him about what this place was like?

The foolish townsfolk were panicking about the so-called creatures emerging from the woods and rampaging through the town. If they could see them now, they wouldn't be afraid. There was something rather pathetic about the whole situation. Especially when the guards triumphantly paraded their captured animals as if they had just wrestled a river gator with their bare hands. Were they really going to round up every animal and try to sell it at the door of the keep, claiming it was a wild mutant? And now a donkey?

Who were they trying to kid?

She came to the end of the row and stopped herself just in time. She had no desire to turn the corner and see the sights she had witnessed on her first visit. The very thought sent a shudder through her body. It wasn't that there was anything particularly fearsome about these last captives. On the contrary, they were the most pathetic of the lot. What made her avoid the final row of cages was the creepy feeling they gave her. Some of the creatures seemed almost human. She didn't know what kind of animals they were exactly, but they certainly were not native to the Kingdom.

The expressions on their faces looked hauntingly familiar. Instead of howling, they had cried as she passed, like they were trying to speak but had forgotten the words. Apart from the fur and the claws, they could have been children. She couldn't bring herself to see that again.

The sound of a gate opening alerted her to the presence of a guard. She needed to get out of there quickly. Retracing her steps, she ran back until she reached the gap in the fence. She had no intention of getting caught trespassing here. After all, what excuse could she give? That the cook had sent her up for meat? The thought sent a shiver along her spine.

CHAPTER 28

It was a strange sensation, to be this close to another human being with the lights out, and for it to be the least intimate moment you had ever experienced. Aimree's muscles had started to cramp from sitting down for so long. And, because her hands and feet were bound together, she couldn't stand up and fully extend her limbs. Periodically she had to turn over to allow the blood from one side of her body to flow to the other.

'Aimree?'

'What?' she mumbled without bothering to look up.

'I've been thinking-'

'That makes a change,' she said, unwilling to be nice to Dren.

'What it is, you see, well, it's a bit of a delicate subject. Since we're in here and we'll have to, you know, I've been avoiding it so far but-'

'Go in that corner, well away from the food, just in case we do decide to start eating it.' Growing up with a brother had taught her how men thought and how lazy they could be when it came to matters of hygiene. It was best to set down clear boundaries from the start. 'This is how Seema must be feeling.' Aimree flexed her ankles.

'Lying down for this length of time can't be good for a person.'

'But it's what she needs right now,' Dren said, trying to comfort her.

'What she needs is the medicine,' Aimree corrected him. 'Which she can't get if we're stuck in here.' She glowered at Dren, ignoring the fact that he couldn't see her facial expression in the dark. It was entirely down to him that they were in this predicament.

Aimree worried that time was passing too quickly without anyone explaining what was going to happen to them. There was no way of telling how long they had been held captive in the small cell. Food came too sporadically to work out when meal times were and, without any windows, she could see neither star nor sun in the sky meaning it was impossible to tell whether it was night or day. Surely Dren had come up with a plan by now. It wasn't like there was anything else to do in here except think.

She was growing increasingly frustrated with Dren. Although he had promised that he would get them into the keep, she hadn't exactly expected him to get them locked up. He was so clueless when it came to- well, everything. It looked as though it was going to be up to her to sort out the mess.

She needed to speak to whoever was in charge and find out when they would be taken to court for a hearing. They hadn't been charged with anything yet. Surely that had to happen soon. Unless today was a day off. Then it must be the following day. Unless that was a holiday. She had no idea when such days fell in the Arcarian calendar. She didn't know how much longer she could hold out, never mind Seema's health. But maybe there was another way.

Her wrists were aching from the rope that bound them together. She raised her arms and brought her wrists close to her face. When they were close enough, she bit down on the rope. She pulled at the bindings trying to find the knot and work it loose. Frustratingly, she couldn't find it and, every time she tugged on it, the rope tightened and bit into her skin.

Blinking back tears, she knew she had to work through the pain. If she managed to loosen her wrists, she could untie her ankles and then take care of Dren's bindings. The obvious thing would be to work together to overpower the guard then they would be one step closer to getting out of here.

Even if her backup plan didn't work, she figured she would rather have something between her teeth to stop her from talking. She could only think of nasty things to say to Dren and she might break down in tears again if she dwelled on Seema lying in her death bed.

She bit down harder on the bindings. It was foolish to waste precious water on useless tears and she had promised herself she wouldn't blame Dren for all of her woes. It wasn't his fault that Seema got sick. But she couldn't help blaming him for dragging Seema into this in the first place. She was a monk after all, not a soldier. She shouldn't even have been walking in the woods never mind climbing trees. What had Dren been thinking?

The day was punctuated by the hatch opening followed by the unceremonial throwing of stale food which invariably landed nowhere near them. None of the guards stayed long enough to strike up a conversation. It was as if the guards were feeding dogs.

By now, she was hungry enough to consider trying to grab the food before it landed on the ground.

How much longer would they have to wait until someone came to speak to them and tell them why they had been arrested? Maybe someone had worked out they were deserters and they were waiting on transport to take them back to the Drabsea Keep for a court martial. She kept on chewing at her bindings, trying to burst the rope a strand at a time.

If she hadn't been running away, she would never have ended up in here. Her whole life had been mapped out for her. She was supposed to pass out of her class with honours and receive her fur cloak then work hard as a soldier and get noticed for the right reasons. When the time came, she would apply to the Kingdom Watch and see out her days protecting the Kingdom. That was how things were supposed to be.

Instead, she was tied up in a small cell with a boy she had only known for a few months, having a conversation about what corner of the room to pee in. She thought of her friends and again her mind returned to Dafine. She felt a pain in her heart. Realising she was coming close to dwelling on that fateful day, she snapped herself out of the dark place.

She tried to keep the emotion from her voice as she spoke. 'We need to make friends with a guard and see if he or she can get some thale for us,' she said, more for her benefit than for Dren's. She would keep fighting, even from in here. She might be down, but she wasn't beaten. Her family depended on her.

******

Beads of sweat formed on her forehead. If the

temperature was rising that could mean it was daytime. The problem was, the smell was rising too. In other circumstances, Dren would have been delighted to spend all of this time alone in Aimree's company. But that was in a world that no longer existed. The relationship was different now. What had started as a tentative friendship had descended into hostility and resentment.

Prison was a strange experience, not at all what she had expected. The overwhelming sensation was not fear or anger. Rather, it was boredom. Sure, if she thought about it, she could work herself up into a rage against the faceless men and women who were keeping them here, shadowy figures who moved in the dark corridors outside their cell. But from moment to moment, what she experienced was the achingly slow passage of time with absolutely nothing to do.

She had already counted the number of spiders in the cell, re-counted how many footsteps the guards took to walk up and down the corridor, and, when she got really bored, she would guess the highest number she could count to before Aimree told her again that she was completely to blame for getting them into this situation. These would entertain Dren for a few minutes at a time and, if she was in the right frame of mind, she could make them last an hour. But these strategies had now lost their effectiveness.

What she needed was a game. However, the only games she knew required a deck of cards and, if they weren't getting any food from their captors, they couldn't very well expect to be given anything that might make their stay less torturous.

'Aimree?' She struggled to sit upright in an attempt

to make herself more comfortable.

'Yes Dren,' said Aimree, taking the binding out of her mouth. Progress on the escape plan was slow. At this rate they would still be here come next year's Blubberfish Festival.

'Do you know any games?' Dren's left foot had developed an unfortunate cramp and she winced in pain as she tried to stretch it out.

'Games? What sort of games?'

'Anything to pass the time with and make us forget the miserable situation we're currently in.'

'Me and Seema used to play this game where you had to try and make the other person laugh. The winner was the one who could keep a straight face.' She let out a long sigh. 'But I don't think anything could make me laugh in here.'

Dren did a perfect imitation of Heron eating the forbidden fruit in the forest. Despite herself, Aimree let out a chuckle.

They spent the afternoon playing the game back and forth until they had laughed so much their sides split. Eventually there came a sharp rap at the hatch.

'Keep it down in there.'

Dren was startled by the response. She hadn't realised they could be overheard. Had there been a guard posted outside the door this whole time? But she could potentially use it to her advantage. She would do what she did best. She would try to talk her way out.

'Hello there,' she shouted at the guard. No response. 'Can you hear me?' But her words echoed back unanswered. Undeterred, she kept up the shouting, hoping that she could engage the guard in conversation.

Aimree joined in and together they talked about

sports, about the weather, about Arcaria's chances in the upcoming King's Tournament, whatever nonsense came to mind, inviting an answer from the human being on the other side of the door. Despite their best efforts, nothing they said got as much as a word from the guard.

But it didn't much matter. Laughing and joking like children, for a brief spell at least, Dren and Aimree forgot the aching in their limbs, the thirst in their throats and the sharp ache of hunger in their bellies.

CHAPTER 29

Now that Cartha the porter had returned to work, Meela was daily reminded of her place at the bottom of the pecking order. As a result, she was forced to spend hours hunched over a barrel in an obscure corner of the kitchen, peeling the skin off vegetables to be used to feed the keep's herd of pigs. Rough calluses had formed on Meela's hands from the repetition of her menial task.

The kitchen porter was the kind of man who thrived upon power. It didn't help that he was lazy with it. The more people he had working for him, the less work he had to do.

Meela remembered the look of panic in Cartha's eyes the day he heard that one of her fellow workers was ill. He virtually dragged the poor boy out of his sick bed still smelling of vomit and demanded he return to work immediately. And all to ensure he wouldn't have to lift his little finger and do any work. The same rules did not apply to Cartha when he required a day off after drinking to excess.

There was something about him that made Meela's skin crawl. Perhaps it was the way his eyes lingered over her longer than they should. But Meela knew it wasn't worth complaining. From the gossip she had heard, he always got away with it. She just made sure to wrap her apron a bit tighter around her when she was within his sight.

As much as the skin on her hands was suffering from the task, Meela did enjoy peeling the vegetables because, if she was lucky and not immediately summoned over to wash the pots, she might be allowed to go outside and feed the animals.

The pigs that roamed freely in the courtyard outside of the servants' quarters always appreciated a bucket of kitchen slops while the hens clucked in anticipation when they saw her coming towards them with a handful of grain.

But today Cartha wouldn't even grant her the few minutes of relief from the heat of the roaring fires. As the day dragged on, she felt as if she was being made to stand there melting, purely because it was within Cartha's power to hold her here. The back door had been left wide open to let out the excess heat. In spite of this measure, tempers were raised even higher than usual. An argument broke out over who had put a pot away without washing it then someone let the sauce boil over. On several occasions Meela had to duck to avoid getting in the way of a stray ladle thrown in anger.

Just when she thought she might pass out with the heat, she noticed Cartha walking in her direction. It triggered her memory of the caller who had enquired about him. She wondered if she should mention it to him.

'If you're going to stand around gawping, you may as well make yourself useful,' he said, raising his voice above the general din. Meela realised, too late, that she had been staring and not moving her hands.

Cartha thumped a wooden bucket down on the bench beside her. 'I'm needing more water. People are just helping themselves to it in the heat.'

As he walked away, shaking his head to indicate his annoyance, she could see beads of sweat trickling down the rolls of excess flesh around his neck. She knew that she best stay out of his way when he was like this. He would be in a foul temper until the sun went down.

She picked up the bucket and walked up the stone steps. Immediately, she felt relief at being outside in the daylight and almost skipped towards the well, glad to have some time away from the oppressive heat of the ovens. She silently thanked Cartha for allowing her this small moment of relief although she knew it was an unintentional gift.

Arriving at the well, a breeze of cool air rushed up to meet her skin. She hooked the bucket onto the rope and let it drop down the shaft and into the deep spring waters below where it made a satisfying splash. Closing her eyes against the bright sun, she savoured these few moments of rest when no one was looking for her.

Her relief was short lived, however, as she heard approaching footsteps in the gravel. Reluctantly opening her eyes, she saw one of the older serving boys chewing on some leaves as he walked towards the well. She had seen him before in the kitchen and remembered how he had deliberately tripped up one of the younger boys for fun, causing him to spill an entire vat of soup for which the boy received a harsh beating. She didn't know the server's name but she recognised his grubby face by the scar on his lip. *Like he had kissed a knife.*

Someone had mentioned he was Cartha's nephew. They certainly had the same bent nose and heavy eyebrows.

As the server came closer, he smiled at her but there was something about his expression that gave her a wary feeling. Maybe it was the way the smile didn't reach his eyes.

'Hot day, isn't it?' he said as if trying to find an excuse to start up a conversation.

'Suppose so.'

Trying to put some distance between them, she took a few steps away from the rough looking boy, careful to disguise the limp in her bad leg as she reached over to grab the rope. She didn't really feel comfortable talking to him alone but she didn't want to seem rude either. 'Have you been sent out to fetch water too?' she said.

Immediately she felt her cheeks redden. He didn't have a bucket with him. She almost kicked herself for asking such a silly question.

He ignored this and walked closer to her until he was leaning against the well, standing between Meela and the direct route back to the kitchen. He stared at her. Meela focussed on drawing the water. Her apparent lack of interest didn't deter him.

'You want to come and see something with me?' he asked in a slow drawl, hooking his thumbs into his waistband.

Meela mentally rolled her eyes. She might be new here but she knew how the world worked. 'I better get back to work before I'm missed.'

'Don't worry, Cartha will never notice you're gone. He's too busy checking the strength of the ale. Anyway, I'm on a short leash too. Got to take some stale bread downstairs before they die of starvation. Two of them in at the moment.' He leant back against the well, dangerously close to the edge.

'Downstairs?' She was unable to contain the surprise in her voice.

'In the basement,' he said without any explanation.

Although Meela had never been down to the basement, she had assumed it was nothing more than underground cold storage for the kitchens. 'You mean there's more creatures down there?'

The man laughed although there was no humour in it. 'No, though I suppose they are little more than creatures. Anyway, I wouldn't be wasting bread on the creatures. It's forbidden to feed them. Don't you know anything?'

'What do you mean the creatures don't get fed? Why are we keeping them in cages then?'

'Cos them upstairs haven't found any other way to kill creatures 'cept by starving them to death.'

Meela's concern wasn't reflected in the server's expression.

'But that's terrible and cruel. Why would we do such a thing?'

'Listen pet, it's them or us.'

Meela very much doubted this was the case. 'So then who are you feeding with that extra bread?' she asked, still trying to make sense of this new information.

But before he had a chance to answer, an angry voice shouted from the kitchen.

'That's my signal. Best get back to it. You know where I am if you change your mind...' He gave her a sleazy wink and disappeared back inside.

She breathed a sigh of relief that he was gone. His musky odour lingered in the air and it left a foul taste in the back of her throat. Walking back to the keep with her bucket of water, she thought about how they were starving the creatures. It wasn't right. She made a mental note to bring more food to the donkey. He really shouldn't be in the cage. It was terrible how a so-called civilized kingdom treated living beings. You wouldn't even treat a prisoner that way, she thought.

CHAPTER 30

Aimree slumbered periodically. Each time she awoke, she would force herself to take the wrist bindings between her teeth and try to pull them further apart. The effort made her cough and the damp conditions got into her chest, making her ill. She felt she was making little progress undoing the knot, but it gave her a little comfort to feel she was at least trying to fight her situation.

The cold of the night was replaced by the sweltering heat of the day. This brought its own problems with an infestation of winged insects attracted by the foul smells in the cell.

'I think I've just seen a ghost,' said Dren swatting at his arm.

'What do you mean?' said Aimree, an involuntary shiver running between her shoulder blades.

'These flies! You kill one, and a minute later it's replaced by another identical fly. I'd swear they're ghosts.'

As if to illustrate his point, Dren managed to squish a winged insect which had been frantically trying to evade capture. He wiped his fingers then, seconds later, another one buzzed furiously past his ear.

'See what I mean!'

Aimree thought about giving up on her plan to chew through her bindings. It just made her wrists red raw and sore. She was slowly giving up hope of ever seeing her sister again. She closed her eyes and the warmth of the dungeon was replaced by the warmth of her mother's kitchen, back in the cramped little flat they all shared above the baker's shop.

Her mind took her back to the sights and smells of her mother making soup. Beside her mother and father, there was Seema, then Telu, Aimree's older brother, then the twins.

Long forgotten tunes filled her ears. She could vividly remember her parents singing to each other as her father peeled the carrots and her mother boiled the stock. Happy sounds filled that house, back before the twins disappeared, before Seema left for the monastery and prior to Telu joining the army. Her mind tried to wander away again but Aimree forced it to stay in that moment, a time before any of those other things had happened.

And then, all of a sudden, she recalled a conversation she had had before she had been old enough to know any better. She was only small, no more than five years old.

'Who lives over the mountains?' she asked.

Her mother stopped rubbing the pan she had been scrubbing. 'Why do you ask, my sweet?'

'Because one day I would like to go see the other side,' she said with a big smile on her young face.

Her parents told her that she had always been a wanderer. From the moment she could walk, they knew that one day she would be lost to the spirit of the wind. As soon as she was old enough to toddle, her parents had to lock the doors to stop her walking out looking for her next adventure. As she grew older and passed the age at which other children had learned to quell this wandering spirit, Aimree just kept on going. Neighbours would return her with a sympathetic smile, explaining how they had found her in their shop or heading down the path that led to the river.

Her parents joked that she would grow to be a travelling salesperson or a wandering minstrel. But the wandering spirit never left the family. Seema joined a mission, Telu the army and the twins with those beautiful blue eyes disappeared and were never seen again.

'Aimree, nobody goes over the mountains. It's just not possible,' her mother said, picking up a knife from the sink and drying it on her apron.

'But we have songs that talk about the lands far, far away,' said Aimree. 'What lands are they talking about?'

Her parents exchanged a look. The kind of look that said: *here she goes again.*

'It must be the frozen lands far away over the sea,' said her mother as she made a start on the carrots.

'But those lands are covered in ice and the song goes *Far far away where the sun warms the grasses.*'

'It's just a song,' said her father in a stern tone, indicating there was to be no more discussion.

As she set the table, her mother unconsciously whistled the chorus of the ditty. Stirring the coals in the fire, her father picked up the tune and hummed it under his breath. Had they turned around, they would have noticed the front door was open and Aimree was out and away.

*****

The next morning, Aimree noticed that Dren's focus had changed. It was as if something just snapped inside him. Whether it was guilt over abandoning Seema or due to lack of food, Aimree couldn't say. But now there was only one thing on his mind. Escape.

'If you claim to be ill, I could attack whichever guard came in to check on you,' he whispered to Aimree, moving about as far as his bindings allowed like an excited puppy on a leash. Dren had been coming up with implausible schemes for most of the morning.

'You would take them on, despite being bound hand and foot while they were fully armed?' said Aimree.

'Can you come up with anything better? Or are we going to die in here?'

'They wouldn't be feeding us if they meant for us to die in here.'

'So we just have to bide our time until they summon us to court,' he said, picking up a couple of small pieces of gravel. 'I might die from boredom. I certainly feel ill with the smell in here. And it can't be healthy to live without sunlight for this length of time,' Dren added as he rolled the small stones around in the palm of his hand.

'Do you really think they'll grant us justice? Even if we did get a fair hearing, we're foreigners and deserters to boot. They'll throw us back in here as soon as they judge us guilty.'

'Why wouldn't we get a fair hearing?' Dren inched further away from the door in case anyone was listening in.

'Have you not heard the stories about Prince Erat?' asked Aimree, 'I thought it was common knowledge that his highness enjoys blood sports. He's well known for his appetite for torture. And then there's all the tales about the people who just disappear after they've spoken out against him in public.'

'No, I didn't know that,' he said in a quiet voice. 'But maybe they're just rumours. Nobody is actually as wicked as that. Are they?'

'It's true. My brother told me. The soldiers used to talk about it in the keep. Apparently, the Arcarian soldiers were made to play an entire game of battleball with the head of a prisoner who had been so badly beaten, they couldn't tell if it had been a man or a woman.'

Dren gasped in horror.

'And I also heard that, this one time, the prince caught a deserter from his army and-'

'Aimree, please. Can we not talk about this? I'm starting to feel worse than I did before and I didn't think that was possible.'

Before too long, the hatch opened again and another stale heel of bread was thrown in their direction. It was a welcome distraction. Also, it was comforting to know that another human being was close by, even one that only offered them meagre kindness.

'Please, before you go,' shouted Aimree, 'can I ask you one question?'

The hatch stayed open.

'Of course you can,' said a male voice

'Thank you,' said Aimree. 'How--' she began but the hatch was promptly replaced.

'Wait!' Aimree called after the voice but no answer

came.

'I think that was your one question,' said Dren.

'Don't be so...' She stopped mid-sentence, realising he was right. That was the moment when Aimree gave up all hope. If her jailors were sadistic enough to play with her like a cat teasing a mouse before it eats it, then there was no realistic chance that they would ever see daylight again. Especially if what she had heard about the prince was true. As for Seema... Aimree curled up into a small, tight ball, blocked out the rest of the world and started to sob.

From then on, she cowered every time the echo of footsteps sounded along the corridor and she would hide her face whenever the hatch opened. She certainly wasn't going to eat any of the bread. Staying alive just prolonged the inevitable. 'I would rather the rats ate it,' she said when Dren quizzed her about not eating. 'At least they have a chance at life.'

'Aimree, you can't give up. What about Seema?'

'My sister will understand. Plus she has the Creator for company. I've got no one and no one will miss me.'

'But I'll miss you.'

'You're just saying that out of pity.' Aimree let out a whine. 'I've thrown everything away. And for what? It's all been worthless. I should never have left the keep,' she continued to sob uncontrollably.

'Aimree, please don't cry.'

'I'm sorry but I just can't help it. If only Dafine was here, she would know what to do.'

There was nothing Dren could do to console her. Her tears ran without stopping.

After a couple of hours, there came the inevitable clattering at the viewing hatch which signalled feeding time.

'Not bread again. The menu said we were having meat today,' Dren shouted.

Aimree swallowed a gasp. What was he thinking?

'That's your attitude, you can starve, makes no odds to me,' came the abrupt reply as the hatch was folded back up with a clatter.

Dren shouted after the voice to come back but the footsteps grew fainter then disappeared. They now faced a long and hungry wait for food which might never come.

CHAPTER 31

Meela returned with the bucket full of water.

'Took your time with it,' Cartha said critically as he ran his eyes up and down her body and stopped when he came to her leg.

Meela knew better than to respond to that kind of comment. It would only be like fuelling a fire.

'Don't just stand there gawping. Put it down over there and help with the chickens.'

A row of dead birds lay on the cold work slab. An older cook was hard at work plucking the feathers. His hands were moving so fast that Meela doubted a starving fox could have done a swifter job. She set her bucket down in the corner and joined in beside the cook. When she tried to copy the quick movements, she found it to be much harder than it looked. She was still trying to pluck the first bird while the experienced cook had already started on a second basin of chickens. Meela didn't like to ask for help and hoped that the older man would explain what to do. But no matter who you were or where you worked in the keep, information was power and the man was not prepared to give up his secrets without good reason.

She spent an hour struggling without making much headway with the birds. Eventually Cartha came back over to inspect her work. She knew that, no matter how many birds she had plucked, he was going to have a go at her regardless.

'Have you even been trying, girl?' he said, huffing. 'We've got a dinner to prepare and hunger won't stop just because you're slow.'

Meela said nothing and focused on her cold, dead chickens, hoping he would move on to another, easier target. Unlike most of the kitchen hands, she made a point of never apologising when she knew she hadn't done anything wrong.

When she was growing up, she had often been teased for being slower than the others. As a consequence, she had spent her life trying to prove she could be better and stronger than those around her. She might not be much of a runner but she could lift twice as much as her lazy brothers and would work all day without complaining while they drank the hours away in some tavern. She would never forgive her father for sending her here.

The dreams of running away still came to her in the night and she had plans to save up the meagre wages they paid her to buy her freedom and passage on a ship. One day she would sail off to faraway lands and never look back.

'You're doing it all wrong,' said Cartha in an exasperated tone.

Her cheeks reddened and she forced herself to take deep breaths, trying to calm her growing anger. She couldn't afford to snap at the man on an impulse. But he just wouldn't leave her alone.

He pointed a thumb in Meela's direction. 'Thinks she

deserves special treatment, that one. Don't know why I put up with it. We've all got to pull our weight around here and she's slowing us down. Why they agreed to take on a cripple, I'll never know.'

That was the last word Meela was prepared to listen to. He wasn't going to get away with saying these untrue things about her without a fight. 'I might be slow because I'm new but at least I'm honest,' she said, interrupting his tirade.

Cartha stopped mid-flow. 'So, she's got teeth. But does she know how to bite or is it just for show?'

But Meela was ready for him. 'I wonder what Jared would say if he knew the kind of man you were bringing to our door.'

Alarm crept over Cartha's face and Meela knew she was on to something.

'I don't know what you mean,' he said, unfolding his arms and clenching his fists.

'Oh, I think you do. The man with the bloodied apron who came calling for you when you were too drunk to be at your work.' She was bluffing here but the expression that flashed across his face confirmed Meela's suspicions.

'He certainly wasn't here to make a delivery,' she added, intent on sending him the message that she knew what he was up to and she would not be taken for a fool.

Beads of sweat formed on Cartha's brow and this time it had nothing to do with the heat. He tried in vain to look like this news was of no consequence but, even if she couldn't work out what illicit plot she was uncovering, Meela could tell she had struck a nerve.

'Oh,' he said trying a different tone. 'But I wouldn't

know him at all. You don't understand the way things work.' Although he tried to sound friendly, his eyes were filled with pure hatred. 'But then you are new here so it's not really your fault.'

Meela wasn't naive enough to believe a word of what he was saying.

'There are often crooks who seek entry or favour from the keep. They try to use a reputable name to gain entry but they are here to rob or steal. I wish I had been there to see to him myself. Did he speak to anyone?'

'No, just me and I told him he wasn't welcome here.'

Cartha visibly relaxed at this. 'You have done the keep a favour by being on your guard.' He gave her a sickly smile.

They both knew that this round had ended in a draw. But Meela also knew, by gaining the upper hand early on in the discussion, she had made a dangerous enemy.

'Leave the cook to get on with the chickens,' he said. 'I've got another job for you. There's flour sacks what need taken down to the basement. I'm sure even you could manage them.' He pointed to a pile of large bags in the corner of the room.

At least she wasn't going to have to wait for the punishment to be dished out. This was clearly it. Meela understood that he had been asked to move them himself. But she was relieved to have an excuse to get out of the kitchen and away from the watchful eyes of its hostile staff. She had simply tried to do the right thing but she had just made life very difficult for herself. Only time would tell whether this gambit had paid off.

CHAPTER 32

Meela was glad to get out of the heat of the kitchen as she descended the stone steps that spiralled down into the basement. But her sense of relief soon gave way to a bone-deep chill. The darkness of the basement set her senses on edge. Water oozed through the mossy cracks in the wall and there was a dank, stale smell. She tried not to let the sack come into contact with any of the surfaces in case the flour inside became tainted.

A figure appeared from the shadows. In the darkness, she could just make out his clenched fists as he continued climbing the stairs towards her. It wasn't until he passed by a recessed flame and the torchlight caught his face that she recognised Cartha's nephew. She was struck by the angry look on his face, his shadowy features distorting into something unnatural and ugly.

When he noticed her, his snarl changed as he contorted his features into something resembling a smile. She avoided making contact with him as she struggled to squeeze by him in the tight space. The weight of the flour sack on her shoulder didn't help and the curved staircase narrowed as it coiled downwards. She felt him press into her as he squeezed through the tight space rather than waiting for a moment to let her by. She didn't know if this was deliberate or not, but it made the hair on her arms stand on end.

Reaching the bottom of the staircase, she continued along the corridor, travelling deeper into the underbelly of the keep. Without any warning, something cold brushed past her face. She didn't want to draw the man's attention back to her so she choked down her fear and tried to walk onwards, away from whatever had touched her. The strangest sensation washed over her. Her body felt numb and she struggled to move as image after image of terror flashed through her mind. She saw blood soaked clothing and an arm dangling by a silken thread. Then came the sensation of falling. Next thing she was deep underwater as a strange sea-monster with razor sharp teeth swam towards her.

And then she blinked and the sea monster was replaced by a tiny spider. Only, this wasn't part of the dream and Meela covered her hand with her sleeve and frantically brushed a whole spider's web from her hair. She realised it was only a dream-spider, its web impregnated with venom which induced daytime terrors. They were a common enough sight within Arcaria, especially in dark, dank places such as a basement. Luckily this particular arachnid was still young. A fully grown dream-spider could send the unwitting victim into a long-lasting coma.

She tried to laugh at her foolishness as she stumbled forwards on unsteady legs but it wasn't easy to erase the images she had seen. Struggling under the weight of the sack, she came to a fork in the passageway. Taking a deep breath, she took a moment to rest the sack on the ground. She wasn't entirely sure where the flour was meant to go. It certainly couldn't be left in the corridor as the leaking walls would cause it to spoil with mould.

She sighed and picked a way at random, trying to keep a mental note of the route she had taken. On the outside, the facade of the keep was decorated with impressive carvings representing the natural splendour of the forest that surrounded it. But down here, deep inside the bowels of the keep, it was distinctly lacking in beauty. Each earthy passageway resembled every other one. She turned another featureless corner. It felt as though she had been walking forever.

Eventually she heard the sound of snoring. She peered round the corner. An elderly guard sat on a fragile looking wooden chair, his bulk spilling over the edges of the small piece of furniture. Meela knew better than to wake him. Soldiers and kitchen staff didn't have the most understanding of relationships.

Loathed to turn and retrace her steps with her heavy load, Meela kept walking in the hope that she was going in the right direction. The sack was growing increasingly heavy but the ground was too wet to take a rest. She needed to find the store room without any further delay.

But, no sooner had she passed the guard, than she heard something that stopped her in her tracks.

'Please, help!' The shout echoed down the narrow corridor and faded away, unanswered. The voice was coming from a hatch in a heavy door.

As her eyes adjusted to the gloom, she noticed a line of doors along both sides of the corridor. They were unmistakably prison cells. Cursing herself for choosing the wrong way, she looked about her, expecting the shout to have roused the guard, but he was out cold. An empty mead jug half hidden behind the leg of the chair suggested he wouldn't wake any time soon. Still, it wasn't her duty to attend to prisoners. It was bad enough she was feeding a donkey without doing the work of the jailors too.

Just as she was about to walk on, the voice called out again: 'Please, maybe I don't deserve food, but my friend does. She's so weak.'

She! Was there someone else in that tiny cell too? The voice didn't sound so confident now, as if it belonged to a boy rather than a man.

Common sense told her she should ignore this and just keep walking. It was no doubt a ruse to try and make a bid for freedom. But the prisoner's persistent cry caused her to hesitate. She spotted the spy hatch in the door. She looked around. The guard was still sound asleep. Tentatively she approached the hatch then slid it open.

It was the stench that hit her first, overpowering her senses and she gagged with the dank warmth. She turned her head to take a deep breath of fresh air, then peered in through the hatch. The small cell was dark, illuminated only by the single shaft of light from the passageway. In comparison, the animal cages outside appeared positively roomy. In here there was hardly enough room for one person, never mind two.

A dirty looking boy was sitting on the filthy earth, clutching his knees up to his chest. On the other side of him lay a girl about her own age. They were bound around their wrists and ankles. Both looked miserable.

'Please,' said the boy again, 'You can't just leave us

here. We've not eaten in such a long time.'

Meela was truly horrified by the conditions. If she were to walk away now, she would be just as culpable as whoever had left them in there in the first place.

'Who's supposed to feed you?' she asked, trying to avoid breathing through her nose.

'Don't know. Some man. He's not a soldier. He's not even very nice.' The boy managed to bring himself up onto his heels, as if trying to avoid contact with the dirt.

'Scar on his lip?' She asked, thinking about the porter who had just passed her on the steps.

'That's him. Only, when I told him where he could shove his food, it seems he took it personally.'

'Well, manners cost nothing,' she said with a smile which faded as she saw a mud soaked heel of bread floating in a large puddle in the floor.

'That might well be true, but, when you're stuck in here, civilities seem rather trivial.'

'I guess that would put things into perspective.' She lowered her eyes. 'How did you both end up in here?' she looked over at the girl who hadn't moved the whole time.

'Me? I came off second best in a discussion with a soldier.'

'What about her?'

'Oh, her mistake was being my friend, that's the only reason she's in here. She tried to help me and they took her too. You don't suppose you could find us something to eat, do you?' The boy's eyes pleaded with her, saying more than words could convey.

Meela hesitated. She knew she had to do something. She just didn't want to get caught. 'I give you my word, I will be back. There's something I need to do first.'

As she closed the hatch over, she knew the boy probably didn't believe her. But she had to get rid of the flour first and then she would figure something out. She swallowed hard. By the look of things, they wouldn't last much longer if she didn't. She might be their only hope. She made a silent promise that she would come back for them.

CHAPTER 33

There was a reason why humans didn't live in tunnels, Meela thought as she tip-toed around the stagnant pools of brown water. Turning a corner, she finally found a raised shelf where she could leave the flour, high above the puddles that seemed to seep up from a source under the ground.

She returned to the kitchen, taking extra care as she walked by the remnants of the web. The spider was busy at work, rebuilding its shattered home. Meela didn't fancy experiencing its terror-inducing silk again.

She climbed the stairs, emerging once again in the kitchen and walked back to the pile of sacks, trying to ignore Cartha but he spotted her immediately.

'You took your time,' he said for the benefit of those around him. 'There's plenty more of those to be moved. And don't take all day with it!' Turning his back to her, he resumed his conversation with the ale wife.

Meela bit her tongue. With the prisoners literally starving to death, it wasn't worth starting an argument. There was too much at stake to risk being sent to do a task that kept her above ground.

As she humphed a second bag of flour down the

stairs, she breathed a sigh of relief that no one had noticed her smuggling the food into her apron. While it was nothing that would be missed, just a few fried hotcakes which had been knocked onto the floor, the penalties for being caught thieving from within a royal keep were almost as severe as those for treachery and murder.

She retraced her steps back to the cell passageway. The guard was still sleeping. She tiptoed around him and kept going until she reached the store cupboard and deposited the flour. When she returned to the cells, the guard was still oblivious to her presence.

She opened the hatch as quietly as she could. The boy's eager eyes looked up at her. Strange as it seemed, his expression reminded her of the donkey anticipating his nightly feed. The boy reached out a hand and she tossed in the hotcakes one at a time. He caught them and divided them up equally with the girl. She had managed to drag herself into a sitting position but the effort had cost her. With her back resting against the wall, she chewed listlessly on the cake the boy shared with her, but she looked very weak indeed.

Meela knew she probably shouldn't get involved but given she was already in this deep she supposed it wouldn't hurt to make conversation. 'Do you live near here?' she asked.

'We're not from this city,' the boy chewed slowly and didn't offer anything further.

'I'm not from the city either,' said Meela, trying to fill the silence. 'My father's got a business in a small village in the countryside. Maybe you've seen his carts: *Sefra and sons*? He's a delivery merchant.'

'No, we're not from near here at all. We ran away,' the

boy hesitated before adding, 'from the Celestial City.'

'Was it worth it?' Meela realised they must be two young lovers, escaping from overbearing parents to be together. She wished she had the courage to run away, rather than being sent here. She supposed she wasn't much better off than the prisoners. At least they had each other. Who did she have?

'I didn't have any choice in the matter,' he said wistfully.

Meela heard a clatter. She looked behind her and saw a heavy bunch of keys had hit the ground. The guard gave a grumble in his sleep. Then his head rolled forward and he gave another snore, oblivious that he had dropped them.

'What's it like living there?'

'Oh, it's nothing like this,' the boy said. 'The streets are made from marble and the buildings from precious stone. Everything glitters in the sunlight and nothing smells of fish.'

'Fish? Why would anywhere smell of fish?'

'It's a figure of speech. Something we say in the Celestial City to mean that everything is rosy. Plus, I imagine that's how Drabsea must smell with the docks and the fishing boats.'

'I understand.' She sensed a sadness in his voice. He must be missing his homeland. She changed the subject. 'How long do you have to spend in here?'

'Well, we've not been in front of the prince yet so we've not actually been found guilty of anything,' said the boy.

'Well, in that case, you'll be here a while. The prince is out of town. In fact, right now he's travelling to your city for the King's Tournament. The finals are next week and he's been invited up to watch them.' The games had been the talk of the kitchens. Not because anyone was remotely interested in whether their soldiers were better than those from the other cities but because it was an opportunity to gamble. Everyone had money riding on the outcome of one event or another.

'Do you think you would be able to get us some water?' The boy coughed.

'I'll see what I can do,' she said and closed the hatch, leaving the prisoners in complete darkness. It was one thing to smuggle a couple of cakes but how would she be able to conceal an entire bucket of water? Then she looked across at the slumped guard. There was no danger of him waking up any time soon.

Approaching the guard as quietly as she could, she bent down to take the jug from under his seat. As she picked it up, something furry shot by her ankle. Startled, she fell backwards and swallowed a scream as she saw the end of a tail disappear into a hole in the floor. As she stumbled, the water jug flew from her hand and crashed to the ground with a metallic clang loud enough to wake the dead.

'Eh, who's there? Watcha think yer doin'?' spluttered the guard. He fumbled for his sword.

'I didn't mean to wake you. I was just going to refill your water jug,' said Meela, which was in fact the truth even if it was unlikely the jug had ever been used to hold plain water. 'I thought you might be thirsty.'

'Well you could try doing it a bit more quietly. You'll upset the prisoners. Got to keep them calm, you see.'

She nodded to the man and then bent down to retrieve the jug. She could have kicked herself for being so clumsy. The girl especially looked so weak. Without her help, she wasn't sure she would make another night.

She returned to the kitchen with the water jug. Her plan was to take her time refilling it and hopefully the guard would be asleep by the time she returned with it. Her heart sank as she walked over to the water tank. Cartha was blocking her path.

'What exactly do you think you're doing with that?' he barked.

'The guard in the basement asked me to refill it for him, he's thirsty,' she stuttered.

'And just who exactly do you think you work for, me or him?' he said, drawing her a look. It wasn't a question. 'You really are thick, girl. Do you think the old guard has the nose of a water drinker? He's wanting you to get him ale. Take water back to him and he'll think you're trying to poison him.

'Anyway, forget that. I have another job for you,' he said, handing her a broom. 'It's getting too hot to be in the kitchen. Go and sweep the paths around the keep. The leaves have been clogging the drains and flooding the basement.'

She eyed him with suspicion. 'But what about the rest of the flour?' she asked as he ushered her out the door.

'It can wait until tomorrow. Now hurry up before I change my mind.'

It was as if he knew what she had been up to. She doubted the girl would be able to last that long and the boy wasn't doing much better. Her heart sank. Life was so unfair.

CHAPTER 34

The hatch closed and the girl left. There was an almighty racket outside the cell followed by an exchange of words, then all went quiet again.

'Right, you can sit up now, you don't need to act,' said Dren looking over at Aimree who had slid down the wall and was slumped with her head on the ground. 'Aimree, are you alright?'

But Aimree just lay there and didn't respond. Dren didn't know if she was ill or had simply given up. For a brief moment Dren had been glad that Aimree wasn't alert enough to contradict her story. She didn't have the strength to play along and probably wouldn't agree with lying to the girl. Well, Aimree would call it lying; Dren would rather call it thinking on her feet. The Celestial City was the first thing that had come into her head. She had never been there but the girl was unlikely to know any different.

Dren thought about what she had just been told. If the tournament wasn't for another week, it could be the best part of a month before the prince was back and held court again. She looked over at Aimree. Dren doubted she had another night in her. Dren needed to do something, she just didn't know what.

Maybe they were lucky that the prince was away. If he really liked to torture prisoners, Dren didn't like to think what could happen to them. Still, it couldn't be much worse than where they were now. Their clothes were drenched in sweat. The corner of the room Dren had been using to relieve herself was in danger of overflowing and it was crawling with flies.

She closed her eyes and took herself back to her home city where, on warm market days, everything reeked of fish oils. She tried to pretend that the heat in here was the warm sun, beating down on her face. It gave her a small amount of comfort until she thought about how cold her friend Artra had been to her. Then she recalled what had happened to the Jade twins. She shuddered. Dren couldn't escape to a rosy past inside her head for much longer.

Things had changed and something was deeply wrong in the world. Firstly there were the earth tremors, then the creatures being rounded up in the city, not forgetting the reappearance of the Wynyms. She had no idea what it all meant but, for now, she had bigger problems.

Aimree was muttering something in her sleep. At first, it didn't make sense but when Dren listened closely, she could hear her calling out her sister's name. 'Seema, it's okay, we're coming soon.'

Dren wondered if she was getting delirious. Then she quietened down which was just as worrying. The thought of the girl coming back with some water kept her going. It was only a faint glimmer of hope but a small hope was better than no hope. She didn't dare go to sleep in case she missed her. The hotcake had been the best thing she had eaten in a long time. She started to imagine what else she might bring them. She closed her eyes and saw slices of thick ham dripping with redfruit sauce, roasted venison steaks and hot toast dripping with melted butter. She salivated at the thought of food.

But, as more time passed, she started to fear that the girl might not be coming back. The last time she was away for no more than fifteen minutes. It had now been much longer than that. Aimree badly needed water, but there was no point shouting out. Not after what had happened the last time.

She had managed to loosen her bindings slightly and shuffled over towards Aimree, an inch at a time. Every movement caused her cramping muscles to ache. White pain flowed through her legs as the blood returned to them. She lay down beside Aimree who looked terrible. There was nothing Dren could do but reassure her. Slowly, Dren brushed a strand of hair out of her eyes. She stirred slightly under the touch but her eyes remained shut.

'Aimree, I promise you I will do everything I can to get us out of here.'

She didn't respond, but Dren kept going. 'I'll find a way to get out of here then we'll get the thale and heal Seema.'

At the mention of her sister's name, she made a noise.

Encouraged by this, Dren continued, 'Seema's depending on you, so you can't give up. I'll come up with a plan, don't you worry,' Dren said with more confidence than she felt. But she knew that if she gave up, both Aimree and Seema were as good as dead.

CHAPTER 35

Meela tried to find the slightest excuse to get back into the kitchen but she was blocked at every turn. At least she had tried everything she could. She did feel sorry for the two prisoners, but they weren't her responsibility and there was nothing more she could do for them.

When her shift was finished for the day, Meela snuck a bag of oats up to the donkey. He recognised the sound of her footsteps and was already waiting at the front of his cage in anticipation rather than cowering in the corner as he had done the first time she visited.

'It's not fun being locked up somewhere you don't want to be, is it?' She knew the feeling only too well. She patted him on the head as she spoke and he allowed her to stroke his nose before he plunged into the bag and greedily ate the oats.

'I wonder who you belonged to before you ran away. Bet you wished you had stayed put.' *Or maybe the soldiers took you.* The soldiers had a reputation for helping themselves to whatever they wanted without paying. They considered it a perk of the job but to Meela it was simply an abuse of power.

As she watched the donkey, she wondered how her father was getting on. He had a taste for gold like some folk had a taste for wine. It clouded their reason and made them do things they weren't proud of. Thanks to his greed, she was stuck in this life. Having seen what the others in the kitchen earned, she realised she would have to work long past retirement if she wanted to buy herself free from her apprenticeship.

Being close to the donkey comforted her. She worked such long hours that she didn't have time to make friends here and there was no one she could really talk to. At least the donkey took her at face value and companionship could be earned for the price of some grain.

In the dim recesses of the cages, she saw the other animals fading away before her eyes as the strength left their emaciated bodies. Few had the energy to let out even a whimper or a yelp. She wondered where they had come from and what was driving them out of the forest. Now they had been caught and put in a cage to starve to death. Meela felt anger.

Distracted by her sombre thoughts, she didn't notice the kitchen server creep up behind her.

'Hello girl,' he said, blowing on her neck.

This made her jump and she spilled a handful of oats. 'What are you doing sneaking around like that?' she demanded.

He just shrugged and looked to see what she was doing.

The donkey gave a warning snort and started to pace back and forwards.

'Hey!' he said when he saw the oats. 'I warned you, we're not supposed to feed the creatures.'

'He's a donkey, not a creature,' she said, not prepared to be bullied by the man, despite him towering over her.

His grey eyes darkened. He wasn't pleased at being challenged. 'You'll be in trouble if I tell. New girl rocking the boat. Nobody likes that. 'Specially not Cartha.'

As much as she was afraid of the porter, she was more afraid of the fact that it was getting dark and the kitchen server had no reason to be sneaking about up here. He certainly hadn't come up to look after the animals.

She looked about her but there was no one else in sight. It begged the question, what was he doing in the restricted area? He must have followed her when she left the kitchen. She could have kicked herself for being so careless and not looking over her shoulder.

She wasn't dressed for lingering outside. She was only wearing short sleeved kitchen whites, both to keep her clothes out of the food and to stop her from overheating. But now the heat of the day had been replaced by the cool night air and, as the wind picked up, she began to shiver.

'Here, let me warm you up,' he said, seizing the opportunity to put his arm around her shoulders.

His arm felt heavy and she could smell the stale odour of sweat. She didn't know how to tell him she didn't want this.

'What's a pretty girl like you doing up here all alone anyway? There's nobody else about.' He looked over his shoulder. 'There's nobody to help you should anything bad happen. Just as well I'm here.'

He started to rub her arm. Instinctively, she tried to pull away but he held it tight.

'No need to struggle,' he said as he pulled her towards

him. His size made it difficult for her to move away from him. 'Don't worry, I'll be gentle. I don't want to hurt you.'

Discomfort gave way to panic. What exactly was he going to do to her?

He pulled sharply at her apron. Frightened, she scratched his arm with her nails, drawing blood.

'Watch what you're doing!' he hissed. 'You don't want to make me angry.'

She realised that no one was going to come and help her. No one would hear her if she cried out for help. Meela was going to have to fight. But he was bigger and stronger than her so she was going to have to pick her moment carefully.

'You're hurting me,' she said, as he grabbed her by the arm and pulled her further away from the torch lights of the keep and towards the darker area of the animal pens. The donkey looked on helplessly as she disappeared from view.

'If you stop struggling, it'll be over sooner,' he snarled.

Still holding her by the arm, he dragged her away from the cages. They got as far as the some bushes when he stopped pushed her roughly to the ground. His expression hardened. 'If you scream, I'll kill you,' he said coldly.

Something inside Meela changed at that moment and she was no longer filled with fear. Perhaps it was the anger she felt against her father for sending her here. Or the helplessness she felt about the boy and girl locked up underground. Or maybe it was simply a realisation that her life as she knew it was about to change. She felt a cool wave wash over her, as if she was nothing more than a pebble on a shingle beach. She was aware of the froth of the wave crashing down on top of her, trying to wash her away but she knew it couldn't move her, no matter how big and how powerful. Like a stone, she was too strong to break. The feeling of being unbreakable gave her power.

Spying a large rock on the ground, she reached out and grabbed it, clasping it with both hands, feeling its smooth coldness against her fingers as she held it beside her head. The man was close enough for Meela to see her own reflection in her attacker's eyes. As he leant down to kiss her, he didn't have a chance to react when Meela swung the rock at his temple. Flesh and stone met with a hollow thud, knocking the man sideways where he struck the ground headfirst.

He lay motionless, blood trickling into his eye from the head wound she had inflicted, Meela let out a deep groan as she realised what had just happened. The rock dropped to the earth below as her fingers went limp. Staggering to her feet, she turned towards the keep and ran as fast as she could.

CHAPTER 36

Meela ran. She ran to escape having to think about what she had just done. It gave her a temporary sense of calm as if she was travelling too fast for her thoughts to catch up with her. But the calmness she was experiencing quickly passed and was replaced by anger. And the anger hit her hard. All of a sudden, Meela was more furious than she had ever been before.

For too long she had just gone along with what other people wanted her to do: her father, Cartha, the unspoken rules that said she had to stay quiet and put up with what other people did to her. But she couldn't stay quiet any longer. Not after what that man had tried to do to her. The rage that couldn't be contained within her spilled over. She felt a sense of great injustice for the donkey, not to mention the other creatures and the two kids in the basement. Her own people had locked them all up and stopped feeding them. The rage forced her towards one conclusion. She had to leave.

There wasn't a minute to lose. When the body was discovered, it wouldn't be long before they came looking for his murderer. She ran back to the servants' tower and climbed the stairs, taking them two at a time. She grabbed the bag she had arrived with and stuffed in a few clothes. She didn't want to take everything or it would be obvious she had run away. Better to let them think she had been taken against her will.

Throwing the bag over her shoulder, she bolted back down the stairs, hatching a plan as she ran. She knew what she had to do. It wouldn't be easy, but it was the only plan she could come up with and it would just have to work.

She sprinted back to the cages. The donkey snorted in recognition and walked towards her. Meela gave a quick glance about her before slipping the bolt from the latch. Hearing the sound of freedom, the donkey paced with anticipation. When Meela opened the hatch to his enclosure he didn't have to be asked twice. He leapt towards her in an excited dance.

She grabbed hold of his rope and led him to the edge of the compound. Then she stopped abruptly. She had forgotten that donkeys don't climb fences and there was no way that he could squeeze through the loose spar. Cursing her complacency, she realised she would have to walk around to the other gate. She hadn't noticed any soldiers patrolling there earlier. She just had to hope that was still the case otherwise this would all be for nothing.

The donkey was more than willing to go with her. When they arrived at the wooden gate, she tugged at the handle but it wouldn't budge. Of course it had to be locked. If there wasn't another way out further round then she might have to rethink the whole thing. Meela took hold of the donkey's rope but this time he resisted her. The harder she pulled, the more he dug his hooves in and wouldn't budge.

'Don't be frightened donkey, I'm trying to get us both out of here. I just need some time.'

But time was quickly running out. Unable to persuade the donkey to move, she had no choice but to let go of his rope and set off to find another way out or at least a carrot to bribe him with. Having just tasted freedom, the donkey wasn't ready to give up as easily. No sooner had Meela turned her back than she heard an almighty clatter followed by a crash. Turning around, she saw a hole in the fence where the gate had stood. The donkey had kicked it clean off its hinges and was now standing on the other side of the fence, chewing on the grass, as if nothing had happened.

Meela ran over to him, stroked his muzzle then picked up his rope. He walked beside her as gently as a new-born lamb. Donkeys were renowned for being stubborn but she had never heard of them being described as loyal before. It gave her an idea for how they might just all make it out of here.

If anyone saw her simply walking around with a donkey, they would know she was up to no good. However, if she was helping with a late night delivery, it wouldn't raise any questions.

An empty porter's cart outside the kitchen was perfect for her purposes. The donkey gave her a questioning look but accepted the harness and a handful of grass. Then she left him and slowly opened the kitchen door.

Meela peered inside. The only person within was Erial, one of the other apprentices. She was tending to the fire in the large stone hearth. It could never be allowed to go out as it heated the water in the prince's chambers and it wasn't unheard of for him to demand baths at strange hours of the night. Even though he was presently absent from the keep, it had been known for him to return at short notice. It wasn't a mistake a person was given the chance to make a second time. Night duty was a long, lonely shift and Erial was keeping herself busy rolling out dough.

She looked up when she heard Meela's footsteps crossing the kitchen. 'It's not like you to be in this late. Don't you have an early rise?' she asked as she floured her rolling pin.

'Yes but I left something unfinished and I don't want Cartha to get mad at me. Not first thing in the morning, at any rate.' She continued walking to the basement stairs as her heart raced in her chest.

Erial stretched out the dough with short brisk motions. 'Well, just make sure you don't sleep in. That'll see you with a mark across your leg judging by the mood that Cartha was in today.'

Meela thanked her for the warning. If everything went to plan she would never have to worry about Cartha's temper again.

The chill hit her face as she descended the stairs for what she hoped would be the last time. She gave a wary glance at the spider which was resting patiently in the centre of its newly completed web. She marvelled at its tireless dedication to its task. There was no sign of the damage from earlier and she almost sympathised with the creature's plight.

But the spider still gave her the creeps as it watched her progress through a multitude of shiny black eyes. And Meela wouldn't easily forget the visions of terror. They were still vivid in her mind as if she had woken partway through a nightmare. She gave an involuntary shudder and continued walking briskly until she came to the storeroom from an alternate route. Luckily, the door was still unlocked from earlier.

Meela spied the two flour sacks that had taken her a whole afternoon to shift and had left her with an aching back. She chose a bag at random and tore at the stitching until it burst. Then she gave it a shove. A white cloud enveloped the small room. Coughing and spluttering as the particles filled her lungs, she emptied its contents into a heap in the corner. Then she did the same with the second bag. The air was thick with flour. It was a regrettable but unavoidable waste.

She folded the now empty sacks and brushed the coating of white from her clothes then made her way along to the cells. As expected, the guard was half asleep. At the sound of Meela's approaching footsteps, he violently nodded awake, almost falling off the rickety chair in the process.

'What, you again!' he said with a gruff tone, his mouth dry from the nap. 'What are you doing creeping about down here?' He narrowed his eyes at her.

She spied the cell door keys that had dropped to the floor next to his chair. She knew what she had to do. 'I would have finished for the night,' she began, 'except there's a giant spider blocking the exit. I can't bear to go near it.' She gave him a graceful smile.

The guard chuckled. 'Never fear lass, I'll kill him for you, then you can get upstairs and sleep soundly in your bed.' He said this as if he was about to go and slay an invading army single-handedly.

'Don't kill it!' That would never give her enough time to complete her task. She also felt a slight pang of guilt.

She had already inconvenienced the spider enough today. It was only doing what came naturally, after all. Did she really want to be responsible for its death?

'I mean, it is one of the Creator's living creatures after all. Can't you take it outside instead?'

'But it'll just come back inside again.' He stopped as he saw the pleading look in her eyes.

'Please?' she blinked a couple of times for effect.

'Well...' he hesitated, 'Okay then. But if any of the lads catch me doing that, they'll think I've lost the plot and have me put out to pasture.' He rose from the chair and walked away chuckling to himself and shaking his head in disbelief.

Meela sighed with relief as she noted that he had left the heavy bunch of keys behind. When the guard's footsteps could no longer be heard, she rushed over, picked up the keys and put the largest one in the lock. Her fingers were shaking. But it didn't turn.

Fumbling, she tried another one in the lock. This one didn't budge either. She looked at the keys in despair. There must have been at least twenty different ones. There was nothing for it but to try them all.

Finally, after trying half a dozen, the right key slipped into the hole and the bolt turned in the lock.

'Are we going to see the prince?' said the boy waking from a fitful sleep.

'We can see the prince if you want,' she said, slicing through the bindings with the paring knife she kept in her apron. 'But it won't be in this keep. We're leaving and we have to act quickly.'

'What do you mean?' he said, suddenly wide awake.

'I've got a cart waiting outside to take you home to the Celestial City but you'll have to trust me. The plan's rather unusual.'

CHAPTER 37

Dren emerged from the cell, supporting Aimree's weight. The girl passed her two empty sacks.

'There's one for each of you,' she said as she locked the empty cell behind them and returned the keys to the guard's chair.

'Quick, get into these. You'll need to hurry, the guard will be back soon. I'll have to carry you one at a time. It won't be comfy but it's the only way to get out of here alive. Just remember to stay absolutely silent.'

Dren helped Aimree into her flour sack and tied the top loosely before climbed into her own. She couldn't help thinking she was escaping from one cell only to be trapped in an even smaller one but she tried to block out the feeling. The rough fabric scratched at Dren's face and her hands were pinned down by her sides. It didn't help that she was now covered in flour and could scarcely breathe without choking. She tried desperately not to sneeze.

'I'm Meela,' said the girl as she secured the top with a knot.

'I'm Dren but please take Aimree first,' she whispered, 'If anything happens and you can't come back she'll be too weak to make it out herself.' She took her lack of response as agreement. Then she waited.

Eventually she heard the turn of the lock behind her and the heavy jangle of keys. Scarcely a moment later she heard a voice.

'Well, you've nothing to be afraid of. Little ole spidey won't be troubling you no longer.' The guard sounded mighty pleased with himself.

'Thank you kindly,' she heard Meela say. 'Now I better be on my way. I've got to take these sacks up to the kitchen.'

'Why didn't you say? Let me give you a hand.'

'No!' exclaimed Meela loudly. 'I mean thank you for the offer but I don't want Erial upstairs to think I can't handle myself.

'Ah!' the guard let out a chuckle. 'You mean your leg. I won't let on that you were scared of the spider, in that case.' And then he added. 'But it'll cost you.'

'What do you mean?' asked Meela. Dren detected more than a hint of steel in her voice.

'I thought I smelled smell some freshly baked sweet buns when I was up at the staircase earlier. If you could happen to let some roll my way, I think we can call it quits.'

Meela's voice relaxed. 'Of course, consider it done.'

Dren heard her footsteps disappear off into the distance and then silence fell. From the darkness of the sack, time passed even more slowly than it had done in the cell. The flour tickled her nose. Unable to scratch it, she tried wiggling her nose from side to side but this just made the itch worse. Her tongue was coated in flour and it made her already parched mouth unbearably dryer.

Dren heard the guard's chair creak. If she could hear the guard moving, could the guard hear her? She started to sweat. The itch in her nose was overwhelming. She felt a sneeze coming on. She tried to hold it in. If the guard heard her, the game was up but the urge was overwhelming and there was nothing she could do to stop it.

She inhaled sharply. The next moment the sneeze escaped her lips. It felt as if an explosion had shaken the room. Dren started to tremble as she heard the guard's voice.

'The Creator's blessing upon you.'

'And also on you,' came the standard reply. It was Meela's voice. 'Sorry all the flour is making me sneeze,' she said. 'Here, I've managed to pinch some buns fresh from the oven. Careful, they're still hot.'

Dren realised just how close she had come to ruining things. The girl had returned in the nick of time.

The next thing she felt was rough jostling and the sensation of being lifted. Dren tried to play dead and resemble a bag of flour as much as she could. Meela was certainly strong.

After a short distance, she was gently lowered to the ground.

'You can walk from here,' Meela said as she untied the sack. 'I've got a cart waiting outside. Aimree is already safely inside.'

Dren opened her eyes. The light from a torch illuminated the underground passageway. She followed Meela up a flight of steps. At the top, she halted suddenly. Putting her fingers to her lips to indicate Dren was to be quiet, she peered round the doorway. Seeing that the coast was clear, she ran out, motioning for Dren to follow.

Dren didn't have to be told twice. She followed her through a well-stocked kitchen, past a hearth where a fire was burning low with a lone figure curled up asleep on a cowhide rug.

On the way out of the kitchen, Meela grabbed a cured ham from a hook. She placed it under her cloak before raising the hood to cover her face. Dren smiled to herself as she realised she was being freed by a kindred spirit.

Dren crossed the flagstones as quietly as she could and followed her up another set of stairs.

Outside the kitchen, a cart was waiting just as she had promised. Meela lifted up a sheet and Dren dived underneath it to safety. Then she waited.

******

Meela climbed onto the high seat of the donkey cart and set them moving at a trot. She held on tightly to the donkey's rope as the cart jostled down the cobbled way that led to the exit. So much for keeping her head down and settling in quietly.

She tallied up the list of crimes she had committed in the space of a day. Most of them were punishable by death. To begin with, she had stolen food. She could lose a limb just for doing that. On top of this she had assaulted a man, liberated a creature, smuggled out two prisoners, hijacked a cart and was now absconding without permission. Not bad for a *cripple*, she thought to herself, ironically. Those were her father's words, not hers.

She knew well enough what strangers thought when they first saw the injury to her leg. Her father had warned her that if you constantly saw pity in the eyes of others, it wouldn't take long before you started to believe in your own inferiority. She knew there was nothing inferior about her. She had certainly proved that tonight.

She just had to head for the Celestial City. Once they got there, she would find someone to take her in and give her some honest work. Maybe the prisoners' families would be grateful for their safe return and offer her a job. Then she would save up her money until she could afford to set up her own business.

She steered the cart towards the gates. She had never tried to leave the keep before but it couldn't be that difficult. People must come and go all the time. She thought about the trips she had taken with her father but she didn't remember delivering things at such a late hour.

Would it look suspicious, turning up at the gatehouse at this time of night? What if they thought she had stolen something? She tucked the ham in close to her side. Maybe it would make more sense to wait until the morning. But then she remembered her attacker. If someone discovered he was missing and raised the alarm, the guards would definitely be suspicious of a hooded stranger trying to leave.

Freedom was now within her reach. She stopped the cart in front of the heavy wooden gates, reinforced with metal studs. Not even the most wilful donkey-kick could open the fortified exit. She would just have to think on her feet.

As she brought the cart to a halt, she was immediately approached by one of the guards. He sounded annoyed at having been disturbed. 'You know the drill, trader. Gate's shut. If you want to leave at this time of night, you have to pay the tax.' It was clear from the gatekeeper's tone that he thought she was a smuggler but was willing to play along if it benefited his pocket.

The guard came closer. Meela desperately hoped he wouldn't ask to see what was in the cart. She tried to draw his attention away from the stowaways in the back. 'How much do I owe?'

'She's asking the price,' he said, turning to the other guards.

Meela could hear the soldiers laughing inside the gatehouse. A couple came out for a closer look.

'Well that depends on what you're carrying, doesn't it,' he said.

Her heart sank as the guard walked straight over to the cart. This time the game was up. The moon was out, bright and high in the sky, bathing the keep in light. There would be nowhere for the two prisoners to hide in the small space. The girl was so poorly she couldn't even move. The two of them would be thrown back in the cells and Meela would be joining them.

Meela couldn't bring herself to look as the tarp was drawn back.

After an anxious wait, the soldier came back round to the front of the cart. His head was bowed. 'Forgive me, I didn't know. I should have realised with the dark cloak and all but nobody forewarned us. Please go about your business and accept our condolences.' The other soldiers looked pale and made a show of blessing themselves.

Meela nodded, thoroughly confused as the guards opened the gates and allowed her on her way. They must have seen Dren and Meela in the cart. Why did they do nothing about it? She couldn't stop to question it though. She climbed back onto the cart, and tugged on the reins. The donkey didn't need to be told twice and, without any more delay, he resumed the journey.

CHAPTER 38

Dren held on tightly to the rough wooden slats that lined the bottom of the cart as it jostled and jolted her over the bumpy ground. She breathed a huge sigh of relief that they had made it out of the keep. There had been dark moments recently when she thought she would never see the Kingdom again.

They were well outside the keep by now and the road noise meant that it was probably safe to talk to Aimree without being overheard. 'I can't believe we actually pulled that off,' she said with a note of triumph in her voice. 'I thought we were caught when the guard heard my sneeze but Meela managed to cover it up nicely.'

There was no response from Aimree. That was strange, maybe she just hadn't heard her.

'How are you doing over there?' Dren tried again, this time louder. Still nothing. She grew concerned. If anything had happened to her, it would be all Dren's fault. Aimree only ended up in there because Dren got drunk. But before she began to panic she felt a hand, weakly gripping hers. She gave Aimree's hand a gentle squeeze, more to reassure herself that she was still there than for Aimree's benefit.

She thought of all the times she would have killed to have a moment like this with her. She chased those thoughts from her mind. She shouldn't be thinking like that now. Especially when she hadn't washed in days. They just had to get out and find Seema.

That's when it hit her. They were driving the wrong way. She had to tell Meela to turn around, that Seema needed them. But then what? They still hadn't managed to get the herb that she desperately needed.

And Aimree wasn't doing much better than her sister, exhausted by lack of food and seriously dehydrated. The few scraps that Meela had smuggled to them in the cells had done little to restore Aimree to health. She cursed Aimree for running away. If she had only stayed at home and not followed her. She had no place coming on Dren's journey. Dren didn't want to be responsible for anyone but herself.

She slammed into the hard side of the cart as the donkey came to an abrupt stop. It was obvious that Meela wasn't used to driving a cart, Dren thought as she rolled upside down. Either that or the donkey wasn't worth the money she had paid for him.

'Sorry about the emergency stop. I've not quite learned how to ride this particular donkey yet,' said Meela.

A moment later, moonlight flooded in as she pulled back the sheet. She looked in and let out a squeal.

'What's so funny?' asked Dren as she climbed out of the back of the cart. Meela was laughing so hard that tears were forming in the corners of her eyes.

'The flour!' she exclaimed, 'You're covered in it from head to toe. You're as white as two ghosts! That guard must have thought you were corpses that I was taking out to bury. No wonder he didn't want to tax you. He probably expects to be haunted for life.'

'Just as well I decided to play dead then. Who knows what would have happened if I had got up and challenged him to a fight?'

Dren stood there for a minute, trying to orientate herself to standing up after days of being chained to the ground. It felt good to have blood flowing in her legs again.

Meela reappeared holding the large ham and grinning widely. As she walked them, the cart lurched forward as the impatient donkey kept moving. It was as if it was doing it deliberately to hurry them along. Dren cursed the animal. Aimree was still lying in the back of the cart and Dren didn't want her to be motion sick.

Dren walked over to grab its rope but the donkey was having none of it. He tossed his head when he saw Dren approaching, moving the reins out of the boy's reach. Every time Dren got within touching distance of the rope, the donkey would nudge them out of his reach with his head. Then to top off the insult, a warm, wet donkey tongue wiped the flour clean off Dren's face.

Dren blinked, ready to unleash a torrent of abuse directed at the irreverent animal. And then she stopped. And so did the donkey.

'Thunder!' cried Dren.

The donkey gave his customary snort of acknowledgement then licked her again.

As delighted as Dren was to be reunited with the beast, she was equally smug that she had managed to sneak a ride on the donkey's back without Thunder realising.

Meela tore off some strips of ham and handed them

to Dren. Before eating her share, Dren broke off small morsels for Aimree and placed them in her palm. She closed her fingers round them. 'You need to eat,' Dren said softly. 'You need to keep your strength up for the journey.' She was almost pleading for Aimree to eat, something which she never thought she'd have to do. Aimree could usually devour her main course and be halfway through seconds while Dren was still blowing on her own to cool it down.

'Well then,' began Meela while they ate, 'I suppose we better make a plan then. I've been heading towards the main road that leads to the Celestial City. Which part of the city do you come from?'

'I've moved around a lot,' said Dren scratching at the ground with her foot. This was going to be awkward.

'Well, where were you planning to go when you got out?'

'To be honest, I wanted to get as far away from the Kingdom as possible.' Realising she had no choice but to trust Meela, she added: 'We planned to travel away to the other side of the mountains.'

'That sounds like a plan. I hadn't thought of going that far but if you're going to escape from it all, you might as well do it in style. I had been hoping you could have put me up when we got to your home but, if you're travelling on, I may as well come with you.' She waited in anticipation of an invitation.

Dren blinked hard. 'Come with us?' She was getting far too skilled at picking up odd travelling companions. She looked to Aimree for backup but she was struggling to chew never mind keep up with the conversation. She turned back to Meela.

'Well, I've managed to get you this far on my own.

You can see I'm more than capable.' Meela waited.

'The thing is,' Dren began. 'I mean, it's not that...' she searched for the right phrase.

Meela threw Dren a dark look. 'I see. You don't have to say any more. I've heard it all before. You don't want to be carrying any dead wood. Is that it?' She turned her head away.

'What do you mean?' asked Dren, confused by her reaction.

'It wouldn't be the first time someone has written me off because of my disability.'

'What? That? No, you didn't think I meant...'

Then a small and quiet voice spoke up. 'I don't care who comes, I just want to find my sister. She needs me, Dren. We have to go back.'

'It's not that I don't want you to come.' Dren decided there was nothing for it but the truth. 'It's just that I haven't been very honest with you. I lied about where we came from. We're not from the Celestial City at all.'

'Well I could have told you that for nothing,' said Meela. 'For one, your accent is completely wrong.'

Dren detected a hint of annoyance in her voice. 'It's just that Aimree's sister is very sick. She's in an Arcarian inn and we need to get back for her.'

'But without the right herb she will die,' came Aimree's feeble voice.

'What herb is that?' asked Meela.

'It's quite rare, you probably won't have heard of it,' said Dren.

'Try me,' said Meela with an edge to her voice.

'Well, it's called thale and-'

'And it grows in the keep garden because we cook with it. Why in Kingdom's name didn't you ask for it before we escaped past a whole garrison of soldiers?'

Aimree glowered at Dren. She felt hopelessly outnumbered. 'Okay,' Dren said, raising her arms in surrender, 'what do you suggest we do now?'

'I'd have thought that was obvious,' Meela replied. 'There's only one thing for it. We have to break back in to the keep.'

CHAPTER 39

Dren was more concerned than ever. Aimree was barely moving. 'We've got to get her to the healer immediately. There's no way she can make it back in to the keep.'

'It will delay us collecting the herbs,' said Meela pointing out the stark reality of the situation. 'This will slow down the production of the potion. Can her sister last that long?'

'It's a risk we just have to take. There's no way we can look after her properly out here. Sorry Thunder, but we're not going to be easy on you.'

It was as if the donkey understood, willingly taking the bit between his teeth and snorting, impatient to get moving again.

Just then, Dren heard Aimree struggling to clear her throat. 'Do I get a say in this at all?' Her voice was weak.

'I'm afraid not,' said Meela, 'Dren's right. You've been weakened by the conditions in prison. We'll take you back to the inn and you can rest there.'

Aimree looked like she wanted to disagree, but didn't have the strength to argue back.

While Meela turned the cart about, Dren slid back

under the tarpaulin and pulled it tight over herself and Aimree. They re-joined the main highway at a trot.

'Which inn is your friend at?' asked Meela.

'It's called the Wayfarers.'

'Eurgh, I hope you didn't drink the water!' exclaimed Meela.

'Well, come to mention it, I... why, what do you mean?'

'Never mind. Forget I said anything.'

'You have to tell me now,' said Dren, not prepared to let it drop.

'If you really want to know, when me and my father delivered food to the kitchen they had a problem with leeches in the well. Guests complained about waking up with the bloodsuckers stuck to their faces.

'Really?' said Dren, in horrified fascination, glad she had stuck to the ale.

'They ended up with nasty bite marks. But it was a while ago,' she said quickly. 'They've surely fixed the problem now.'

Dren pulled back the tarpaulin and snuck a glance at unfamiliar streets. The whole city smelled of pine. It was fresh and clean compared to the odour of fish that Dren was used to. She said as much to Meela.

'You think that now, but just wait 'til it gets hot and the sap starts to melt. Then you can't touch anything without sticking to it. The mess gets everywhere.'

It didn't take long before they arrived at the inn. Dren hoped that they didn't bump into the soldiers who had captured them. If the troops drank there regularly, there was every possibility they could meet them again.

Meela parked up round the back of the inn then helped Aimree out of the cart. All of Aimree's weight rested on Meela's arm. Dren felt a knot in her stomach but she couldn't afford to worry about Aimree's condition. The healer would fix her up, Dren was sure of it.

'How is Seema?' asked Dren when Meela reappeared.

'She's stable but her pulse is becoming difficult to locate. Listen, it's the middle of the night. I think you should take a room and get some rest. You haven't eaten properly in days.' She paused as she looked Dren up and down. 'And you need a bath. If I'm being brutally honest, you don't smell too good.'

'But we can't afford the time!' Dren said.

'Do you actually have a plan to get back in the keep?

'No, but-'

'In that case, I suggest you sleep on it. In the morning, things will be clearer.

She didn't answer her. Something was nagging at Dren. It was like the humming of an insect inside her ear, a physical sensation that she couldn't quite locate

'So, are you coming then?' asked Meela.

Dren ignored her and wandered off round to the back of the inn. Her attention was drawn to an area that seemed familiar. A brief twinkling caught her attention, almost like a spark of light glinting off a jewel.

She walked over to a pile of weeds in the grass and prodded something solid with her foot. A tangle of vines partially covered a wooden object lying on the ground. Could it be her bow? Frantically clawing at the undergrowth to free it from the quick-growing mosses, she eventually pulled it loose. Not questioning why the soldiers hadn't taken it or how it had become so overgrown in a matter of days, she picked it up and hugged it tightly against her chest.

Noticing that Meela was observing her from a distance, Dren pulled back her cloak and slung the bow over her shoulder where it sat comfortably.

'Okay,' she conceded as she walked back to where Meela was standing. 'Let's get cleaned up, and have a few hours rest. There's something I have to collect when the shops open in the morning so it seems we will be spending a few hours here after all.'

Dren was apprehensive about being recognised by any soldier but it was late at night and there wasn't a soul around other than the innkeeper.

The burly male stood in front of Dren, blocking the front door, just as he had done the night they had first arrived. The innkeeper didn't mince his words.

'Just be glad your friend pays well otherwise I wouldn't have had any one of you back, not after that stramash with the prince's guard.'

The man looked Meela up and down as if weighing up Dren's chances.

'If we're paying you so well, see to it that you bring us a bath of hot water each,' said Meela, emphasising the fact that they would not be sharing a room.

Dren admired her directness. When the bathwater arrived, Dren checked each bucket thoroughly for leeches and other undesirable parasites before filling the tub. She lowered herself in gently. Her skin had grown sensitive over the last few days and the temperature was almost unbearable. She slid her body under the surface, inch by inch until a grimy layer of prison dirt floated on the surface of the water. She lathered herself with the soap and rubbed at the dirt until she felt clean again. Then she lay in the bath as the water grew cold, trying to work out what her next move was going to be.

Eventually she began to shiver and got out of the bath. She dried herself with a rough towel then sat down on top of the bed. As tempting as it was to curl up under the blankets, she didn't dare close her eyes for fear of over sleeping. She would use the time to figure out a plan. She tried to savor a half loaf of bread that had been left out for her. She broke off bite-sized pieces which she dipped into a bowl of pork fat. She tried not to drop the crumbs on her blankets as she thought about tomorrow. The idea of coming up with a plan was hurting her head and, before long, she had nodded off.

The urgency of a crowing rooster woke Dren from her unintended sleep. She hadn't meant to doze off, even though her body clearly needed a good night's rest. Leaping from the bed as if it was on fire, she grabbed her cloak and put the bow over her shoulder before racing out of her room to find Meela. She found her, ready and waiting at the top of the stairs.

'I'm used to early starts,' she said by way of explanation.

'Is Aimree still asleep?'

'Don't worry,' she said sensing Dren's fear, 'She won't try to join us. She wouldn't leave her sister's side even if the inn was on fire.'

Dren followed Meela out into the stables where Thunder had been tied up next to the cart.

'I think we'll have to leave him and go on foot,' said Dren as she picked up an armful of fresh hay and dropped it into the donkey's feeding trough.

'I agree,' said Meela, stroking Thunder's side. 'There's no telling who might be looking out for him, thinking that he's an escaped creature.'

'Creature?' asked Dren quizzically.

'I think your soldier friends sold him to the keep under false pretences. That's why I had to break him out.'

'I see,' said Dren, although she didn't. There was clearly more to this story than they had time to discuss just now.

'In that case, he's definitely staying here. Let's get a move on before it gets much lighter.'

She looked for anything left lying around the stables that might come in handy and spotted a long length of rope. It was thin and strong and she looped it across her body, underneath her cloak.

'I'll put it back when we're done,' she said when she noticed Meela's disapproving look. 'I mean, it's not like I'm thieving someone else's donkey and cart.' Her comment was rewarded with a sarcastic smile.

Leaving the stables, they took up a brisk pace towards the keep until Dren recognised the fletcher's shop. A crack of light coming from the dimly lit workspace was the only sign of life.

'Wait here,' she said to Meela, gesturing to an empty doorway, 'I'll be back in a minute.'

She had to contain the desire to run, opting instead to maintain a smart walk. She knew that nothing drew attention more than someone running in a city. And, if the Kingdom Watch examined the contents of her pockets, she would be arrested as a thief without any questions being asked. It was crucial that every part of her fledgling plan came together without a hitch.

Arriving at the shop, she pushed open the door with both hands and entered to the sound of the ringing bell.

The fletcher was already seated at his workbench.

'They're not ready yet,' the man said without even looking up.

That was not the response Dren wanted to hear. 'It's just that I'm in a bit of a hurry, do you have anything else I could use that would be more-' she searched for the right word. 'Useful?'

'If it's useful you want,' said the grey headed man looking up, 'I can certainly do that for you.' He reached down into a sack on the floor and picked out half a dozen round headed bolts.

'It takes a certain type of individual to be able to take another person's life and I doubt that, for the moment at least, you're that kind of person.'

Dren had never thought about it in those terms before. Although she had spent countless hours practicing on targets stuffed with straw, she hadn't given a thought to the difference between a painted target and deliberately taking a life. She was no killer. That was, if she excluded the death of the Wynym which had been an accident.

'These bolts will stun an opponent, giving you time to escape. Which means you can reuse them should the shaft remain intact. But be warned, an ill-timed head-shot from one of these can be every bit as fatal as the armour-piercing kind. I can assure you that the death which follows is neither instant nor painless.'

Warning over, the fletcher handed one arrow to Dren to examine and placed the rest of them into a discrete quiver. As Dren turned it over in her hands, the fletcher named a small fortune in coin. The colour drained from Dren's face. She knew they would be expensive but this was beyond anything she could have imagined. She simply didn't have the money.

The fletcher saw the hesitation and withdrew the quiver from display, realising then exactly what Dren's situation was.

Dren was left holding the solitary arrow. There was no arguing that it was a very finely crafted arrow but it was certainly out of her price range.

'Perhaps, you would accept payment for this one arrow now and if I like it, I will come back and buy the rest,' said Dren, trying to rescue the situation and disguise her financial position.

The man reluctantly agreed and, after adding on a hefty commission, named his amended price which Dren could scarcely afford. She was in no position to argue with the man who could just as easily turn her in for carrying a weapon without written authority. She had a horrible feeling that, should she fail to pay, she'd be back in a deserter's cell quicker than she could blink.

She handed over half of her remaining coins in return for the solitary arrow. There was something about the nature of the work that gave her a chill in her bones. As she closed the door behind her and re-joined Meela, she hoped she'd never have to deal with the man again.

CHAPTER 40

As they crossed to the edge of the city, the vast silhouette of the keep loomed into sight. Back-lit by the sun, this feat of engineering dominated the city. It was surrounded by a mighty perimeter fence so smooth that it looked as though it had been carved from a single tree.

Dren caught a glimpse of the top of the keep's tower. It was covered in intricately decorated wood carvings but Dren didn't have any time to marvel at its detail. The height of the watch tower meant that invaders were visible from all sides and she knew the orders would be shoot to kill. There would be no room for mistakes.

So, how do you suggest I get back in?' asked Dren, looking up towards the mighty fortress.

'You're asking me?' said Meela unable to keep the astonishment from her voice. 'How in Kingdom's name am I supposed to know? I've only ever gone in once and that was through the front gate. I wasn't supposed to leave until I was too old to get married or to have any chance at happiness.'

Dren was sorry she'd asked. Meela clearly had unresolved issues.

'And we can't very well go in through the front door in case they're looking for me,' she continued.

'Will they not expect you back after you've buried the bodies?' Dren asked. This stopped Meela dead in her tracks.

'But there was only one!' she cried out before she had a chance to think about what she was saying. 'How did you know?' Her hands started to shake.

'Don't you remember? You said we looked like corpses when we came out of those sacks covered in flour.'

'Oh yeah, right. I remember now,' she said, relief flooding across her brow.

'What did you think I meant?'

'I killed a man, but it was an accident.' She covered her mouth with her hands as if trying to take back what she had said.

It wasn't exactly the response Dren had been expecting. She tried not to sound shocked by what she had just admitted.

'Is there anything else you haven't told us?' asked Dren, not sure what the appropriate response was.

'Nope, that's all.'

'Would you care to expand on how you accidentally killed someone, or do I not want to know?'

'Well, if you must know, I was provoked. He tried to attack me and let's just say I wasn't going to let him do that to me.'

Dren thought she knew what Meela was hinting at and didn't press her further. 'So, I've been thinking about a plan to get back in.'

'Not before time. How are we going to do it then?'

'You worked in the kitchens, didn't you?'

Meela nodded.

'I need you to tell me what time the soldiers eat at.'

'That's an easy one. The bell for breakfast is due to sound in about...' she looked up at the faint hint of daylight and held her hand up to the sky. 'Two fingers of sun.'

'Then that's when I'll do it. The best time to storm a castle is when the soldiers are either busy eating or on guard duty counting down the seconds till it's their turn for a feed. Chances are they won't be paying a great deal of attention to a whole lot else,' Dren took off the long length of rope she had wrapped around her shoulders.

'What do you mean storm the castle? There are only two of us, not a whole army.'

'But the principle is the same.' She started to tie knots in the rope. 'I'm going to go in through a window. That's why I'll need you to give me directions to the gardens.'

Meela looked at the rope.' Dren, are you sure you know what you're doing?' she asked.

'Nope, but unless you can come up with something better in the next few minutes, we're just going to have to do it my way. What's in that black tower in front of us?'

'You mean the prince's tower? It's the most heavily guarded section of the keep. The prince is paranoid about being assassinated so he's careful to keep soldiers around him at all times.'

'Perfect,' said Dren, rolling the knotted rope up into a ball, 'that's exactly how I'm going to get in.' Dren concentrated hard as she waited for the breakfast bell to ring. Crouching low, she tried to stay out of the sight of the patrolling soldiers. Then she felt a tug at her sleeve.

'What is it?' she hissed, trying to keep totally still.

'Did you not hear what I said? The prince's tower is the best protected part of the keep.'

'Yes, I heard you,' Dren said as she continued to look straight ahead at her target. 'You said the prince is paranoid, I was listening. That's the whole reason why we're going straight in through his tower.'

'I don't understand.'

'Just think about it. If the prince is away to the tournament, this tower will be almost empty. He will have taken most of his troops with him. Which will, in theory, make it the easiest way to get back into the keep.'

'Oh,' said Meela, 'I hadn't thought about that. That's quite clever.' Then she added under her breath. 'For you.'

The rising sun worked against them as it burned bright and low in the morning sky. It would only get worse as it continued to travel across the sky, getting brighter with every passing minute. Dren could only hope that her theory was right. If not, and the soldiers were doing their job correctly, she would be dead before she even saw their arrows coming.

And then she found what she had been looking for. It was a blind spot. 'Look!' She pointed to a wooden pillar. 'See how the patrols don't quite overlap there?'

Dren watched as the guards walked along two opposing walkways. Because of an ill-placed beam, their patrols stopped short of each other before they about-turned. This meant there was a very narrow angle where neither patrol had full view of the surrounding area. If they stayed within this area and luck was on their side, they could get close to the perimeter without being detected. From there, they could move round to the prince's tower without alerting anyone to their presence.

'When I give the signal, follow in tight behind me. Unless-'

'Don't even go there,' Meela said in a warning tone which stopped Dren mid flow.

Dren knew better than to make an issue of Meela's ability and resolved not to ask her if she could manage the run. Of course, she had no choice but to leave Meela at the bottom of the fence. With the description of where the herb garden was situated, Dren should be able to find it by herself before re-joining Meela again on the outside. That only left the small matter of an escape plan but there was no point in wasting thinking time. Better to focus on getting inside.

Eventually, the two patrols met at either side of the column. When they parted, Dren seized her chance and ran from the cover of bushes, through a section of open ground. All the while Meela followed at her heels. Dren dived behind a tree where she collapsed, trying to get her breath back. Very carefully, she peered round the old tree that shielded them. She bit her lip. They were very close to the edge of the tower now and she knew that, even if the next part of her plan worked, she still had to get over that imposing perimeter fence.

She took the knotted rope from her bag and tied her single arrow onto one end before slotting it into her bow. Her palms were moist with sweat. She hadn't felt this nervous since her spear-throwing heat back at the keep but this time it wasn't a game. The tip of the arrow was coated with a thick bulb of rubber. It wouldn't pierce but it would hit with some force.

Even though it felt oddly familiar, she reminded herself that she had never actually fired the bow before.

She took aim and waited, chasing all negative thoughts from her mind. The bow felt cool and steady in her hands. She was ready.

At the sound of the bell she released her arrow. It flew directly towards the prince's suite, as if rushing to meet its twin reflected in the window. It carried on through the glass, dragging the rope behind it like a tail. Dren could only hope that the breakfast bell would mask the sound of the window smashing.

It didn't seem to have attracted any attention. She gave the rope a tug, but, to her disappointment, it came straight back out. Not having a backup plan, there was nothing for it but to try again. The arrow and the coil of rope fell at her feet. This time she aimed a little higher through the broken window and held her breath as she watched the rope disappear into the room.

Giving a tentative pull, the rope moved a little then stopped, as if it had snagged on something. She yanked a bit harder and this time it didn't budge. It was wedged!

She wiped her brow with her sleeve then tied the other end of the rope around the tree they were sheltering under, anchoring it tightly to stop it swinging. Then, to see whether it could hold her weight, she gave one final pull. To her great relief, it held firm. She had created a temporary but effective ladder. The only thing missing was a safety net. 'If I'm not back out in an hour, try to make your way back to the inn. I'll come find you when I make it out.'

'What do you mean? I'm coming with you.'

'Meela, I'm a soldier, which means I'm trained to do things like this. You're not. End of discussion.'

'You're not leaving me here,' she said with a scowl that could have curdled milk.

'Listen, I don't have time to discuss this but-'

Without warning, Meela jumped up and grabbed the underside of the rope with both hands. She briefly struggled to wrap her legs around the rope but eventually managed and started to pull herself up, reaching from one knot to the next.

Dren could only watch in disbelief, silently fuming. This had been her idea, now she was having to wait while Meela attempted to make it all the way up. There was no way that she would trust the arrow with their combined weight and she couldn't shout up to her in case the soldiers heard. What had Meela been thinking? She didn't have to prove anything to Dren.

But, as she looked on, the anger drained away. She was impressed by the way Meela's strong arms carried her up the rope, as if she had done this before. Eventually, she made it to the top and removed the broken shards of glass from the window ledge then climbed into the room. Dren let out a massive breath she didn't realise she had been holding.

It was now her turn. The rope swayed furiously beneath her as she hooked her ankles around it. She pulled herself along, carefully placing one hand over the other, aware that she didn't have much time. If anyone happened to so much as glance out of a window, all this would have been in vain.

Climbing the rope was harder than it had looked from the ground. She felt her arm muscles strain. Still, with Meela watching, she wasn't going to let it show. After all, Meela had made it look easy. But the higher she climbed, the more movement there was in the rope. She tried to calm herself down. *A castle made of wood has to sway,* she thought as the wind picked up and she swung dangerously over to one side. It took every bit of strength she could muster just to keep going. The sun was blinding and she paused for a brief rest, taking the weight onto her crossed legs. This caused the rope to cut into the sores on her ankles, digging in where the blisters had formed over the tender skin. Then she pressed on until she could hear Meela's reassuring voice close by.

'That's it Dren, just a few more steps now, you're doing well.' Meela extended her arms and helped her through the window. She had never been more relieved to feel solid wooden floor boards beneath her feet.

This trip better be worth it, Dren thought as she looked out the window at the ground below and realised the height of the tower they had just scaled. And then she ran to the corner of the room where she threw up.

CHAPTER 41

'If it's all getting too much for you, why don't you stay here and I'll go get the herb?' said Meela. She didn't seem to be trying very hard to keep the edge of triumph from her voice.

Trying to regain her dignity after losing her last meal, Dren pretended she hadn't heard the remark. She straightened up, snorted and spat on the ground, then shook out her arms, trying to get them to work again after the nerve-wracking climb.

Concentrating on the decor of the room rather than her weak stomach, she noted they were now within a large bedroom dominated by a giant four poster bed. The golden crown motif on the headboard indicated that it did indeed belong to the prince. The dark wood panelling gave the room a cold feel. Bearskins, antlers and the stuffed head of a snarling rock lion adorned the walls. The prince clearly liked to hunt. Dren didn't understand why anyone wanted to display the heads of the things they had killed. It seemed disrespectful to what had been a wild animal minding its own business.

Dren saw the arrow had wedged snugly between a chest and the wall. She walked over and gave a tug, but it didn't budge. She nudged the heavy wooden chest but it would take more than her fatigued arm muscles to move it. She wasn't going to be able to retrieve the arrow anytime soon.

'I presume we go this way,' said Dren, turning the handle on a heavy-looking door.

'I know you don't want my advice,' Meela interrupted him, 'but it's probably safer to use the servant's door.'

'What do you mean? There's a different door for the servants?'

'Of course there is. You think the prince wants to see how things get done? All he cares about is the end result. If he wants to eat an egg while he's lying in the bath, he just clicks his fingers and one appears. He's not interested that three dozen eggs were wasted before that one just in case he happened to get peckish. He just wants a quick egg.'

This certainly fitted in with what Dren had heard about the prince and it reinforced her poor opinion of him.

Meela opened the small door in the corner of the chamber. It was made out of the same wood as the wall panels but it made an audible click when it was opened.

'So the prince can hear anyone coming,' she explained.

They exited onto a landing where they were met with a bewildering network of servants' corridors which lead off in at least six different directions. Meela walked over to a table and picked up a pot. She passed it to Dren.

'What's this for?' Dren turned the plain, earthen coloured vessel over in her hands.

'Pretend you're a gardener,' she said brushing a hand

through Dren's hair. A twig and a couple of leaves fell to the floor. 'It's the only explanation for why you're this dirty. And you should never walk about without carrying something or you'll get shouted at for being idle.'

Dren realised that soldiering had been a privileged occupation. No one would have given her a second look in the Drabsea keep if she didn't seem to be gainfully employed. She glanced down at her clothes. The sweat marks that stained her shirt added to the general impression that she belonged outside.

'This should take us all the way down,' said Meela as they came to the top of a spiral staircase.

'You seem to know this place pretty well. Did you work up here?'

'Only once or twice. I've had to bring food up to the royal chambers when the other servants were too busy.' She took off her own apron and scrunched it into an unidentifiable heap. 'But I'll need to avoid being seen. There are too many people who know me and I didn't turn up for my shift this morning so I'll be in trouble if I'm caught.'

At the foot of the stairs, Meela opened the door which led out into the garden. Despite the danger in just being here, Dren immediately felt her spirits lift at the sight of so much greenery.

'Come on!' Meela hissed.

At the far end of the garden, they came to a walled area. Meela stopped and turned to Dren. 'That's the herb garden. We should find what we're looking for. Unless there's been a massive demand for salad overnight.'

Dren smiled half-heartedly at her joke. She couldn't shake the ominous feeling that this had all been too easy. But maybe it was about time that things finally went in their favour. She followed Meela to the gate which led into the herb garden. The air was infused with the fragrance of mint and wild garlic. A second later they heard voices.

Instinctively, Dren grabbed a bamboo cane which had been propping up a sweet pea plant. She still carried the pot that Meela had given her and clutched it so tightly it was in danger of shattering against her chest.

The voices came closer. Dren tucked herself against the edge of the wall next to Meela. There was nothing to do but wait helplessly in the hope that whoever was there would move on without noticing them.

Time stood still. The longer Dren stood here, the greater the risk of being discovered by anyone making their way through the ornamental garden and the longer Seema would have to wait for her cure.

'I'll sneak in and try to see what's happening. You wait here,' said Meela.

Dren tried to gesture that she hadn't yet heard the voices move away but Meela had already set off towards the garden. Dren moved closer to the entrance and listened. There was nothing she could do now without drawing attention to them. For a couple of minutes all was quiet. Then she heard a scream.

Ignoring the danger she might be putting herself in, she sprinted at full pace into the garden, still clutching the cane and the pot. She hadn't gone very far when she saw Meela standing opposite two large figures. Dren came to an abrupt halt on the soft path, spraying up a shower of bark as she dug her heels into the ground to avoid slamming into two solidly built men who blocked her way. The younger man's face was a mess of small cuts and bruises. One eye was swollen shut.

'Come back for more, have you?' he said addressing Meela. He hadn't yet noticed Dren and he sounded very drunk.

'Look what you did to my nephew,' said a taller man, holding a glass bottle. He gestured wildly, sloshing liquid onto the path as he spoke.

'Yeah, well, I should have finished him off, after what he tried to do to me,' came Meela's reply.

'You're overreacting as usual. Typical female!' the younger man said.

Dren could see spittle forming on the man's lips. She doubted that that bottle had been the man's first drink today.

'You can't speak to her like that,' said Dren, stepping forward from the shadows.

Both men looked over at Dren, noticing him for the first time.

The older man laughed. 'Who's this, your boyfriend?'

'Don't be daft, what self-respecting man would want her? She's feral, this one.' The younger man cleared his throat and launched a glob of spit at Meela.

Without thinking, Dren swiped at him with the cane. It made a whipping sound as it caught the young man clean across his arm, leaving a deep red mark.

He hurled a curse at Dren and looked around for something to grab. At the same moment, both he and Dren noticed a pitchfork stuck into the soil. Despite being drunk, the man was much closer and made a successful grab at the wooden handle, pulling it clear of the earth.

The older man clapped his hands in malevolent glee. Dren looked about for something to defend herself with but there was nothing. She was left holding the small stone plant pot in one hand and the garden cane in the other. Both would be virtually useless against a pitchfork, and they all knew it.

She turned and looked to Meela but all she saw was the back of her head. Meela had seized her chance and was running off to safety. Dren felt anger flowing through her veins. She hadn't expected much from Meela but she certainly didn't expect her to abandon her when things got difficult. *Coward.*

She thought about how brave Meela had been when they scaled the wall. It must have been a one off. But it didn't matter now. Dren would have to rely on her own resources as usual. She was back to being a lone wolf.

The prongs of the rusty fork were thrust towards her chest. The man might be drunk, but it didn't take much skill to wield the weapon he was holding. Dren took a step backwards. The older man laughed as if he was watching a stage show. The fork came towards Dren once again, forcing her backwards towards the edge of the garden.

The thick woven branches of hedges extended left and right meant there was nowhere for Dren to go but backwards. Unable to think of a better plan, Dren raised the pot and launched it with all her might towards her attacker. It flew through the air and bounced against the fork before shattering into several pieces as it crashed onto the path. Now Dren was left holding only the cane.

The attacks were coming with more fury. Every blow that failed to connect just encouraged his assailant to try again. Without stopping to look behind her, Dren turned another corner in the decorative maze. Too late, she realised the path came to a dead end, blocked by a carved standing stone. There was no escape through the thick hedge. The thorny branches would tear at her flesh if she tried to crawl through.

Maybe her luck had finally run out. Meela had deserted her and, in turn, she would let down Aimree and Seema who were both relying on her.

Just when she was at her most vulnerable, she remembered the bow hidden under her cloak. As if guided by an unseen hand, she slipped it off her shoulder, placed the bamboo cane on the string and drew the tension back to her ear.

Her attacker wouldn't have had a chance to see it coming as he charged around the corner and came face to face with Dren who immediately released the bowstring.

Cutting through the air, the makeshift arrow flew straight towards her attacker, catching him in the middle of his chest and knocking him off his feet. The pitch fork fell from his hand with an almighty clatter followed by the man who landed hard on the ground, his skull colliding with a rock.

Giving only a cursory look down, Dren ran past her fallen attacker. The man was out cold. Dren felt a pang of guilt. Her mind raced back to the encounter with the Wynyms but there was no time for regrets. She had to get out of there.

When she saw the older man running towards her, Dren almost changed course. But he was no longer interested in Dren. He had spotted the younger man lying on the ground and ran to tend to him.

CHAPTER 42

Dren's legs continued to gather pace as she turned sharply towards the exit. She looked over her shoulder and was relieved to see that she wasn't being followed. But she knew she was running on borrowed time. Once they learned what she had done, the soldiers would soon hunt her down. She headed for the tower. It was the only way she knew to get out of this dangerous keep.

She was so preoccupied with survival that the search for the herbs went completely out of her mind.

'Dren, wait!' It was Meela's voice. She ran towards Dren, carrying a brightly flaming torch.

'Why did you leave me in there?' Dren shouted as Meela caught up with her. She could still feel the adrenaline from the fight coursing through her body.

'What could I have done? You said it yourself, you're the soldier, not me. Anyway, I've got an escape plan. Follow me!'

Dren followed her back inside the prince's tower. Dren took the stairs two at a time with Meela following closely behind. As they made it into the prince's suite, a bugle sounded and a shout went up. Dren knew that news of the intruders must have gotten out and all available persons were being mustered to assist with locating them.

'What do we do now?' shouted Dren. She heard heavy boots on the steps outside. Although the rope ladder was still attached to the outside of the window, it would be too dangerous to try and escape down it, given the time it would take. If someone cut the rope, Dren and Meela would plummet to their deaths.

'I need that arrow,' Meela shouted.

'I've tried, but it's wedged tight,' said Dren.

'Try harder and this time I'll help.'

Under the watchful eye of the stuffed beasts whose macabre pelts decorated the room, they set about pushing and pulling the heavy chest every which way but it was stuck fast. Dren's eyes were drawn to a tusked wildhog. If it was going to watch them, it could at least be useful.

Dren let go of the chest and ran to the wall. 'Sorry about this, pig.' Standing on the tips of her toes, she reached up and pulled the mounted head off the wall.

'What on earth are you doing?' shouted Meela. The heavy footsteps outside were getting closer. If the green-cloaked soldiers were searching room by room, it wouldn't be long before they were discovered.

Dren ignored Meela's protests as she dragged the stuffed head over to the chest and dropped it onto the ground, smashing the tusk.

'Are you daft? They'll hear us now!'

Dren picked up one of the long curved tusks which had snapped off. She thrust it underneath the ornate chest, wedging it tightly.

Meela watched on as Dren jumped up and down on

the exposed end of the tusk. The chest give a creak as it moved ever so slightly with the makeshift lever Dren had created.

'Give me a hand!' she shouted, straining with the effort. Could they move it enough to free the arrow?

Meela grabbed hold of the arrow which was still attached to the knotted rope. This time when Dren jumped, she pulled the arrow and it fell free.

Dren uncoupled the arrow and the knotted rope then re-secured the end of the makeshift ladder to the prince's bed frame.

Meela looked out of the broken window and pointed at the thatched roof of a neighbouring tower. 'Think you can hit that?'

Dren peered out. It didn't seem to be too difficult a target. She nodded.

Meela grabbed the arrow from Dren and held it against the flaming torch she had brought from the garden. The finely crafted tip smouldered then burst into flames. 'Aim low and the fire will spread upwards,' she said, handing the burning arrow back to Dren.

'What if I hurt someone?' Dren protested. 'There could be innocent people inside.' The flames starting to burn her fingers.

'It's just the roof. The soldiers are trained to put it out quickly. In the meantime it will draw everybody in the opposite direction from us.'

The servants' door gave its warning click. It was a matter of seconds before they were discovered. Dren had no option but to trust her. Taking aim, she drew back the string until the arrow was level with her cheek, then released it and watched it fly straight towards its target. The flaming tip buried itself deep into the thatch. Wisps of smoke rose from the roof as the dry material started to smoulder followed by bright fingers of orange flame.

Almost immediately the fire bell sounded. Fire was the natural enemy of forest dwellers and the keep would now put all its resources into extinguishing the flames. The hunt for the intruders would have to wait. The door behind them remained closed and the footsteps got further away.

Meela picked up the loose end of the rope ladder and threw it out the window. She gave it a tug to make sure it was secure. 'With all of the commotion it should be easy enough to slip out through the gates. The soldiers will be too busy dealing with the fire to care about who's leaving.'

Dren peered down to the bottom of the makeshift ladder. 'You go first.'

'I'll catch you up, there's something I have to do first.'

'I'm not leaving you here. I've not even got the thale. I can't go back empty handed.'

'I know,' said Meela, removing a bunch of leaves from her pocket, 'That's why I picked some when I left you in the garden. That should be plenty.'

'I'm not leaving without you.'

But Meela shook her head. 'There's still something I have to do here. But your friends need you and you can't delay getting the herbs to them.'

'At least tell me what you're doing.'

'I'm going to free some more prisoners,' she said with a glint in her eye.

CHAPTER 43

By the time Dren arrived back at the inn, she was scarcely able to speak. She sprinted up the stairs and knocked on Seema's door without any breath left in her body.

'Enter,' said a voice she didn't recognise.

Tentatively she opened the door and scanned the dimly lit room. The window shutters were closed and the room was dark save for the soft orange glow of a fire burning low in the corner. Above the fire hung a metal pot suspended from a chain. Clouds of steam filled the air with the smell of damp grass.

An unfamiliar woman mopped Seema's brow, wringing out her cloth in a copper bowl. She didn't acknowledge Dren until her task was complete. Her braided hair came down to her waist and her sandals reminded Dren of something Seema would wear. But more importantly, she had a kindly disposition.

Aimree lay next to her sister in the bed. She appeared to be in a deep sleep and didn't even stir when Dren came in. She tried not to think about what that might mean and forced herself to swallow. 'I've brought you the thale,' she said, her mouth as dry as dust. She held out the bunches, silently praying it was the right herb.

The healer nodded. 'This is indeed what we require but I just hope you're in time. You can see for yourself that they're both very weak.' She pointed to the cauldron. 'Add half of the leaves to the pot and keep stirring it. Don't let them stick or they'll burn and spoil.'

Dren didn't have to be told twice. She added the leaves to the pot then stirred it until the water bubbled and turned green. After a few minutes of stirring with the long wooden stick, her arms were aching but she wouldn't stop until it was done.

Eventually the healer appeared at her side and peered into the pot. She took the stick from Dren and gave the mixture another couple of stirs then took a deep sniff. She nodded in approval. 'Now pour it into a cup and add a little cold water so it doesn't scald the patient.'

Dren did as she was told then handed her the wooden cup carefully so as not to spill a drop of the precious liquid. The healer lent over the bed and held the cup up to Seema's lips. At first she just lay there, lifeless but, as the healer uttered soothing words in an unfamiliar language, Seema's eyes flickered open and she managed a small sip.

Her eyes closed over again and she screwed her face up with the pain of the effort. The healer encouraged her to take a few more sips and then, exhausted, Seema laid her head back down. The healer placed the cup down on a small side table.

Dren was relieved that Seema had taken the medicine but she was concerned at how ill Aimree looked. 'What about her sister? Why aren't you giving her anything to drink?'

'Aimree doesn't need the infusion. She wasn't

scratched by the bat.' The healer tucked in the bedclothes around Aimree's sleeping form.

'But look at how white she is. You don't need to be a medic to see that she's sick, she can hardly move from the bed.'

'It's difficult to explain to those who don't-' The healer looked Dren up and down. 'She is sick and she is not sick. You see, deep down she's linked with her sister. It's her sister's pain that she's feeling, not her own.'

'How can that be?'

'It can happen when two people who share a close bond are separated whether through distance or illness. The mind tries to reach out to re-establish the link which has been broken. It's exhausting.'

Dren wasn't following this explanation at all. 'So it's all in her head.'

'No, the symptoms are real, it's merely the origin of the pain that is different. When Seema regains her strength, Aimree should recover too.'

Dren could only hope this was true.

'I will return in the morning,' said the healer as she gathered up her herbs and folded them away inside a cloth wrap. 'Give Seema the cup again at dinner time and encourage her to drink as much as she can.' Instructions given, the healer left.

Dren was physically exhausted but didn't dare sleep in case she missed giving Seema her medicine. She slumped down into a chair and felt nothing but guilt for causing this whole situation. And to top it off, there was still no sign of Meela. After a long, anxious wait, the time came to wake Seema. Dren gently roused her, put the cup to her lips and begged her to take some. Encouragingly, she managed to drink a little more this time.

She mopped Seema's brow just as she had seen the healer do then offered her some more of the potion. She looked up as Dren tilted the cup against her lips and she continued to drink until the cup was empty. Then she lay down, exhausted with the effort. Her stomach gave a groan and she let out a massive belch before falling fast asleep.

Dren looked over at Aimree, hoping to see even a slight improvement but she was still in a feverish sleep, tossing and turning and kicking out. Even when Seema fell into a deep sleep and started to snore, Aimree didn't respond. There was nothing Dren could do for her but wait as she fought against her invisible demons.

Dren sat back down in the chair by Seema's bed and swore she wouldn't rest until they were both awake and healthy again. And then exhaustion took over and she fell into a deep, dark sleep.

Daylight flooded into her eyes and she realised the shutters had been opened. It was now morning and the healer had returned. She panicked. What had she missed?

'How are they?' she asked anxiously.

'Why don't you ask Seema yourself?' she said with a smile.

Dren looked up. Seema was sitting up in bed, yawning. 'How are you feeling?' Dren held her breath.

'That's the best sleep I think I've ever had,' Seema said, rubbing her eyes.

Dren's smile faded as she looked over at Aimree's bed. It was empty. She felt a pain in her chest. 'Where's A-?'

The door to the room opened and in walked Aimree carrying a tray of hot buttered toast.

'Good morning, Dren,' she said. 'Unfortunately these are only for the patients so you'll have to get your own.' Her eyes sparkled.

The healer spoke again. 'My work is done though the healing is far from complete. Seema must have complete rest for at least a day before getting up. The potion will tire her as it forces the rest of the poison from her body. Aimree will be spared the worst of this but she should also stay inside until all of the symptoms have disappeared.'

Dren thanked her for all she had done. She turned to speak to Aimree only to hear the healer give a small cough.

'I find the healing is also more successful if the healer is paid for her work.'

Dren blushed. 'Of course, I'm sorry, I didn't...' she patted her pockets. She only had the few coins in her pocket that she had been saving for arrows. The bow would have to remain useless for a while longer. She handed the payment to the healer who uttered a blessing and then departed.

Once the healer had left, the sense of relief once again turned to apprehension.

'Where's Meela?' asked Aimree. She was looking and sounding like her old self again.

Dren explained what had happened in the keep. Both sisters became very concerned as Dren described how she had run back towards the garden and that was the last she had seen of her.

'At least she knows where we are. It's not as if we're going anywhere for the next few days.'

Morning turned to evening and then the next day dawned. Eventually, Seema regained her strength and was able to get out of her bed and walk around but Meela still hadn't reappeared.

'We should think about moving soon,' said Seema. 'Our presence will start to draw attention and you two are not safe in this city.'

Although Dren agreed with her words, she was loath to leave Meela behind. They owed their freedom entirely to her heroic actions.

'It seems like Meela has made her choice and we must move on without her,' Seema continued. 'Plus the innkeeper seems to be billing us by the minute. Grandmothers don't attract the same discount as monks, it seems. I don't think we can afford to stay here much longer.'

Reluctantly they began to pack for the journey. Dren tried to draw it out but there was still no sign of Meela. Eventually she could put it off no more. The time had come to leave. Dren walked out to the stables to ready Thunder for the journey.

As she approached the barn, she could see Thunder curled up asleep in the corner. She called the donkey's name but, predictably, Thunder ignored her. Then Dren noticed something buried in the straw. Upon closer inspection, it appeared to be a bundle of clothes.

As Dren got closer, a head appeared in the straw. 'What the-?'

'Morning!' came the sleepy reply. It was Meela!

'I got back late last night and didn't want to wake anybody up so I decided just to kip down here,' she explained, brushing the straw from her hair.

'Where in Kingdom's name did you go?' The relief at seeing her safe was tinged with a hint of annoyance that she had put them through so much worry.

'It doesn't matter now. My work here is done.' Then she added, 'But we should probably leave town quickly. How is Seema?'

'She's made a full recovery, thanks to the herbs you found. I'm just loading up the donkey and then we'll be ready to leave.' Dren walked over to Thunder. 'Do I smell smoke?'

'That'll be from my clothes. I had to burn a few other things on my way out.'

Dren knew better than to ask her for an explanation. She led Thunder from the stables. Aimree and Seema were waiting for them at the front of the building. Dren introduced Meela and Seema thanked her for saving their lives.

For once, Meela looked embarrassed. 'I only did what anyone would do.'

'That's not exactly true,' said Aimree as she threw her arms around Meela. 'You risked everything to get us out of there alive. I can't think of many people who would have done that for two complete strangers.'

Hitching the cart onto the donkey, Dren grew sombre. They were leaving the relative safety of the inn for a dangerous unknown. She turned to the three girls.

'Probably best if you all travel underneath the tarp again until we're out of the city. There's no telling who might be looking for us.' She cast a glance at Meela but she said nothing.

They climbed aboard and Dren raised her hood, assuming the guise of a simple merchant making his way to the Celestial City to sell his wares. As they set off, she couldn't help notice something didn't feel right. Apart from a few people hurrying between doorways the streets were empty and they hadn't passed another cart in some time.

They had only been on the road for about ten minutes when a road block came into view. There was no way to avoid it without arousing suspicion. Dren approached slowly and was brought to a halt by a soldier wearing the forest-green tunic. The soldier walked towards her, sword drawn.

Keep calm, Dren told herself as she steadied her breath. *Don't give the game away*.

'Good day soldier, what can I do for you?'

'What is your business in the city?' The soldier eyed Dren up and down intently.

'I'm travelling up north for the King's Tournament. Just looking to offload some of my wares to the rich city folk.'

'You don't sound as if you're from around here.'

'No, that's right, I've come from Drabsea. Business isn't too good down there at the moment.' Dren couldn't gauge whether the man believed her or not.

'You've come far then?'

'That's right, I only stop when my trusty steed needs a break. But the journey is long. I've been on the road for a good week now.'

'I can see from the state of your clothes you're not lying. Let me give you a warning then, since you seem like a decent fellow. There's been a breakout from the jail.'

'Really?' said Dren, hoping to sound appropriately shocked.

'Yes, two dangerous criminals made off. They're armed and violent. I don't want to alarm you but they've also released a number of wild animals into the city.'

That would explain what Meela was doing in the keep.

The soldier was clearly looking for two people travelling together. A single traveller didn't arouse suspicion. They had made the right decision to travel this way. But she knew she still had to keep her wits about her. They weren't out of danger yet. 'What kind of animals, if you don't mind me asking?'

The soldier leaned in closer and looked her in the eye. 'They call them creatures,' he said in a hushed tone. 'No one is sure what they are or where they came from. Some want to use the word ma-'

Even under his breath he couldn't bring himself to use the forbidden term. *Magic.* 'Let's just call it dark forces. But make no mistake, however they got here, they're very dangerous and now, thanks to the lawless actions of two undesirables they are free to prowl the streets.'

'Anyway,' he said, his voice returning to its normal volume, 'I'll just need to give your cart a quick search and let you on your way. What was it you said you were selling?'

Dren hesitated. She could not let the soldier look inside the cart. And then she saw movement in the distance. This might be her only chance to escape. She had to act quickly.

'Creature!' she screamed at the top of her lungs. The soldier looked up, panic in his eyes at the sight of the animal in the distance.

'Run for cover!' shouted the soldier as he drew his sword and ran in the opposite direction to save his own skin.

'Thunder, run!' roared Dren.

With a twitch of his ears, the donkey came to life and

trotted on like a brave steed, completely unperturbed by the stray dog that was happily rummaging through the bins up ahead.

CHAPTER 44

The overnight rain had only recently stopped falling and an early morning light mist lingered. It coated the Kingdom in a shimmering carpet of dew that the low spring sun was struggling to burn off. Dren's cloak was muddy and damp from spending yet another night lying on the ground.

She was tired from her broken, restless sleep and her head was pounding. But that was nothing compared to the pain in her feet. She now questioned the decision to abandon the cart in favour of continuing on foot. She could have done with a bit of comfort now even if, deep down, she knew that travelling with a stolen cart was too risky.

Ditching the cart made their group less recognisable which could only be a good thing. Dren hadn't wanted to worry the others by mentioning anything but she was convinced she was being followed. It was an uneasy feeling that had travelled with her from the moment she had left Drabsea. But each time she turned around, there was no one there. Maybe it was just her overactive imagination but she couldn't shake the feeling of being watched.

At least Thunder was now tolerating Seema's weight. The ill-tempered donkey had stubborn days where he wanted to do nothing other than to dig his heels in and eat grass. But he had a definite soft spot for the monk. Today he hadn't even snorted when she lowered herself onto his back and whispered gentle encouragement into his ear.

Dren took a step and something sharp stabbed into her heel. What had started out as a mere irritation, rubbing her skin every time her left boot struck the hard path, had grown worse over time. Now it had become almost unbearable.

Still, Dren was determined that nothing was going to get in the way of her reaching her destination. 'I think we'll make it by tomorrow,' she said, trying to keep an upbeat tone to mask how she was really feeling. 'I'm almost definitely sure of it.' Her attempt at sounding confident trailed off as she realised none of the others could hear her as she now lagged far behind.

Despite her aching foot, she quickened her pace to catch up. 'I'm sure we must be nearly there,' she said after several minutes of struggle. Each step only served to increase the crippling foot pain. 'I'm sure I can sense we're near the Celestial City which means we're getting closer to the mountains.'

'You're limping!' said Aimree noticing Dren's uneven strides. 'Do you need to stop?'

By now she must have gouged a sizeable hole in her foot and common sense dictated that she should do something about it, but she wasn't going to give in. Stopping would be as good as admitting weakness and she didn't want the others to think she wasn't capable of keeping up with the pace. After all, if a civilian like Meela could manage it then so could Dren. If she stopped to remove her boot and shake out the pebble, it would just as soon be replaced by another one and they would only have to stop and wait for her again. For now, she resolved to grin and bear the pain.

'No, why would I be limping?' she said through gritted teeth.

'Do you want a shot on the donkey?' asked Seema, giving Thunder's head a pat. 'I'm over the worst of my illness and I could probably do with the exercise.'

'Just another bend in the road and we'll get our bearings, I'm sure of it.' Dren chose to act as if Seema hadn't uttered a sound. 'And I'm not planning on stopping until we see the misty clouds hovering over the tops of the summits and we know that we're on the right track.'

Dren hadn't ever seen mountains up close. She had read somewhere that the mountains were misty so she figured they should be looking out for clouds, which would then lead to the mountains. This was easier said than done as they were surrounded on all sides by established forest, which blocked out the sun and prevented them navigating the dense woods with any confidence. The only thing she knew for definite was that the Celestial City was bordered by the mountains so surely they wouldn't be that hard to find.

Aimree tried a different tact. 'When I climbed up that monkey puzzle tree earlier looking for nest eggs, all I could see were more trees. This forest is massive and we're all tired. Maybe it wouldn't kill us to take a rest.'

Seema gave a wistful sigh. 'It would be nice if we could just get a warm bed tonight, and maybe some food that we haven't had to pick from the ditch.'

'We've been pushing our luck with too many days on the road and not enough time off to rest,' said Meela. 'We need to think about resting up for a few days. If we are to cross into the mountains, we'll need to be fully fit. We'll also need provisions. It's not a journey to be undertaken lightly.'

It now became a battle of unrelenting stubbornness. All knew they needed to rest, but no one was prepared to admit weakness and be the first to stop. Then circumstances took the decision from them as Thunder stopped dead in the middle of the path.

'Woah!' exclaimed Aimree, as she narrowly avoided colliding with Dren. 'Please give me a little warning before you do that next time.' She shook her head and tutted at Thunder.

'For the love of...can't you get that donkey to walk in a straight line for once?' said Dren, thinking Seema was dithering again. But, as she looked closer, she put her hand to her mouth and swallowed her scream. For once, she couldn't blame Thunder for stopping. Dren stared at the horrifying sight that lay across the path.

It was the body of a man, lying on his back, face up to the sky. The most striking thing about him was his bare skin, which was stained a deep red. It looked as though someone had thrown a goblet of wine over him except that the dark liquid had the viscous texture of blood. The pungent scent of early decay hung heavy in the air. He was unquestionably dead.

Dren's hand instinctively grasped the amulet hung around her neck.

Blood pooled from a deep head wound, offering some clue as to the violent manner of his death. A first inspection revealed that the deceased was an older man.

Fine wisps of long grey hair stuck to his skull with clots of red matter. Although Dren hadn't seen a dead body for a long time, there had been a period in her life when the sight had been commonplace. In the city, death tended to come from extreme hunger and exposure to the elements, and violent death was thankfully rare.

The gory death had a hypnotising effect. Her first reaction was to stand and stare. It was no different to seeing a chunk of meat laid out on a butcher's slab at the market. It was fascinating and repelling in equal measure. It dawned on her that this had once been a living person with hopes and dreams and talents. Dren felt a sense of shame for staring but she still didn't turn her head away.

Seema led Thunder a short distance away and tied him to a tree, facing away from the scene of horror. Then, very carefully, she approached the dead man from the side, swatting away a death beetle that was hovering in the air, attracted by the scent of the open wounds. She surveyed the scene, her hands crossed over her heart.

'Without emotion, the world would be flat and featureless. To have hills you must also have valleys, land would not exist without sea and darkness is necessary for there to be light.' Seema walked around the man who was face up towards the heavens. 'And without death, there would be no life.'

There was something so striking about this figure that it was hard to look away. 'Aren't those tattoos the markings of a priest?' asked Dren.

Although the priest was clearly dead, it would be a mistake to describe the corpse as being without life. An opportunistic crow was pulling off pieces of flesh with its razor-tipped beak. But even without the help of the bird, nature had already started the process of reclaiming what belonged to her. Flies buzzing around the corpse wasted no time in feasting on nutrients that the priest no longer required.

Dren took a step forward to shoo away the bird and give the deceased a little bit of dignity. It was all she could do for the stranger.

'Stop!' screamed Seema, causing the crow to pause and raise its blood-soaked beak. 'Don't touch him!'

'But I was only...'

Seema was still shrieking. Dren took a step back.

'Seema, what is it?' asked Aimree, puzzle and concern showing on her brow in equal measure.

But Seema didn't answer. Instead, with quick fingers, she refastened the sash that bound her brown robe, pulling the folds of heavy material tight around her waist. Then she rolled up her sleeves, held out her carved wooden staff and waved it over the body making slow circles in the air as if stirring a pot full of thick chewsan.

At this, the crow flapped its wings and took off, abandoning its free meal. It chose a tree overlooking the crime scene and wrapped its claws around a sturdy branch. The bird's yellow eyes peered at the intruders interfering with its dinner.

Dren, Aimree, Meela and the bird watched Seema place the tip of the staff in the earth and trace a circle around the body.

As the end of the circle met its beginning, Dren felt a sharp pain on her back as if she had been stung by an insect. She gave it a scratch but it didn't sooth it. She hoped it wasn't the rash flaring up again. It hadn't bothered her since she had left the keep and she wanted it to stay that way.

When Seema had finished her work with the staff, she took a step back. Dren didn't want to stare but it was hard to take her eyes away from the macabre scene. The man was naked, save for a small cloth around his waist which was preserving the last of his modesty. His priestly garments had been torn off and were lying in tatters around him. Some pieces had caught on thorny bushes and were blowing in the breeze like ribbons at a fair.

Seema walked around the outside of the circle, her eyes closed and head slightly bowed. Then she clapped her hands and paused. After the momentary silence, a soft moan escaped from her lips. The sound intensified until she was taking in huge gulps of air to produce unholy warbling sounds as she wove her way around the circle she had created.

'Do you think she's alright?' asked Aimree, squinting in the daylight.

'If you ask me, I don't think she's ever been quite right.' Dren, raised an eyebrow. 'I'm sorry, I know she's you're sister.'

'No, this does not run in the family. I'm just as confused as you.'

Seema's noises increased in intensity until they filled the space completely.

Dren was growing increasingly concerned by the noise. Did Seema have no awareness of the situation they were in? What if the killer was still nearby, hiding in the trees? A shiver ran through Dren's body. It was the same feeling of being watched that she got every time they were in the woods.

'You know she's warding off the spirits of the dead so they stay with the body and don't haunt the living,' said Meela. 'At least, that's what I've heard they do.'

'Who told you that?' said Dren with a half sneer. But, as soon as it was out of her mouth, she realised how insensitive her question was.

'I don't remember. I was quite young when my mother died.' The pain in her voice was obvious to all and it killed the conversation.

CHAPTER 45

At least Seema's chanting filled the awkward silence that Dren's thoughtless question had caused. Even though the whole procedure was decidedly odd, she accepted that other people took comfort in rituals. It may be strange to her but she was happy that such rituals existed for the benefit of others like Meela, even if they didn't make any sense.

Dren had seen first-hand how people went out of their way to avoid causing harm to Seema in case a higher power took revenge. If someone had killed the priest, they would have been well aware of what supernatural forces they were messing with. Was it an accident? More likely a robbery gone sour. Perhaps the priest had fought back, refusing to give up the gold that belonged to the church. But what kind of person would be capable of such a vile act?

However it happened, a violent death didn't bode well for continuing on this road. As well-meaning as Seema's actions were, she had just announced their presence to any cold-blooded killer who might still be lurking in the vicinity. Or, for that matter, to any other thief, bandit or robber who happened to be passing.

They had already stayed longer than they could afford and now they were sitting targets. Dren felt a shiver and rubbed the back of her neck. Maybe it was just the birds in the trees but something was watching them.

She called out to Seema but she was lost in some kind of a trance. Dren struggled to maintain her composure as Seema, hopped from one leg to the other whilst shaking her fists. Why did Dren always get the urge to laugh at the most inappropriate moments?

'Is that really necessary?' she whispered to Aimree, who was trying to maintain a dignified silence despite her sister's antics. Seema was throwing herself into the strange dancing and writhing about as if her own life depended on it.

Once again it was Meela who surprised them with her knowledge. 'She's recounting the story of the man's life so that the good spirits tell it to the Creator. It means they will seat him at the correct table in the afterlife.'

'How does she know his life story? She's never met him,' said Dren.

'You mean, never met him as far as you know. Technically, he's a colleague,' said Aimree managing to keep a straight face as Seema swung her arms about as if she was tossing pancakes. 'It's probably a pretty generic description of a holy man's life. There's not much room to improvise in the church.'

'Are you sure this man wasn't a champion sword-swallowing javelin thrower?' said Dren. 'I don't know about the Creator, but I'm certainly confused as to what the priest did in life. Thank goodness I'm not in charge of heavenly seating arrangements.'

Dren wasn't going to waste the opportunity to rest. She sat down on a tree stump and wrestled off her well-worn boot. She turned it upside down and a stream of gravel tumbled out. The boot had let more stones in than it had kept out. She gave it a good shake, unable to tell which stone in particular had been causing the most pain.

Cursing the ground for being so stony, she pulled the boot back on over her filthy sock. Grunting with the effort of standing back up, she stretched out her aching muscles and took a few steps forward to test her foot. The pebble may have gone but it had been replaced by a blister. The pain reminded her how much it sucked to be her at that moment in time. Then she stopped herself. It was probably worse to be the priest.

'What do you reckon he was doing out here?' said Aimree.

'My father would often sell medicinal herbs to priests,' Meela explained. 'But it wouldn't be unusual to see the older ones embarking on long foraging trips into the wilderness to gather rare varieties for their rituals.'

'Why don't they just grow them in a garden?' asked Dren. 'Seems a waste of time to go hunting for things you can just plant in the ground.'

'If only it was that simple.' Meela shook and kicked a weed with her foot. Instantly, its yellow petals disappeared inside a tightly wrapped bud, frustrating a bee that had been attracted by its scent. 'Some need the thin mountain air to bloom. Others grow where the animals graze so that their seeds will be carried to all four corners of the Kingdom and beyond.'

'Look, can we focus here?' said Aimree losing patience. 'A man's dead and you two are discussing gardening.'

'I'm sorry,' said Dren, 'but I thought it was a valid

point. If we can work out what the priest was doing out in the middle of nowhere then maybe we can work out what killed him.'

'And, more importantly, avoid the same fate. Are those scratch marks on his face?' Meela pointed towards the man's head, which was lying at an unnatural angle.

Dren was careful to keep her distance as she knelt down to get a closer look. The blood on his face had made it difficult to discern the marks but, as she focussed, she saw that the side of the priest's head was indeed criss-crossed with a series of fine lines.

'Surely that wouldn't have been enough to kill him?'

'Could it have happened after he died?' asked Meela. 'Maybe a bird's claw?'

'I don't think so,' said Dren, trying to recall her battle training. 'There wouldn't have been as much blood if it had happened after his heart had stopped pumping.' The death was looking less like a tragic accident and more like a crime scene.

'So it was either a person or an animal that attacked the priest,' said Meela.

'Or a creature,' said Dren.

'There's no such thing as creatures, just sorry animals that folk have mislabelled.' Meela shook her head.

But Dren took one look at Aimree who was thinking the same as she was. Meela hadn't seen the shadow creature at the Drop. The snake-like shadow had killed a whole herd of cattle. Who knew what else those things were capable of?

A bird called out overhead. The shrill tone echoed through the trees, mocking and irreverent.

'Flesh-eating birds give me the creeps.' Aimree looked

up at the trees where long thin claws curled impatiently around the branches. The flock cawed and flapped, impatient for the interlopers to leave so they could continue with their business of recycling flesh.

'They do call them a murder of crows,' Meela continued. 'But they only feed off dead meat. I've never heard of them attacking someone. Maybe a bigger bird. Something like a hawk...' Aimree tailed off, seemingly lost in thought.

'Whatever it was, it looks as though his face has been sliced open.'

'With a filleting knife?'

'Or razor sharp claws,' said Aimree.

'No, I think it was definitely a blade but the head injury might have been caused by a club which would suggest more than one attacker. My money is on highway thieves.' Dren lowered her voice down to a whisper. 'Have you two not felt something watching us for the last while?'

Meela looked confused but Aimree nodded. 'I know what you mean. I've felt it too. But every time I've turn to check, there's nobody there.'

This admission confirmed Dren's fears. They were being followed. 'We need to get out of here fast,' said Dren.

'And what about his-' Meela began.

Dren noticed the missing body part at the same instant. 'His eyes! Or where his eyes should be-'

'They've been pecked clean out.' Aimree finished the sentence that neither of them wanted to say.

But Meela was nowhere to be seen. She had disappeared into the undergrowth. The churning sound gave away the fact that her stomach was not accustomed to sights like these. A moment later, she re-emerged. She gave an apologetic wave and covered her mouth with her hand. She was saved from explaining her weak stomach by the unexpected sound of silence. At last, Seema's fervent chanting had stopped. The ritual was complete.

CHAPTER 46

A hush descended on the group. The silence suited Seema. Some things needed to be done in a certain order and the quicker she could carry out the ritual, the sooner the man's spirit could move on to where it was supposed to be. At last she felt useful.

As she wiped her hands clean on her robe, her fingers brushed past something cold and hard. It was the stone egg that her friend and mentor had given to her before she had left the monastery. It was a strange parting gift and she had almost forgotten it was there. She had no clue as to what it was or why Petra had chosen to give it to her. But whatever she was supposed to do with it, Seema trusted that she would know how to use it when the time came.

Just like life, the egg didn't come with a set of instructions. Although, sometimes, a little bit of guidance would have been nice. She chastised herself for letting her mind wander. She cleared her head of thoughts and allowed her mind to focus on the work that required to be done.

Aimree cleared her throat. 'Now Seema, I don't mean to hurry you but we really need to keep moving in case whatever attacked this man comes back.'

But Seema ignored her sister and carried on with her ritual as if nobody had spoken.

'Will I find a spade and start digging a hole?' said Dren.

Abruptly Seema stopped and opened her eyes as if coming out of a trance. She blinked a few times, her eyes readjusting to the daylight.

'Don't touch him!' she shouted out in an alarming voice that caused the crows to flap and retreat to a safer distance. The unexpected ferocity in her voice shocked Dren.

'I need salt!' she growled in a low voice barely loud enough to be heard. Then she went back to gesturing around the body.

Dren rummaged around in their bags. 'I don't think we have any in here,' Dren shouted back. 'I've only got a couple of stale pieces of bread.

'None here either,' said Aimree, tying up her pack with a piece of rope to keep it dry.

'I've got some.' Meela unwrapped a bulging cloth parcel. Nestled inside the square of material was a good handful of grey-white crystals.

'Where did you get those from?' Aimree's eyes opened wide.

'Oh, it's just an old habit I picked up working in the kitchen.'

When this was met with blank looks, Meela explained. 'If someone wants to sabotage your cooking, they switch the salt for the sugar so you get blamed for ruining the food. So we all made a habit of carrying our own supply. I've got some sugar crystals too in another safe place. I was keeping them for Thunder.' She blushed at her own admission and handed the salt parcel over to Seema before retreating to safety.

Seema licked the tip of a finger and dipped it in the salt before bringing it to her lips. A nod indicated it was fit for purpose.

She folded the cloth into a funnel shape then poured the salt into the groove she had made in the dirt. She walked around the circle, turning the furrow of earth into a complete white band around the body.

Aimree turned to Meela. 'Now, I'm not trying to be critical,' she said addressing Meela in a tone which indicated she was about to be exactly that. 'But you should think about the consequences of your actions.'

'Can't we save the lectures for some other time?' said Dren, not wanting another argument.

Aimree tensed her shoulders and then took a deep sigh-like breath. 'I'm sorry but I think it's important not to let wounds fester. It's just, I'm thinking about the salt. You know, Meela, we have to work as a team and you didn't tell us you had it. We could have sold it to buy some food. None of us have eaten properly in days.

'Of course, I'm not accusing you of deliberately concealing it. Maybe you weren't thinking straight given how hungry you were?'

Meela looked hurt but Aimree didn't pause to hear a reply. Now that Seema had completed the salt-circle, Aimree's criticism moved to her.

'And Seema, I'm sure you meant well but did you really have to waste the salt? Now if we catch anything we hunt in the woods, there's no way of preserving it. I know you take your job seriously but we really needed it more than him. We're still alive, for now.'

Meela might have been left speechless after the

verbal attack but Seema was having none of it. 'Are you quite finished little sister?' she said, her good-natured smile replaced by a much less forgiving expression. 'Then let me open your eyes to something that will make the rumblings in your over-privileged belly seem a little less important.'

Aimree gasped open-mouthed at the unaccustomed rudeness.

'That man was murdered,' Seema continued. 'Of that I am quite sure. And what's more, it looks as though whoever killed him did so trying to steal the very essence of magic from his body.

'Woah, back up! What do you mean *steal his magic*?' said Dren.

'How do you know he was murdered?' asked Aimree. 'I mean, it could have been an animal?'

'This was not the work of an animal.'

'How can you be so sure?'

'Just look at the mark on his chest.'

At first glance the red spot looked like nothing more harmful than a bee sting.

'Someone has pierced him with a needle. It's a very unusual type of death but it's unmistakable if you know what to look for. A wishbone needle would be sharp enough to pierce through to his vital organs. It's crude but it tends to do the job. And Dren, to answer your question, what I'm talking about is theft of magic. But, of course magic in its purest form is of no use to anyone, except to the poor man who used to have it coursing through his veins.'

Seeing Dren's blank look, she continued: 'The needle would have drawn out the essence from his vital organs. However, to be useable, the magical essence must be distilled. This means the perpetrator had access to an illegal still. All it then takes is some refining fire to burn away the impurities and you have yourself a bottle of pure magic.

'Nasty stuff in the wrong hands. Thankfully it looks as though something scared him off before they managed to get very much of it.

'Really, how can you tell?'

'If you're at all squeamish then you probably don't want to know the finer details of how the body responds to the very essence being sucked from its being.' Seema let out a sigh. 'Poor man. Imagine being killed for the contents of your soul.'

CHAPTER 47

Perhaps it was a coping mechanism to stop her brain from melting with the new information, but something inside Dren burned with the desire to find out what had killed the priest. The fact that magic was a banned subject made the question all the more interesting.

'But why would anyone want to steal his magic?' asked Dren. 'If it's as dangerous as you say, surely you would leave well alone.'

'And given that the mere mention of magic is strictly forbidden in the Kingdom,' Aimree gave her a hard stare, implying she should stop talking about the subject, 'it's not something that you can just sell in the market.'

'I would imagine whoever attacked him was either stealing it to order or had wanted a shot of it for themselves.'

'Shouldn't we warn the other priests?' Meela asked. 'If the killer wasn't successful, maybe he'll strike again.'

'Don't worry about them, they'll have felt his loss when I completed the ring of salt. The circle has a magic of its own and those with the sensitivity will react to it.'

Dren scratched an imagined itch on her back.

Aimree folded her arms. 'We do need to keep moving. There's an ill-feeling in this wood and we've already been here a while. That will attract attention that we can do without.'

But Dren still wasn't satisfied with Seema's explanation. 'You seem to take it for granted that magic exists. I thought that the issue of magic was the most contentious subject in the world. Aimree, please back me up here.'

'Well Dren's right. We were taught about the great war of our parents' generation, you know, the Uprising. It split families right down the middle. Those who believed in magic fought against those who denied its existence. Those who said that magic was greater than the king were chased from the Kingdom and those with any magical ability were banished along with them. So how can there be any magic in the Kingdom left to steal?'

'You two use the word magic in the same way that you use the word religion. Like you've never experienced either. Magic can mean different things to different people.

'For some, magic happens during the Blubberfish Festival. We give thanks to the Creator and She ensures the seas remain full of fish. In the monastery, magic is the daily conversation with the Creator through meditation.

'Some folk may see it as the reason behind every war that's ever happened but, without magic, the sea would be dry and the stars wouldn't twinkle. Magic created the earth.

'I thought the Creator created the earth,' said Dren.

'Indeed, and magic was the tool She used, a bit like an artist's paintbrush or a surgeon's knife,' Seema continued, her eyes gazing fondly into the distance. 'Magic keeps the seasons turning and the rain falling and the waves crashing down on the beach. There's magic in the birth of a calf, and in the birdsong in the trees and-'

'Yes, yes, and there's also magic in the organs of the unfortunate priest. At least there very well might have been until some crazy monster disembowelled him,' said Aimree. 'Listen, we don't have time for a lecture. We need to get on the road without delay. There's no telling what killer is on the loose out there and the last place we want to be is here where there is unfinished business.'

'But let me get this straight,' said Dren blocking the path, unable to let it go until she understood what Seema was saying, 'Let's say whoever did this managed to get a small amount of magic and then distilled it. What would happen then?'

'It varies from person to person and depends on the amount.'

'Well for argument's sake, say they only got a drop,' she persisted.

'For a time after they ingest it, they will wear a mantle of greatness. They will feel more powerful than the king and mightier than the mountains. But the effects are only temporary and magic has a funny way of acting on the body. When it goes, the shock of it leaving your body can even be fatal.'

'What do you mean?'

'People are wrong when they say magic lets you do miraculous things. Magic merely sustains the ordinary functions of your body. When you're high on magic, it breathes for you. You don't need sleep or to drink or even go to the toilet. Magic takes care of all of these routine functions for you so that you can spend your energies on higher things. Your mind can reach places you've never been to before. It doesn't change you in so much as it lets you be the best version of you.'

'You talk about it like it's a drug,' said Dren.

'I'd compare it more to a dream. Have you ever fallen asleep and dreamed that you can fly? You stretch out your arms and suddenly you're soaring with the hawks.'

'Of course, hasn't everybody?' she said.

'Well, that's what you can do with magic, except it's not a dream. It's your own arms that are propelling you upwards, the magic just keeps your heart beating. That's why it's dangerous if it leaves you suddenly. You can forget to breathe.'

'It would explain why someone was so desperate for magic that they would murder a holy man in cold blood,' said Aimree.

Seema nodded. 'It could be that whoever killed this priest had become addicted and was running low on magic. The thief would have felt as if his or her own skin would dissolve without a top-up.'

'So how do priests get their magic? Surely they don't rip out each other's organs?' Dren was itching to ask Seema if she had magic but she couldn't seem to form the question.

Before Seema could answer, Meela interrupted. 'Listen, there'll be time for talking later. But Aimree's right. We need to get out of here and quick. We're already in plenty of trouble. And, if anyone finds us here, they'll probably blame us for killing the priest too.'

'We won't be safe until we make it through the

Celestial City and get over the other side of those mountains out of this blood-thirsty kingdom.'

'I agree we need to get moving but we can't just leave the priest like this. Shouldn't we at least bury him so that no one comes back to steal the body,' asked Aimree.

'No, they would just dig him up given half a chance and you really don't want to get too close to him even with the salt ring. Better leave him exposed to the elements and let the ritual do its work.'

'What about the animals?' said Dren as she untied Thunder. The branches overhead was bending under the weight of the crows.

'Don't worry about them, they'll know to respect what has happened,' said Seema as she washed her hands in the stream.

As they set off, Dren heard the cawing of the crows and the rush of air under their wings as they took flight. She gave a final glance backwards. Bright sunlight was obscuring the body but she would have sworn in that moment that it was glowing.

She shook her head. Her eyes must have been playing tricks. But, when she next looked back, the body was gone. That was the moment when Dren realised that the magic Seema talked about was more than just a word. It might just be real.

CHAPTER 48

Thunder raised his nose skywards and drew in a long, deep sniff of late morning air then he bit down on the rope that was looped around his neck and refused to budge.

Dren bristled with annoyance as the rope strained in her hands but she said nothing. She sensed that the donkey was looking to goad her. If she acknowledged the misbehaviour, it would only encourage the beast to act up.

Thunder continued to walk but, rather than moving forward in a straight line, she trotted sideways. The temporary truce was over. It was time to remind him who was boss. Dren grasped the rope with both hands and pulled sharply.

Thunder responded by shaking his head and, with a wilful tug, lurched violently away from Dren, throwing her off-balance. Had Seema not been straddled across his back, Dren sensed that the animal might have chosen that moment to bolt, but, as luck would have it, he was anchored down by the full weight of the not-so-delicate monk.

'Stop it!' Dren's brow creased in annoyance as she

turned to face the donkey. Before she knew what she was doing, she lifted her arm towards Thunder, threatening to strike him. There was something about the donkey that just got under her skin and invoked an ugly response in her. But Seema cried out and Aimree and Meela both turned and shot Dren a look which stopped her in her tracks.

'I wasn't really going to...' she said, her arm hanging limp in mid-air. She lowered it back down to her side.

'You can't punish the donkey,' said Aimree. 'Animals have better intuition than us humans. What if he's sensing danger and trying to warn us?'

Meela added: 'Maybe he's been here before. He might even be leading us into the city.'

'We don't even know where we're going ourselves, never mind relying on the stupid donkey,' said Dren in frustration. She was quickly losing patience with them all. It was a struggle to look after herself, never mind four strong opinions. Or five if you counted Thunder.

'We need to keep going straight. If we take too many turns we'll end up even more lost than we already are.' Breathing deeply, she opened and closed her fists, trying to contain her annoyance.

'Give him to me.' Aimree sounded exasperated.

But Dren held tight, not willing to be beaten by the animal's stubbornness. 'He's fine, he just needs to know who's boss.' Dren gave another sharp tug on the rope.

Thunder stopped dead causing Dren to stumble forward. She turned around and made a rude gesture at the donkey.

Aimree tutted. 'Give him here.' She held out her hand.

Reluctantly, Dren passed her the reins. She knew she was well and truly beaten when the two of them ganged up on her. Thunder trotted next to Aimree like a contented puppy for the next few miles.

However, when they came to the next crossroads, Thunder stood still and took a long look to the left then turned back to look at Aimree. She patted Thunder gently on the soft patch of fur under his chin then leaned in close. 'Why don't we walk on till we find some of that sweet grass you like?' But he didn't even twitch at the promise of food.

'And then a nice inn with some fresh straw to sleep on?' She left the question hanging in the air like bait dangling on a fishing line. Usually, he would have responded to her gentle tone, but this time there was no reaction.

'What is it you want? Are you ill?' Aimree rubbed his soft muzzle. The only answer he gave was another long look down the road to the left.

'Is everything okay?' Seema shouted from the rear. 'Should I just get off and walk?'

'No, you stay put,' said Aimree rather firmly.

Dren was irritated by the way that Aimree had assumed the role of parent since recovering from her illness. She treated her travelling companions like her own children despite one being older than her and one being covered in fur. But Dren's annoyance soon gave way to concern. Could Thunder be sick? They had been travelling many miles without a proper rest. What if he had eaten something poisonous among the grass? Dren didn't have the first clue about how to treat a sick animal. In the army, they would just have replaced him but the donkey had become more than just a piece of equipment.

'I think maybe we should listen to him,' said Aimree.

'Animals have a natural sense for danger. He could be trying to warn us of something up ahead.'

'Or he could be getting lazy.'

As if on cue, Thunder gave a snort.

'Shh, he's sensitive. He knows when you're mad at him.' Aimree petted Thunder's ears and he purred like a cat, nuzzling into her hand.

Dren glared at the donkey although it was some consolation that even Aimree couldn't persuade him to move. Eventually, Aimree managed to get Thunder walking a couple of steps but he pulled so hard to the left that he left her with no choice.

'That's settled it, then,' said Aimree. 'We're not continuing along the main road. We'll just have to turn off this way. Who knows, maybe it'll be for the best.'

'I don't think-'

'Unless you're volunteering to carry both him and Seema?'

'I told you I'm happy to walk,' shouted Seema from behind her.

'Just shut up, and keep out of this. You're too ill to have an opinion.'

'But this is madness,' Dren protested. 'The bridge to the Celestial City is just up ahead and the Celestial City leads to the mountains. If we turn off here, who knows when we'll come to the next crossing? Meela, don't tell me you agree with her?'

'Don't look at me, I'm only here for the ride. You two just sort it out and I'll follow wherever you decide.'

Dren fell behind, preferring to stay quiet and sulk than keep up a losing argument.

Aimree steered Thunder to the left and he visibly perked up. He picked up the pace, confirming Dren's suspicion that he wasn't actually ill.

Meela slowed her pace and approached Dren. 'For what it's worth, I don't think we should be following him at all.'

'Why didn't you say something to the others?' Dren moaned.

'Because if the donkey don't want to move, then we ain't gonna move the donkey. Some battles aren't worth the cost.'

'So you're saying I've lost the battle but I might win the war?'

'Hopefully there won't be any war.'

CHAPTER 49

The path chosen by Thunder followed the line of the river and Dren should have been pleased that they were close to a source of water. However, something about the path unsettled her. Again, she felt the eerie sensation of being watched. She glanced back over her shoulder every couple of steps, trying to catch out whoever or whatever was tracking them but each time there was nothing to see but leaves floating in the breeze or a thrush landing on a branch.

Up ahead, Thunder had once more come to a halt. Dren muttered under her breath as she hurried to catch up with the girls. If this was another donkey-related issue, it would be the last one.

But this time it was nothing to do with the animal. Meela was crouched down at the side of the path, rubbing the smooth surface of a round grey millstone, half sunk into the earth with only the moss-covered top visible.

'Look! A waymarker. It should tell us how far we have to go to get to where we're going.'

'That'll be useful then, since we don't have a clue ourselves,' said Dren.

Aimree knelt down beside Meela. 'It's very old. See there, some of the letters have worn away.'

'Hey, isn't that arrow pointing back the way we came?' Dren's face fell.

'We wanted to avoid the main roads,' said Seema trying to sound cheerful. 'Isn't that the whole reason we're sticking to these disused paths?' She slid down from the makeshift saddle to take a closer look.

'Wait. It's indicating something ahead of us too.' She scraped away some of the spongy green moss with a fingernail. 'See the arrow? I can't make out the place name but, wherever it is, it's only half a day's walk away.'

'I bet it's another bridge,' said Aimree.

'Good luck with your navigation by wishful thinking,' said Dren. 'Let me know how it works out for you. Personally, I'd stick to reason and logic, and maybe a map if we can get our hands on one.'

'It was your reason and logic that got us thrown into prison last time, if you recall.'

Dren flinched. Aimree's comment had hit a sore spot. But Dren was only wounded. 'I think you'll find it was going after the donkey that got us into trouble in the first place.'

'But he also helped us to escape from the keep,' Meela reminded her.

'Listen,' said Seema. 'Unless we put Thunder on wheels and give him a push, we don't really have a choice but to go this way. We're responsible for bringing him along with us so we can't just abandon him. It might take us longer but, one way or another, we will get across the river. All of us.'

They set off again. Dren's pace quickened as she spied a pair of stone pillars in the distance. Even Aimree's tired feet were spurred on by the thought that their goal lay just over the water. She almost ran the whole way, as if to confirm that following the donkey had been the right thing to do.

However, as they came within touching distance, their hasty sense of joy was replaced with bitter despair. A piece of mouldy wood broke off in Aimree's hand, throwing a cloud of yellow dust into the air.

'It's completely rotten,' said Aimree sinking to her knees in disbelief.

The shattered remains of an old wooden bridge was strewn across the banks of the stream. It was hard to believe the moss-covered pieces had ever fitted together to provide a safe crossing to the other side.

'I told you,' said Dren unable to keep the triumph out of her voice. 'That's what happens when you trust a dumb beast with map reading.'

'We'll just have to keep following the stream,' Meela said resolutely. 'I mean, this can't be the only crossing.'

'I disagree,' said Dren. 'We should turn back before we get completely disorientated.

But the others had already walked out of earshot and were continuing along the path.

The riverbank meandered haphazardly through the trees. Curve after curve made it impossible to see more than a hundred strides ahead. Despite knowing they were going the wrong way, there was still something satisfying about being in the right. The problem was, being in the right didn't stop the ticks from biting. It was hard to walk more than a few strides without having to brush away a speck-sized spider that may or may not have teeth.

Then there was the danger of treading on venomous

water lizards. Although not fatal, a single bite could paralyse the leg muscles. Dren wished she hadn't been so keen to learn during her time in the keep's garden. Ignorance would have been better than knowing the dangers but still having to walk through the long grass.

By the time the sun reached the half-way mark in its journey across the sky, a large wedge of doubt hung in the air. 'They could at least put some signposts in,' said Aimree. 'How anybody is supposed to find their way around here is beyond me.'

Just then Aimree gave a shout. 'Look at this.' She pointed to a young tree.

As Dren came closer she could see that the bark had been shredded. 'What are you thinking did this? Maybe deer?'

'Deer nothing. Look!' Aimree pointed to the next tree in the row. Two large, unmistakably claw-shaped stripes marked either side of the tree. 'That's the right size for a mountain lion.'

Meela let out a gasp. 'But I'm allergic to cats.'

Dren and Aimree turned to look at her.

'Sorry, I'm just stating a fact. Why is everyone staring?'

'Meela, do you think you'd manage to sneeze before it ripped your throat out.'

'I was just making conversation. I am particularly allergic to cat fur you know.'

'We'll have to go back to that fork and take the higher ground, I'm afraid,' said Aimree. 'The lions must come down to the water to drink. I wouldn't like to get stuck down here at night and have to share the path with something that wants to eat us.'

Dren was travelling with little more than the clothes

she slept in. However, the bow which she carried over one shoulder and the half-filled waterskin slung over the other meant that her muscles were on fire. The mere thought of even one unnecessary mile was torturous.

'But they're called mountain lions,' said Dren. 'Doesn't that mean that we're more likely to find them on higher ground?'

'They might sleep up high but they come down the hillside to hunt. It gives them an advantage over their prey. They like to chase it back uphill to tire it out.'

'I don't think we can argue with the claw marks,' shouted Seema, looking uncomfortable on top of the saddle.

'Maybe when we reach the top of the hill we'll catch a glimpse of the mountains,' said Meela.

Dren rubbed the tendons in the side of her neck and unconsciously rubbed the bow she kept hidden. It would have been the perfect defence against a hungry carnivore. However, without any arrows it was worse than useless. She would have to find a fletcher in the Celestial City and, more importantly, a way to pay.

Without further delay, they about-turned and retraced their steps until they came to a path that branched off the main track and rose high above it. Climbing the steep gradient took at least twice as long as walking on the flat and they made slow progress.

Dren paused to mop the sweat that was stinging her eyes. What had started as an overgrown but passable route had quickly turned into a challenging scramble. She had to use all four limbs to navigate safely over the boulders.

Even Thunder was showing signs of exertion, snorting hot breath as he carried Seema who was clutching on for dear life and pleading with Aimree that she was now fit enough to walk. Every bump threatened to bounce her out of the improvised saddle they had cobbled together from blankets and old rope. But performing the ritual had taken its toll on her and Aimree was adamant that Seema would ride Thunder to the very end.

'No wonder this road was abandoned. There's no way a donkey could drag a cart up here,' said Seema. 'Speaking of which, I must insist that Thunder gets some rest. His hooves are slipping and sliding and the poor beast is exhausted from the effort.'

Aimree didn't look happy but she couldn't argue with the facts. 'I suppose we can rest just for a little while.'

Dren passed around the waterskin then they continued their journey up the hill. It took another hour of effort before the roofs of a hilltop village came into sight. At last their hard work was going to pay off. But, rather than the expected relief, it held an unwelcome surprise.

'What the...?' Dren cried out as she sank to her knees in despair. A landslide had washed away the path ahead, leaving the ground littered with large boulders. Mighty trees had smashed through windows and entire house walls had fallen down revealing empty shells of buildings. Cut off from any access roads and damaged beyond repair, the village looked to be totally abandoned.

Dren's heart sank at the sight and she fought back bitter tears.

CHAPTER 50

Despite their flagging spirits, turning back was not an option. The threat of lions meant there was no choice but to continue through the abandoned village.

Seema climbed down from Thunder to examine a broken piece of pottery lying on the ground.

'We should have a look about in case there's anything we can use,' said Meela.

'I'm not sure I like the sound of that,' said Seema. 'These are people's homes.'

'Were people's homes,' Meela corrected her. 'If they've abandoned them that's their choice.'

Dren's feet stumbled over the rough terrain, past the remains of walls that once belonged to farm houses, the village school, a shop. The fields had already been harvested and anything of any worth had been carried away. Frustratingly, the promised view at the top of the hill didn't materialise. The tree coverage was as thick up here as it had been in the valley. However, the presence of stone was a reassuring sign, it meant that they were getting closer to the Celestial City.

'It must have been the earth tremors that destroyed

the village,' said Aimree.

'Don't you think it's strange no one repaired the damage or rebuilt the houses?' said Dren. 'It's as if they've all just upped and left. Couple of little earth tremors and an entire village leaves, never to return. Don't make sense to me.' Dren counted at least forty houses in the village.

'Careful,' said Aimree in hushed tones. 'I saw movement.'

Still out of breath from climbing the steep hill, Dren stood very still, trying hard to quieten her breathing. She strained her eyes but there was nothing.

Aimree pointed at one of the houses. Apart from some missing roof tiles, it stood mostly intact. Bundles of firewood were stacked up ready for lighting. Its damaged stonework had been patched with straw. Out of all of the houses, it was one of the few that could still have been inhabited.

'Remember, there could be highway men camped out in there,' said Aimree. 'I'll go round the back with Meela.' Then she pointed at Dren, 'You take the front door and Seema can back you up.'

'Why do I get the front door?' said Dren but Aimree was already out of earshot.

As she approached the front door, she noticed scorch marks on the stonework. Her mind instantly turned to dragons. Then she checked her imagination. Of course the burning was more likely to have been caused by flaming torches rather than the mythical beasts of old. Dingwall's dragon egg must have been playing on her mind.

Dren turned the handle and pulled open the front door. An alarming beating of wings blew wind into her face. It was a dragon for sure! She ducked, expecting to see the fire-breathing lizard of her nightmares. It was a relief to see nothing more harmful than a pigeon fly out.

She took a moment to compose herself, relieved that her fear was unfounded. But this relief was short lived.

'Who goes there?' cried a voice. 'I've got a knife and I know how to use it. Show yourself in the light or I'll kill you.' The words may have been spoken with force but the elderly voice trembled as it uttered them, casting doubt over whether the speaker was a threat at all.

'We mean you no harm,' said Dren slowly pulling open the door. But when a large hunting knife appeared in the gap, Dren instinctively took a step back.

A frail-looking figure peered out from behind the door frame. He was hunched over with age and his cloudy eyes looked around blankly. Dren was struck with pity. The torn rags would barely have kept the wind off his body.

'We just want to speak to you, can you put down your knife?'

Dren knew the man was no threat to them. His leg was barely the thickness of Dren's arm.

'How do I know you're not going to push me over and steal all my food?'

'Because I give you my word. We just want to talk.'

Dren's words seemed to have the desired effect and the door opened slightly wider. The man gave a resigned sigh and grudgingly let the intruders into his home. 'Whether you're going to try and rob me or not, makes little difference to me. There's nothing left to take.' He gestured into the single-room house.

Apart from a chair, there didn't seem to be anything inside the tiny house, not even a bed. It looked like the man slept on a bundle of straw on the ground. Save for the light that came in through the holes in the roof, the inside of the low house was pitch black which confirmed Dren's suspicion that the man must be nearly blind.

'Please take a seat if you can find one. I don't have anything to offer you to eat but, if you fill up my bucket from the well, you're welcome to a drink.' The man was clearly starved of company and seemed grateful for the intrusion.

There wasn't enough space for five people in the small cottage so Aimree remained outside while Meela made several trips to the well to refill the water cistern.

Not wanting to reveal too much, Dren gave the man minimal details about who they were, concocting a story that they were travellers living off the land. The man seemed satisfied with the explanation and didn't display the expected hostility when the word traveller was mentioned.

Content they didn't pose a threat, the man launched into his own story, clutching the arms of his wooden rocking chair as he spoke.

'I was born in this village and, as I always tell folk, I will die here. Probably in this very chair. In its day, this was a prosperous town. We mined the ground below the hill for minerals. We caused our own problems, really. See, the earth under our feet is riddled with tunnels. And I don't have to tell you what lurks in tunnels.'

Dren vividly remembered the shadowy creature she had seen at the drop. Would this explain why there were no animals left in the fields?

'When the earthquakes struck, we were the first village to be affected and we were hit hard. Night after night whole buildings fell down. Then the school wall collapsed and crushed the schoolmaster. People started to leave saying it wasn't safe anymore, the foundations of the buildings weren't strong enough to withstand another shaking.' There was little emotion in his voice as he spoke. It was as if he had told it many times before and was no longer affected by his own words.

'Those with relatives in the cities packed up and took their young families away with them, promising to return when the school reopened. They were the lucky ones. They got out before it got a whole lot worse.

'Another half moonspan of tremors passed before they started to appear.' He lowered his voice to a whisper. 'At first, the only evidence of their existence was a fleeting glance of something moving through the trees. People started finding the bones of small animals turning up in the morning. Cats and owls, that sort of thing. Then rock rats, forest martins and the occasional octaclaw started turning up half eaten. All kinds of nocturnal creatures were being hunted. But once they developed a taste for human flesh, that was the game changer.'

Dren felt a shiver run along her spine. 'But what was doing this?'

'That's exactly the question we asked.' Although the old man was looking in Dren's direction, he stared straight through her as if she wasn't there at all. 'The only noises that you would hear were the screams of their victims. No one ever saw them coming.

'One morning a mother woke up to find her young son had been snatched from his bed. She had forgotten to bolt his window shut. There was uproar in the town. Bands of villagers volunteered to keep watch at night.

Night after night they patrolled the streets, looking for any signs of the mysterious monster that had taken the child.'

Aimree was silhouetted in the doorway. At the old man's words, she pressed her body closer into the walls of the house as if they could somehow protect her.

'But after a few days, the morning head count showed that one of the vigilantes had not returned home. He turned up the next day. At least, his body did, some way off down the hillside. After that, every able man and woman was expected to arm themselves and take up a torch to root out the evil from the village.' He clasped his hands tightly as he brought the memories back to life through his words.

'For weeks, no one caught anything more than fleeting glances of eyes in the woods. During this time, the creatures claimed another three victims, each one taken without anyone noticing. The bones were dumped down the hillside without a scrap of meat left on them.'

Dren grew cold at this. She had frequently sensed that she was being watched along the way. Now she knew it was more than just her overactive imagination.

'No one wanted to leave but, since they couldn't keep themselves or their children safe, what choice did they have? Tried to convince me to leave too but where would I go? What would I do? I'm an old man now and I'll leave this world alone same as I entered it.'

'How do you manage by yourself?' asked Dren.

'I forage in the woods by day and I lock my door tightly at night. And so far, I've been alright. My eyesight is dim so I can only work for an hour in the brightest part of the day but I think that's what's kept me alive. It seems the creatures prefer the darkness.'

'Is there nobody else here? Do you not have anyone to help you?' asked Seema.

'My neighbours all promised they would return and not forget about me, not a one has ever come back. Only visitors I get now are the soldiers on patrol and the occasional travellers such as yourselves.

'I did have a young man come to visit not that long ago. A nice fellow, called himself a priest. He was my last visitor before yourselves. A kinder man you never did meet. He promised he would visit again on his return. It will be good to see him when he comes back this way.'

Dren felt her blood run cold at the mention of the priest. She thought it kinder not to explain that the holy man would fail to keep his word.

A noise made Dren jump. She pulled back the dusty curtain that kept the light out and saw two crows fighting over a stick of wood. It was too heavy for either of them to carry but that didn't stop them trying to take what had once been part of someone's house.

'It's just me and the birds left here now and they'll outlive me. Smart creatures, so they are. Sometimes too smart for their own good. But take my advice. Do not tarry here overlong. You must be away come dusk. Beware the creatures that come out at night.' The man closed his eyes as if remembering the pain of all he had lost.

Dren thanked him for his story. 'We don't have any plans to return, but if we do, we'll be sure to look in on you.'

But the man with the eyes dimmed to almost the point of blindness was staring straight at Dren. 'The creatures of the night have no use for an old man like me. They feed on the young and the vital and won't hesitate to come for you young ones.' He straightened a crooked finger. 'Especially you,' he said pointing directly at Dren.

CHAPTER 51

They bid farewell to the old man and left him to sit alone in the darkness twitching at every noise outside. It was no way to spend your fading years on earth. But Dren was particularly unsettled by the man's parting words to her.

'Are you sure they don't have special powers of sight?' she asked, as they headed back to the main path that would take them out of the village and down into the next valley.

'Special powers? What are you talking about?'

'You know, blind people. Don't they have some gift that lets them see into the future?'

'I've never heard so much nonsense in all my days. Have you never met a blind person before?' said Aimree. 'Plus, you don't know for a fact that he's blind. Some people do just sit in the dark. Saves lighting candles. And I'm sure he wasn't just talking to you. He must have meant you plural.'

'But it felt like he was aiming it at me,' said Dren. The visit had given her the chills.

'Well it hardly matters. It's not like we're going to ditch you.' She glanced away from Dren. 'Anyway, as he said, we need to get off this cursed hill. Let's saddle up Thunder and get well away from the forest before it gets dark.'

'I'll be quicker on foot,' said Seema. 'No point in me holding us all up if the donkey's not willing.'

Aimree was clearly not happy about this but it was the donkey who had the final word on the matter.

'Where is Thunder?' asked Aimree, casting her eyes around the abandoned village. The field where they stood was quite clearly missing a donkey.

'I thought you had him,' said Dren turning around. Previously she would have been quite delighted to be rid of the smell of animal breath. But she had started to form a sort of affectionate tolerance for the beast. Not that she would admit that to anyone, of course.

'What do you mean you thought I had him? You've been standing next to me the whole time.'

'It's all my fault!' Seema cried out in panic as she remembered. 'He was thirsty. I let him off next to a puddle. When we went to the house, I must have forgotten to tie him up.' She looked distraught. Second only to caring for the sanctity of human life, she took her responsibilities towards the donkey very seriously indeed.

'Don't worry, I'm sure we'll find him. There's not many places he could have gone.' Dren sincerely hoped that Thunder hadn't run away on purpose. Surely Thunder would panic when he realised he couldn't see them.

They split up and walked in opposite directions calling out his name but there was no sign of the donkey anywhere in the village. Eventually they met back in the middle. But no one had heard as much as a snort.

'Hmm,' said Aimree, 'He must have continued along the path in the direction he was trying to take us earlier. They have a sixth sense, these animals. Maybe he's trying to avoid the creatures?'

Dren shook her head in disbelief. Why they let some women be soldiers was beyond her. Aimree was too soft by far. She almost said as much out loud, then saw the two sisters staring at her and, for a split second, wondered if they had read her mind. It was probably best to err on the side of caution and assume they at least suspected what she was thinking.

Now that her disguise had been with her for so long, it was also part of who she was. It had become second nature to see herself the way others saw her. She reminded herself that she, too, was a girl and the things she was thinking about Aimree could easily be applied to her too. She still hadn't worked a good way to talk about who Dren was.

Meela looked around at the stony terrain. 'The ground's too hard for footprints. We're never going to be able to see where he's gone.'

'I don't think he'll have gone back the way we came,' said Dren. 'He was too insistent about going this way. We should continue along the path. He can't have gone too much further under his own steam. I'll bet he's just munching on a cabbage patch nearby.'

'I really hope you're right,' said Meela, patting the thread-worn shirt that covered her empty stomach. 'I don't know how much further my blistered feet will carry me.'

It wasn't like Meela to complain but this had been a particularly hard day. If truth be told, Dren was beginning to worry about how much more misery they could take. Working in the keep's kitchen, Meela was probably used to going to bed exhausted but never hungry. Was she beginning to question whether she had made a mistake leaving her old life behind?

Dren's foot sank into a patch of wet mud. She didn't need to look down to see where the gaps in her boot were, the cold water had already seeped in between her toes. If they had to put up with these conditions for much longer, she wondered at what point the others would turn around and walk back to where they had come from. If she had any other option available, she would certainly have taken it.

Her musings were cut short as they came round a bend.

'Looks like we're on the right track,' Meela cried out. A steaming pile of manure gave a clue to the whereabouts of their donkey.

A high pitched screech indicated that something badly needed a good dose of oil. As Dren turned the next corner, she saw where the noise was coming from. A rickety wooden waterwheel attached to the side of a mill house turned slowly in the low river.

Dark-coloured hens pecked about the yard looking for insects in the straw. It was the first sign of life since leaving the abandoned village and they had no choice but to halt their search for Thunder and seek hospitality. A grain mill meant there would be a market nearby as well as houses. And, if fortune was being kind to them, perhaps there would be a bridge over to the other side. But more importantly, a mill wouldn't be short of a loaf or two. At least, that was the order of things where Dren came from. Surely Arcaria wouldn't be that much different.

'I've got a funny feeling I've been here before,' said Meela examining the giant waterwheel which sat in a shallow channel of the river, bolted on to the side of the single storey building. A couple of cats played outside in the long grass, hissing and baring claws at each other. Whether this was a game or a hostile stand-off Dren couldn't tell. She had always been more at home in the company of dogs. As long as you treated it kindly, a dog would warn off intruders and keep your feet warm at night. Even if you treated a cat like your own child, it would still sink its claws into your bare skin just for fun.

'I can't help thinking I've been here before with my father, back when we sold grain from town to town.' Meela shrugged. 'But no matter. Let's knock and see if we can't get ourselves something to eat.'

Dren was already salivating at the prospect of dinner. But it was Seema who tempered their enthusiasm with caution. 'Do I need to remind you that there's a killer on the loose. If they fled this way, he or she could still be in the area.'

Dren's stomach was preparing for a mutiny if she delayed eating any longer but she forced herself to swallow the hunger. She hated to admit that Seema might be right. But before they had time to decide on a plan, Meela was already running towards the front door, skipping like a child tempted by some sugar vine.

It took so long to get any kind of response to Meela's knock that Dren had started to give up hope. Eventually a key turned in the lock and a bolt was pulled back. The door opened slowly and a tall, narrow woman with a face as flat as a shovel stared back at them. The cats took the open door as an opportunity to scurry inside. Can I help you?' asked the woman, speaking entirely through her long nose.

Peering out from the dark interior of the mill, she scowled at Meela standing in the bright daylight. When she noticed the other three loitering nearby, her face grew even darker.

'I wonder if you could.' Meela began her pitch. 'You haven't seen our donkey have you?' Meela continued without giving the woman a chance to answer. 'Thing is, he bolted with all of our bags attached to his saddle and we've not got a thing to eat. And what's more, we couldn't cook even if we bought more food, the stubborn beast's run off with our pans.'

The woman gave a nervous glance over her shoulder as if expecting someone to join her.

Dren admired Meela's ability to embellish the truth. It sounded just the right side of far-fetched. But would it convince the stony-faced householder?

'I'm sorry but we don't usually entertain beggars at the door.' The woman's tone was anything but kind. 'I'll need to check with my husband but...' She gave another lingering glance over her shoulder and it seemed like they were out of luck. But Meela wasn't for giving up.

'Beggars indeed,' she said with a snap in her voice. 'If you think we're beggars then I'll be having no business with you or your husband. I'm not after charity and I'll bid you good day. I fully intended to pay you back for any kindness. But, if you take me for a pan-handling vagabond we shall just be on our way.'

Meela sounded utterly indignant. She had already proven she was not to be underestimated and once again revealed a shrewd and calculating side. As Meela motioned for the others to leave, the subtle but unmistakable sound of chinking metal tokens came from her pocket.

The woman's expression changed. Her mouth, lubricated by the promise of a couple of coins, mustered up a crinkled smile. 'I'm sorry, I meant you no disrespect.' The fleshy part of her neck wobbled as she spoke.

Meela turned back to look at the woman.

The woman continued. 'I took from the state of your clothing that you were down on your luck, but of course, that's just the dust from travelling. Poor things, you must be exhausted.' The woman beckoned them in. 'Come and have a seat by the fire and get warm. I'll see if we haven't got some bread and cheese in the cupboard.' She pulled open the wooden front door revealing a dark interior behind her.

Dren and Aimree exchanged cautious looks but Meela strode straight in ahead of them.

CHAPTER 52

A few shafts of sunlight made it through the dirty square windows illuminating the dust particles in the air. The smell of damp flour hung heavy in the air and the sound of trickling water was a constant reminder of the threat of flooding.

As she ducked under a low beam and sat down on the wooden bench, Dren felt the hair on the back of her neck standing to attention. She glanced up at a dark cupboard. The glowing ovals of the cats' eyes scowled down from their hiding place.

The woman disappeared through to the other side of the wooden partition that divided the workspace from the living space.

'Who'd have thought she'd have fallen for such an old trick,' said Meela patting her pocket. 'It's amazing how far a pocket of odd metal buttons and some shiny river stones will get you.'

Dren sat on the edge of the hard bench, muscles poised, ready to move at short notice. She felt uneasy accepting the begrudged hospitality and whoever the woman had been looking for over her shoulder still hadn't materialised.

'But how will you pay her when she demands it?' asked Aimree.

'Like I told her when she was trying to slam the door in my face, I do fully intend to pay her. That wasn't a lie. I equally told her that the donkey has everything I own so she can't possibly expect anything right now, can she?' She blinked and looked at Aimree with sad wide eyes, trying to keep a straight face.

Seema looked positively ill at the deception going on in front of her. But Dren knew how much she needed to eat to keep her strength up and she hoped that she would stay quiet. When it came to food, the end justified the means.

After a couple of minutes, a slamming door alerted them to the woman returning. Aimree nudge Meela with her elbow, cautioning her against saying anything further. Their host carried half a loaf of bread and some slices of cheese. But she was no longer alone. An equally tall, gaunt man walked at her side balancing a jug of milk on a plate of tomatoes. The veins twitched in the back of his hands as he set the food down on the dark wooden bench. The woman nervously encouraged them to tuck in while the man peered down at them over the top of his moustache.

Seema was the first to grab the knife and slice off a piece of bread. Greedy as a field mouse, she gnawed down on the dry crust before looking up guiltily from her feast and passing the knife on to Aimree.

The man creased his face up as if he was concentrating hard. 'Do I know you?' he asked Meela in a rasping voice.

'I was wondering the same thing myself,' she replied as she swallowed a piece of cheese.

'Must just have a familiar face,' said Dren with a forced smile, nervous that she would reveal too much.

'We don't get many visitors nowadays,' the miller continued. 'You'll have noticed they don't maintain the roads around here.' He produced a serrated blade from his waistband and began slicing the tomatoes. 'We've been mostly forgotten about since they built the bypass. People can move quicker between the two cities on the highway,' he explained as he sawed through the crust, 'They don't pass by this way anymore.' He poured the milk into half a dozen wooden beakers.

'The towns out west used to have a lot of passing trade. Now, they're ghost towns. The young ones are leaving to seek their fortune in the city. I s'pect that's where you folk are off to, or am I wrong?'

He was probing a little too much for Dren's liking. Perhaps Meela did know the man from helping her father in the grain business, but Dren knew better than to ignore her nagging feeling and there was something about the man that she just didn't trust. It might have been the way his cold eyes contradicted his smile.

'Young folk love the draw of the city, you don't have to be a mind reader to know that.' His wife joined in with a nervous, hollow laugh despite the lack of humour in his remark. A toothy grin revealed gaps in her gums that had been filled in with semi-precious gemstones. It must have been fashionable at one time but her rainbow tinted smile only enhanced the feeling of falseness.

'You said you're from Drabsea?' said the man. 'Of course then you won't be familiar with our ways out here.'

I don't think we said-' Dren started to correct him but

Seema gave her a dunt in the ribs.

The man's words had stirred something inside of Seema. Maybe it was carrying out the death rite but part of her old life was awakening inside her. Her inner mind switched on and she focused on the man standing on the other side of the bench from her. There was a ringing in the distance like a wire being whipped by the wind. The ringing sound increased in intensity until it became a high pitched whine.

Everything went dark and Seema realised it was happening again, that she was unwittingly using her gift and being sucked inside the man's head. She knew it was dangerous but, as she was already in elbow deep, where was the harm in lingering there, just for the briefest moment? If she stayed inside too long, he was going to notice her intrusion. But now that she was inside, she had to leave the ethics to afterwards and concentrate on finding something, anything, to justify intruding into his private thoughts.

She concentrated hard to filter out the noise in the room and sensed that the man was tallying up figures in his head as if he was approximating the value of something. The problem with seeing inside the mind of a stranger was that their thoughts were full of symbols and hidden meanings she didn't have time to investigate.

Although, it was unlikely that the man would notice her soon. He was totally transfixed by a pile of gold coins. A series of numbers raced through his mind followed by a set of weighing scales. He was trying to place Dren on the scales as if trying to gauge his worth. But what did that mean? It wasn't as if he could butcher his visitors and sell them for meat. People in the city weren't exactly known for being ravenous flesh eaters, not to mention they were so undernourished they'd hardly fetch a decent price. Seema tried to shake the ridiculous notion and clear her mind.

The image of a chalice came into his mind. The miller mumbled something to his wife but his words were muffled as Seema's senses were trained on hearing only his inner thoughts. The vision then jumped to a small bottle on a high shelf, stopped up with a cork.

All of a sudden the image faded and she saw herself reflected back in the dark centres of the man's eyes. He was staring straight at her and his wife was gone.

Seema was annoyed with herself. She hadn't meant to use her gift in the first place. After all, it wasn't exactly reliable and she had promised herself she would only use it when she really had to. Did Thunder's disappearance justify the intrusion? She wasn't sure but she felt the same sense of guilt and shame as if she had been caught cheating.

The man was still looking right at her. She had no idea whether he knew what she had been up to but she had to say something and quickly. Her cheeks flushed crimson and she started to sweat. 'Well I'm not thirsty at all,' she blurted out without thinking.

She certainly hadn't meant to say that, it just came out as if she had forgotten to put the filter back on her subconscious.

Dren looked up from the bread and cheese and looking mildly confused at her remark. However, the miller's wife picked that same moment to emerge from the kitchen. And, luckily for Seema, she was carrying a wooden cup in outstretched arms.

The woman handed the bowl to her husband who

took it, cupping his thin hands around the wide vessel. He gave it a sniff. 'Vera, what have I told you? This is far too cold. Good Thwardian wine should not be served at the temperature of stone. Excuse me a moment.' He shook his head and walked off clutching the chalice.

'He's only upset because hospitality is such an important part of our culture,' explained the woman. 'The cup we offer visitors is called a quaich. You'll have noticed it has two handles. It's offered as a cup of welcome because a host can't hold it and brandish a sword at the same time. When the guest takes it, he too must put down his own sword. It's the ultimate symbol of trust,' she said looking at the floor.

The woman's delivery seemed stilted and forced, as if she was just repeating a story. If they had this special cup designed for visitors, it made no sense that she had made no move to be hospitable when they first knocked on the door.

An alarm was sounding in her mind as the pieces of the puzzle started to fit together. What was in the bottle that the miller kept on a high shelf? If she could just concentrate on the images she had seen in the man's mind, she knew it would all make sense. This was one of the reasons why her gift was more of a curse than a blessing. She could never trust what she saw yet she always felt the heavy weight of responsibility on her shoulders.

If the woman hadn't been sitting within earshot, she would simply have told the others not to drink anything they were offered. They were all capable of telling untruths and could have feigned some kind of religious observance. But, on her own, Seema was not a convincing liar. The man was already suspicious of her.

If she came out with any more strange comments, he would realise she knew more than she should have and that could spell disaster.

It was up to her to fix this. She made up her mind to do something quite out of character. It would be embarrassing for them all and there wouldn't be any guarantee that it was the right thing to do. But the journey had changed Seema and there was no going back. This was her chance to prove she had finally managed to break out of the box she had been kept in for all of these years.

The man returned carrying the quaich, hot wisps of steam rising from the surface. Seema closed her eyes and silently counted to three. Saying a final prayer for forgiveness, she stuck out her leg.

As soon as he made contact, the tall man let out a groan and stumbled forward. He could only watch on helplessly as the cup shot out of his hands and flew through the air. A moment later, it landed with a clatter, its liquid contents forming a puddle on the dirt floor.

The opportunistic cats ran over to feast on the spilled wine but the man hissed to shoo them away. Seema detected a look of panic in his eyes. Was it because he didn't want them drinking wine or was there something harmful in the liquid? Again it was hard to be sure.

Aimree looked at her big sister with something akin to abject disgust in her eyes, waiting for an apology that Seema couldn't offer. It was the same look she would have given had Seema hitched up her robes and peed on the floor. All things considered, Seema could just about handle her sister's disappointment. But she needed to convey the imminent danger they were in and worry about explaining her actions later.

The man's face flashed anger but he managed to control it and covered his rage with the flimsiest of smiles. He ran to retrieve the quaich while his wife fetched a bunch of rags. They finished mopping up the spill and disappeared into the kitchen together.

'I think they're trying to poison us. Don't drink anything,' were the only words Seema managed to say before the miller came back out from the kitchen.

Dren and Aimree exchanged a worried glance but there was nothing for it but to wait and see what happened next. They sat in an uneasy lull until the miller's wife reappeared carrying a teapot and a stack of cups on a tray. She sat them down on the faded lace mat in the centre of the table. Her arm shook involuntarily as she filled up the cups with a hot liquid that none of them wanted to drink.

When he saw that the cups of tea were growing cold, the miller filled the silence. 'Say, young man, perhaps I could show you how the mill works. I bet you haven't seen anything like it before.'

The invitation sounded more like an order than an offer. There was no warmth in the words and more than a hint of danger. After Seema's odd behaviour, Dren wasn't in a position to refuse.

Dren nodded politely before following the man who was already holding open the door to the rear of the room. He gave a last glance towards his companions as he left the room.

CHAPTER 53

Dren didn't want to be separated from the group but there wasn't much she could do about it. In the distance she heard Seema give a dry cough. Was it a signal or merely a dry throat as a result of the dust in the air? She hoped she would survive long enough to find out.

As Dren left the living quarters and passed by the kitchen, the floor sloped down sharply. The patches of damp on the wall meant that this part of the building sat below the water level of the river.

The passageway opened up into a dingy basement room. Two massive grey mill stones dominated the cramped space. A gritty residue was left over from grinding down husks of grain although, for the moment, the giant cogs were still. Even without any technical knowledge, Dren could still appreciate the power of the milling machine.

A high pitched squeak alerted her to a rat sprinting from one side of the room to the other, an unavoidable part of building in the river. She just hoped it couldn't smell the cheese she had tucked into her pocket to nibble on later.

'She's a beauty, isn't she?' The miller patted the metal gears that connected the giant crushing stones inside the room to the wooden blades outside.

The rat paused in the corner of the room to sniff about an empty sack, scavenging for crumbs. At the sound of human voices, it looked up, its red eyes reflecting the light let in by the sky light. The rat lifted its whiskers to sniff the air then turned back around and continued its nibbling, hunger giving it a sense of fearlessness.

Dren had had many a fight with the sewer rats back when she lived on the streets. The rodent population felt it had as much of a right to the crumbs in the market as did the street children. You had to admire the animals' persistence. Through sheer determination, they managed to get into the smallest of places and, if you didn't tie up your sleeping bundle properly during the day and hang it up high, you were liable to have an entire family of rodents making their nest in it by sundown.

Dren couldn't blame the animal. She was hungry too. The meagre hospitality hadn't filled the hole left by days of travelling and, after Seema's warning, she didn't dare touch the tea despite her raging thirst.

A lever was sticking out of the ground. The miller tried to pull it first in one direction then the other but it didn't seem to move.

'What does that do?' Dren asked, realising she better start sounding interested.

'It raises up the top crushing stone so you can add the grain you want to grind. I would show you it in action, 'cept there's something stuck in the gears.' He gave another half-hearted tug at the lever then looked at Dren expectantly. 'You couldn't give me a hand, could you?'

Dren laughed nervously. 'As long as I don't lose my hand.'

The miller ignored the joke and continued, 'I'd do it myself, 'cept I'm too big. Needs a nimble paw with a slender bone structure and my boys won't be back til later.'

Dren's pulse started racing. The weight of the stone could crush her arm. She could see why the miller didn't want to do it himself. She unconsciously patted the cheese in her pocket. She supposed she did owe the man something. She just didn't want it to be at the expense of a limb.

'Times are hard and every day these stand still is a day I can't feed my family.' The merchant patted the side of the mill stone. 'It's totally safe, so long as the brake is on.'

'And is the brake definitely on?' Dren cast a wary eye over the mechanism. The teeth would rip the flesh from her arm if she got on the wrong side of it.

'Of course it's on,' he snapped. 'I take safety very seriously.'

There was something about the way he spoke that unnerved Dren. Maybe it was just the way Arcarian people were, but it felt like the man was backing her into a corner. She could hardly refuse this small request and she didn't see what other choice she had. They had just spilled the man's good wine all over the floor.

Then she had a brain wave. 'Of course I'll help you.'

The man's face lit up.

'I'll just need a little help.' She cupped her hands around her mouth and hollered, 'Seema.'

The man's face fell, 'I'm sure there's no need to trouble the-'

But Seema had already responded to the call. The *tap tap* of her walking stick could be heard striking the flagstones as she walked. Through the open door, Meela and Aimree's worried faces stared down the corridor.

'Is everything okay?' Seema asked.

'I'm just doing a spot of fixing but I need a favour, can I borrow your stick for a moment?'

Seema nodded and held out her carved walking staff. Dren knew how much it meant to her. Still, she offered it without a grumble.

Dren took the beautifully carved branch and held it tightly at one end, squeezing her fingers around the intricate designs. Then, feeling like the rodent who was on the brink of outfoxing the mousetrap, she pushed the stick between the two heavy wheels and gave a sharp nudge.

The sound of a metal object hitting the floor was followed by a blood curdling squeal as the machinery started up and the gears began turning. Instantly, the lever gave way, dropping one heavy millstone onto the other, trapping Seema's stick. Dren gave a tug but the stick wouldn't budge.

'Well, that was a narrow miss there, wasn't it, she said turning to face the miller. 'Thought you said the brake was on? I could have lost my arm there.'

'Please don't hurt me!' the older man gave an involuntary cry.

It was a pathetic sight. The man looked terrified with his arms outstretched to shield his face.

Dren paused. She hadn't threatened this man in the slightest. Did she really look that dangerous? Then she felt the walking stick being pulled away from her by the force of the stone. If she didn't do something, it would be ruined.

'Seema!' she shouted without letting go, 'See that lever by the grind stones? I need you to pull it to open the stones.'

Seema rushed over to the wall and yanked the lever. The stones lifted for a split second sending Dren flying across the room where she landed on her back, still clutching the walking stick.

When Dren got to her feet and raised Seema's staff to return it to her, the miller started to back away, fearing that Dren was about to attack him with the staff. Dren didn't correct him.

'Just take whatever you need and good luck finding your donkey.' The man sounded on the verge of tears. He scampered up the ramp. Dren ran through to where Aimree and Meela were sitting with the miller's wife, nursing their cold cups of untouched tea, completely unaware of what had just happened.

The miller held open the front door. 'Come to mention it,' said the miller as the door to the mill room slammed shut behind Dren, 'I think I saw a four legged animal walking by just before you came. It was heading in the direction of the town.'

'Thanks for nothing.' Dren signalled to the others to leave with her.

Aimree jumped up and tried to follow Seema outside but Meela blocked her way as she made a show of thanking their hosts for their hospitality and promising to pop in and see them if they were ever passing by this way again.

As soon as they were away from the front door,

Aimree's rant started. 'So let me get this right,' she said to Meela. 'You saw what they tried to do to Dren and yet you still smile and shake hands then say you'll visit them next time you're passing?' Aimree looked thoroughly disgusted at Meela. 'I don't understand how you can stand to be so polite to a pair like that, not to mention two-faced.'

'Not to mention he nearly crushed my arm,' Dren said, rubbing her hand.

'To be fair,' said Meela, 'We did smash his best wine.'

'Maybe I should tell you-' Seema started to explain but Aimree didn't let her finish.

'I don't know where you come from or how you were brought up but where we're from,' she grabbed Dren and Seema, throwing her arms around their shoulders and pulling them towards her in a vice-like grip, 'we value honesty. You merchants might sleep on piles of money but, morally, you're bankrupt.'

'I'll stop you right there before you go on making a fool of yourself.' Meela straightened her shirt and stood tall. 'That was purely business. You don't think for one moment that I actually like that woman or that I trust her to be a friend?

Aimree folded her arms. 'It's dishonest to pretend you like her when really you don't.'

'And that's how you all operate is it?' asked Meela.

Aimree nodded.

Meela continued: 'And exactly which part of your moral code lets Dren fill his pockets with the cheese of the people you hate so much?'

Dren looked down at the ground. A blush of shame rose in her cheeks.

Meela clicked her tongue. 'Thought as much. Not one

of you declined to join me when I tricked the woman into letting us in.'

'No, but-'

'For goodness sake Aimree! Don't you understand none of it is personal? They have something you want and, in exchange, you give them something they want. It comes down to money, not love. We don't have to like each other but we do have to be civil.'

'Are you talking about the millers or are you talking about me?' said Aimree

'Why would you think...?'

But Aimree had already stormed off.

CHAPTER 54

All at once the mountains came into view. The immense jagged peaks that rose high in the distance took Dren's breath away. No one had expected the journey to be easy but the scale of the challenge that lay ahead was truly intimidating. A low grey mist shrouded the base of the hills in a featureless curtain making it impossible to discern any obvious path up or around it. For a moment, Dren shared Seema's sense of awe at a Creator who had the imagination to form all of this out of the nothingness before time began. Everyone in that small group felt it too, a sensation that the air had suddenly gotten heavier.

Dren drew a long deep breath. Then she shook herself. This was no time for getting all religious. Particularly when she may have to resort to tactics which the church wouldn't exactly endorse. All of her hopes for future happiness lay outside of this narrow-minded Kingdom, on the other side of the seemingly insurmountable hills that enclosed the land.

They descended a hill and the lights from a village came into sight. 'About time too, I was wondering when we'd see civilisation.'

'I wouldn't think about making dinner plans just yet,' Seema announced. She was staring at a piece of paper which had been nailed to a fence. 'Dren, you better take a look at this.'

As Dren read the notice, her heart pounded hard and fast and her mouth was as dry as if she'd swallowed a bucketful of sand. At least it made sense. The miller and his wife were just plain scared of the man on the wanted poster who had been standing in their home.

Never before had she come face to face with herself. There was no denying it was her image that was affixed to the fence post along with her name, height and age, even if it labelled her sex as male. The artist had given her dark hair the untameable strand that defied gravity and any amount of combing. They had managed to find a shade of blue to match her uncommon eye colour. This attention to detail was unnerving.

'They've captured that sullen expression of yours perfectly.' Aimree seemed to be quite amused by the situation, much to Dren's annoyance. 'But I'm just not convinced by the ears. Yours stick out more.'

'Aimree, this is not funny.' Dren pointed along the street to a dozen other identical posters. 'My mug shot is on every gate post in the village.'

'It says here you're wanted for murder, arson and desertion from the Drabsea Army,' said Seema with more than a hint of worry in her voice.

'Plus they're offering a year's wages to anyone who captures you alive,' said Meela with a grimace. 'Usually you'd be wanted dead or alive, but I guess someone really wants to torture you.'

Dren suppressed a shiver. Now that money was

involved, everyone was a potential enemy.

'I get the arson and desertion,' Meela continued, 'but murder?' Her voice faltered, as if suddenly scared by the company she had unwittingly found herself in.

Dren looked at Aimree trying to communicate how worried she was without alarming the other two. Until this point, she hadn't ever thought that she had actually killed her attacker. She assumed she had merely wounded the Wynym when she rescued her classmates.

Why hadn't someone said something? She felt sick to her stomach but tried not to show it. If Meela became frightened she could easily turn them in to the authorities.

'It wasn't Dren's fault,' said Aimree. 'We were kidnapped by a large group of Wynyms in the forest. Dren had no choice but to act to save us.'

This was clearly too much for Meela to take in. 'Wynyms? Why not just tell me he was captured by six inch pixies! Everyone knows that they're mythical beings. But, just supposing for a minute that they did exist, they're half the size of you. What kind of threat would they pose? It'd be like harming a child!' She tutted in disgust.

'Except that they're anything but mythical. The ones we met were heavily armed and extremely dangerous. We were outnumbered and they were desperate men who were willing to do anything to get a ransom for us.'

'Whatever the ethics of the situation, I suggest we disappear and quickly,' said Seema. 'These posters will be up in every shop and a group of strangers will naturally attract attention. If anyone recognises Dren we'll have a riot on our hands.'

'They've given me fangs,' said Dren, still studying the

poster. 'I don't have fangs, do I?'

'I'd be more worried about the nose if I were you,' said Aimree.

'What's wrong with my nose?' she asked ripping the poster down from the nail and holding it with both hands. 'You're right, it does look squashed, doesn't it.' She exhaled loudly. 'Whoever sketched this must have only seen me after I'd taken some knocks on the training ground. Defence was never my strong point. I look like a criminal.'

'But they've got to make you look mean, so that people believe that you could be armed and dangerous.'

Just then something occurred to Dren. 'I suppose Aimree's wanted poster will appear after a few days. I did go missing first, after all.'

'Yeah and you also broke into the Arcarian Keep and tried to burn it down,' said Meela. 'That's certainly one way to annoy the authorities.'

'Only because you told me to do it.' Dren couldn't help but smile at the memory of how they had saved Seema's life.

'However,' said Seema taking stock of the situation, 'Unless you fancy being chased out of town by a baying mob, I suggest we make a plan. It's funny how folk who wouldn't ordinarily take the king's blood money might be tempted by the thought of cleansing their town of a murderer.'

Unsurprisingly, it was Aimree who took charge. 'The safest thing is for Dren to stay hidden while the rest of us scout the route ahead and look for any sign of the donkey,' she said decisively. The others nodded their agreement.

While Dren didn't much like the idea of waiting like

a sitting duck, it wasn't as if she had any other option. It was yet more proof that they should never have trusted the donkey's instincts in the first place, though she avoided saying this out loud.

Seema turned to Dren and pointed in the direction of a field up ahead. 'Looks like there's a barn at the edge of the village. I suggest you hide out there.'

Dren realised she didn't have much of a say in the matter. Her presence would put the whole group in danger and she couldn't be responsible for that. She didn't relish the prospect of her own execution which was, without doubt, the only fitting punishment for the crimes she was accused of. Then she had a thought. 'Aimree, what's to say there aren't posters up for you too and we just haven't seen them yet.'

'That's a good point,' said Seema. 'You better stay with Dren just in case. Stay out of sight and stay safe. We'll be back before you know it. I don't want to lose you again.'

CHAPTER 55

Dren bid farewell to Seema and Meela as they left in search of Thunder. 'We don't want to wander too far from where they left us,' Dren cautioned as Aimree cleared a path through the brambles, 'Or they might not be able to find us again.'

'Never mind that. I don't want to be too close to the road. If anyone sees you, we're done for. We want to have a good view of anyone approaching.'

Aimree fought her way through the overgrown field as Dren followed reluctantly behind her. The long grass was damp from the last fall of rain and every step soaked the lower half of her trousers. Bramble thorns sliced her arms to ribbons. She sighed but said nothing. It was not worth the fight.

A stone barn sat at the end of the overgrown path. It had probably housed cattle at one time. Cows had a notoriously strong kick and anything less than heavy stone would have been too easy for them to escape from.

Aimree prised back what was left of the rotting wooden door and held it open for Dren. The barn didn't look as though it had seen any agricultural use in Dren's lifetime. The thatch had collapsed years ago letting in the daylight that encouraged giant spineweeds to grow. Jaggy nettles and thorny brambles choked the dirt floor.

Despite its dilapidated condition, it was cleaner than some of the inns she had stayed in. Surprisingly, there was nothing to indicate that anyone else had visited recently: no charred remains of fire circles, no discarded food waste, no flattened pile of straw. It was strange that no other traveller had made use of the shelter.

'I can't believe we have this place to ourselves,' said Dren, her voice echoing around the empty space. As if on cue, a noise like a knife ripping through fabric took her by surprise. She ducked as a flock of silverwings took to the sky, startled by her voice.

Aimree laughed. 'Just us and the birds then.'

'But don't you think it's odd that, apart from some birds roosting in the roof beams, no one is living here. Not even a stray farm cat.' The barn may have been missing a complete roof but it was right beside the river. A person could fish, hunt and live here in reasonable comfort.

'Maybe the owner doesn't like folk camping here,' Aimree said.

'If they cared that much surely they would either knock it down or repair it and use it themselves. But why would such fertile land not be farmed?'

'Maybe it's cursed?' said Aimree. 'Maybe that's why no one uses it.'

'Cursed?' Dren laughed. 'Curses are for the weak and suggestible. Come on, let's get a fire going and brew some tea. All these nettles are just going to waste in here and there's plenty of firewood about.'

'I could do with a heat. There's a dampness inside

here that gets into the bones.' Aimree shivered and rubbed the exposed skin on her arms.

'If you gather up these sticks, I'll go out and fetch some water,' said Dren. 'Just make sure the wood is old and dry. Anything that's still green will give off too much smoke and give away our position.'

Aimree rolled her eyes as if to say *Tell me something I don't know.*

Dren turned her back and walked to the door to retrieve an old metal bucket she had seen lying outside. It would make an ideal kettle provided it hadn't rusted through.

An almighty scream pierced the stillness.

'What's wrong?' Dren turned around to see Aimree standing on one leg, frozen in fear.

Aimree tried to form words but the only sound that came out was frantic panting. Slowly she raised her arm and pointed to a pile of wood.

'What is it?' Dren grew concerned. Was she hurt?

'S-s-s-snake,' was all she managed to say.

Relief flooded over Dren. It was only a little reptile. 'Don't worry,' she said with a smile. 'I'll get rid of it for you.'

She walked towards Aimree and bent down to pick up a long stick from the pile. She couldn't believe that someone who had trained as a soldier could be afraid of a creature some people kept as pets.

As she reached down, she stopped. Things were swimming in front of her. She could have sworn that the sticks moved. She must just be tired. Hoping that the spell of dizziness would pass, she rubbed her eyes then stood up and took a step to the side. As she did so, she stepped on a stick. But, instead of snapping underfoot, the stick gave a warning hiss. Dren jumped backwards. The 'stick' she had trodden on was in fact the tail of a snake with mottled brown scales.

The rest of the snake was slowly uncoiling itself and bearing its fangs. Dren looked around in horror. All about her the piles of seemingly harmless sticks were slowly coming alive. The barn was hoatching with coils of snakes the colour of grass and tree bark.

'Aimree.' She tried hard to keep her voice low and calm. 'We need to get out of here.'

But Aimree was paralysed. She let out a soft sob. 'I don't think I can move. They're everywhere!'

She wasn't exaggerating. The idyllic-looking barn was teeming with snakes. Those who had been peacefully hibernating in the shade were now coming alive, and the air was filling up with the sound of their collective hissing.

'Maybe they're not poisonous?' Dren said as a couple slithered towards her inspecting the trespasser who had disturbed their lair. Half a dozen other snakes rose up towards her in a strike position, heads back, tongues tasting the air.

Aware that her next move could be her last, she inched backwards, looking behind her for something she could use as a weapon, praying she wouldn't grab hold of anything that was alive. The snakes' eyes were trained upon her. It was as if they could hear the terror in her heart and they were using it to track her. Every step she took, they advanced towards her at the same pace.

She took another step backwards and then another until she felt her back coming up against the cold stone wall. There was nowhere else to go.

They were trapped.

CHAPTER 56

Brown furrows of ploughed earth stretched outwards from the edge of the path to the horizon. In the countryside, life was practically indistinguishable from work. Each depended on the other. But today the ploughs were oddly still even though there was still daylight left to work by.

'Where d'you suppose everybody's at?' said Meela, expressing out loud what they had both been thinking. 'Sitting on their hands waiting for the crops to grow themselves? As my father always said, an idle tool earns only rust.'

'Yes, it is most strange,' said Seema as they walked through the deserted village. 'Very strange indeed.'

Meela hadn't spent much time alone with Seema. The monk's other-worldly manner of speaking was a sure sign that she had lived a sheltered life far removed from normality. And yet, rather than being detached from reality, Seema had proven herself to be quite practical. It made Meela want to know more. Now that they were finally alone, she seized the chance to satisfy her curiosity. 'Are you really a monk?'

'Are you really a kitchen hand?' Seema replied with a

teasing smile.

'Well, no,' Meela hesitated. She looked down at her feet as she figured out what to say. 'Not really. I mean, it's just temporary. I was born to be a merchant in the family business but my father fell on hard times.'

'So what you're saying is that you're a merchant-in-waiting?'

'No, not that either. I used to be a merchant but it's complicated. Trading is in my blood. Just because I'm not doing it at the moment... Wait, are you avoiding answering my question?' she looked up to meet Seema's tall gaze and was rewarded with a knowing smile.

'Not at all. I'm merely showing you that there's not always a simple answer to a simple question.'

'Oh, I see. But are you really a monk?' she persisted.

Seema conceded defeat. 'Yes, I'm really a monk.'

'That is so great,' Meela couldn't keep the excitement from her voice. 'I've never met a real monk before. Well, not up close anyway. I mean I might have seen one during the Blubberfish Ceremony. I do like all of the ceremony: the blessings, the invocations, the incantations-'

'Not to forget the exaltations,' Seema added smiling brightly.

'But it's not like any of you go out of your way to speak to us ordinary people.'

Seema's smile faded. 'We do tend to keep ourselves to ourselves, that's the nature of the calling,' she conceded. 'But I suppose that's why I was excited about coming on this adventure. I went into the monastery young. Don't get me wrong, it was the life I was called to live and I didn't dislike a minute of it. But as an adult, I realised I'd never actually spoken to anyone from the outside other than the farmer who delivered the milk each morning and, until last month, I hadn't so much as been over the front door by myself.

Meela gave her a look of disbelief, as if assessing whether or not she was going to be a liability crossing the road in traffic.

Their conversation was interrupted by the sound of a drum beating.

Seema inhaled sharply. 'What was that?'

'Absolutely no idea,' said Meela looking about. 'But we better be careful. It's a bit close for comfort.'

They moved over to the soft verge, trying to stay out of sight while avoiding the ditches filled with frogs, dragonflies and knee-high puddles. As the houses came into view, the rhythmic banging grew louder. Up ahead a thick cloud of red dust filled the air, kicked up by the many pairs of feet that were lining the street.

'It looks like an army going into battle,' exclaimed Meela but she could see that Seema wasn't paying her the slightest bit of attention.

'Over there!' Seema's eyes grew wide. 'A bridge! Finally, a way across this river.' Relief flooded over her face. 'We should go back and get the others.'

'Not so fast,' cautioned Meela, grabbing her by the arm. 'Let's find out what's going on first. Dren's a wanted man, remember and there's a bounty on his head. You'd be just as well handing him in and claiming the reward money for yourself if you took him down here in broad daylight.'

The reward poster flashed through Meela's mind but she quickly dismissed it. This was not the time to be thinking only about herself even if the money would come in handy when she started her new life. She was not that kind of person.

Up ahead, a crowd had gathered. Even the smallest children ran from their games to squeeze between the legs of the adults for a better view. Meela and Seema joined the back of the throng. Seema was tall enough to get a clear view over the heads and they could still sneak away when the time came.

A line of soldiers in emerald green cloaks held back the crowds. Beyond them, a formation of soldiers marched down the street in time with the drum beat. Some wore the blue of the Drabsea Keep complete with Winterhawk motif while other groups were dressed in the green of Arcaria which bore the tree insignia.

A cheer went up as a procession of elegant carriages rolled slowly across the bridge. Soldiers flanked the carriages, each one pulled by a team of decorated mules. Seema studied the animals closely but instinctively knew that Thunder was not among them. No amount of coaxing would get him to wear a full harness and walk in an entirely straight line.

The crowd waved green paper flags and clapped as the soldiers walked by. Hordes of excited children snatched up colourful sweets thrown from the carriage windows by gloved hands.

Seema counted at least a dozen gilded carriages all heading towards the Celestial City. She didn't know much about the military but, judging by the livery, she suspected these wagons contained more than just plain colonels and generals. It was definitely worth a closer look.

Seema pulled up her hood to cover her face. 'I'm going to investigate what's going on. You stay here.'

'No offence,' said Meela, 'But you're a bit too obvious,

hood up or not. Why don't I try to blend in with the kids and get a bit closer? Any trouble and you'll be able to see me from here.'

Without waiting for a response, Meela squeezed through a gap to make her way to the front of the crowd.

Seema turned to a couple next to her. 'Can you tell me what this procession is for? I thought the Feast of the Blubberfish concluded last moonbirth.'

The man just stared at her. His wife answered, 'You're not local to these parts, are you traveller?'

'No ma'am, you guess correctly. I'm not originally from here.' Seema silently cursed her thoughtlessness and pulled her cloak closer, wrapping it around her head. 'I've come from the South,' she added.

'That explains it then,' the woman nodded, apparently satisfied with her answer. 'The soldiers are transporting the noble families to the King's Tournament in the Celestial City. A couple of village kids got selected to compete so we're making sure they get a good send off.'

'But why aren't they using the main highway?' asked Seema. 'Surely it would be faster.'

'Same reason I'm going to be notching my belt in come harvest,' said the man joining in the conversation. 'These wretched earth tremors have destroyed most of the bridges and the main roads are impassable.'

'Times are hard,' his wife added. 'We've never known it so bad, have we? You must have had similar trouble in the south.'

Seema nodded in agreement before the couple turned their attention back to the parade.

Seema looked over the heads of the crowd and scanned the crowd for Meela. Just where had she gone?

CHAPTER 57

Meela emerged from the crowd clutching two halves of a broken pie. 'Would you believe it, someone dropped this and just left it there on the ground for the dogs to fight over. I had to grab it from the jaws of some great big drooling hound.'

She looked down at her hand and flexed her fingers. 'Yup, still got all ten.' She grinned and offered one of the pieces to Seema who, after rubbing the crust to remove any trace of canine saliva, took it gratefully.

Seema bit down and the taste of home filled her mouth. The filling was a comfortably familiar mixture of meat and vegetables. As she took a second and then third bite, a thought occurred to her. 'Should we not save some for Dren and Aimree?'

'Sure,' said Meela, her mouth full of flaky crust, 'You keep as much as you want for them. But I figure, it's probably best eaten while it's still hot.' She gave a shrug as she shoved more pie into her mouth, barely chewing as her body absorbed the nutrients.

Seema took another look at her pie, hot steam rising from the filling. She took just one delicious bite. She probably could keep a little piece of the pie for her sister.

She was still chewing and pondering that thought when she realised there was no pie left. Meela was right, it probably was best eaten hot. Otherwise the pastry would have been soggy. She sucked the last of the evidence from the tips of her fingers.

'I overheard some news in the crowd. Apparently they've doubled the security measures in the Celestial City because of some dangerous outlaws on the run.'

'Really? Outlaws?'

'That was my first reaction too,' Meela continued. 'Until I realised they'll be meaning Dren.' The expression on her face grew serious and she took a step closer to Seema then lowered her voice. 'But really, how well do you know him? I mean he is a trained killer. Maybe we should be wary.' She looked over her shoulder as if he might creep up on her at any moment.

Seema took a deep breath. 'I understand your fear,' she replied, 'But Dren saved my life. That's a debt I can never repay. Plus, if I had any doubts, do you think for one minute I would have left him alone with my only sister?'

'True. If he's really all that dangerous, then I'm sure he can find his own piece of pie. Speaking of which, now that we've found the bridge, it's probably time to go back for them. Meela finished her pie and wiped the grease from her lips with the back of her sleeve.

Seema was moving about as if in a daze, but Meela had come to realise that this didn't necessarily indicate that anything was wrong with her. It just seemed to be the way that monks were. The other thing she couldn't help but notice was that, for someone gifted with such long legs, Seema managed to dawdle an awful lot. In other circumstances, Meela would have simply attributed this to a misplaced act of kindness. Because of Meela's noticeable limp, some folk felt they had to slow down their walking pace to match her perceived weakness. But what they failed to appreciate was that, after her accident, Meela had done her utmost to ensure her disability would never give people an excuse to take advantage of her. She never walked when she could run and she never took a seat when others were standing.

The only thing that made her different from her peers was the way that people looked at her with pity and prejudged her ability. But one thing she was well aware of from the short time she had known her was that Seema was utterly blind to social convention and niceties. So any dilly dallying was all about Seema and nothing to do with Meela's leg.

She scanned the crowd around her. Most people were still watching the procession. Although the king's soldiers would have scoured the road ahead for any bandits and thieves to ensure the procession could proceed without incident, this didn't mean that their own onward journey would be entirely without danger. The road may have been safer but the crowds attracted travelling gangs of criminals hoping to cut a few purses or pick some pockets.

Plus, there was always the risk that, being strangers in town, they themselves might get mistaken for common thieves. And worst of all, should one of the townsfolk recognise Dren, she would be considered guilty of aiding and abetting a known criminal and thrown in jail.

Meela took Seema by the hand and gently guided her out of the crowd, leaving the townspeople to their celebrations.

* * * * * *

'Aimree,' Dren spoke without turning her head, 'We need to get out of here.' She kept her voice as soft as she could but the noise of hundreds of hissing snakes drowned out her words.

She had always had an immense respect for the natural world. Dren knew how the beetle and the worm were just as important as the cattle and the corn when it came to ensuring there was enough food all year round. The few snakes she had seen around the keep had been harmless corn snakes which kept down the rat population. They were small and completely harmless to humans, unlike the terror they were currently facing.

Whatever way Dren turned, all she could see were unblinking black eyes assessing when to strike. Dren swallowed back her anxiety and tried to stop it growing into full blown panic. She knew that most animals reacted to movement and could sense fear.

One of the larger snakes slid closer to her foot, its forked tongue quivering, exploring the air, trying to taste its prey remotely. Dren stood completely still. Predators attacked when they sensed weakness. The snake was waiting patiently for the right moment to strike.

Dren made a quick calculation. Those closest to her were too small to constrict anything larger than a small rodent and yet they weren't backing off from the much larger humans. Her internal voice was screaming that this meant they were venomous.

She had to avoid panicking Aimree. 'Stay as still as you can and don't make any sudden movements.'

Aimree couldn't have moved even if she wanted to.

She was frozen to the spot, paralysed by the kind of fear that overtakes the senses and overwhelms all capacity for rational thinking. 'Sn-n-nakes!' was all she could manage through trembling lips.

Dren counted four earth-coloured reptiles who were already too close for comfort. A further half dozen lurked no more than a step behind them. The closest one had started swaying from side to side, its dark eyes glistened like polished lumps of coal but without the promise of warmth. Was it trying to hypnotise her or was it warming up its neck muscles, preparing to attack? She glanced towards the corner of the barn. There was a narrow channel of broken tiles that was currently snake-free.

Dren took a half-step to the side and then stopped. There was no sense in backing herself into a corner. Her best option would have been to sprint in a direct line towards the door they had come in through, but Aimree was too far from the exit to make a run for it, and there was no telling how fast these things could move. The muscles in Aimree's jaw trembled and she struggled to hold back tears.

Dren's main fear was that Aimree would panic and do something unpredictable. Or worse, she would faint. If Seema had been here with her stick, she would have whacked them out of the way. Dren pictured snakes diving out of the way to avoid being crushed under one of Seema's giant sandals. She relaxed ever so slightly.

Dren forced herself to think logically. Being cold-blooded, the snakes must be coming to life as the midday sun filtered through the rafters and heated their smooth dark bodies. The situation would only get worse as the temperature rose and their blood warmed.

Braver now, a stray snake inched closer. Dren felt the rough stone wall behind her with her hand. Could she climb it?

'Do you think you can move?' she asked Aimree, tentatively. The snakes became animated, responding to vibrations from her voice. They started slithering towards Dren en masse. She had no more than thirty seconds before the first one came within striking distance.

Aimree let out a faint whimper. And then, from out of nowhere, the call of a bird sounded. Not just any bird, but a winterhawk, the natural enemy of the snake. Instantly the snakes shrank back, eyes scanning for the danger overhead. The call rang out again, deep and echoing. The snakes decided lunch would have to wait and vanished under every rock and into every available hole.

As soon as the last snake retreated, Dren wasted no time. She lunged towards Aimree and grabbed her tightly by the arm. Together they ran towards the blinding daylight and out of the barn and didn't stop running until they had crossed the overgrown field and reached the road.

Finally she let go of Aimree's hand and breathed deeply.

'Do you think there's someone watching us?' Aimree mopped the sweat from her brow.

Dren wiped her mouth with the back of her hand. She held her hand up to shield her eyes from the sun and peered towards the outer stone wall. But she saw nothing more than trees and shadows.

'I swear I saw someone standing there a second ago,' said Aimree.

'Just the stress of the situation.'

'Maybe,' replied Aimree. But her tone of voice suggested otherwise.

CHAPTER 58

'Get down,' hissed Dren tugging at Aimree's sleeve. 'We need to stay hidden.'

'What we need to do is to make sure Meela and Seema don't end up going into that cursed barn when they come back,' said Aimree shaking her arm free. 'There's no point staying hidden if it means they end up bitten by a snake. Give me a hand up.'

Much to Dren's dismay, she started to climb up a seal-grey stone that stood out on a high point overlooking the road. This was one of the few natural things not covered with a thick coat of forest moss. It was a good vantage point to watch the road from but it left her exposed.

'Pssst, get down from there,' Dren said sharply. 'Someone's going to see you. Plus you shouldn't be clambering around on a standing stone. Those things are supposed to be respected.'

'I'm just trying to get a better look at where we're going next.' All of a sudden Aimree jumped down from the rock as if she had slipped.

'What is it?' asked Dren concerned that she was hurt.

'I'm not really sure,' she said, dusting down her

hands. 'Well, I mean it's hard to explain. It's just-' She stopped herself as if she were frightened to utter her thoughts out loud.

'What?'

'I just got that strange feeling again. You know, like someone's watching us.'

Dren looked around but there was no sign of movement anywhere. 'If you think we're being followed then why on earth were you exposing yourself up there? Why not just paint a target on your back?' Given there was a reward offered for her capture, she was duly worried by Aimree's remarks.

'It's hard to explain.' Aimree hesitated. 'You know, it's like that thing my sister does. She looks at you and then there's this chill inside your head as if she's looking right through you. I don't think she's even aware she's doing it.'

'Maybe it's something they teach them at monk school,' Dren.

'There's no such thing as monk school it's-,' she started to explain and then noticed Dren's wide grin.

'Stop it! I know I'm probably an easy target but I've had a rough day.' She laughed and the tension melted.

Dren looked up as the light faded from the sky. It would soon be dark and there was no telling what other creatures lurked around these woods after night fell. If it was anything like the abandoned village, they wanted to be safely out of the forest by the time it got dark.

'You're right, of course. I'm probably just being paranoid,' said Aimree. 'But I've got a bad feeling. Those two have been gone a long time. What if they're injured? I mean, they're not used to being out by themselves. And they're not exactly soldier material, are they?'

'I'm sure-'

'I should go and try to find them. Hopefully they'll have found out where the bridge is and we can all get out of this viper-infested town before there's any more trouble.'

'I don't know, shouldn't we-?'

'And maybe they've found the donkey. I really better go and help them. I won't be long.'

'Aimree, I really don't think-'

But it was too late. She was already up and running in the direction of the houses. There was nothing Dren could do except stay hidden. She searched around for a hiding hole and settled on a hollow beside a cluster of trees. A bundle of green ferns provided a screen to hide her from view.

Tucking herself into a small ball, she inhaled the relaxing scent of the forest. It only took a few deep breaths before the nagging fear in her head subsided and her lids grew heavy. She hadn't planned on sleeping but the last thing she heard was the sound of birdsong and the nagging thought that she had to stay awake and keep watch for the others returning.

Dren awoke from her feverish sleep with a start. Her hands brushed the dirt floor and she felt earth beneath her nails. She thrust her hands out as if reaching out of a green tomb. Had she been buried alive? Then the terror passed as her eyes adjusted to the darkness and she saw the leaves keeping her safe and hidden.

But the feeling was replaced by a different kind of panic.

Where was Aimree? Why was she not back yet? Her mind spiralled into worry. Anything could have happened to her.

As she scanned for danger outside her hiding place, her eyes were drawn to a large willow tree, bending under the weight of ripening seed pods. It took up a prime position on the edge of the riverbank, its long branches leaning towards the water. Silhouetted by the sky behind, it looked like an elderly figure holding out its two cracked branches to welcome her.

But this wasn't the time for seeing ghosts in the shadows. A distant rumble of thunder confirmed the worst. A storm was brewing. As each successive crash got louder, she knew that it was coming this way. Thick grey clouds in the sky obscured the light of the moon.

Closer by, a twig cracked confirming that she was no longer alone. She called out towards the half-light. 'Aimree?' I'm here.' But her voice echoed around without reply.

By shouting out, she had just ensured that any predators, animal or otherwise were aware of her position. A shiver ran through her body. All around her, moon shadows were blowing in the wind and heavy drops of rain soaked the muddy ground. There was nothing for it but to make sure she was as hostile a target as possible.

Another sensation ran along her skin. It was warm and familiar and she suddenly became aware of her bow, sensing its carved wooden body wrapped comfortingly around her back. It possessed a certain aura that was intoxicating. She enjoyed the feel of having it pressed against her body, hidden under her cloak.

The others thought she was daft lugging it around without any arrows. Deadweight was what Aimree had named it. But Deadweight had already come in handy and it would have been foolish to part with it.

She noticed a long straight branch just within reach. Confident it was actually a stick rather than a viper, she picked it up by its foliage. It didn't bite which was a good start. Working quickly, she plucked most of the greenery from the branch until it was almost recognisable as an arrow.

She tried to sharpen the end to a point by rubbing one end of the branch against the tree trunk. But the soft bark was no good for the task and the end stayed blunt. She examined her handiwork. It was a sorry excuse for an arrow and looked more like something a dog would fetch. If she was going to be able to fire it, it was going to have to look a little more arrow-like.

Another crash of thunder sounded, this time much closer. It meant she couldn't hear whether whatever was watching her was getting any closer.

Reaching into her pocket, she brought out her spark-stone. She touched the tip to the stone and turned the arrow between her hands until it picked up speed and she smelled freshly milled wood. When the heat threatened to set fire to the arrow, she stopped and touched her finger against the tip. It was pleasingly sharp. Then she attached a couple of bird feathers to the tail to ensure it flew straight. Using a fingernail, she scratched a notch into the tail.

She felt an immense sense of satisfaction as she placed the finished arrow on the bow. But she told herself she would only fire it if she absolutely had to.

Peeling back the ferns, she looked out across the dark woods, scanning the trees for danger. If the lightening hadn't chosen that moment to light up the sky, she would have missed the slight movement of a shadow in the woods. Instinctively, she raised the bow and tracked the threat but, as soon as the sky darkened, she lost it again.

Barely breathing, she held perfectly still, her weapon pointed in the direction of her target, waiting for the next burst of light in the sky. Any creature choosing to be outside in these conditions was not something to be messed with.

And then a white bolt of lightening came crashing down, striking a tree in the near distance and lighting up the sky as if the very heavens were on fire. The shadow moved and a roar filled the space inside Dren's head. Time stood still. She felt a whoosh as the arrow shot forwards and she was gripped by a sense of loss which grew.

As a deep hunger gnawed at her insides, her next thought was to fire another arrow but she looked down to see that her bow was now empty and the single arrow was gone.

Then she heard a high-pitched scream.

CHAPTER 59

An imposing monument stood on a raised stone plinth at the heart of the village. Closer inspection revealed a group of chiselled figures dressed for going on a journey. With rucksacks fastened to their backs and tightly laced boots, the artist had captured them mid-stride, heading purposefully towards the city.

Over time, nature and the elements had weathered the aging stone, eroding the finer detail. This made it impossible to tell whether the group was male or female, young or old. The only thing certain was that those depicted in the memorial would all be dead by now. If a substance as strong as stone had become so pitted and worn, what hope would mere flesh have against the passing of the years? The date carved into the base confirmed as much.

Shrines to the dead were not unheard of but they were unusual. As a rule, mourning happened quickly so that the memories of the departed could be released to travel along the river until they met with the keeper of the spirit world. Superstitious relatives felt that preserving the image of their loved ones could hinder their journey from this life to whatever awaited them beyond.

'To the memory of those who disappeared,' Meela read the inscription aloud. 'What's that even supposed to mean? If something's lost, why not just look a bit harder for it? Don't waste your time building a useless statue.'

'Have you ever had a dog?' asked Seema in response.

'A dog? What's that got to do with anything?' She wished that Seema would ditch the riddles and get to the point. But just at the thought, a memory came into her mind. 'My father had a mongrel once. Well, it started off as mine. I found her running loose as a stray. My father kept her to scare off thieves. One day she stole a sack of meat. My father gave her away the next day. He was not one to be sentimental.'

She was surprised at how she hadn't thought about the dog for a long time but now the same feelings of sadness and loss came back to her along with that very familiar feeling of betrayal.

'The thing about dogs is that they understand death,' Seema said, in a soft, low voice. 'To them it's a perfectly natural part of life. They mourn the loss and then they move on and continue to live. But the thing is, they have to see the body.'

'And what does this have to do with the statue?' asked Meela.

'Until you see the body with your own eyes, it is almost impossible to accept that someone is dead. We think we are smarter than the animals with our words and our language but, deep down, we all want to sit by the front door and whine. Without proof, we don't know how to say good bye.'

'So you think that people built this statue to help them mourn?' Meela's nail caught underneath the edge of a large piece of moss. A chunk of the spongy substance came loose. Just like picking off a scab, it came away in one satisfying piece. Then something caught her eye.

'What *is* that?' Meela said, rubbing at the newly exposed stonework with her fingers. A design which had lain hidden under years of mossy growth was now on display.

She bent down to take a closer look. 'It looks like it's some kind of symbol. But it's not a shape I recognise.' Although Meela wasn't the most accomplished of readers, she knew what the numbers and letters were supposed to look like and she didn't recognise this one. 'What do you think it-?'

No sooner had Meela started to form the question than the monk virtually shoved her out of the way.

'What's a rune doing in a village like this? Have you got a knife?'

'Was there any need to push me?'

'Or any kind of blade?'

'I've only got this kitchen-'

Before she could get the words out, Seema had snatched the blade from Meela's waistband and began cleaning some more of the moss from the statue. Next, she laid down her staff on the ground in front of her. Then, with one eye half shut, she squinted at the mark on the statue and stuck the point of the blade into her ornately carved staff and copied the design from the plinth onto her staff.

But their actions had attracted attention. A dishevelled woman made her way towards them, her sandals kicking up a cloud of dust as she stumbled over the path. Dark strands of wispy hair flew across her wild eyes and the strings of her stained apron hung loosely by her sides.

'Have you seen my baby?' she pleaded.

Seema stepped forward to help. 'My poor lady, where did you last see your child?'

The woman's eyes narrowed like a cat's. 'A monk!' she pointed accusingly at Seema. 'You've stolen my child.' She turned to anyone in earshot and wailed accusingly, 'The strangers have taken her away!' Her breath was heavy with the scent of alcohol and she slurred her words. She brandished her fists as she tried to focus on the target of her wrath.

Meela's first reaction was to pity the poor drunk woman. However, the woman's wild cries had started to attract attention from the dispersing crowd. In honour of the procession, most of the village had been drinking since the first rays of morning sun had crossed the horizon.

'Evil spirits have sent strangers to my home and they've taken away my baby.'

Drawn by the sound of the woman's screams, a number of villagers rushed to her side.

'We've not stolen your child,' said Seema. 'But we will help you look until she is found safe and well.' She reached out an arm to steady the woman.

A restless murmur ran through the crowd and the woman realised she had now found an audience. 'Thieves and vagrants,' she shouted as she took a mistimed swing at Seema. Luckily, Seema had seen it coming and was well out of her reach.

Colliding with nothing more solid than air, the

woman stumbled backwards. This was met with a collective curse from those standing nearby who shouted out that Seema had in fact pushed the woman.

Meela weighed up their options in the face of the swelling crowd. Reasoning with the drunk mother was like wrestling with the wind and soon they would be surrounded with nowhere to run.

'I only let her out to play,' the woman's sobs continued. A rock landed on the ground next to Meela, followed by an angry shout.

'They've got Sonja,' shouted a voice from the crowd.

'Please,' Meela raised her hands. 'We've not done anything wrong.' But her voice was drowned out by the angry shouts of the advancing villagers who had both Meela and Seema trapped against the stone plinth with nowhere left to go.

Suddenly, the warning tones of a siren sounded. Immediately, the crowd lost interest in the scene that had been unfolding and the villagers scattered like hares scampering for cover at the calling of the circling hawk. Young and old alike ran at the sound, elbowing neighbours out of the way in their haste to disappear inside. Parents made brief detours to pick up small children but no one gave a second look at the bedraggled woman and the pair of strangers.

'No, come back!' the woman shrieked.

Meela grabbed Seema by the sleeve. 'Run!'

CHAPTER 60

The scream sounded like the cry of a feral cat and, at first, Dren thought she had wounded an animal. Then to her horror, she saw the outline of a little girl pinned to the tree by her makeshift arrow. What have I done?

She leapt to her feet and sprinted from her bolt hole through the torrential rain. The screaming didn't stop. She stumbled over tree roots and pot holes without giving any care to the danger she might be putting herself in.

As she approached, she could see her arrow stuck firmly into the trunk of a heavy oak tree. Despite being rudely crafted, the arrow had flown a fair distance before it found its target. But this was no time to admire her workmanship.

A lifeless shape dangled underneath, both feet suspended off the ground. The screaming had stopped. The colour drained from Dren's face and she felt sick to her stomach. *I've killed her,* she thought. She could see the small figure of a child hanging from a cloak which her arrow had pinned tightly to the tree.

Her fear was short lived, however. A stone the size of

a potato flew past her head, narrowly missing her. She ducked to avoid a second stone but failed to anticipate the third which smacked into her face taking a chunk of skin with it. 'Ouch!' she exclaimed, her worry turning to rage. 'What do you think you're doing? You could have had my eye out there!'

At first, she couldn't work out where the stones were coming from. Then she noticed the bulging pocket. She pounced as she saw the girl reaching in for another handful.

'Your eye?' the girl screeched, quickly dropping her clutch of pebbles onto the ground. 'You nearly killed me and I'm meant to worry about your eyesight!'

'You're not injured, are you?' I'm sorry, I thought you were going to hurt me or I wouldn't have fired first.' As luck would have it, the arrow had missed her flesh as well as her vital organs, merely ripping her clothes.

'Hurt you? Why would I hurt you?' the girl said. Although there was a spark of fury in her voice, she sounded very young. Dren was beginning to realise the power of the bow and how badly this situation could have gone.

She looked up at the girl from her crouched position. Just what was the girl doing out in the woods in this weather? A wave of nausea rose up in Dren's throat and it took all the strength she could muster to hold it back. She spat on the ground then wiped her mouth with the back of her arm.

'Don't you dare throw up,' the girl said. 'Get me down at once!' Then the steel went out of her eyes and she looked as though she was about to cry. 'Please,' she added in a small voice.

Dren lent over her and took hold of the arrow with

both hands. It was pinning her jacket tightly through the sleeve. She pulled hard but it was deeply buried in the gnarled trunk and didn't budge.

Dren pulled again but the arrow was stuck for good. There was only one other option she could see. 'Unbutton your jacket.'

'No! I'm cold,' she shot Dren a defiant look. 'Why did I have to be shot by the weakest hunter in the woods? Can't you just try a bit harder?'

'Take your jacket off or I'm going to leave you hanging there til the bears find you and take you down with their teeth.'

'Okay,' she said, close to tears as her bravado drained away, 'I'll take it off. Just get me down.' As she fumbled with the awkward fastenings, a dozen small spring-apples rolled out of their hiding place and bounced onto the ground one after the other.

'Is that your dinner gone?' said Dren with a laugh as the miniature apples rolled downhill and out of reach. But immediately she felt shame at her actions. She had been hungry before and knew the physical pain that came with losing a meal.

A scowl creased the child's brow as she wriggled out of the jacket and down onto the ground. Knowing she needed her coat, torn or otherwise, Dren reached up to grab it from the tree. At the same time, she felt a sharp pain on her left leg as the child's foot collided with her shin bone.

'You kicked me!' Dren shouted as the girl started to run. The rush of adrenalin gave Dren a surge of speed and in a few strides she had caught up with the small girl and scooped her up in her arms, careful to avoid putting her fingers anywhere in reach of her mouth.

The child hissed. 'Put me down right now!'

'What's that, you want me to drop you?' Dren said in a mock serious tone. 'I can toss you where the apples went if you like.'

'No, please.' In a small voice she said, 'May I have my coat back please?'

'Do you promise not to bite, kick or scratch me again?'

'Yes.'

'Can you promise that again without crossing your fingers behind your back?'

The child paused. Then she nodded and this time it seemed genuine. Dren slowly placed her feet on the ground. The fact that she didn't instantly run felt like a minor victory.

'What's your name?' Dren asked, trying a different tack. She hadn't had much experience with young children, not since she had been one herself. She supposed she might be quite scary for someone who barely came up to her chest. She wondered why the girl was out by herself after dark and realised that, in the absence of any other grown up, she was now responsible for getting her home safely. 'And where do you live?'

The girl clamped a dirty hand against her mouth. It was covered with mud and cuts, most probably from climbing trees to steal young apples. 'I'm not supposed to speak to strangers when I'm out playing,' she said.

'Oh, well in that case, I'm... Artra,' said Dren, remembering at the last second to conceal her identity. She held out her equally dirty hand for the girl to shake.

The girl just stared at it then, reluctantly as if her fingers might go on fire, she gave it a limp squeeze.

'Why do you have a boy's name?'

'A boy's n-' Dren paused. She wasn't going to lie. Her hair must be giving her away.

'Just because. Now that we've been properly introduced, I reckon we're not strangers anymore.'

The girl mulled this over, wondering whether she had been tricked.

Seeing her hesitation, Dren continued. 'But I still don't know your name. I suppose I could call you half-size, since you are so small.'

'I am not.' The girl strained to full extension on her tiptoes. 'My mother says that I'm tall for my age.'

'Well this is my deal. If you don't tell me what your name is then I get to pick one for you.'

The girl gave a dramatic sigh and rolled her eyes. 'My name is Essme.' She continued without allowing for any interruptions. 'You're not from here are you? You speak funny. So does that lady. Are you foreigners?' The girl placed her hands on her hip and looked at her as if aware she was circling the edge of a trap but not wanting to lose the attention.

'What lady are you talking about?'

'The lady who you want to kiss.'

'I don't know where you got that from. Where did you see her?' Had the girl seen Aimree recently? Perhaps her luck was changing for the better.

'Earlier when you two were fighting. That's how you know two people like each other, they're always fighting. Is she your wife?'

'I don't really think that's how it works and no, she's not my wife!' Dren said, with surprising protest in her voice. 'She's just my friend.'

Essme grew bored of the topic and the subject was

dropped.

'Someone's going to be worried that you're not home in this weather.'

'Nope, mama's away watching the procession and too busy sucking on the wine bottle to notice I'm gone.'

A crash of thunder rumbled in the distance, signalling the continued threat from the storm. As the rain battered down, the trees overhead provided little shelter. People always warned against sheltering under trees when lightning was around. Here in the middle of the forest, the advice was difficult to follow. At any rate, it was time to get out of the woods.

CHAPTER 61

It was getting late, and the dank smelling riverside path was in complete darkness. Apart from the odd drunken reveller looking for an out of the way spot to relieve themselves, Aimree was alone. There had been no sign of Meela or Seema. Perhaps this was a good thing. It meant they were staying hidden which meant they were safe. A thought flickered into her mind. How long would it take for anyone to notice if she just kept going? What if, instead of simply finding the bridge and turning back, she crossed it?

She had arrived at a fork in the road. Judging by the noise of merry-making, the wide left-hand path led to the village. Alert for danger, Aimree peered down the lane. In the glow of the far-off street lamps, she could just about make out the remains of a carnival. Discarded bottles littered the path and she could see couples swaying as they walked together, arm in arm. The crowds seemed jovial but she couldn't run the risk of a confrontation. When the happy phase of the drink wore off, it would be safer to be out of arms reach.

She selected the narrow right-hand fork and continued following the river. As she got further away from the festivities, the sound of drunken hijinks subsided and soon only the gurgling of the river could be heard over the nighttime insect chatter.

Overhead, the stars twinkled in the night sky. Had she paid more attention in class, she might have been able to use them to navigate by, but the theory taught in books had failed to grip her imagination. The pin-pricked canvas of celestial bodies provided a map that she could not read.

The cooling air made her shiver. The drop in temperature indicated the dry weather was coming to an end. Before long, clouds rolled in and raindrops the size of small stones fell around her, instantly turning the dirt path into a sticky quagmire. Her feet squelched along the path and the sticky mud meant she left very distinctive marks that could easily be followed by anyone with a less than honourable intent.

The path she took wound around the back of dark buildings. These looked like workshops and Aimree guessed they would be unoccupied until morning or whatever time the workers eventually rose after tonight's festivities.

The village boasted a sizable industrial quarter with weavers, dye makers and wheat brewers vying for space along its banks. Her nose told her that the river attracted anyone who required a quick place to dump whatever waste they produced.

A cold wind picked up carrying with it an unholy smell. Aimree covered her nose with her sleeve and quickened her pace. A shiver of fear ran across the fine hairs on her arms. This was not a pleasant place to linger. Overhead, flashes of lightning illuminated the sky over the forest. At least she now got an occasional glimpse of the path ahead. In the background, the thunder rumbled on, like a clumsy cook dropping a large pan onto a stone floor. This continued for several minutes with the wind gusting to match the ferocity of the thunderbursts.

Then, as the echo of the thunder faded, a rasping sound cut through the air. Aimree strained her ears to pinpoint the origins of the sound. Was it made by animals or insects? She couldn't be sure. But it was coming from somewhere among the tall reeds. They lined the path, tight-knit and uniform like sentinels standing guard, their roots bound together under the river-silt. Buffered by the storm wind, their razor-like stalks swayed violently towards Aimree like hundreds of accusing fingers pointing at her.

Something sharp scraped along the side of her neck as if she had brushed against a needle. She swatted at it with the back of her hand but felt only air. She hurried onwards, pulling her cloak up around her ears.

Once again something brushed against her skin, this time across her exposed wrist. Then it happened again. Could it just be marsh flies hiding in the reeds? She rubbed her arm. To her disgust, her fingers came away covered with sticky sap.

The droning noise increased steadily until it sounded like an orchestra of tiny flies buzzing but she could see nothing other than wild reed fronds rasping in the wind. She stopped at the edge of the path and pulled back a couple of the fronds. Peering into the body of one of the plants, she observed a pair of shoots sticking straight upwards. As the two fronds rubbed together, they mimicked the sound made by insect wings rubbing together.

Hidden deeper in the reeds were dozens of curled shoots. One was wrapped around the tail of a dragon fly, while another held a wasp. She heard a snap and something struck her on the ear. In quick succession, three coiled reeds launched straight for her face. That's when it dawned on her. The reeds were mimicking the sounds of insects to lure their prey into striking distance before using these sticky shoots like a frog catching flies with its tongue.

She had to step back to avoid being struck. It seemed like the carnivorous plant was deliberately aiming for her. Her blood ran cold. The plants *were* aiming for her. She didn't know if they could successfully catch something her size but she wasn't planning to hang around long enough to find out.

She took to her toes and sprinted and didn't stop running until she was out of reach of the hungry reeds. The itchy sticky sap clung to her skin, impervious to the rain. She had to find a way to wash it off before she started to attract flies.

She rounded a corner and to her relief, spotted a solid looking bridge spanning the river. The bridge was constructed on wooden stilts which arched high over the path.

Although she had at last found the way to cross into the Celestial City, she couldn't afford to get too excited about it. Without her three fellow travellers, there was no point in crossing the bridge. She knew she couldn't make it much further by herself. She could only enjoy a brief pause before it would be time to retrace her steps and return to the others.

The area under the bridge was well tended and the vegetation had been cut back to allow access to the water. This should have rung alarm bells but Aimree was too tired to think logically.

She knelt down by the side of the river and dipped her hands into the cold water. The rains had churned up the riverbed and the water was cloudy, concealing all manner of hazards. She decided not to give too much thought to what lurked underneath the surface. Particularly when something resembling a dead rat floated along in the current.

She was so engrossed in washing off the sticky reed sap that she failed to notice the dark figure creeping up behind her.

CHAPTER 62

Essme couldn't have been more than seven years old. She had the look of a child who was used to being left alone for extended periods of time. Grazed knees showed through the cuts of her worn-out trousers. Like most children in the out-lying villages, the skin on the soles of her feet was hardened from running around without shoes.

'Be careful!' Dren shouted as she danced in the direction of the barn. 'Watch you don't stand on any snakes.'

'I'm not scared of snakes,' Essme scoffed, stopping mid-hop. She turned towards Dren to ensure she was watching then raised two clasped hands to her lips. She wiggled her thumbs and exhaled sharply. The unmistakable sound of the winterhawk call rang out through the woods.

'That was you earlier?' Dren asked, surprised by how easily she had been fooled into imagining the presence of the bird.

'I can do all of the animals.'

Dren turned her head sharply to see where the owl was hooting from. Then realisation dawned and she laughed at how easily the child had fooled her twice in such a short space of time.

'So,' said Dren, changing the subject, 'do you always sneak up on people like that?'

'Yes,' she said, unable to contain her excitement at the implied praise. 'I'm training to be a Shadow, like my brother.'

'A Shadow?' This time Dren was careful to keep any note of surprise from her voice. The Shadows were the seldom discussed royal spies. She was intrigued to learn more but didn't want to scare her off with more questions. Instead, she tried a different tack. 'I don't think a girl can become a Shadow.'

'You wouldn't know. You're not a Shadow.' She emphasised the last word. 'And why shouldn't a girl become a Shadow. I'm just as strong as all of the boys and I'm smarter too.'

'There's surely more to being a Shadow than just being tough and clever.'

'Well of course there is, that's why I've been practicing. I can sneak into any room without being noticed and then I listen to what people are saying and I write it down in a secret code so that no one 'cept me knows what it says.'

'Hmm, that does sound pretty clever, I'll admit that. You must have heard lots of secrets then.'

'I have but I can't tell them to anyone until I die because you never tell a secret.'

'But that's not true is it?' said Dren trying to work out how to milk her for information. 'Because a Shadow's job is to find out secrets to keep the city safe, isn't it.'

'Yes...' she said, trying to work out where Dren was going with this line of questioning.

'But how can he do his job if he isn't allowed to tell someone the secrets he discovers.' Dren tried to sound confused. It seemed to be working.

Essme tutted, 'Well, of course he's allowed to tell the important people like the spymaster. And he can tell the other Shadows too. And I suppose he could tell the king if he asked. But he couldn't tell me, even though I'm in training to be a Shadow.'

'But you know his secrets because you're smarter than him?'

Blinded by the praise, Essme kept talking. Dren knew it was shameful to exploit an abandoned child desperate for the attention but she couldn't help herself.

'It's not just secrets. I also hear news. And you can tell news because it's not secrets. As long as it's not gossip.' She said this in the manner of someone older than her years. Dren wondered whether she spent much time with children her own age.

'So you hear gossip too?'

'Yeah, soldiers love gossiping. I've been listening to them all day. Mostly they talk about really boring things. But there was this one group of really stupid soldiers. They were boasting about looking forward to the war. I mean, who in their right mind would look forward to killing people?'

Dren felt her blood run cold. War? That was a concept known only in history books. She had been too young to remember the Uprising a decade before and there had not been any war in her lifetime. Even though soldiers trained for battle, the Kingdom had closed its borders and there was no one to fight except each other.

'Oops, I guess I'm not s'posed to say that out loud. But

that was just gossip after all. Not really a secret.'

The thought that she was failing in her responsibilities as a trainee Shadow clearly troubled her. 'I can trust you, can't I?'

'You told me your name. You wouldn't have told me that if you couldn't trust me,' said Dren, trying to keep her on side.

The young girl mulled this over, deciding whether Dren was telling the truth or trying to con her.

The storm continued to rumble overhead. Then, as if the sky had developed a crack, a great bolt of lightning split the heavens, illuminating the ground and bathing everything with a bright white glow. Essme let out an almighty scream.

'It's okay,' said Dren trying to calm the terrified child, 'the storm'll pass soon.'

But it wasn't the lightning that was causing the problem.

'I can't be seen with a traitor,' she pointed a quivering finger at her. 'You're the outlaw!'

'What do you mean?' said Dren keeping her voice soft as she took a step forward. But this only made things worse and the child continued to back away, her tiny legs trembling beneath her slight frame.

Essme had only panicked when the storm lit up Dren's face. This meant that she must have been shown the wanted posters and memorised the face of the murderer who was now walking towards her. Given that Dren had already tried to shoot her once, her fear wasn't entirely irrational.

'Murderer! Don't hurt me!' she shouted before taking off, sprinting in the direction of the distant houses, two sodden pigtails flailing behind her in the wind.

Dren had no option but to catch the terrified child before she alerted the whole village. This was easier said than done since the girl had the advantage of a head start and was familiar with the uneven terrain.

The ground was sodden and the ankle-deep mud slowed her down and threatened to pull off her boots. By the time they had reached shouting distance of the houses, Dren was struggling to keep pace with her.

And just what was she going to do when she caught her? For a start, the girl could fight like an animal. Dren would come out of this chase in a worse state than she had gone in to it, most likely with teeth marks and scratches to show for her troubles. Maybe she should just keep running and hope she could make it out of town before the small girl alerted the soldiers.

But, just as she was resigning herself to failure, a warning siren rang out over the town, stopping them both in their tracks.

As people started running in all directions, Dren's first panicked thought was that the siren was for her. There was no coordinated effort, just a lot of shouting as people disappeared into doorways. She didn't have time to take it all in when the ground erupted and she was catapulted forwards.

She hit the dirt with a thud that knocked the wind out of her lungs. All around her, ancient trees, uprooted by the unstable earth, crashed to the ground, flattening anything in their way. Then she saw Essme just ahead of her. The gap was closing. Dren sensed her opportunity and, with a final effort, leapt to her feet and surged forward to grab her.

Just then, she experienced a strange premonition, like a sixth sense that she couldn't explain. It was an unexpected sound that made her hesitate and this hesitation may just have saved her life. A dark shadow covered the area where she was standing and she leapt backwards in time to avoid being crushed under a mighty oak which fell at her feet. It had only narrowly missed her.

But where was Essme? In a panic, she sprinted around the exposed root system of the fallen tree. When she made it around to the other side, she stopped dead in her tracks. The small frame of the child lay trapped underneath a branch.

'Essme!' Dren shouted.

'I can't move,' came the weak reply between tiny gasps for air.

The massive branch had pinned her across the chest but at least she was still alive. Dren uttered a silent prayer that she wasn't seriously injured but there was no way to tell until she was freed from underneath the oak tree.

'Please. Help me. It hurts.'

But Dren couldn't even look in the child's direction. Whilst she didn't want to ignore the pleading cries for help, there was no way she could lift the tree by herself. In any case, the accident would soon draw the attention of the villagers and it wouldn't take a minute before they recognised Dren from the posters. This was no time to be sentimental. Dren turned back in the direction of the barn. That's where the others would be looking for her. She straightened her cloak and walked away.

CHAPTER 63

She regretted her decision as soon as she had committed to it. She felt sick to the pit of her stomach and the sensation didn't leave her, even when the child's muffled crying ceased. Her guilty feet felt like lead and refused to move any faster.

Dark figures moved swiftly in the distance, hurrying into buildings, some seeking safety from the dangerous effects of nature, while others threw buckets of water onto small fires.

She spotted two familiar figures silhouetted against the streetlights. Seema stuck out head and shoulders above the crowds, her holy robes billowing as she ran with Meela by her side. Dren rushed out to meet them and instantly her joy turned to shame. Neither of them would have chosen to save themselves at the expense of Essme. And now she was contaminating them with her selfish decision.

It was time to make things right.

'There's no time to explain but I need your help,' she said.

They followed Dren without asking why. Their looks of delight at being reunited were now mixed with confusion.

If she hadn't known where to look, she would have missed the child who was no longer making any noise. More worryingly, she had stopped moving. The girl lay motionless in the earth as if the life had already gone from her tiny body. Dren felt nothing but shame. Was it too late?

'I couldn't lift the branch,' she said feebly. 'I couldn't lift a tree that size by myself.'

But rather than waiting for any further explanation, Seema stepped forward and took charge. 'There's no sense in trying to lift an impossible weight.' She threw herself onto her knees and started shovelling fistfuls of earth with her bare hands. 'The tree is crushing the child into the earth. The only solution is to dig her out.' She clawed at the earth around the child.

Her chances were slipping away with every minute that passed. But, rather than dwell on the unthinkable, Dren threw herself into the task, digging through rocky soil with her bare hands until her fingers bled and her nails were no more.

'We have to clear a ditch alongside her and roll her out,' said Seema.

Meela didn't need an invitation. She had already dropped to her knees and was removing as much earth as she could.

Underneath the oak, the ground was packed hard. They could have done with some tools to help break up the earth. But there was no time for that. What's more, they couldn't risk digging directly underneath the child in case this caused the tree to move and crush her.

It took what felt like an eternity for the three of them to clear enough earth to create a hollow around the child. Dripping with sweat, Seema got to her feet. 'That should be enough digging. If we waste any more time, her life flame might extinguish. That is, if it's not already too late. Dren, help me lift the branch, Meela, you slide the child into the hollow.'

But Dren interrupted. 'No, I'll do it. She knows me. Plus it's my fault she's in this state in the first place.

There was no time for discussion. Seema grabbed hold of the branch that was pressing down on top of the child and Meela crouched down and positioned herself so the branch rested on top of her shoulder.

'Dren, when you're ready, we've got the tree.'

As Meela and Seema lifted the branch, Dren half rolled, half pulled Essme into the ditch. As soon as she was free, they let go of the bough. It sprung back dangerously but the trunk stayed in place.

Essme didn't as much as groan when Dren lifted her out of the ditch. She placed her down gently on the ground. Essme's face was pale as ash. The only colour came from the blood that ran down her nose from a head wound. Her thin arms were scratched with a crisscross of red cuts where the branch had scored her flesh.

'Wake up!' Dren shouted at her, praying that she would give even a flicker of her eyes to signal there was still life in her young body. 'Come on Essme, we need to get you home.'

'Essme!' Meela said. 'We've spoken to your mother. She wants you to come home. She's been looking all over town for you.'

But there was no response from the small figure. Dren couldn't bear to look any longer. 'I think we've lost her.'

Then Seema knelt down and placed her hands on the girl's shoulders. She rocked her from side to side then took a deep breath. She whispered something so quietly into the girl's ear that Dren couldn't make out the words, then she exhaled, blowing strands of dark hair away from Essme's face.

'I swear her chest just moved!' Meela cried out.

Dren looked but couldn't see anything. Had Meela just imagined it? Then she heard a rasping wheeze.

'She's breathing, Seema, she's breathing!'

Essme sat up and looked about her. Then the young girl stretched out an arm and rubbed her head.

'I want mama,' she said in a firm voice. Her lip quivered and she stuck a dirty thumb in her mouth in a valiant effort to avoid shedding tears in front of strangers. Maybe it was the knock to the head but she seemed to have forgotten that Dren was a wanted outlaw and she was supposed to be afraid of him.

'We'll need to take her home,' said Dren, still amazed by Seema's talents. One day she would sit down with the monk and ask how she managed to make the impossible look so easy.

'We'll get you home, don't worry little one,' said Meela.

'Will you tell me your address now that I'm not a stranger and I've saved your life?' said Dren.

Essme burst out laughing.

'Well you're definitely feeling better,' said Dren. 'But what's so funny?'

'You didn't save my life. Those ladies saved my life.'

Dren looked crestfallen. Seema and Meela couldn't keep the amusement out of their faces.

Trying to redeem her self-respect, Dren tried again.

'But if it wasn't for me shooting you, those two wouldn't have been able to save your life so, really, when you think about it, it is all down to me.'

Essme was struggling to puzzle it all out. However, for now at least, the child's distrust was overridden by the trauma she had suffered. Even though she was growing up wild, left on her own for long hours at a time, she needed Dren's help and, for now, seemed willing to trust him.

'You're funny,' she said with a smile and offered out her hand to Dren.

The child giggled as Dren picked her up and threw her up onto the back of her neck, one leg dangling over each shoulder.

'So Essme, which of these fine houses is yours?'

'If you mean where do I live, then it's the brown house next to the bakery. It's not really mine.' She screwed up her face. 'It's mama's sister's house. But she lets us stay there since my father left.'

'Well hold on tight and we'll have you back with your mother in no time.'

A sharp voice called out. 'Just where do you think you're going?' It was Meela. 'You need to stay hidden.'

'We've seen the mob. They'll kill you,' Seema added.

'And maybe I deserve it.' The feeling of shame and self-loathing returned. 'I left that child there, alone and frightened.'

'But you had no choice, you had to leave to find help.'

It was shame and guilt which stopped her correcting Seema. The truth was better left unsaid. 'Look, it's my fault she got stuck there in the first place. I have to fix this.'

Now was not the time to admit the whole truth,

that she had been planning on leaving Essme to fate. That she was nothing more than a coward. She had to do something to regain her humanity and putting herself in danger might just be enough to cleanse her conscience.

'We've got no choice,' said Meela. She stared at Dren with an intensity Dren hadn't seen in her before. 'Let's make this quick and hope we all get out alive'.

CHAPTER 64

'Halt! Who goes there?' The voice couldn't have been more than half a dozen paces behind her. Aimree could have kicked herself. Why hadn't she considered that a bridge across to the Celestial City would have been guarded?

'State your name and your business.'

'M-m-my name?' Aimree turned around very slowly, buying a little more time to think. The most embarrassing thing was that the border guards had always been the butt of every joke in the keep. They were the unit that those seeing out their last days of service were sent to. It was a refuge for the lazy who could manage nothing more taxing than collecting the toll fees. It was not somewhere to aspire to if you wanted to have a successful career.

Aimree had already formed the opinion that the unit would be full of old-timers waiting for retirement while doing as little work as humanly possible. Surely, it wouldn't be too hard to bamboozle this guard with a sob story. But the soldier who had managed to catch Aimree unawares didn't look daft, just incredibly mean. 'And I expect you to tell me the reason why you've been skulking around down here underneath my bridge,' he said through a full beard.

Aimree stood, dumbstruck, unable to think of any plausible reason why she should be washing herself under the bridge in the middle of the night.

'If you were going to blow it up, you've missed your chance.' He eyed up her slim backpack. 'The procession has already passed.'

That gave her the inspiration she needed. 'The procession! Don't tell me I've missed it!' She racked her brains trying to figure out what kind of procession he meant.

His expression softened. 'That's a shame lass, it was quite a sight to see. The carriages were decked out in all their finery. There was even a royal escort, the whole works.'

Aimree still had no clue what this was all about. She had to stall for time. Luckily the guard was enjoying having someone new to talk to on the night shift and he didn't need prompted to keep talking.

'And the athletes are going to do us proud.'

Of course, the athletes' procession! How could Aimree had forgotten that the games were scheduled for next week?

'I've travelled all the way from the countryside. I can't believe I missed it!'

'The countryside, you say? Unusual accent you've got there.'

A warning sounded in Aimree's mind. Was this a test? She would need to tread very carefully. 'My parents were from the south and I've been landed with their accent but I'll be rooting for the team in green, have no fear.'

This explanation seemed to satisfy the man. 'There was a good turn out, you'd have been lucky to get a space by the roadside. Never mind. Who were you here to wave off then? A brother?'

'Oh no, I wasn't supporting. I should have been travelling with them. I'm supposed to be competing. I just overslept and missed the convoy. Do you think I can still catch it up?' Feeling bolder than usual, Aimree embellished the truth a little. Then instantly regretted it as she saw the man's mouth fall open.

'You? Competing! Well, I suppose it takes all sorts. What's your event?

Aimree looked around for inspiration. When none came, she said the first thing that came to mind.

'Archery. I'm an archer.'

The man processed this information slowly. 'In that case, it's a shame you missed the procession. But you might just be able to make up the distance overnight. You'll need to hurry though. You'll miss registration if you don't get to the Celestial City in time.' He gestured over to a set of stairs cut into the side of the steep bank that led up to the bridge and the toll booth.

'That's the quickest way over to the city. I'll even waive the toll fee since you're one of our own.'

'It's very kind of you,' she said as she climbed onto the roughly hewn catsteps that led up to the bridge. They were no more than sharp ledges cut into the steep riverbank.

As she climbed, the wind picked up and she caught the scent of something on the breeze. 'Has someone burnt the toast?' she asked, her mouth watering at the thought of hot butter.

'What did you say?' the border guard's jovial

expression changed as his eyes narrowed.

'I'm sorry- I didn't mean anything by it, I only-'

'You can definitely smell burning?'

'Yes, like toast but-'

'Where is it coming from? Answer quickly, there's not much time.'

She took a quick sniff of the damp air. 'The village, I s'pose.'

The guard looked alarmed. He cupped his hand around his mouth and bellowed orders towards the toll booth. 'Sound the alarm!' Frantic movement came from the small hut which controlled the entrance to the bridge. Aimree saw a couple of stools being carried inside.

'Quickly, come with me,' he said as a shrill siren on the bridge rang out a warning. 'We need to get away from this loose rock.'

When they had climbed the last step, the border guard took hold of her hand. He pointed towards a rock. 'There's a natural shelter over the other side. We'll be safe in there, if a little crushed.'

Aimree was in no position to argue. Giving a final look heavenwards, she saw a flash of light and the sky changed colour. She followed the guard into the cave and all went dark.

The light of a candle appeared followed by another and then another, each one illuminating a soldier.

'Please, have a seat,' said her host indicating a stone bench carved into the wall of the cave. The stripes on his shoulders signalled he was in charge. 'Let's just hope your nose was keen, eh.'

She smiled at the guard but still had no idea what this was about.

Everything went dark and she was thrown violently onto the floor.

CHAPTER 65

Aimree covered her head with her arms and curled up into a ball on the ground where she had landed, waiting to receive a kicking. She had been foolish to have expected them to believe her story. She had learned her lesson the hard way. Next time she would have a story prepared, ready for any unexpected enquiries. That is, if there would be a next time.

When no assault came, she peered out into the gloom of the cave.

This was met with hearty laughter. 'Are you all right down there, lass?' The deep baritone of the border guard filled the small space. 'At least you can have the satisfaction of being right.'

'What just happened?' said Aimree, sitting up slowly.

'That? Strange you say you're from these parts and yet you don't recognise an earth tremor.'

Aimree felt her throat closing and it became harder to breathe in the confined space.

He continued, 'Bit of a nuisance really. No reliable way to predict them but you seem to have the gift. They come from underground, see, from the very core of the earth. I'm told the earth releases a particular odour just before they strike. It's like charcoal, hence the smell of burnt toast. Strange thing really, very few people can detect it.'

'Well, if it's over, I should probably be heading on my way.'

'Oh, I wouldn't do that not just yet.'

'It's just you said I would need to hurry to make the games.

'Like the sergeant says, you can't go just after a tremor, it's when the creatures come out.'

'Creatures?' said Aimree.

'For some reason, the creatures appear at the same time as the tremors. It's nothing to worry yourself about lass, you'll be safe in here. In fact, I shouldn't even mention this but rest assured, there is an extermination program in place. Hopefully they won't trouble us for much longer.

One of the other guards piped up, 'We're usually okay down here because they tend to drown in the river.'

'Aye,' said another. 'And make more work for us. We're forever having to fish the bodies out of the water.'

Although it was probably still safer than being outside, she became aware that she was now trapped in an underground stronghold filled with half a dozen border guards and a whole lot of suspicion.

She didn't trust the soldiers and needed to leave here as soon as possible. But if she crossed the bridge, there would be no way for the others to find her and who knows how long they would wait for her. This could get tricky. Then she had an idea.

'You'll be looking for survivors after the tremor. If you like, I can come and help you,' said Aimree, hoping she could encourage the guards to move outside to give her an opportunity to escape.

'No, we're border guards, clues in the name. See, that's not our jurisdiction. We're just here for the bridge.' There was a round of laughter.

'Aye, help them out once and they'll expect you to do it again. Then before you know it, we're not just patrolling the border but halfway down the town too.'

'It's just I thought that you were sworn to protect human life-'

'Dinnae worry lass, you don't need to understand how it works.' The old sergeant frowned. 'We've got the benefit of years of experience behind us. We know what's best.'

'You're welcome to stay, though,' said another one of the guards from behind his candle. 'That nose is a handy tool to have around. It means the villagers get some warning when we sound the alarm.'

'I'm sure it's not just her nose that would be good to have. Just look at h-'

'Thanks really,' she said not wishing to hear which of her attributes he was going to comment on. 'I'm flattered but I've got to get to the games.' She wished she hadn't gone off on her own looking for the others.

'Ah, these games,' said the sergeant rubbing his beard. 'Well now, I've been wondering about that. You say you're an archer but I can't help but wonder where your bow is?'

'My bow?' Aimree's mind raced to find an explanation but the guard had caught her out. She clearly hadn't given enough thought to her story.

'Come on now,' he said with a menacing smile. 'You dinnae take me for a fool do you? How can you be competing in a tournament without any equipment? You're never from round here and I doubt if anyone about here knows your family. You a traveller or a runaway?'

Aimree tried to muster all of her military training and keep her face unreadable. The man was just bluffing, she told herself.

'I admire your attention to detail. I bet you also noticed my nails are too long to draw a bow.'

The man looked at her hands. It was a valid point. They had grown rather long over the time she had been away from the keep.

'You see, it's a tradition that we don't cut them until the night before we compete. It's silly really, but you know how superstitious athletes can be.' She could tell he wasn't swallowing this but she had run out of excuses. She couldn't see any way out except by buying more time.

Then the sound of a small explosion echoed under the bridge, startling a swarm of bats that had been roosting in the wooden rafters.

'You stay with me.' The sergeant pointed a finger at her chest and gave her a look that implied she was somehow responsible.

'Troops, it's time to get to work. We're under attack!'

CHAPTER 66

Mama!' the child started wailing and wouldn't stop. Dren tried to shush her but, as they walked through her half-destroyed village, Essme became more and more vocal.

It wasn't hard to understand why she was so unsettled. There was scarcely a building left intact. Broken branches littered the paths along with debris from damaged houses. It was as if a giant had rampaged through the town, breaking anything in sight.

'I want mama!'

The shrieking had reached a pitch where it could cause serious hearing damage to those in range. As a soldier, she was well out of her comfort zone. She had no idea how to calm a distressed child. Did you give it something to eat? Or maybe she wanted a toy. In reality, it would be easier to put a dark sack over her head and hope she fell asleep but that was likely more suitable for caged songbirds than children. Plus she didn't have a big enough sack.

'Give her here,' said Seema. She stretched out her arms and Dren passed the small child over. Instantly the child stopped crying as she nestled into her neck.

Relief flooded over Dren. As sympathetic as she was trying to be, she didn't want their little group to attract any unwanted attention. She pulled the hood of her cloak up tightly around her face.

'Just tell me where to go and we'll get you home little one, I promise.' Seema instinctively spoke to the child in a tone she understood.

'Are you from the south too?' said Essme once she had wiped the tears from her eyes.

'What makes you say that?' said Seema.

'The posters say he came from the Winterhawk Keep,' said Essme using the local nickname. She turned back to Seema. 'Do you come from there too?'

'You managed to read that all by yourself?' asked Seema giving Dren a worried look.

'Not all of it but some of it. Mama helped read it to me. She said I need to keep myself safe.'

'It sounds like your mama is a very sensible lady.'

The child sniffled. 'I want mama.'

The mournful tone would have been enough to soften the hardest heart given any other set of circumstances. But this child presented the greatest danger they had faced recently. The girl sucked on her thumb, content for the moment to nuzzle her face into Seema's shoulder.

While Seema struggled with the weight of the child, Dren was burdened with darker thoughts. Was the child going to turn her in? And not just her but the others too. What if she had just left Essme under the tree? No matter how hard Dren tried to bury the thought, the darkness still lurked there just under the surface.

Small towns could quickly turn hostile. It didn't take much for a crowd to form. Before long even elderly grandparents could be out on the street brandishing pitchforks and flaming torches. However, Dren's overriding concern now wasn't for her own safety. Rather, it was for Aimree who was probably still searching for her by the snake infested barn.

'We should go back to the forest and wait for daylight. Aimree will be looking for us.'

'No!' Essme shouted, blinking hard. 'We can't go back that way, it's not safe,' she said, her voice muffled with the fabric.

'What are you saying?' said Dren, 'What do you mean we can't go back?'

She looked up. 'You can't go back to the woods, not after dark.' Her voice lowered down to a whisper. 'That's when the creatures come out.'

Were her fears grounded in more than just childish imagination? The warning echoed what the blind man on the hill had been describing. The terror in her big brown eyes looked real enough to unsettle Dren. She tried to probe further but all she got was a whimper in response to her questions before she returned her face to the thick fabric of Seema's cloak.

'Thank you,' said Seema, trying to sooth the child's fears, 'you've been a good help to us.'

'I didn't help you!' said Essme punching Seema's shoulder with her tiny fists.

'But of course you helped us.' Seema held her tightly to stop her wriggling loose from her arms. 'Without you sharing your knowledge we could have been devoured by a creature in the woods.'

The mention of this act of kindness seemed to worsen the child's anxiety. 'I promise I won't tell anyone I saw you.' Her voice wavered. 'I don't think you're bad.

You can't be that bad if you helped me. But you can't tell anyone that I helped you.' She trembled as Seema held her tightly. Essme burst into tears. 'I don't want to go to prison.'

'What do you mean?' asked Seema.

The girl sniffed and wiped her nose with a dirty sleeve. 'When Mama read the poster, she said anyone who helped the man would go to jail and now I've gone and helped you. So if you told anyone I helped you avoid the monsters I would go to jail.'

Dren smiled at the child's logic. That fear might just be strong enough to ensure they got out of here alive. She turned to Essme who was still cowering in Seema's arms. 'I think the safest thing for you is if we disappear, wouldn't you agree?' She could see Essme doing the calculations in her head. 'And I reckon, if we don't tell you where we're going then you can't be accused of helping us anymore.'

She frowned in solemn concentration. 'But you'll help me find my mama first? It's not against the law if you help me, is it?' She looked at Dren, her young eyes full of fear.

'That's a fair point you make, young lady. There's nothing in there says I can't help you.' Dren reached over and took one of her tiny hands and shook it to confirm the agreement.

'Then we have a deal. I'll help you find your mama.' She lowered her voice to a half whisper. 'And I won't tell anyone you might have helped us a teeny tiny little bit.' Dren was relieved to see the cheeky smile had returned.

CHAPTER 67

They walked towards the centre of town, Seema still carrying the child in her arms. Dren looked for the landmarks that the child had mentioned. The town had changed after the quake and her directions were no longer up to date. Eventually, they found the bakery by the carved sign depicting a hearty loaf. But something was obviously missing.

There was no house beside the bakery. At least, nothing that would be recognisable as a building. All that remained were the ruins of what must have been Essme's house. It could best be described as a gap since it was nothing more than a higgledy-piggledy pile of logs liable to roll and crush a person at a moment's notice. Despite this threat, townsfolk hurried to free whoever might be buried inside, clambering over rubble and lifting the logs which only moments before had been walls and a roof.

Dren leapt in front of Seema, trying to block Essme's view so she wouldn't see what had happened. But the child's eyes were keener than Dren's tired legs. She immediately spotted what was wrong with the scene and tried to wriggle out of Seema's arms. But the monk held her tightly against her chest.

'Let me go!' she sounded indignant.

'Stay here, it's not safe.'

'I have to go and see.'

'Don't worry, I'm sure they won't be long in finding your mother,' Seema crossed her fingers in hope.

'Oh, mama won't be in there.' The scorn in her voice took Seema by surprise.

Seema paused. 'I'm sure your mother-'

'Mama is not in there! If anyone is crushed, it'll be my aunt,' her tone was scornful. 'Let me go!'

'Well, if your aunt is in there, I'm sure your neighbours are doing all they can to get her out. Listen, I know you want to help but you're safer over here.'

'I don't want to help get her out, I want to check she's really dead.'

'I don't understand.' Seema made a face as if the child had bitten her.

'My aunt was mean. And she was too stubborn to leave her house when she heard the siren in case thieves stole her valuables. I won't miss her. And Mama's not daft enough to stay inside a rickety old house when the ground is shaking. She's probably out looking for me.

'Well, even if you're right, I'm not sure you should be so happy about your aunt being crushed to death under the weight of her own house. Even if she was mean,' said Seema. She recalled the woman she had seen earlier in town and suddenly it all made sense. 'Essme, do you know how to get to the statue from here?'

'The walking people statue? Of course I know where it is. I know where everything is in the town.'

'Can you show me it? I think I know where your mother might be.'

Essme nodded. She jumped down from Seema's shoulders and pointed northwards.

'Essme, do you know the story behind the statue?' asked Seema.

'Mama says it's a warning, not to run too far from the town, or you won't come back.'

'And who were the people?'

'Mama calls them idiots. They wanted to climb over the mountains but they never came back.'

Dren felt a chill run through his body. Whether this was just a story told by an anxious parent to a wandering child, it hit too close to home to be dismissed.

With the help of Essme's directions, they found a town square in disarray. The statue was lying on its side.

Before Dren could probe any further, a woman's panicked cry called out Essme's name. Essme slipped free from Seema's grasp and ran the length of the town green to find her mother. Seema, Dren and Meela crouched down out of sight behind the statue and watched as a woman covered in a film of grey dust picked up the little girl and kissed her on the forehead.

Hand in hand, mother and daughter walked off together. Essme didn't so much as glance back. It seemed that, for now at least, she was keeping to her word.

Dren looked at the fallen statue. Was the story merely a parent's warning to an errant child? Then Meela reminded them of their priorities.

'Aimree's been away a long time.'

'Yes,' Seema agreed. 'It's time for us to get out of here.'

They hadn't bumped into her in the town which

hopefully meant she had found the bridge and was waiting for them. Either that or she was back in the woods by herself. Dren put the thought away to the back of her mind. She knew Aimree was more than capable of surviving on her own but there was no question of leaving without her.

They came to an uprooted signpost that pointed to the Celestial City. This meant a crossing. If Aimree had seen this, there was a chance that she would have gone that way to look for a bridge.

'What way do you think it's meant to point?' asked Meela.

'It's hard to tell,' said Seema. 'There's an opening down there, looks like it leads to the river.'

'No, that's not it,' Meela shook her head. 'You'd never get a cart down there. We should go the way the procession went earlier. That's where we saw the road bridge.'

'Far too dangerous,' said Seema. 'We'd be spotted a mile off. We'd be better off going towards the river and follow it till we get to the bridge.'

The path down to the river looked dark and uninviting and Meela didn't look happy at being overruled. 'Better just hope she's down there then.'

Oblivious to her tone, Seema just nodded and they set off at a quick pace.

The earth tremor had been powerful, breaking up the ground and covering buildings with a coating of fine dust. Fearing secondary tremors, residents only emerged from their houses to pour buckets of water over small fires, a major hazard of living in the woods.

Those who didn't have to venture out again remained inside, at least until first light when they could look for damage in the daylight.

'Did I ever tell you the story of how I met Seema?' said Dren as they walked.

'Yes, Meela replied. 'Several times.'

'I had to rescue her from a sinkhole caused by a tremor,' Dren continued, ignoring her sarcasm.

'I thought it was only a small crater!'

'We should be thankful for the earth tremors, really,' said Seema, before Dren had a chance to think up a reply, 'Otherwise we would never have met.'

'That, I can agree on.' Dren gave a sniff to clear the dust which tickled the inside of her nostrils.

'Are you coming down with something?' Seema touched the back of her hand to Dren's forehead. 'You don't seem feverish.'

'I'm not ill,' Dren sniffed again, suppressing a sneeze. Then she rubbed her eyes which were full of grit. 'It's just all the dust in the air.'

They followed the dirt track down to the water's edge. The river was high and full of debris. Whole trees floated on the current alongside all manner of unidentifiable rubbish. She hoped that Aimree hadn't been close to the water when the quake had struck. Surely she possessed the common sense to move away from the hazard and had managed to find shelter in time.

'Watch your step along here,' said Dren, avoiding a couple of cracks that had opened up along the river bank. By now it was so dark, it was almost impossible to find a safe path.

'Should we find somewhere to sleep for the night and continue at first light?' said Meela.

'No!' said Dren. Her nose was so stuffed up from the

dust that the words sounded strange in her mouth. 'We need to find Aimree.'

'I'm not saying we abandon her.' Meela forced a smile. 'But we'll be no use to her if we end up taking a tumble into the river. It's flowing so quickly you'd never make it out again.'

'Ou can give up if 'ou 'ave 'oo,' said Dren, struggling to breath. She gave a sniff to clear her nose. 'But I'm not quitting until I've found her. I'd never forgive myself if something happened to her while we were sleeping.'

Her perseverance was rewarded around the next corner as the dark shape of the bridge loomed overhead.

'Ook, the bridge!' Dren exclaimed with the smug look that came with winning an argument.

'Keep quiet for goodness sake, you don't know who's up there,' said Meela sharply as they hurried towards a set of stairs that had been cut into the embankment.

'Achoo!' The sneeze crept up without any warning and took Dren by surprise as the force cleared out her tubes. The sound reverberated under the bridge startling a colony of roosting bats.

CHAPTER 68

Before long, the guards who had been sent to investigate the noise came back. And they weren't empty handed. Aimree could see the lead guard was dragging something behind him. He had a strangely triumphant expression on his face.

As the lamp light illuminated his catch, Aimree felt a knot of terror in her stomach. Three figures followed behind the guard in single-file. They were tethered together with a length of rope looped tightly around their wrists. If one fell forward, she would pull the other two to the ground.

Aimree could clearly see Meela and Seema along with a third figure sandwiched in the middle. The figure was wearing their hood up but, from the height and build, she was pretty sure it was Dren. Aimree shuffled nervously as the sergeant examined the three prisoners. Would he recognise Dren from the wanted posters?

'Caught these three lurking under the bridge,' the guard said, patting the tree insignia on his chest with his gloved hand. 'Would you believe it, they tried to bribe me so I wouldn't turn them in?'

The sergeant tutted his disapproval.

'I mean, what do you take me for?' said the guard, speaking more for the benefit of an audience than his captives. 'A beggar holding out his hand for a couple of coins?'

Seema blushed. 'I apologise for my clumsiness. I meant no harm.'

'You may call it clumsiness, but in this part of the world, we call it a criminal offence,' said the guard, no hint of compassion in his voice. Clearly this man played by the rules and Seema had put her foot in it.

This wasn't looking good for any of them. Aimree had to do something.

'Untie them at once,' she said, addressing the guard. 'Unless you want our city to lose out on a medal?'

The sergeant looked confused. 'What do you mean? Do you know these prisoners?'

'Do I know them? That's my training team you've captured there. They've been carrying my bow and the rest of my supplies.'

'But if you're an athlete, why can't you just carry it yourself?' the sergeant's voice had an edge of suspicion.

'I wouldn't expect you to understand.' Her voice softened. 'You are twice my size after all. But, when you're as short as I am, you have to save your energy for the competition. I'm not allowed to carry any weight other than my small backpack.'

She saw the sergeant weighing up whether there was any truth in her words.

'You asked me earlier why I didn't carry a bow. I didn't want you to think I was lazy.' She turned to Dren. 'You there! Show the man my bow.'

The guards put their hands to their swords but the sergeant waved at them to stand down. He nodded at the guard who was holding the rope that chained the three together.

'Untie them!'

The gruff man did as he was told and released the three prisoners, although his body language warned them not to take another step.

Aimree watched Dren remove his cloak and lift the heavy wooden bow over his head.

'Give it over boy, the sergeant's waiting,' said the guard.

Dren hesitated until Aimree interjected. 'He's really not supposed to let it leave his possession.' She smiled apologetically. 'Not until I need it for the competition, at any rate.'

The sergeant's gaze lingered over Dren a little longer than was comfortable. Could he be wondering why his face seemed familiar?

'What do you need the other two for?'

'The others, right, well...' Aimree thought for a moment. 'The tall one is my medic. She heals my muscles between competitions. The smaller one does my cooking. I have a very specific diet when I'm competing.'

'I've never heard the likes of it.' The sergeant shook his head. 'You mean to say you can't carry your own bow or make a pot of soup? The whole point of firing the bow is to catch your dinner!'

Aimree's nerve teetered on the edge. Had she gone too far with this?

But the sergeant's laughter broke the tension. 'Well well. It's certainly changed a lot since I was a boy. Back then we had no more training than a slap on the back of the head when we missed the target. I remember when we had to make our own bows by bending water cane. None of your fancy wood carved technology.' He chuckled and shook his head. 'Now they can't so much as carry their own bows! We're living in strange times. But I don't want it to be said that the border guards got in the way of your victory, so let's see if we can't get you into the city in time for registration.' He signalled to one of the guards who nodded before disappearing out of sight.

Aimree muttered a silent prayer of thanks to a god she hadn't previously had much regard for. Could she just have pulled off the greatest deception of her life? Aimree was thoroughly embarrassed. She should have been more careful. She hated it when others had to step in to rescue her.

The sound of a cart rumbled towards them. Could they be getting a free ride to the city? She could think of nothing better. This would make up for the humiliation of being rescued by Aimree.

But the inward celebration turned to horror as the van appeared from around the corner. It was indeed a mule-drawn carriage but the windows were covered in iron bars and the door was padlocked shut. There was no mistaking it. This was a jail cart.

To make matters worse, Aimree recognised one of the donkeys pulling the cart. Thunder was harnessed alongside another donkey. The animal's eyes stared downwards and didn't give even a flicker of recognition. Aimree felt sick to the depths of her stomach. The guards must have crushed the animal's spirit to get him into the harness, never mind have him actually pull the cart. He looked as downtrodden as Aimree felt inside.

Aimree wasn't able to hide her face. The sergeant saw

her look of disgust but misidentified the source.

'The last mule went lame,' he explained. 'This one's not much better. He's new so he's not yet used to the feel of the cart but don't worry, it'll be a smooth ride. It's amazing how quickly they learn when they're hungry. This one's surprisingly compliant when he wants to be.'

He brought the whip down on Thunder's flanks. Aimree winced in sympathy but managed to avoid crying out. There was not one hint of protest as the donkeys turned the cart until the padlocked door was facing the sergeant.

The sergeant produced a key from a chain around his belt and opened the door of the prison van. The cage door swung open and the sergeant held out his arm, gesturing for them to climb in. Although they weren't chained together, Aimree didn't doubt they were no longer free.

The sergeant sensed her hesitation. 'I know it's probably not the comfort that you're used to but it's the only transport we have available at short notice. The rest of the troops are part of the convoy taking participants and officials to the tournament. Watch your head as you get in.'

With no other option, Aimree ducked as she led the way. Dren followed and sat down beside her, positioned away from the mesh hatch that afforded those up front a view of the prisoners. Meela and Seema took the seats opposite. The lock clicked into place as the door swung shut behind them. The whole coach shook as the sergeant jumped into the front passenger seat. He uttered a command and the coach started on its way.

To say that it didn't smell fresh inside the small cell would have been an understatement. Previous occupants had been less than fastidious about their hygiene and Aimree suspected that the odour of urine wasn't coming from the donkeys. She tried her best not to touch the insides of the cage with her bare hands. The names of former prisoners were etched in scrawling letters on the hard wooden bench, as a reminder of the time spent here against their will.

The coach turned onto the highway. The sound of gravel rumbling beneath the wheels set Aimree's teeth on edge but it did give a brief window of privacy where they could talk without fear of being overheard by the guards.

'I know I've gotten you back behind bars again, but aren't you the tiniest bit glad to see us?' Dren said, trying to inject a little bit of poorly-timed humour into the situation. It was the wrong thing to do.

Aimree nearly exploded. 'I expected my sister to have a moral compass that pointed somewhere above the average petty thief. But bribing guards? I had the situation under control. If it hadn't been for *her*,' she pointed a finger at her sister, 'We would have been on our way by now.'

Dren tried to play peacemaker. 'But what choice did she have? We didn't know where you were?'

Aimree was in no mood to listen to reason. 'Where did a poor monk get so much money anyway? I thought you were meant to live a life free from material possessions and yet you have so much money you can afford to make some really poor decisions and still have change left over!'

Seema spoke for the first time since being inside the prison van. 'It's quite embarrassing, really.' She looked up awkwardly at the other three. 'People like to donate to the monastery. I suppose it appeases their conscience. You think I'm generous with my money? You should see just how generous people can be when they've had an affair with a neighbour or pushed a relative down a flight of stairs.

'Does that happen?' said Meela.

'It did once,' said Seema, not expanding further.

'I've heard that, if someone confesses to you that they've murdered someone, you're sworn to secrecy,' said Dren. 'Is that really true?'

'Well now, that depends-'

That's not the point,' Aimree cut Dren off. 'Seema had no right to do what she did, flashing her cash around when we just needed to talk our way out.'

'Can we please just stop?' said Meela. 'Seema has bought us some time. We need to acknowledge that for what it is and spend our efforts on working out our next move rather than on bickering.'

'I'm sorry but there are principles at stake here and she has crossed a line.' Aimree wasn't about to let go of her argument without a good fight.

'It's all very good and proper having principles,' Meela countered.

'Yes but-'

'But it's no good staying true to your principles if it means that you die and take us down with you.'

'Don't you see-'

'What good does it do if you take your principles to the grave? All very noble but not much use to anybody.'

Aimree had run out of fight. She sulked but didn't fire back.

'Look at it this way,' Meela continued. 'There's a bigger principle at stake in all of this. It's called self-preservation. Animals understand it. You just have to look at Thunder. He knows how important it is to cling onto life for as long as you can, even if it means putting up with the harness for a while. The guards'll probably just issue us with a hefty fine and we'll get to walk away with nothing worse than a lightening of our purses.'

'Why would we get a fine?' asked Seema.

'You don't think they're going out of their way for nothing, do you? Did they strike you as being particularly public spirited?

'I suppose they-'

'No, they're not doing this because they're generous. Since we offered them a bribe, they suspect we're wealthy. It'll cost us but we should get out of this unharmed.' Meela sat back against the hard bench.

Aimree wasn't so sure but she let the subject drop and gazed out at the dark landscape through the window bars. No one had the appetite for small talk.

CHAPTER 69

The fields of the countryside soon gave way to buildings. Densely packed neighbourhoods swallowed up every available piece of ground in the approach to the city.

After what seemed like an eternity, they finally entered the city walls. Dren had never come face to face with so many people in one place before. Despite the late hour, people wove in and out of the traffic like a swarming ant colony. She pulled her cloak even higher up around her ears and sank down in her seat. Judging by the glazed-over eyes and the way they weaved dangerously close to the wheels of the moving wagons, there was little chance of any of the revellers recognising Dren from the wanted posters. Still, it was best to take precautions. Just because the border guards hadn't recognised her didn't mean she was safe here.

There was no time for sleep in a city preparing to welcome in the games. In spite of the evening's earth tremors, business carried on regardless, with traders selling all manner of goods. Mountains of fried food were sold from the back of hand drawn carts while coopers rolled ale barrels along the street to ensure the drinkers didn't go thirsty. Messengers dressed in velvet cloaks hurried between doorways carrying bundles of rolled up parchments while soldiers in black leathers patrolled every street corner.

The towering heights of the Celestial Palace loomed into view, its tall spires dominating the capital city's skyline. They were getting closer to the palace with its cells and torture chamber and Dren had no idea whether this was a taxi ride or whether she was being driven to her own execution. She nudged Aimree in the ribs and tried to tell her they didn't really want to get much closer than this but Aimree gave her a blank look.

Just then the cart lurched violently as the wooden wheels slid over slick cobbles. The driver let out a curse and pulled sharply on the reins. A drunk pedestrian had stumbled into their path.

The donkeys ground their hooves into the road to kill the speed of the coach and they passed within a finger's width of the man. The pedestrian staggered on oblivious to the tragedy his family had been spared.

'We need to get out,' Dren whispered into Aimree's ear as she landed on her shoulder. 'Do something.'

Aimree seized the opportunity. 'Thank you for your help, sergeant. I believe this is where we should be getting out,' she hollered through the mesh observation hatch. Her shouting should have caught the attention of even the deafest guard but there was no response from any of them.

Aimree gave Dren a worried look and knocked on the mesh hatch. 'I said, we'll just get out here, if you can find somewhere to stop.'

But the man with the sword on his belt and the stripes on his shoulder didn't even turn around to acknowledge her. Was it really that difficult to hear at the front? Either the guards were deliberately ignoring them or they genuinely couldn't hear the passengers over the noise of the road. The cart picked up speed and rounded a corner.

Aimree cleared her throat loudly then tried again, 'I said, thanks for the lift but I think I see our campsite.'

Dren's mind raced. Could it be that the guards had recognised her after all? She had wrongly assumed that border guards were less astute than other soldiers.

She tried to still the voice of panic that was hollering inside her head. They were running out of time. Dren looked about. Could they break open the door and jump out of the cart? They risked injuring themselves on the hard cobbles but it might be their only chance. Then she looked closer and realised there were no handles on the inside of the doors. She cursed herself for getting sloppy. Having a bad day was no excuse for failing to pay attention to basic details.

There was no other way out. The bars on the windows were heavy and designed to ensure that no passenger could leave mid-journey. The wooden floor and ceiling were covered over with a lattice of metalwork. At first glance you could mistakenly think it was purely decorative but the curls and flowers were made from hard iron. There was no doubt that the wagon had been adapted to convey dangerous prisoners. They were well and truly trapped.

Why had she been so quick to accept a lift? Was she so dazzled by Aimree's quick thinking that she hadn't seen through the guards' trickery? Through the bars she could see that the Celestial City hadn't been spared the wanted posters either. Her image fluttered in the breeze from every other lamp post and shop window. Her heart sank. Any realistic chances of the guards not recognising her were dwindling to almost nothing. Had she been a gambler, she would have stopped taking bets by this point.

'Maybe I should knock on the hatch?' whispered Meela, creases of worry lining her face. Like Dren, she had already worked out the predicament they were in.

Before they had a chance to communicate further, the sergeant interrupted them. 'It's not a patch on how the city used to look which is a shame really. It used to be a sight to behold.' He continued his guided tour. 'After the worst period of tremors, they rebuilt the damaged parts but the new buildings were thrown up in a matter of days using the cheapest material possible. You can literally poke a stick through the walls and yet the houses are piled three and four high. Look at them all living one on top of another. They'll be lucky if they last the year. One more big tremor'll bring the whole thing down.'

'I really think we better walk the rest of the way,' Aimree tried again.

'There's no question of you walking. You need to keep your strength up for the games,' said the sergeant coldly.

'It's just I think you've taken a wrong turning,' said Aimree. She couldn't disguise the worry in her voice. 'The campsite appears to be behind us. I'd be very grateful if you could drop us in the shadow of the palace and we can sneak back to camp before anyone notices I'm late. And, we will reimburse you, of course.'

The sergeant turned to face them. Pressing his forehead against the mesh, his dark eyes looked menacing. 'Don't you worry, my dear athletes. We're not going the wrong way. The driver knows exactly where we're headed. And don't fret, not a soul will notice you're late. Where I'm dropping you is well out of the way, no one will see you. It's what you might call... discrete.' His voice tailed off.

The sergeant barked a couple of commands to his team and the cart veered sharply to the right. There was no doubt that the guards knew exactly who Dren was. The only question now was where on earth were they being taken?

CHAPTER 70

When they came to a halt, the sergeant jumped down from the driver's bench and pulled up his hood. Dren looked out through the window bars. It wasn't raining.

The carriage had stopped near to a tavern, although they hadn't pulled up directly outside the entrance. Clearly the guards were no strangers to drinking on duty and the driver was well trained. A casual observer would notice that the border patrol had business near to the drinking den without anyone being able to draw a direct conclusion about which establishment they were visiting.

'Wait there, I won't be long,' he said through the bars of the window, as if those locked inside had any other option.

Dren shrank back, trying to keep out of the light in the hope that the border guards really were so isolated that they hadn't recognised her. She exchanged a worried glance with Aimree.

'Does anyone else smell cabbage?' said Seema, seemingly out of the blue.

'What are you talking about?' said Aimree.

'Has nobody else noticed that this city has got a reek of cabbage to it?' I mean, I suppose people have got to eat something. It's a shame that it had to be that. The smell is quite unpleasant.'

Well guess what,' said Meela. 'They break wind, same as the rest of us.'

'Well, that would be inevitable, what with all this cabbage they're eating.'

Dren groaned inwardly. Trust Seema to be paying absolutely no attention to their current predicament.

'Quiet in the back!' boomed a voice from the driver's seat.

'I was only saying-' Seema protested but a sharp elbow in the ribs from her sister was enough to silence her. The other guards were still sat up the front and it wasn't safe to talk freely in case they were overheard.

For the second time in as many weeks, Dren was trapped in a confined space with Aimree. It was strange to think back to the time when she and Toran had fallen out over her. Back then she would have given anything to spend this amount of time in such close quarters with her.

When it came down to survival, romance didn't rate all that highly. What Dren admired was Aimree's quick thinking and determination. It made a mockery of the bards' heroic tales where the hero would do anything to save the pretty girl. Here the pretty girl was every bit the soldier.

The sergeant rapped on the closed door of the tavern with the hilt of his sword. The sound echoed down the street. At first, Dren couldn't put her finger on what was wrong with the scene. But the more she thought about it, she realised that the closed door was decidedly odd.

Usually a tavern was designed to draw you in. But here the opposite was true.

Any stranger passing by would give it half a glance and then walk on by, believing it to be an establishment for other people, locals perhaps, or someone belonging to a different trade guild. They would have no inclination to enter through its faded doors.

Eventually a young child answered the door. After a brief exchange, the sergeant was ushered inside. The child stuck its head outside for a moment to give the cart and its occupants a visual inspection before quickly closing the doors behind the visitor.

Dren couldn't imagine an existence where she worked for twelve hours a day, just to spend the few remaining hours of daylight drinking her life away in some windowless building which smelled of other peoples' sweat. One day, she supposed, she would buy a piece of land, build a house and raise some animals. But for now, her entire focus was on escaping from the Kingdom.

Escape, the word echoed in her mind. She needed to slap herself awake. Why wasn't she trying to escape? After all, she was a wanted man with a price on his head. Her head. She was struggling to manage so many layers of disguise.

She looked through the metal hatch. While the sergeant was away, they were left with only two guards. If they could just trick a guard into opening the door, they would outnumber their captors two to one. The soldiers may have the advantage in terms of strength and the fact that they were armed but, if Dren could manage to disarm them or even trap them in the cell van, she could unhitch Thunder and make a bid for the mountains.

Seema had her walking stick and Dren had her bow. But she reminded herself that she didn't have any arrows. Plus Seema was no fighter. However, before she could begin to form a plan, the door to the tavern opened and the sergeant appeared holding a package. He quickly tucked this inside his cloak and headed back towards the van.

Dren's spirits plummeted. There was no doubt in her mind, the sergeant had sold them out. Dren's mind raced with one question. Why, with a bounty on her head, had they not just been driven to the prison at the keep?

* * *

Aimree's mind was also occupied with thoughts of escape. The problem was that her freedom and Dren's were incompatible with each other. She felt the place where she had sewn the scroll into the lining of her cloak. She trusted it would ensure safe passage for her at least. Maybe it would guarantee Seema's safety too. But then again, maybe not.

She hadn't thought it would have taken so long to accomplish her mission. She hadn't realised it would have felt like the wrong thing to do. If she had just been able to follow the plan and hand over the scroll when they had reached the Arcarian Keep, she would already be back home with Dafine and Wudsam.

The problem was, when she thought back to the time when she had passed out, Dren was the one who had risked himself to save her life and her sister's. But, if she played her cards right, maybe Dren would never know that she had been the one to betray him.

The other problem was that her sister and Meela

were now part of the equation. Aimree tried to justify her actions, telling herself that she didn't owe Meela anything. But she knew that wasn't true. Without Meela's ingenuity and daring, she and Dren would still be lingering in some damp cell in the Arcarian Keep. Maybe she would hold onto the scroll for just a little while longer.

* * *

The sergeant returned to the coach. He snorted and spat a ball of snot from the back of his throat onto the ground. Then, without saying a word, he jumped back up onto the front seat.

The wagon gave a lurch as the donkeys walked forward, throwing the four captives back in their seats. The wagon sped around the corner, jolted over cobbles and turned down a narrow alley.

The driver pulled up sharply on the reins. The donkeys' hooves slipped on the slick stones, almost throwing Dren off the smooth bench. She would have bounced onto the floor had Aimree not reached out and grabbed her shoulders to stop her from sliding forward. On the opposite side of the cabin, Seema hung on tightly to the window bars and was saved from the indignity of falling but Meela wasn't so quick and slid clean off the bench to land in a tangled heap on the floor. Her teeth clattered together violently.

'I think I can taste blood,' Meela complained, wiping her mouth with her sleeve.

'Sorry about that,' said the sergeant, glancing back over his shoulder. 'Slight change of plan. There's a fellow in here that wants a word with you.' The sergeant's feet thudded on the flagstones as he jumped down from the front of the wagon.

Dren reasoned that, if they were being turned over to the king's soldiers, then they would have already been handcuffed and taken to a cell. It didn't mean they were safe though and she knew that there were worse fates than simply being arrested.

The cart had stopped alongside a trap door. It presumably lead to a beer cellar where barrels of drink would be rolled down into a cool underground store. Dren scanned the cul-de-sac but there was no exit from the narrow alley. From her early days spent on the streets, she was good at finding creative uses for drainpipes and chimney breasts but, frustratingly, there was nothing which would give her a hand or foothold out of the reach of the guards' blades.

They were trapped in an alley with no witnesses. Her mind wandered down a dark path but she pulled herself back to the present moment. She was still worth something alive. Surely the other guards wouldn't let anything happen to her, not when there was still reward money at stake.

The only way out was the narrow close that led back to the main street but this was covered by the driver and the third guard. There was nothing subtle about the way they positioned themselves, blocking any possible escape. Dren knew there was no point trying to make a run for it or fighting their armed captors. The guards would not hesitate drawing blood first and asking questions later.

The two flaps covering the trapdoor opened outwards and slammed on the ground, startling a couple of birds in the courtyard. The sergeant turned the handle on the door of the prison van then ushered them out.

No one wanted to make the first move. Then Aimree stood up. The sergeant held out a hand towards her. 'Watch your step, it's a bit of a drop.' She ignored his arm and climbed out unaided. The other two girls followed her, leaving Dren to follow along at the rear.

By the time Dren had made it out of the cell van, Aimree was already disappearing down into the cellar hatch, closely followed by the other two. Dren walked over to the hatch and peered down.

A shadowy figure stood in the cellar below holding out a flickering candle, indicating where she should jump. Dren slid her body down into the cellar until her feet touched something soft. The doors slammed shut above her head, plunging her into darkness. This was followed by the screech of a bolt closing. She was now trapped underground.

It was obvious that they had just been sold to the highest bidder. Which begged the question, who could outbid the king?

For more books in the series check out my website at SLGERVAIS.com

Printed in Great Britain
by Amazon

23891265R00235